Bouncer

A Fox & Thayne Mystery

This book is a work of fiction. Any resemblance to actual events or persons, living or dead, is entirely coincidental.

"Bouncer," by Tyan Wyss. 1st Edition. ISBN-978-1491225349

Manufactured in the United States of America

Bouncer

(A Fox & Thayne Mystery)

by

Tyan Wyss

Prologue

Tuesday Night, September 10th, 2002

Escape! There had to be a way out! The groggy mayor glanced over his shoulder and knew it was now or never. Flinging his portly body over the windowsill, he cringed at the distance yawning below him and bordered by mature roses with long, treacherous thorns. An odd coughing sound pursued him, and in terror, he flew from the window, flapping his arms like useless wings before crashing to the ground. He numbly crawled on battered hands and knees, seeking escape. A strange snarling off to his left struck terror into his rotund frame as he propelled his corpulent mass like a shrieking pig along the ground. A sudden command followed by an obedient hush forced him to raise his bleary eyes in terror. Amazement at that final image quickly blurred as acute pain made night envelop the day forever.

Gasping and choking for breath, he awoke in terror from his night vision, the heavy headphones pounding out *Metallica* in a feeble effort to block out the voices and visions. Stumbling to the bathroom cabinet, he grabbed two migraine pills and chomped them like candy. He staggered over to the police scanner and flipped the switch before lowering himself into the office chair. He poured out a generous dose of bourbon and listened and waited, the image of the magnolia pulsing inside his brain. When dawn peeked through the shuttered window, he gave up. *All comes to he who waits*.

Chapter 1

Earlier that month

"Ba? Ba? Ooohh . . . see ba." Thunk. "Where ba? Ooohh . . . hee, hee, snag. Me Bonsir. Ba! Ba! Wher ba? Eedd! Eedd!"

Philemon, the African-American gardener, was excruciatingly bored. He'd been hired by the prim and arthritic Mrs. Simms to manicure her lawn and garden three times a week when one would have sufficed. Every Monday, Wednesday, and Friday morning from eight until noon, he cleaned, swept, and maintained her already immaculate garden. To fill in time, Philemon moved as slowly as the snail he methodically removed from a hydrangea bush, crushing its amber shell beneath his worn yellow work boots. His calloused fingers searched a *Mr. Lincoln* hybrid tea rose and pulled off two slightly yellowing petals. The flowers still bloomed in full glory this early Fall in north-central California, and even though the evenings were growing cooler, the garden still glowed in layers of finely tuned color. He placed his hands upon his jean-clad hips and surveyed the emerald green lawn before him with faded chocolate eyes that reflected the smile of a man who knows he has achieved a superior result.

Philemon turned his still-astute eyes to the main house and studied its distinct lines. It was built in classic Tudor style with tall white-washed walls and black wooden face-boards crossing in attractive Xs. The stately anthracite roof reached towards a tall ash tree centered just left of the expansive lawn. The cobbled walkway gently meandered up to the triple steps of the front porch, which overlooked an oval-shaped lawn. The quaint path was painstakingly lined with lovely tree roses bursting with color. Mrs. Simms only allowed only *Peace* and her pink cousin *Chicago Peace* to hedge the perfect pathway, and their alternating copper pink petals and bronze-tinged yellow flowers contrasted beautifully. Mrs. Simms demanded perfection in her garden, and Philemon willingly obliged.

Hydrangeas and camellias vied for space under the shady eaves, both species blooming in brilliant purplish-blue and mauve arrays. It was to be their final display before the winter set in, but for now, their amazing depth of color startled the eye and nourished the senses. The proscenium of the house hosted not only the beautiful ash tree but a silver maple as well as a lush cluster of liquid ambers, whose pointed leaves were now tinged pink and orange by the advent of cool fall evenings. Lastly and perfectly, a huge, mature cottonwood shaded the already cool interior of the two-story domicile Mrs. Simms called home; standing tall near the left back fence bordering the vacant lot.

An ivy-covered, split-rail fence surrounded the front yard, and pink, cream, and scarlet creeper roses crept around its vertical poles, promoting the desired impression of peace and tranquility. A garden worthy of a Monet painting, Philemon was thankful Mrs. Simms remained open to his suggestions. Whenever her dedicated gardener suggested replanting a flowerbed or trimming a tree, she almost always agreed. As long as the final result proved stunning, Philemon was allowed a free hand. Mrs. Simms was obsessed with beauty and perfection, and because of it, her yard remained a showpiece.

Philemon Jenkins had been a gardener for nearly four years and loved the outside work. Before that, he'd stood on the assembly line in Detroit for twenty-two years laboring for a major motor company before his foot had inadvertently caught in a gear chain, crushing thirteen bones in the process. The company had paid him off while discreetly suggesting he should retire, motivating him with what is so affectionately called the 'golden handshake.' Philemon had cheerfully pocketed his money and limped off to California, where the weather proved less stressful to his often-aching bones. Detroit held sour memories of mislaid loyalties and unrelenting demands, and he'd been relieved to finally break with the too-stressful city.

His gentle wife, Darcy, had accompanied him to the Golden State and loved it immediately. The African-American community was large, and their modest home, located near the Southern Baptist Church, beckoned to her energetic though gentle nature. Every Sunday, Philemon stood ramrod straight as he listened to his plump Darcy lifting her lovely voice to God, for she had truly been blessed with the gift of song. Each and every Sabbath, he counted his belated blessings and praised the Lord for his recent redemption and cleansing baptism only three years earlier. Positive God had cracked open a door for his salvation, Philemon remained eternally grateful for the luxury of feeling entitled to a pleasant afterlife. In repentance, he dutifully deposited a generous sum into the offering plate each and every Sunday under the rapturous eyes of his relieved wife.

Their three children had retreated years earlier to states south and west from chilly Detroit and seemed more inclined to visit their ageing parents in the warmer sun of California, so Philemon contentedly gardened, worked on his expanding stamp collection, and every Saturday afternoon, headed to the nearby Indian casino to play bingo and Blackjack. His devout wife grimaced every time he sauntered off to his weekend obsession, but relented graciously since Philemon remained a faithful, loving husband; and Darcy couldn't deny him his one sinful passion. Nickel gambling, the warm sunshine, and an occasional whiskey were minor sins compared to others.

So, Philemon worked ever so slowly in the perfect garden and squinted occasionally at the fiery sun. His blue lopsided hat covered the graying hair that remained on balding head and shaded his dark face from the fearsome California heat. Soon, it would be time to head home for lunch. Darcy had promised to serve up his favorite chili and beans with green peppers, which had been gaining fire all morning. A thump and a crackle of fallen leaves indicated something had landed close to Philemon's feet, and he turned towards the sound. A red rubber ball, just larger than a softball, lay guiltily in the leaves near one of the liquid amber trees, and the gardener tried to ascertain where the child's toy had originated. Only the distant barking of a dog and the slight lift of a breeze rustling the liquid amber leaves disturbed the silence of the late morning. No one called to Philemon for their ball.

It was always quiet on this cul-de-sac at 612 Chester Street in Central California in the lovely, small city of Monroe. Cars rarely visited the gently curving dead end unless they needed to turn around, and the nearest neighbor was 614 Chester Street—an imposing monstrosity of a two-story gothic house surrounded by ten-foot high walls. Razor sharp spikes protruded from the top and defended white washed walls fronted by a huge black cast iron gate, which reminded the aged gardener of a portcullis fronting a castle. Philemon instinctively knew this was where the ball had originated.

Philemon picked it up and bounced it absently upon Mrs. Simms' cobbled walkway while squinting at 614 Chester Street. The child's toy sprang delightfully into his coffee-colored hand, and he bounced it rhythmically for a few moments, pondering whether to throw it back over the wall. Philemon had only a half-hour until quitting time, and he still needed to rake up some of the leaves scattered underneath the large cottonwood tree. Finally, his mind made up, he drew back his arm like a baseball pitcher and threw the ball high into the air, then watched it arch perfectly and land well beyond the spike-clad wall. Immediately, he heard the rustle of leaves scattering as if someone chased the ball.

"Hello!" he called. "I threw back your ball. Did you find it?"

Silence was his only response. Philemon shrugged and adjusted his hat. Perhaps it was just as well, so he reached down to pick up his discarded rake. Suddenly the red ball sailed past his ear, landing near the arbor where Philemon had carefully trained a *Joseph's Coat* to trail over thin slats of brown trellis. He scurried over as quickly as his stiff legs would allow and bent down to retrieve the ball once again. Someone was playing an impish game with him, and he smiled. The visits from his grandchildren were few and far between and he missed the laughter of little children.

Philemon moved closer to 614's driveway, and this time tossed the ball underhanded over the towering fence. Instead of returning to work, he waited, one hand shading his eyes as the telltale rustle of leaves indicated his playmate was as intent on the game as he. Sure enough, within less than a minute the ball whistled over the fence again, and he grinned triumphantly to himself. He once again retrieved the ball and tossed it. This time, the ball sailed back in less than thirty seconds.

"So, you wanna play ball," he called out. "Well, here you go!"

This time, Philemon threw the ball nearly straight up. It rose more than twenty feet into the air before sailing over the wall and plummeting straight downward. He swore he heard a slight chuckle before the ball was returned in exactly the same manner.

"Not bad," cried Philemon. "Now, why don't you try this?"

Drawing his arm back, he threw his best spinner. As he watched it whiz over the fence, he smirked with a certain amount of satisfaction. Not too shabby for an old man! The ball zoomed back so fast he barely had time to react, the round orb smacking him right in the forehead. As he rubbed the aching spot, Philemon laughed out loud.

"Good shot from wherever you are. How did you know exactly where I was?"

But once again, no answer came, only the slight, nervous crunching of the unseen dead leaves. Philemon glanced toward the house speculatively. Mrs. Simms likely still puttered around her backyard greenhouse, tending to her precious orchids, and he concluded it was worth taking five minutes to play with the lonely child behind the wall.

For the next few minutes he tried all sorts of different throws; underhanded, over-handed, spiked, and short tricky lobs that missed the spikes by a scant three inches After five minutes of frenzied, creative play, he called out once again.

"My name's Philemon. What's yours?"

The trees rustled slightly, but this time, the ball was not returned. Philemon waited for a full two minutes before turning sadly away and reluctantly retrieving his rake. He would have loved to play more, but still had twenty minutes of work left. After raking up the leaves scattered over the quartz colored gravel, he watered the hydrangeas again since the rains hadn't begun, and finally headed towards the front door of the huge two-story house occupied by the elderly Edith Simms. He briskly knocked and the wide door opened almost immediately. Mrs. Simms peered out at him over expensive gold-rimmed glasses.

"Are you finished for today, Philemon?" she asked, flashing him a big smile.

"I sure am, madam," he returned. "I put all the tools away, and since Wednesday is trash day, I'll set out the trashcans as soon as I arrive. We're starting to collect quite a few leaves."

"We most certainly are," said Mrs. Simms, sighing deeply. She wore faded old overalls upon which potting soil clung. "Even the most perfect of plants fade." A frown passed over her weathered face, but Mrs. Simms mentally shook herself and added perkily, "I believe Friday is payday!"

Mrs. Simms always smiled as if payday was the most delightful day of the week and paid Philemon punctually every Friday after work, usually adding a plate of chocolate chip cookies, fudge brownies, or occasionally, her amazing butterscotch fudge to his already generous pay. Philemon knew that Mrs. Simms delighted in sharing her baking, so he graciously received whatever she doled out even though his own wife Darcy was a phenomenal cook.

Mrs. Simms had probably been a decent-looking woman in her younger days, but now, at sixty-five or so, was skinny and frail, the veins protruding bluely through her pale skin. Her long and brittle nails were always stained with gardening chemicals and dirt, and her clothes didn't fit her properly any more. While a well-off woman, she lived simply and seemed to have no family, rarely entertaining guests. Philemon knew she must be excruciatingly lonely in the huge, echoing house.

For the past three Christmases, he and Darcy had joined his employer for some eggnog and seasonal cheer. He always took the opportunity, while his wife and Mrs. Simms chatted, to wander through the expansive house, marveling at the collection of furniture and unusual artifacts she'd collected through her many years of traveling. Edith Simms had been a librarian, but after the untimely death of her husband—a biology professor at UCSB—she'd finally obtained the money to travel and enjoy those places she'd only read about. Unfortunately, her once-adventurous mate could no longer accompany her, and in many ways, his absence had made her more daring; encouraging her to visit the Congo, examine the unique flora and fauna of the Galapagos, and venture to obscure Hindu temples in the remotest regions of India. Her hair was dyed that hideous silver-blue of the elderly, and Philemon sensed she would like to chat for a few moments before he took his leave, so he thought it appropriate to bring up a question that had bothered him more than once.

"Who lives across the street Mrs. Simms, at 614?"

Mrs. Simms seemed startled. "Well, I only know their name is Collins, but I've never met them. They seem practically barricaded inside that old house of theirs."

"Do you know if there's a child?" asked Philemon. "A ball came bouncing over the wall today, and I thought there might be."

Mrs. Simms shrugged a bony shoulder. "I really don't think so, but then again, maybe. I'm positive they don't have a dog, since I've never heard one, but once, a furniture truck from that Oriental Trading Company was parked out front; delivering furniture, I guess. And I once saw the most beautiful ginger cat perched on the wall. She stepped so daintily over the spikes. High walls like that can't keep everything out." Mrs. Simms spoke in that fluttered train-of-thought style of hers that was so difficult to follow.

Philemon nodded to indicate he agreed. Personally, he despised fences and bars of any sort and thoroughly enjoyed the wide openness of the Big Valley in central California; the breadbasket of the West. He loved how the flat valley stretched almost as far as the eye could see until it reached the two opposing mountain ranges; the Sierra Nevada's on the east and the Coastal Range on the west. It amazed him how this little residential area in Monroe reminded him so much of the high class suburbs outside Detroit with their beautiful large houses, spacious yards, and towering trees that looked like they'd been planted a hundred years ago.

"Only wondering," he said dismissively. "I tossed the ball back over the fence anyways. I'm sure they must have a guest or something."

"Most likely. I'll see you on Wednesday, then, Philemon," said Mrs. Simms. She gave him a friendly wave before shutting the huge door against the midday heat.

When Philemon arrived on Wednesday, he quickly put out the trash because the truck usually arrived by 9:00 a.m. It was amazing what a difference two days had made, for it had gotten much cooler at night, and the liquid amber leaves had turned a brilliant orange umber. He worked hard for over two hours in the backyard, helping Mrs. Simms with her roses and carrying several sacks of potting soil into her greenhouse before the pair turned their attention to the vegetable garden.

They harvested radishes and carrots today and placed them in a large wicker basket. Philemon knew from experience he would be the recipient of some of the choicest vegetables. Mrs. Simms tended to weary easily, and after only ninety minutes, she straightened, indicating she needed to go into the house to lie down. He placed the large apple basket on her back porch filled with vegetables and moved to the front yard. Many leaves had fallen over the previous two days, and he worked quickly, raking and trimming dead branches. He loved when fall arrived. The constant litter of dropping leaves kept him busy and content.

His back was turned to 614 Chester Street when the red ball thumped a mere 18 inches away, barely missing him. He smiled to himself before chasing after it, finding it lodged under a camellia plant, whose bright shiny leaves still looked healthy this late in the season. He gripped the ball tightly before throwing it over the fence. This time, he heard a definite chuckle, and the ball came sailing right back as hard as a baseball pitch. He caught the simple toy and returned it deftly, and for the next ten minutes played ball with the mysterious child behind the high, white fence. Finally, he paused and approached the wall before tossing it over.

"Hello," he said gently. "Do you remember me? You and I played catch last Monday? My name's Philemon, what's yours?" There seemed to be vast hesitation as if the child was afraid to answer. Finally one word drifted over the wall.

"Bon . . . Bonsir."

It was hard to ascertain whether it was a male or female voice, or even whether it was young or old.

"Bouncer," Philemon repeated. "That's a fine name for such a great pitcher." He in turn bounced the ball high before tossing it barely clear of the high spikes upon the wall. They played for another five minutes until, just like on Monday, the game stopped abruptly.

"Bouncer, do you want to play some more?" Nothing but the distant complaint of a mocking bird's chatter filled the morning air. With great reluctance, Philemon returned to his tasks, the game with the lonely child occasionally returning to his mind as he tidied and trimmed, ensuring Mrs. Simms' garden remained the most beautiful on the block.

And so it continued through that week and into the next. On Monday, he played three separate times with the silent child who seemed quite skilled, if his creative tosses and rapid, scrambling retrievals were any clue. On Wednesday, Philemon had just thrown a high spin when he heard Mrs. Simms' brittle voice behind him.

"What on earth are you doing, Philemon?"

He turned guiltily. "I'm sorry, Mrs. Simms. I'll make up the time. Bouncer and I were just playing some ball."

"Bouncer?"

"The little kid on the other side of the wall. We've been tossing the ball back and forth. It's a harmless game."

Mrs. Simms' pale blue eyes narrowed as she studied the high wall. "I've never heard of anyone called Bouncer living there."

"That's the name he gave me. Assuming he's a male, of course. I remember playing catch with my own two boys, and it brings back pleasant memories. I didn't mean to be negligent on the job."

Mrs. Simms swung her faded eyes back to him and smiled sweetly. "I could never accuse you of that, Philemon. Will you come around the back and carry some bricks for me into the greenhouse?"

Philemon took a relieved breath. He loved his job and didn't want to jeopardize it by annoying Mrs. Simms. Luckily, she was an easygoing, uncomplaining sort. He didn't return to the front yard that day and wished he could have told little Bouncer goodbye.

Friday Morning, September 20th, 2002

BOUNCER

The end of the week stayed busy. Mrs. Simms had a million projects, and Philemon started his day by pruning the myrtle shrubs and removing the heavy purple-black berries nearly ready to drop when Mrs. Simms showed up at his elbow.

"I have to go to the bank, Philemon, and dump off some clothes at the hospice shop. Here's your money for the week, and I'll see you first thing on Monday. Make sure you hang up the tools, won't you?"

She'd dressed in a bright pink frock that made her look old and tired. More rouge than necessary gave her pallid cheeks some life, and she resembled a manikin with the falsely painted colors.

"No problem, Mrs. Simms. I'll see you Monday, then."

He kept working as she backed her huge blue Chevy out of the driveway and waved in return when she lifted a pale hand to him.

Finished, and with just over an hour to kill, he wandered into the front yard. He wondered if Bouncer wanted to play.

"Hello, Bouncer," he called. "It's Philemon! Would you like to play ball?"

There was an immediate response as that breathless chuckle again rose above the fence.

"Fil, Fil."

"Yes, it's Philemon." Philemon was a damn hard name for a child, and 'Phil' was close enough for him. He'd been called that more than once by many he hadn't liked half as much. "Throw me the ball, Bouncer."

It spiraled and plopped not three feet from the curb, and they played merrily for several minutes. The wind picked up, and a couple times whirled the ball off course. As Philemon approached the high wall, a putrid scent assailed his nostrils, and he grimaced before returning the ball. It didn't come back, but Philemon knew to expect that now. Their game always randomly started, and as abruptly, ceased. That was simply the fickle nature of children. Philemon turned to leave when he swore the raspy voice said, "Phil . . . Mag . . . mag … nolia."

Magnolia? What on earth did that mean? "Hey, what's that? Bouncer, are you there?" Not even the crunch of gravel or the whisper of wind through the huge maple trees lining the street whispered back.

Poised in the middle of the cul-de-sac, Philemon peered about. The two large end houses dominated the large circular curve of the street separated by the unclaimed area. Too small a lot for another house to be built and too large to be simply classified a dog park; it remained a nature reserve for the residents. Shaped like a piece of pie, the narrowest part opened to the cul-de-sac and the widest backed onto the shrub oak forest that sloped gently to eventually meet the gentle

Monroe river that flowed only periodically. During drought, nothing existed but a trickle, but at the whims of the fickle rains during winter, the river actually rose one to two feet as it flowed towards the Sacramento River.

Within this large wedged piece of land, a huge magnolia tree of at least fifty to sixty years old dominated the landscape. It cast a huge circle of shade, and its massive trunk measured twice a grown man's arm span. Abundant large white flowers opened towards the sun, a marvel indeed in this sparsely treed piece of land. The magnolia seemed to defy the scrub nature of the oak forest and reminded the gardener more of the deep South than semi-arid California. This tree must be what Bouncer had referred to.

He vividly remembered that, in his childhood, his parents had had a large climbing tree growing in their backyard. He and his two brothers had built a rough shack among the broad branches and called it their hideout, though it was obvious to everyone where they disappeared every afternoon. Perhaps Bouncer had his own special place among the shady leaves and twisting trunk of the magnolia, and Philemon decided that after work, he would check out the old tree. Perhaps he'd find some clues to Bouncer's identity, or better yet, find a small child playing there. Housed deeply inside Philemon's soul was the need to return to innocence, and that possibility of reliving some of his own lost childhood made him anticipate quitting time. He wondered if Darcy would mind him bringing some Legos or something for Bouncer out of the hoard they'd collected for his grandchildren.

Philemon worked diligently for the rest of the morning before heading to the pie-shaped field. He'd told Darcy more than a week ago of his pleasant game with the child so she wouldn't be surprised if he was a mite late. Philemon was a natural with children, so she laughed and encouraged him. She knew how much Philemon missed his grandchildren.

At roughly 12:05, Philemon waited under the heavy shade of the magnolia tree. Someone had been busy here, for a great deal of loose dirt and rocks were piled about. He remembered that, as a boy, he'd dug tunnels into the earth, pretending he was a pirate burying his ill-gotten treasure in deepest secret. Apparently, Bouncer had done the same. Philemon moved closer. The dirt seemed grossly disturbed, the sparse grass bent between the white river rock scattered liberally over the newly upturned soil. He knew from his own experience digging in Mrs. Simms' garden that the rocks were a major nuisance. Philemon suddenly stopped abruptly, his throat paralyzed.

There, situated between a small cluster of river rock and savaged earth, poked one partially unearthed human hand. Philemon gave an inhuman scream and backed away, resisting the urge to run. Seeking to control the burst of fear and revulsion threatening to paralyze his whole being, he moved forward on leaden legs as a horrible wave of déjà vu overwhelmed him. It was indeed a hand upon closer inspection; curled and grossly pale with just the faintest trace of black human hair evident above the knuckle of three protruding fingers. The bile rose in his throat, and he rushed to the edge of the street, his brow and back suddenly soaked with perspiration. Philemon clumsily retrieved his cell phone from his jeans' pocket and with a shaking dark finger punched 911.

Chapter 2

Friday afternoon, September 20th, 2002

Monroe had always been touted a peaceful town by the locals. Therefore, Police Chief Richard Rollins, who had hoped to obtain an eventless retirement in less than five months, was thoroughly pissed off. This couldn't be happening now! He observed the heavy body being slowly unearthed by his three grim-faced deputies wearing protective masks and gloves against the gagging stench. Inspector Roger Chung, Monroe's second-in-command, hovered to one side, shaking his dark head. He had briefly interviewed the visibly shaken Philemon Jenkins before moving on to the site, and it had taken him only a couple minutes to suspect the identity of the bloated corpse. A white-faced Randy Phelps, the newest officer on the small force, snapped photos, the whirring sound of the camera vying with the hum of persistent flies.

Thad Fisher hadn't been seen for nearly two weeks, and Roger had personally been of the opinion that the ex-mayor had finally left his overbearing and persnickety wife for his mistress. Thad Fisher had been a big man at over 6'1" and two hundred-fifty pounds. He'd possessed a large, soft belly and boisterous laugh, and as the dirt slowly disappeared, his once-white dress shirt half-revealed a hairy abdomen that forced Richard Rollins to lurch off, his stomach churning. Roger examined the area under the magnolia tree meticulously, ordering his junior officer to take more photos before allowing the others to dig.

Even though he instructed the stoic senior officer, Brian Stevens, to mix plaster of Paris for a smeared footprint in the dirt, Roger harbored no hopes that it would reveal the killer. He was certain the print belonged to the helpful gardener now being interviewed by the force's only remaining on-duty officer, Jesse Steele. A small crowd of interested bystanders from the posh neighborhood remained at a respectful distance, and Roger was grateful the magnolia tree was located a good two hundred feet from the curb. There was little the crowd could discern or disturb, thank goodness. Roger Chung hunched down and examined the body, steeling himself against the reality of what an extended time underground produces in this hot weather.

His dark eyes widened as Thad Fisher's left arm was finally unearthed; it flopped heavily upon the dirt and Roger leaned forward, suddenly intent. One of the ex-mayor's five digits was missing, that of his ring finger. It had been neatly and precisely hacked off, and in addition, a feminine ring consisting of shiny silver braiding rested on his pinkie. Inspector Chung had, upon occasion, played small-stakes poker with Thad and had never before noticed evidence of any such ring, though Thad Fisher had been just the personality for it. Thad loved to flaunt his financial success and prominent position in the small city. Loud and opinionated and blessed with a notorious roving eye, he'd been a colorful, though highly ineffective mayor.

Roger straightened up, a sharp pain forcing him to push harshly at his right abdomen. The pain decreased after rubbing it for a few seconds and nearly back to normal Roger took a deep shaky breath. He readjusted his Ray-Bans and strolled up to Richard Rollins, who, as he peered down the cul-de-sac, kept his back turned both to the magnolia and the grisly remains of Roger's one-time poker partner.

"It's Thad, isn't it?" asked Richard, already knowing the answer. He fished out his handkerchief and mopped his heavily lined brow. This damn heat sucked the moisture from the living and caused the dead to stink.

"I think there's little doubt," said Roger in his usual, quiet way and described the missing finger as well as the ex-mayor's strange acquisition of the tiny pinkie ring.

"You'd better call your wife," stated Richard, wishing this day was already over. He'd have to contact the Realtor and reschedule his long awaited meeting regarding selling his house. “Looks like we’re in for the long haul here. Time for you to do that magic we pay you all those big bucks for.”

Both knew the big bucks were a wishful joke, but Roger’s incredible skills as a detective were not. Richard Rollins made no secret about his intense admiration of his second-in-command’s methods. Roger had graduated in the top five of his class in San Francisco, and even though the detective hadn’t had the opportunity to use his skills much here, Richard was highly impressed by what he’d seen. He studied the stocky Asian man, who once again analyzed the vacant lot. His subordinate was hardworking, dedicated, and so intelligent one would feel intimidated if Roger wasn’t such a nice guy.

He should have felt complimented, but instead, Roger felt only a mild wave of dizziness. Usually, the heat didn’t affect him like this. It was high time for summer to release its grip on the Big Valley and usher in cooler days. He needed to continue this conversation in the shade, so Roger gently tugged at Richard’s arm until his chief followed him reluctantly to the gravesite.

Richard stood over the corpse and examined a man he’d had little respect for. Roger watched the play of emotions drift over his superior’s face. Another sharp twinge twisted his side, and Roger Chung shoved his palm forcibly against the pain. What the hell was wrong with him? He’d seen corpses before, and they’d never affected him like this. He should feel exhilarated by the first apparent homicide in Monroe County in over six months, not dizzy. The last had been a drunk who'd been dumped on the highway just past the northernmost potato fields. While it had screamed possible homicide, it later came to light that a remorseful farmer, one John Houghton, had deposited the body by the road after giving a ride to a derelict that'd ungratefully died of a massive heart attack in the bed of his battered pickup. John had panicked and later admitted to what happened, but the body had lain in the sun all afternoon and been an awful sight to behold.

Roger pressed at the pain again. The nausea persisted along with a queer clutching ache on his right side no matter how hard he massaged the area. He forced himself to study the crime scene now being efficiently taped off by Randy Phelps. Thad Fisher lay totally exposed upon his back, his partially unbuttoned shirt stained with blood and dirt. Randy, finished with his task, waited for new instructions. The entire department consisted of only five officers, a dispatcher, one secretary, and two clerks along with Roger and the chief. In a situation like this, every man had to pitch in. The highway patrol governed the long stretch between here and Modesto, and until now, Roger had felt the department grossly over manned.

"Start taking close-up pictures," instructed Roger, "while I record what I see." He removed his small handheld recorder and began a monotone recital as Randy snapped away. Roger always recorded his first impressions on tape.

"Rigor mortis unapparent, which means body has been dead well over 24 hours. The skin of his abdomen has taken on a greenish tint, also placing time of death to several days, perhaps even a week. Bloodstains liberally splattered over victim's shirt and hands. A small, deep entry wound is evident on the left side of the throat."

Roger squatted closer, the stench of death causing his stomach to swirl as he studied the unearthed mayor. The dirt and debris made it difficult to determine if there was an exit wound, but it was apparent, by the lack of burn marks and precise symmetry of the entry wound, that Thad Fisher hadn't been the victim of gunshot. In addition, no blood stained the earth near the body, but even so he instructed Randy to take soil samples. A mild clench of excitement joined the vague nausea. Clearly, the mayor had not been killed here. He dictated his findings into his recorder as Richard, now in control, studied Thad Fisher.

"The bastard cut off his finger as a souvenir. How sick is that?"

"Serial killers often take trophies," said Roger. His hand shot to his side, pressing hard. His black eyes closed for a moment in pain.

"Good God, Roger, are you all right?" asked Richard Rollins, momentarily shaken from his perusal of the dirty puffed body.

Did his chief really have two double chins or was he seeing quadruple? “Of course,” Roger responded until another acute attack doubled him over, and he pitched face down onto the short dry grass of the vacant lot, barely avoiding striking his head on an unearthed rock before losing consciousness.

“Ah, shit,” said Chief Rollins before crying out to the paramedics who had just arrived on the scene. “Something’s wrong with my man!”

Friday afternoon, 3:00 pm

Chief Rollins was livid. He knew he should only be concerned about the health and upcoming appendectomy of the city’s only detective, but strangely felt only inconvenienced. Roger’s willowy wife, Susan, leaned near her husband, holding his hand in support, and Richard felt a twinge of envy. Susan Chung was exotic and lovely in the way only East-Asian women can be, and it always startled him when she spoke, her voice sounding as Californian as any other born and raised here.

“All will come right,” she whispered to her husband, who felt rather well after the mega-dose of painkillers.

Roger turned his head towards his Chief. There was something important he had to say, and he frowned, concentrating hard. Ah, yes, the body of their ex-mayor and the now stifled investigation.

"I've put you in a fine pickle," he stated, his voice slurred from the numbing barbiturates.

"It's okay," Chief Rollins mumbled, knowing he couldn't utter anything else. What the hell was he to do now? He hated to call in the boys from Cameron, 50 miles away. They were all so pompous and depreciating now that they had their new state of the art forensics lab, and that blowhard, Bill Peters, with his smug demeanor and condescending voice, always put him on edge. But it was clear he had no choice; he had to call in someone before the crime site turned cold.

"Thayne," slurred Roger. "Call in Nick Thayne."

That name seemed familiar. "Nick Thayne . . . that hotshot detective from Frisco?"

"He's freelance now. Works in Girard, not 60 miles from here. Quit Frisco because of a personality clash with the chief. He'll help you out."

Richard Rollins fiddled with the bleached sheet nearest him, his florid face mirroring his unease. He'd heard about Nick Thayne and the rumors surrounding his dismissal from the San Francisco Police Department. An old friend, Gerald Hopper, who'd retired last year from the force, had joined Richard for some trout fishing last winter and told him all about the renegade.

"They called him the *spook* because of his odd methods, but only behind his back. He'd pissed off Chief Martin royally because we nearly had what should have been an airtight case thrown out because of lack of hard evidence. He sent the entire homicide division on what appeared to be a wild goose chase during the Gonzalez murders out beyond the wharf. Lo and behold, there appears the murder weapon. We knew only someone directly connected to the gang could have obtained that information. If it weren't for a latent fingerprint, we'd have been thrown out of court. That, and the fact Sanchez's mistress squealed.

"Figure I know how Thayne got her to squeak, considering his reputation with women. After that, the DA refused to work with him. Everyone swore she'd only put up with his shit until then because he was bonking her, and Chief Martin was livid. Swore Thayne was playing both sides against the middle and fired him. Thayne's explanation for everything, get this, was that he'd had a *hunch*. Spooky hunch, *I'd* say. Same thing happened in that child trafficking case we'd worked on 14 months earlier. Three weeks into the case, and suddenly, he just leads his partner to where the Wiederitz twins were stashed. No one could have known to look in the old warehouse beyond the wharf, but *he* did!"

Gerry had spit into the muddy water of the Colorado River and popped more noxious chewing tobacco into his already bulging cheek.

"Was he on the take?"

"No one's positive, but I think so. Sure never seemed to be hurting for money, if his vintage cars are any clue. And you know how cheap they are! Out of a job now, and if he comes prowling around your area sniffing for a new situation, you'd be best to send him packing!"

Richard shook his head, which was shorn to marine standards, hoping to dissuade Roger. "If he's not officially working for the police, I can't use him."

Roger closed his eyes for a second trying to think through the haze of painkillers. "I remember now. He's contracted out to the Girard Police department as a consultant. Girard has only 15,000 inhabitants, and he's a private P.I. as well. We have that $10,000 for special services right?" It was becoming increasingly difficult to speak, since his lips felt numb.

The present mayor, Cindy Perez, had allocated the department $10,000 for an emergency. Richard couldn't think of a bigger emergency than Roger undergoing the knife in 30 minutes and having Bill Peters step in. He could pay the P.I. to head the investigation while Roger recuperated.

"He's good?"

"The best. Of course, you could always use Fox."

"Over my dead body!"

"Well then, you have no choice but to give him a call. Susan has his number. We've been friends since detective school, so I can vouch for him."

"Well, I don't know. You're the best man for the job."

Roger coughed, his handsome Chinese face contorting

in pain. "Probably, but just not at the present moment. Call him, okay? He'll solve this case. He's never been known to fail."

A white-clad aide rolled in the gurney as Dr. Samson popped in his graying head. "Get him to pre-op right now. Who knows when that appendix is going to pop."

Roger gave him dizzy thumbs up while a pretty young nurse with two noses swabbed his arm.

"You're still in charge," growled the chief. "As soon as you're remotely coherent, he answers to you."

Was it his imagination or did Roger grin?

"Yeah, right," he whispered as they wheeled him away under the twitching florescent lights. By God, that was rich. Roger chuckled to no one in particular as things began to fade.

Nick Thayne sounded highly professional on the phone and indicated he could be in Monroe within 90 minutes. Chief Rollins gave him directions to Chester Street and breathed a sigh of relief half-mixed with trepidation. He'd already called the Mayor and explained the situation, and she'd immediately agreed to the temporary arrangement. She didn't like Bill Peters much, either.

"Get a handle on this case before the press has a field day," was her only admonishment. Cindy Perez hated negative publicity, and Chief Rollins had felt the acrid side of her tongue only three weeks ago when his rookie officer had been pulled over on a possible DUI. What a fricking mess that had been. Thank God Phelps had only had the flu. He crossed his fingers and suddenly prayed. *Make this an open and shut case*, he asked the God, who always seemed to be just around the corner and never quite near enough to help. Richard's ever-present ulcer flared, and the burning irritation in his rotund stomach indicated that this might just be the case he'd dreaded all his life.

Nick smiled at his good fortune. With his utility bills directed to a collection agency, the car agency threatening to repossess the love of his life, and his current squeeze dumping him for some middle-aged real estate agent with more money than brains, he was in dire straits. Nick figured he could last another two weeks without real income. The check he had just tried to deposit from one Jason Oswald had bounced. He'd done exactly what that overbearing lout of a salesman had asked and followed his cheating wife around town, snapping pictures. He'd presented Oswald with the torrid evidence, not that he blamed the wife, Beverly, one bit. Her husband was a boar of a man, and he wondered for the umpteenth time why women stayed with men who were bad for them.

Heading to Monroe on a job not only got him out of town and away from the bill collectors but would legitimately stave off those self-same jackals for a couple of months. For one brief moment, Nick remembered his mother's offer to help and gritted his teeth. No way! He'd make it on his own, his family be damned. He rubbed the back of his neck and gulped down a migraine-strength pain tablet before tossing his overnight bag, computer, and sketch book into the small trunk. He swung his long frame into his cherished, cherry-red Mustang and checked the map, noting the long, straight highway. If he could avoid the CHPs, he'd sail down the road at 100 miles an hour—this baby could take it! He flipped on his radar sensor and gunned the engine. Things were looking up.

By the time Nick arrived at the vacant lot on Chester Street at 5:15 p.m., the body had been removed, though several bystanders still stood respectfully behind the yellow tape. *Oh, how America loves the violent and ridiculous*. From the fascinated stares reflected on the faces of the residents, they probably thought this was just another episode of the *Jerry Springer Show*. He was slightly irritated that the body had been removed before he'd had a chance to examine it, but didn't blame the police chief, who'd suddenly had this mess dumped on his plate. Besides, it was blazing hot and no body lasted long in heat like this. A young officer named Randy Phelps followed him about and showed him the Polaroid's he had taken of the crime scene before Roger had been whisked off to the hospital.

"So, how's Roger doing?"

"Don't know," said the rookie. "Getting his appendix out is all I've heard. Keeled over right there near the grave. Said the body had been killed elsewhere and was buried here later."

Nick didn't need the rookie to tell him that, since it was so obvious, but he smiled anyway. You never knew who would turn out to be a top-notch investigator if they just got some practice. Nick squatted and studied the freshly turned earth. Police disruption was everywhere, and his irritation intensified. In this dry weather, there might have been a good footprint.

"So, you're going to help me out?"

The young man looked surprised. He had the washed-out, freckled face of the very fair and couldn't be much older than 25.

"Sure."

The young man followed Nick around like a housebroken puppy. Finally, the substitute detective paused and pointed to a vague indentation resembling a very narrow tire track.

"Pour plaster of Paris here and search the area for a discarded shovel, though the likelihood is slim." He faced the opposite direction. "What's down there?"

"The onion and potato fields. The field slopes and then runs into some of the Agrit-Empire's fields just past the river. Of course, it doesn't have any water in it this time of year."

Nick followed the direction of the rookie's finger and studied the area. The steep incline guaranteed no vehicle could have managed a getaway in the crumbling dirt. He traced the perimeter of the entire field, but no disruptions of the earth were evident. He was positive the killer had not battled the rough scrub but transported the body from the street. He scanned the elite neighborhood. Beautifully manicured gardens, towering trees, and the gentle curve of the cul-de-sac didn't seem a prime location for a brutal murder.

"Whose house is that?" he asked the deputy silently following him around.

The youth checked his notes. "The house to the left belongs to someone named Collins. It's apparently vacant—from what the neighbors can tell. The body was discovered by the gardener from the house over there, owned by one Edith Simms. She returned home about forty minutes ago from a shopping trip and the news nearly put her under."

"Elderly?"

"Yeah, plus her gardener found the body. She was quite beside herself when the chief spoke with her. We had to let her go inside because of the heat. Thought we might have a third casualty on our hands."

Nick enjoyed the young man's sense of humor. "I'll speak with her later."

"Oh, just remembered. I'm supposed to give you Inspector Chung's notes and this." Randy presented him with a small notepad and a hand-held recorder.

"Thanks. I need to see the body."

"Yeah, you're supposed to follow me to the coroner's. The chief's gonna meet us there. He's at the hospital now, checking on Roger. Oh, and a lady from down the street said to give the investigating officer this." He handed Nick a scrap of paper with a name and phone number. "Said her daughter saw some activity at that vacant house earlier this week and someone should come talk to her."

Nick pocketed the paper and recorder. "I need you and that gent there."

"Officer Steele," Randy volunteered.

"Yes, Officer Steele. You're to visit each one of these houses and impound their wheel barrows."

"Wheel barrows?"

"Yeah—the mayor was lugged to his final resting place in a wheel barrow—see that narrow tire track. It could have originated from any of those houses—or none at all. So get cracking."

The freckled junior officer appeared like he wanted to salute, but instead, headed towards his ostentatious police car. Nick hated police cruisers. It was one of the reasons he'd quit the force, amongst a hundred others.

Chapter 3

Friday, 6:00 pm

Chief Richard Rollins met Nick outside the coroner's office. Upon being introduced to Nick, he stammered, "I . . . ah . . . sorry. You're not quite what I expected. I met your father once." He flushed and glanced down.

"Then, I sympathize with you. At least you could keep your association brief."

Richard seemed disconcerted by the quip. "I need to say thanks for helping us out. Please keep in mind that Roger will be on his feet in no time, so make sure you take careful notes so he can jump right back in. Right now, the details are sketchy at best and will remain so until the coroner's report comes back. If you'll follow me, Mr. Thayne?"

"Nick. You can call me Nick." Nick took an instant dislike to the chief, whose agenda was clear. He was to serve as an interim investigator and no more. To top it off, the asshole was probably a closet bigot to boot. Nick's notorious temper nearly flared, but he managed to keep himself in check.

The coroner's office consisted of two rooms filled with the inevitable stainless steel tables, an office, and a tiny lab. No wonder he'd been called in. This was Amateurville. The puffy, decomposing body had been dead for days; it didn't take the stench or grayish-white tint of the body to tell him that. The coroner was a tall thin Asian-American with pleasant features and opaque eyes named Dr. Koh. After two seconds, Nick had to eat his words about Amateurville.

"Fourth digit, left hand surgically removed. Finger not found with body. Been dead 72-96 hours, since no rigor mortis is apparent. Appendages are starting to appear mottled, and you can see the veins of his hands are very conspicuous. Cause of death was a blow to the throat with a narrow, blunt instrument. He likely died of massive blood loss, since the thoracic artery was severed. Bled out within a couple minutes. See here. Weapon wasn't a knife—a screwdriver I'd say—likely a Phillips. I'll investigate the circumference of the entrance wound to determine the exact shape of the instrument. You can see the weapon was thrust so forcefully it exited through the rear of the mayor's throat at an upwards angle. The killer was shorter than the victim, but strong and probably right-handed, since the wound is on the left."

Dr. Koh changed subjects abruptly after noticing the chief's pallid face. "This ring was found on the left pinky finger." He pointed to the braided silver ring already bagged and tagged. "Roger indicated before his surgery that Thad Fisher never owned such a ring."

"So his name was Thad Fisher?" asked Nick.

Richard broke in. "The ex-mayor, of all things. Been missing for quite a while. Everyone thought he'd taken off with his mistress, Connie."

"Has this Connie been found?"

"No. I'll supply you with all the details I know about her once we finish our examination." Chief Rollins took out his handkerchief and wiped his pale forehead.

Pansy, thought Nick. "So, the finger was surgically removed?"

"Perhaps. I can't be certain except that no bone or skin fragments were left hanging. Very clean. Removed after death."

Nick thrust his hands into his trouser pockets. "A good chop of a cleaver could do the trick I'd imagine. Did the mayor wear a wedding band?"

"Yes. He had a designer ring," supplied Chief Rollins. "A thick gold nugget band with a full carat diamond in the center. It was a real beaute. Probably set him back eight to ten thousand dollars."

"You've seen it?"

"Couldn't miss it, being so big. Must have had that ring for seven or eight years. Really stood out. Maybe he refused to hand it over and a robber retaliated."

"Hmm, *Murder itself is not interesting.* It's the *reasons* for it that are interesting, gentlemen."

"What?" said Chief Rollins, clearly annoyed.

"Just a quote from a book I read once; it discussed why people murder. A must read for any detective, by Ruth Rendall."

"Well, glad *you've* read it," stated the Chief crossly. He didn't particularly care for smart aleck pseudo-intellectual women who told men how to do their jobs. His Nancy had been quite content staying at home these past thirty years and knew her place.

Dr. Koh handed Nick a Polaroid. "I took the liberty of taking a candid of the ring. It's important we discover the real owner, I take it?"

Nick nodded.

Dr. Koh smiled. "If you don't mind, gentlemen, I'd like to continue my examination further, and you might not enjoy its thoroughness." His dark eyes playfully pinpointed the aging chief as he reached for the shiny bone cutters atop his metal tray.

Nick instantly took a shine to the tall, thin coroner. At least he possessed a sense of humor about his morbid profession.

"Of course. What's your theory, Chief Rollins, or is it Chief?"

"Doesn't matter. You can call me either or. Everyone

else does."

They moved away from the examination room, and Nick spied Dr. Koh carefully slicing into Thad Fisher's chest cavity.

"I suspect," said the chief, warming to the subject, "that Thad was mugged, and the murderer couldn't get the ring off, and therefore had to remove the finger violently. That alone would have been motive enough for the crime, considering the value of the ring." The police chief kept jingling change in his pocket as if he wanted to say something more but was afraid to.

"Though you must agree, a screwdriver is a strange instrument for a mugger to choose, isn't it? And a screwdriver can't remove a finger, so the murderer must have had access to several tools. Plus, the wound was relatively dry—the mayor was murdered elsewhere. I believe he was buried under the magnolia tree during our full moon this week. The murderer used a wheelbarrow and worked alone. Is there something else you wanted to say, Chief?" urged Nick.

"You *are* quick. Roger said you were good. Well, I'm sure it means nothing, but there was another you know," offered Richard vaguely.

"Another?" asked Nick blankly. "What do you mean?"

"Another body we found, twenty-five years ago when Jeremy Fox was police chief."

Nick had heard about the legendary Jeremy Fox. He'd

been a massive man at 6'5" and totally white-haired by age thirty. The police chief of Monroe for ten years before he'd quit and started his own investigative firm, his integrity and grit were still marveled at by his successors. He'd worked for a while in Berkley and then come back to his hometown of Monroe City. While Nick had never met the man, his reputation had permeated all the law enforcement agencies in the area—that, and his spectacular murder. He and his son Lane had been investigating a Russian gang seeking to infiltrate several of the large agricultural firms that dotted the Big Valley. Jeremy and Lane had been found hanging from a makeshift gallows near Rancho Mandesto, far from their home. The sensational crime had made headlines, even in San Francisco.

His interest now thoroughly aroused, Nick turned his dark brown eyes to Richard's watery blue ones. "Another similar murder where the ring finger was removed happened during Fox's day?"

"Yes," whispered Richard, suddenly visualizing the victim. "It was horrible indeed. The victim was a young runaway by the name of Ashley Peebles found buried by an irrigation ditch out near Highway 4. Two scumbag drifters, Luke Cambridge and Deke Rhodes, were convicted of the crime. They'd been working the spinach fields not two miles from the main highway where her body was dumped. It didn't seem just like the normal murder-rape story; in fact, the girl didn't seem to have been recently assaulted. The unusual thing was that her left-hand ring finger had been hacked off.

"Interesting. But you say her murderers were apprehended?"

"Yup. Sentenced to the Big House for life. Deke died about twenty years ago in prison. Bled to death in some brawl inside the prison laundry, but Luke, he's still serving time."

"So, what was their motive?" asked Nick.

"Motive?"

"Yeah, you know, the reason she was killed? Most killings outside sexual assault, robbery, or unbridled passion have a reason."

The Chief bristled. "Wise guy, aren't ya? Of course there was a reason. It was jealousy. One was seeing her, and the other got jealous. Girl got caught in the middle. Simple as that. Don't go getting any of your weird ideas about a closed case. It was cut and dry."

So, the portly police chief had heard the rumors surrounding his methods. Nick ignored the barb.

"And what did Chief Fox think about all this?"

The chief shifted his feet. "Well, that's the strangest part about it all. He was always under the opinion they'd convicted the wrong men. In fact, when he and his boy Lane started Fox Investigative Services, Jeremy said that one of the things he wanted to do was delve deeper into the Peebles' murder.

Apparently, both Luke and Deke had contacted him swearing their innocence, but nothing came of it after Fox and his boy were murdered. For the best, really. Those guys were guilty as sin. Deke had her blood all over him." It was obvious Chief Rollins didn't agree with his ex-chief's doubts about the two men's innocence.

"Do you still have the file regarding the case?"

"Of course. Figured the likes of you would still want to dredge up that murder, so be my guest. You'll find everything pertaining to the case in the Monroe County records at the back of the courthouse. But I'm telling ya, it's probably just a random coincidence. I'll walk you over. And, Thayne . . ." He paused on the hot sidewalk. "I want you to be clear. When Roger is fit enough, he'll take back the case. You're to relay everything you learn or suspect to me and him. Your pay is $400 a day. No expenses, and it's a one-time deal. My budget is ten grand. You're done when the case is solved or the budget runs out. And . . . none of your weird, front page methods, okay? You got that?"

His barely disguised animosity was real, and Nick pondered the reasons. The man was clearly a traditionalist, and new or shaky methods made men of his type highly uncomfortable. Nick strolled along the long wide sidewalk next to Richard, lost in thought. It should have been only a three-minute walk to the County Records Office, but took closer to six with all the Chief's huffing and puffing.

Richard paused in front of the building and pointed. "Take the stairs at the rear. They lead down to the records section. Priscilla Smith is in charge. She might be a bit grumpy, since I asked her to stay late a Friday afternoon. I have to return to the station to phone Mrs. Fisher, who's going to be devastated by her husband's death."

Nick found the records room without any trouble, but Priscilla Smith proved no pushover.

"So, you work for the Monroe County Police Department. Then why don't I know you?"

"I'm taking over for Roger Chung, who's in the hospital with appendicitis. We were friends in detective school, and I'm helping him out on a case until he recovers."

The sixtyish woman softened somewhat. "I didn't realize he was ill."

"Just happened this afternoon. It's obvious you don't know me from Adam, but feel free to call Chief Rollins to verify my identity. I can clearly see you are a woman who is very conscientious about her job. I wish our records clerk in Girard was as dedicated as you."

Miss Smith did something no one had ever seen her do before and blushed. Nick smiled his most charmingly, and the lady led him to the stacks like an eager virgin enticing her first lover.

"Well, it's after hours , but let me help you. Hmm, the Ashley Peebles' murder. Quite a sensational case, one of the best we've ever had. Of course, the best mystery around here was the Fox murders. Never was *really* solved you know. Now, *that* was a tragedy."

Miss Smith talked non-stop for the next 30 minutes. At the end of the torturous search, both Nick Thayne and Miss Smith were in equal states of consternation. Nick felt frustrated and highly suspicious while Miss Smith was just plain livid. Ashley Peebles' records had disappeared, and Nick suspected they couldn't fault Priscilla's filing system for the truant records.

"Could Jeremy Fox have taken them?" asked Nick.

"Well, he might have, but I'm certain if he *did* he would have only taken a copy. That man was the most law-abiding, straight-and-narrow police chief and detective you ever met."

Nick swore Priscilla Smith was about to set off on a special fantasy just her own. "And look where it got him," he said between even white teeth. "Thanks so much for your help, Miss Smith. I'll know who to turn to in time of need. '*The public does not matter—only one's friends matter.*'"

"You read Yeats, Mr. Thayne?" Her suddenly interested pale-blue eyes lit up.

"Cover to cover," he lied. He read quotation books religiously because an appropriately placed quote seemed to convince people you were well-read and intelligent; something every private investigator needed desperately in his line of work. The only things he read religiously besides those quotation books were the Sunday paper and the daily sports page.

"He's one of my favorites. Please *do* come back for a chat sometime. Maybe we can share our favorite poems."

"I'll do that," said Nick, gallantly raising her hand to his lips and kissing it. He wasn't certain that women still swooned (his mother had always said that it was simply a symptom of too-tight corsets) but Miss Smith looked damned close. It was good to know he hadn't lost his touch after his last fiasco.

Nick recognized he should tell Chief Rollins the Peebles' files were missing, but the urge to consume a good meal and check on his old friend Roger trumped everything else. Chief Rollins would just have to wait.

Roger was resting comfortably when Nick arrived nearly an hour later. Nick had read Philemon Jenkins' statement and listened to Roger's meticulous oral notes over a greasy burger and an enormous plate of French fries. Later, he'd flirted with the pretty blonde waitress with the gorgeous implants and the outrageous name of Chastity. He'd tucked her number in his pocket and was pleased to note this otherwise sleepy town might have some possible diversions.

Roger, hooked up to the ominously dripping IV pouch as Susan sat nearby holding his hand, stirred at the sight of his friend. She rose when Nick arrived and gave him a warm hug. She smelled of lilacs and fresh oriental rain.

"It's nice seeing you again, Nick. Are you behaving yourself?" she purred.

Nick had the uncomfortable feeling that Roger may have shared a few too many of his escapades with his curious wife, and grinned sheepishly.

"Of course not, but at least I'd not horizontal and hooked up to one of these."

Roger smiled. "You'll have your day. Just make sure you have someone sweet to hold your hand." He shifted uncomfortably. "You sure they didn't take out the wrong thing, Susan? I feel kinda funny."

"Of course not, Roger, they just removed your appendix. Nothing else." Susan smiled at Nick. "He's absolutely paranoid about doctors."

"Can't trust 'em," growled Roger. "I wonder what extra charges they've added to our bill. You file the papers correctly, Susan?"

"Yes, love. Everything's taken care of."

"I read just last week about some guy who had cancer. His insurance company dumped him, and he later had to declare bankruptcy."

"Your children's college funds are safe, Roger." She smiled prettily at Nick.

Nick remembered what a worrywart Roger was. It felt

like old times.

"So, did you get to the site?" said Roger.

"I did. And a fine mess they've made of it. Footprints and disturbed soil and the usual lookie-loos on the sidewalk. Whatever possible clues were there are history now. The body's at the coroner with a Dr. Koh. He seems competent enough."

"I glad you feel that way," said Susan smoothly, "since he's my brother."

Nick's already good-sized feet seemed to expand a couple of inches and inch closer to his mouth. "I'm, er . . . waiting on his report. Dr. Koh says the mayor was probably stabbed with something like a screwdriver. We had to leave before he could get down to real business—the chief was suffering from a little *indigestion*."

"Doesn't have the stomach for it," stated Roger. Obviously, this wasn't a new revelation for him.

"I jotted down a few notes and will leave a copy of Philemon Jenkins' statement as well as both Officers Phelps' and Stevens' interviews of the neighbors for you to read when you're up to it. I did learn something interesting, but was unable to follow up on it. Thad Fisher's ring finger was hacked off. Chief Rollins stated a similar thing happened to a young woman murdered 25 years ago. An Ashley Peebles."

Roger's blurry eyes sharpened. "That had to be the most sensational crime to hit the area until the Fox murders. I believe two drifters were convicted and put away. There was something about a missing ring. That's right. She had a silver rope ring that her father said was missing from the body, and Thad had a ring like that on his pinkie. Did you check the files?"

"Couldn't. They were missing as well, and my new girlfriend Priscilla and I searched for over thirty minutes for them in the Records' Room."

"Priscilla? The records clerk? You've got to be kidding. She's an insufferable old prude."

"Oh, really? I thought she was quite fetching. Wanted to have my children, she did."

"So, you're already bestowing your undeniable charm upon the women of this otherwise staid town? Watch yourself, Nick. You saw what happened to the mayor when he fooled around."

"Ha, Ha, you *must* be feeling better. Anyway, my gut instinct says this is too much of a coincidence, and unfortunately, I can't speak to the man who headed the case before our time—the ex-chief of the police department."

A burly nurse pushed her way past Nick. "It's time to send your visitors home Mr. Chung. And here's your medicine. Open wide."

Roger obediently swallowed the two blue tablets and almost immediately his black eyes lost their focus.

"Great timing," murmured Nick annoyed.

"You can still get the records," slurred Roger. Susan had risen and caressed her husband's hand. "Lee Fox still runs the P.I. Agency and . . ."

"Roger, I don't think . . ." soothed Susan.

"And . . ." prompted Nick as Roger's eyes momentarily closed. "Roger?"

"Yeah. Lee is a handful, but I'm sure the files are there. Lee is . . ." Roger's eyes closed and didn't open again.

"Oh well," said Nick. "I guess I have to give this guy a call. Thought Jeremy Fox's son was murdered along with him."

"He had another child." Susan smiled strangely. She tucked her husband's unresponsive hand under the covers and placed the file Nick had brought for Roger's review on the side table.

"I suggest you tread lightly, Nick. Lee Fox doesn't share information or anything else without a price. There's a few things you should know before . . ."

"Leave it to me. There isn't a guy I can't persuade."

"Right," said Susan and forced a smile. Nick had the annoying feeling she was mocking him, and he was loathe to know why.

Chapter 4

Dr. Koh called before Nick made it to the parking lot and asked him to stop back by.

"I haven't finished my complete examination, but so far, some very interesting tidbits have surfaced. Do you see this here?"

"What is it?"

"They must be at least ten or so half dissolved barbiturate tables."

The white flakes floated in the jar of vomit-colored material. Nick could only hope that Thad had been nearly unconscious when he'd been murdered, since the weapon had been the lethal end of a Philips screwdriver. Dr. Koh illustrated how it had been shoved upwards through the throat embedding itself in the nasal passages behind the nostrils before jutting out the rear of the mayor's skull. Thad Fisher had bled to death, but mercifully had probably felt little pain because of a brain numbing dose of barbiturates.

"And look at this." The coroner pulled back the linen sheet from the bloated feet of Thad Fisher. 15 or so cuts were evident upon his hairy feet and ankles.

"What caused those?"

"The mayor was found without his shoes. I speculate he tried to escape his murderer and ran through some rough terrain. I pulled two of these out." He thrust what appeared like a rose thorn in a pair of tweezers towards Nick.

"Anyway to tell what kind of rose bush this came from?"

"Only that the size indicates they were hybrid teas. I'll call you when I learn more."

Voices sounded in the reception area. "Take the back entrance. I'm sure this is Thad Fisher's wife and the chief. Might not be a pretty scene to witness."

"Got it," voiced Nick gratefully. He hated hysterical scenes involving women. Tears made him feel helpless, and they were so goddamn useless anyway. The stoic Dr. Koh seemed used to weepy women and plastered a sympathetic smile upon his pleasant face as Nick scooted towards the back alley.

He settled into the front seat and closed his eyes before reaching for his pencils. Twenty minutes later, he recognized how imperative the Peebles' records were. It was time to call Lee Fox. Nick just wished he had something to bargain with in case the man proved to be difficult, which made him reflect on a far less important mystery. Why had he been called in when the city had its own private investigator?

Within the hour, he had checked into Louise's Boarding House. Nick had actually stayed here nine months before during a missing person's case. He lugged in his suitcase and the large portfolio containing his drawings and pencils and placed them on the business-sized desk provided by the red-cheeked Louise.

"It's *so* nice to have you here again, Mr. Thayne. I'll make sure I make more of my special rhubarb and cherry pie you enjoyed so much last time," gushed Louise.

Louise Martin was a poster ad for Dexatrim. She was, however, the cheeriest and most generous of hostesses. He smiled back, examining her bottle-blonde hair. Marilyn Monroe *was* alive.

"I'll certainly look forward to that, Louise."

"You'll want breakfast and dinner each day?"

"Most likely. Let's start tomorrow. Tonight I'll be busy."

She smiled prettily, lipstick staining her upper teeth. "I'll make some Eggs Benedict."

"I can hardly wait."

"Ohhh! You draw?" Her chubby fingers reached for his packed portfolio.

"A little."

"Can I see?" She actually clapped her hands in anticipation.

"No!" he responded more gruffly than he'd meant. "That is, I'm shy about my drawings, being such an amateur, and all. Maybe some other time?"

Louise didn't take offense. "Well, I'll be *waiting* for that. Hope you enjoy the room. It's the best in the house." She toddled off, and he grinned at her outfit, which consisted of a short, flowered dress pulled too tightly over her heavy breasts and exposed masses of cellulite. She wore bright, matching pink sandals with spiky heels. Louise had style, all right, and seemed to have no trouble with body image.

The room was indeed spacious, offering Internet access as well as a cable TV with a large screen. It possessed a small sitting area as well as a tiny kitchen equipped with two burners, a microwave, internet access, and best yet, a huge coffee pot. The king-sized bed fit comfortably into the beige wallpapered room. This would do just fine. He put some coffee on before settling himself down to call Lee Fox.

After the second ring, the clear, strong voice of an efficient secretary resounded even though it was well after normal business hours.

"Fox Investigative Services."

"Hello," said Nick without preamble. "My name is Nick Thayne from Thayne Investigations in Girard, and I'd like to make an appointment with Lee Fox. This evening, if possible. I know it's late, but I've heard his father spearheaded a case regarding one Ashley Peebles—a seventeen-year-old runaway who was murdered about 25 years ago. It's come to my attention that certain specific details from that case are similar to one I'm working here, and I thought maybe your agency could help me out, since the original casebook seems to be missing."

After a long pause on the other end of the line, the efficient voice returned. "At what time would you like to stop by?"

"9:30 p.m.? I know it's late but would that work for Mr. Fox?"

"That would be fine. And you are, again?"

Nick ground his teeth exasperatedly. "Nick *Thayne* of *Thayne* Private Investigations in Girard," he repeated. "I'm on special assignment with the Monroe Police Department. Tell your boss I'll see him promptly at 9:30."

Lea Fox hung up the phone and leaned back in her chair, her thin hands clasped before her. Nick Thayne wasn't the first man to have mistaken her gender and wouldn't be the last. She recognized the case he'd inquired about and sat for a full five minutes thinking furiously before removing the file from the top drawer of father's old wooden filing cabinet and settling herself down to read. Her eyes widened, and she nodded. After a few minutes, she tossed the well-read file upon the too-clean desk and fired up her computer, her short fingers punching in the noted P.I.'s name. When the facts and surrounding speculations came up, the information caused her to grin broadly. *Well, well, Mr. Thayne.*

On the bright sunflower pattern of the breakfast tablecloth, the cluster of drawings would have put anyone off their lunch. The first depicted a red brick fence bordering an abandoned field shaded by an immense magnolia tree. The small red ball rested not two feet from the upturned claw of a hand. The second, as riveting as the first, could have served as an advertisement for never drinking and driving. The good-looking man horribly ravaged by a large oak tree trunk and a close encounter with the front windshield leaned against the still form of a teenaged girl appearing merely asleep by him. The final drawing showed an abandoned crib, its only occupant a chewed-up teddy bear floating in a huge twist-top jar. The artist flung down the garishly colored drawings and scooped up his keys, but not before swigging down three extra-strength aspirin. It was going to be a long evening.

Nick paused before the modest yellow stucco house, standing for a moment on the pleasantly wide front porch and admiring the early evening neighborhood. His ring was answered by a lovely African-American woman, who, although clearly aging, boasted fine bones in a gentle face.

"I'm Inspector Nick Thayne," he said extending his hand.

"And I'm Darcy Jenkins. Philemon is waiting for you inside. Do come in."

The beige furniture, though inexpensive, was comfortable, and Philemon rose from his favorite recliner, sticking out a calloused hand to Nick Thayne.

"How are you doing?" asked Nick kindly.

"Fine *now*. Please, won't you sit down?" Philemon gestured to the plaid couch across from him. "Darcy, bring Mr. Thayne some of your award-winning lemonade. My wife captured the title in the Monroe County Fair's lemonade contest three years in a row. She's an expert at achieving just the right mixture of sugar, water, and lemons."

"That would be lovely," said Nick sinking upon the worn but comfortable couch. He studied the African-American man. For a man nearing sixty, Philemon was in excellent condition. Only the faint lines engraved upon his dark face and the gray wiry hair cut very short around an increasing bald spot indicated his age. His glasses emphasized an intelligent if wary face. Darcy returned presently, bearing a tray with two glasses and a pitcher whose ice cubes clanked freely. She poured two tall glasses of lemonade and discreetly left the room. Nick opened his briefcase and took out Roger's notepad.

"Thank you for being so detailed about your rather gruesome discovery, Mr. Jenkins. How long have you worked for Mrs. Simms?"

"Well, it's been going on to three years now," said Philemon. "I enjoy the work, and Mrs. Simms is a first-class employer. I have my retirement, and Darcy her Social Security, but the extra money helps us afford trips to visit our grown children."

"Had you ever seen the ex-mayor in the neighborhood before?"

Philemon had hung around long enough to see the unearthed body of Thad Fisher and shuddered as he remembered the bloated, stinking corpse. "No, I can't say I have, but I may not have recognized him—his features were . . . ah . . . distorted."

Nick nodded. "He'd been dead a few days."

Philemon continued. "Chester Street is very quiet, you know, and because I work only mornings on Monday, Wednesday, and Friday, most folks aren't around. And Mrs. Simms, she's retired, and all. I remember, I did see him a couple years ago at the Country Fair, delivering some speech. I don't pay much mind to politics."

"Do you ever work in the field next to Mrs. Simms' house?" asked Nick.

"Sometimes. She often has me take the weed whacker and trim the edge of the fence, but it isn't her land, after all. I spend most of my time in her garden."

"And the neighbors across the street? You reported

that someone mentioned the word 'magnolia' to you?"

"Why, yes," said Philemon clearing his throat. The whole topic of Bouncer made him strangely uncomfortable. After all, he might have been mistaken about the lisped words coming from the unknown child, but decided to confess everything to the broad-shouldered detective. The Lord demanded it. "I've been playing ball with someone behind the fence during my breaks. I think it's a little boy. Mrs. Simms said someone named Collins owns the property, so it's probably some relative of theirs."

Nick glanced at the plot numbers and nodded. "Yes, Mrs. Simms was interviewed by one of the officers and reported she is inclined to believe the house is vacant. She rarely, if ever sees or hears anyone in the house. I guess this murder was quite a shock to her."

"Mrs. Simms is frail, and the heat has been intense lately. May the Lord give her strength. She's so often told me how the peace and quiet of the street keeps her from moving into one of those fancy retirement homes. This must have been a blow; a blow, indeed."

Nick nodded. "So, about this neighbor? You've been playing ball with someone inside the fence?"

"I know it's highly unusual. A child's been tossing over a red rubber ball, and I've been bouncing it back.

"You said a red rubber ball?" A peculiar look flitted across Nick's face.

"Yeah, a bit bigger than a softball. The child doesn't say much, usually just chuckling and giggling sometimes, and well, when I asked their name the only response I got was Bouncer. So that's what I call him."

"How long have you played ball with this faceless child?"

"Not even two weeks. We played for about fifteen minutes today, and towards the end of our game, the boy said the word *magnolia*. I got to thinking that maybe the kid had a hideout or fort in the magnolia tree located in the vacant lot, so I decided after my work to just saunter over there and maybe meet my little friend in person. Instead, well, you know what I found."

"I do indeed," said Nick. "I'll check the records on the Collins' house."

Philemon took a long swig of the tart lemonade, gulping as if it was the finest Kentucky bourbon. Nick joined him and smiled in appreciation. This really *was* good.

"Just one other thing, Mr. Jenkins. Deputy Steele asked you to come into the Station to make a statement, and you refused. Why?"

Philemon gazed at his work-worn hands a long time before answering. "I just don't like police much. My cousin was killed a couple of years prior to my moving here, and the police weren't very helpful. Just said it was gang related and dropped the case flat. He was only forty and left a wife and three children. His lady never did get over it"

"That was where?"

Philemon cleared his throat and glanced up. Darcy hung in the doorway, looking fretful.

"Detroit. We used to live in Detroit."

Nick smiled soothingly. "I've not always had the best of luck with the police myself, Mr. Jenkins. I'm actually just contracted out on this case and am a freelance P.I." He flipped open his black leather wallet and handed Philemon his card. "Only call me on my cell. I'm usually located in Girard, but I'm camping out at Louise's Boarding House during my stay here. You can reach me anytime, day or night."

Philemon appeared vaguely reassured. "Thanks, Inspector Thayne. I'll certainly call if I remember anything else."

"Oh, one other thing. Does Mrs. Simms own a wheelbarrow?"

"Yes, a rusty old yellow one. I keep having to pump up the tire. It gets a lot of use."

"I'll have someone take a peek at it. Thanks so much, Mr. Jenkins."

"Please call me Philemon, or Phil, if you like. Mr. Jenkins sounds like an old man."

Nick grinned as the gardener escorted him to the door after the detective made a show of drinking down the rest of the sweet lemonade.

"My compliments to your wife, sir. She certainly deserves all the rewards and accolades she's received for this prize-winning lemonade. I've never tasted better."

As he strolled to his red Mustang, he wondered why Mrs. Jenkins seemed so nervous. Of course, finding a body in the shape of the ex-mayor's was enough to rattle anyone, but it might be wise to delve deeper into the life of Philemon Jenkins.

Nick's next stop was back at Chester Street. He squinted at the scrap of paper. Number 621; the home of Lindsey and Mark Lyons. The beautiful two-story brick house with its imposing foyer impressed him as the door opened to reveal a stout, red-faced woman who wiped her face with a dishtowel.

"Hello," she said tentatively.

"My name is Inspector Nick Thayne. You indicated to one of the officers that your daughter saw something earlier this week. I'm sorry it's so late but I'm here to follow it up immediately since it sounded so important."

"Oh, yes, Officer. Please come in."

"I'm afraid I'm not an officer," Nick explained as he strolled into the immaculately clean living room. "I'm a private investigator working on contract for Monroe City Police Department, and I run my own private investigative company. The MCPD's only detective had to have some emergency surgery, and since it is a small police force, I'm helping them out."

"I see," said Lindsey Lyons nodding, obviously not caring a rat's ass about whom he was affiliated with. "I'll go get Katie right away, and she can tell you what she saw."

A little blonde girl was led out by the hand by her heavyset mother. Her hair parted down the middle, and her nose and cheeks were badly sunburned. When she parted her lips to smile at Nick, two spaces existed where front teeth should be. She couldn't have been a day over six, and Nick felt his heart sink. A small child would not exactly be the most reliable of witnesses. He'd been hoping for at least a teenager.

He sank down into the mauve and couch and patted the cushion beside him.

"Why don't you sit beside me, Katie?"

"Okay," said the little girl. "So you're a policeman?"

"I used to be, but now I'm a private investigator. So, you say you know something about the body?"

"Well, kind of," she answered and glanced up at her mother, who nodded reassuringly.

"Tell him everything you saw, Katie."

"Well, it was Tuesday evening," said Katie. "I saw this big old car, one I had never seen before. It was all long and black and shiny."

"A limousine," interrupted her mother, who had flopped down on the oversized couch to listen to her daughter's lisping speech.

"Yes, a lemonusine," repeated the little girl. "I was skipping rope with my friend Jeanie."

"Jeanie," said Nick, "and where does she live?"

Lindsey Lyons blushed, her round cheeks turning even redder. "I'm afraid that Jeanie is Katie's invisible friend."

Nick closed his notebook and decided it might be best to just listen to the little girl's rendition of whatever she thought had happened.

"Anyway," said Katie. "Jeanie and I saw this lemonusine drive down the road, and it parked right in front of the ghost house."

"The ghost house?" asked Nick peering questioningly at Mrs. Lyons.

"She's talking about the big house across from Mrs. Simms' place—the one that looks kind of like a fortress with its high fence and spikes on top. It certainly doesn't fit in *our* neighborhood."

"Well, anyways," said Katie unperturbed by her mother's interruption. "This big old man got out with this woman, whose hair was really red, and she was wearing this dress that was just as red as her hair was and big old high heels. I remember her shoes went clickity, clickity clack."

Nick smiled at her description of Thad's redheaded mistress. "And what else, Katie?"

"Well," said the little girl, realizing she had a captive audience. "They went into the house, and it was almost dark, and my mom called Jeanie and me in for dinner, but after dinner, I went out and then I saw it. I was chasing Celeste down the street and had to bring her in."

"Celeste?" asked Nick.

"Our cat," sighed Mrs. Lyons.

"Anyway, I was chasing Celeste down the street when I heard this really weird sound like a 'woo woo woo' and weird laughing, and then on the second floor of the ghost house, there was a light flickering in the window, and I saw a ghostly ghoul standing in the window."

"A ghostly ghoul?" repeated Nick, realizing this verged on incredible. Katie's pale eyes gleamed. She was obviously into her story.

"Yeah. He was standing in front of the window. His hair was all spiky and red, and he had big, fat cheeks just like the Pillsbury Dough Boy. He had his hands on the windowsill and was howling at the moon, 'woo, woo, woo.'"

"Would you please tell me the night again, Katie?"

"It was Tuesday because it was the day after my Daddy's birthday."

If she was right, Thad could have been dead since the beginning of the week.

"When you saw the ghostly ghoul, Katie, was the limousine still around?"

"Nope, it had gone. There was nothing there but the ghost, and he looked something awful, like a monster with a big old head and short body. Kind of like Uncle Fester on *The Addams Family*."

"Katie watches old reruns with her granddad," said Mrs. Lyons apologetically.

"Katie," said Thayne, "all of this is very interesting. I really want to thank you for your information. What you have told me has given us a time frame when we know that Mr. Fisher was on the block. Thank you so much for your help."

He rose politely and stuck out a hand to the little girl, who amazingly took it before dropping into a pretty little courtesy while holding his hand. Nick grinned. He wasn't the only one blessed with charm.

"I'm glad to help, officer," said Katie in her best TV voice. "I'll keep an eye on the ghost house and let you know if I see anything saspicious." She had trouble pronouncing the final word.

Nick bid the family goodbye after handing them his business card and easing his long legs into his Mustang. He hoped he'd have better luck with Lee Fox.

Chapter 5

9:30 pm, Fox Investigative Services

Fox Investigative Services ended up being in an older and more pleasantly established part of town than his boarding house. Once a rundown section near the railroad depot, the neighborhood had been renovated and restored to its former, quiet dignity and in the heart of this discreet but tasteful business district, Nick found Lee Fox's office. Five minutes to early, he arrived at Suite 7, 1257 W. Mesa Street. He wrapped his knuckles upon the glass door and tried to peer through the frosted panes. The door opened abruptly and he nearly fell inside.

A short, nutmeg-haired woman stood before him. Her hair, cropped in pixie cut, would have looked fine on a child or teenager but seemed abruptly out of place on a grown woman. Bug-eyed glasses with rims too dark and oversized perched upon her short, upturned nose. Her dress was an awful blue-checked affair, cut way too long and loose over her slight frame with huge shoulder pads. It dwarfed the already small woman, who glanced at her tiny gold wristwatch as if hoping he were late. Nick felt a childish satisfaction that she seemed disappointed.

"I'm here to see Mr. Fox. I'm Inspector Nick Thayne." He sincerely hoped Lee Fox was a little more with it than his frumpy secretary.

"I'm Lea Fox," said the short woman and Nick blanched. "And the name is L-E-A Fox, short for Lea. Do come in." She led the way into a rear office, a strange thumping noise accompanying her slow progress. Nick's dark oval eyes shifted downwards to note the metal half-crutch she used to help her progress. She set down across from an expansive polished desk, leaning the crutch against a filing cabinet.

"You had an accident?"

"Years ago, but I re-injured it a couple days ago. So, what do you want?"

Her violet eyes shrewdly analyzed his slender, handsome features as he lowered himself into her brother's old chair much as a fox might do before it was about to attack a chicken. Lea noted he was incredibly attractive, the kind of man women view as a sinful indulgence for the eyes. Some women, however, probably labeled him simply as an exotic treat; the kind you sample at an ethnic restaurant but never take home. The more racist among them would probably shift uneasily in their seats, uncomfortable with that tightening sensation in their lower regions, the kind of heat their own overweight WASP husbands could no longer inspire within them. Lea Fox felt none of these.

Charm was his best friend. “First, I must apologize. I’m sorry about before. I just assumed Lea Fox was a man.”

“It’s a common mistake. There’s no offence taken. You’re here because you want the files on the Peebles’ murder?”

“You have them?” asked Nick leaning forward in the squeaky chair.

“Just copies. Their originals are in the County Records Office behind the courthouse.”

“They may have been at one time,” said Nick, “but they’re certainly not there now.”

She chose not to comment about the missing records and just continued staring at him. He wanted to smooth back his hair or something under her unwavering gaze.

She finally asked, “And why would you be so interested in a twenty-five-year-old murder?”

“It has a lot to do with your ex-mayor. Mr. Thad Fisher was just found murdered this afternoon in an empty field on Chester Street. His finger—his ring finger to be exact—was hacked off exactly like Ashley Peebles’. I’ve been informed by Police Chief Rollins that she was reported to have been missing a silver ring. A similar silver ring was found on Thad Fisher's pinkie finger, and I'm hoping you might have a photograph of the original ring so I can see if it's a match."

"I might," said Lea, not seeming inclined to stir from her red-cushioned swivel chair.

"May I look at the report?" asked Nick, wondering what on earth was wrong with the woman. She was that kind of female who made a man acutely uncomfortable, and he was uncertain whether to ignore her, throttle her, or sign her up at a beauty resort for a weekend hoping it might have some modifying success. Yet, there was something acutely odd about her. The glasses were too large and obscured her eyes, which were truly lovely. In fact, she was almost pretty, but he got the strange feeling that she didn't want anyone to recognize that.

"No, you can't," responded Lea defiantly. "Since you've indicated the original records are missing and I possess the only remaining records regarding the Ashley Peebles' murder, it's apparent that the Monroe City Police Department should now deal directly with me."

Nick Thayne had not expected this. "I'm just asking for a simple favor," he said in his most charming tone. It rarely failed to work on an attractive woman, though this one seemed determined not to warrant a second glance. "I thought as one P.I. to another, we could help each other out."

"We're not one P.I. to another," stated Lea Fox

sharply. “You don’t even live in this town, so I needn’t deal with you. Where’s Roger Chung?”

Nick noticed that Lea Fox’s teeth were small and straight and even, but for all the mildness of her tone, he recognized them for what they were really were; retractable canines.

“Roger’s in the hospital. Appendicitis. I’m filling in while he recovers. So, I’m asking you, as the Monroe Police Department’s substitute investigator, to share the documents with me. I know your father Jeremy worked long and hard on this case, and I need his insights.”

“My father’s dead,” stated Lea abruptly.

“I recognize that,” returned Nick as evenly as possible, “but because of the similarities between the Mayor’s case and the Peebles girl, I would like to go over those documents, and my suspicions have been doubly aroused since they’re now missing from County Records.”

Lea Fox rose to her full 5’2” height and stared Nick Thayne straight in the eye. “And just what makes you think I’d share them with you? I know your reputation and barely disguised male chauvinism glossed over by your oh-so-delectable charm. I’ve read all about your escapades in the papers and heard your smugly disarming voice on Juniper Cox’s radio show. I believe a recent spellbinding segment covered how you located her long-lost father, who just happened to be a multi-millionaire living in luxury down in

Costa Rica, though God knows where you got *that* information. You're just an ex-hotshot police detective with a rich daddy and a Stanford education, and now you've been contracted out by the Monroe Police Department on special assignment. I'm smart enough to know what that translates into. You're just one of the good ole boys. Why didn't Chief Rollins come to me himself, as if I didn't know?"

Nick bristled at her tone. "Maybe he knows my reputation and trusts Roger's referral. After all, I worked on the San Francisco City Police Force for over four years before starting my own P.I. firm. I get the job done."

"Ah, that must be it. So, he turns to you, a relative stranger, even while knowing that three generations of Foxes have lived in the area for over forty years. As a matter of fact, no one understood the ins and the outs of the Peebles' case better than my father and brother. Now that I've studied their notes, I'm quite as expert as they were." She crossed her arms defiantly.

Nick, sick of fighting, settled himself more comfortably into the stiff wooden chair and stretched out his long, gray-clad legs before responding.

"Do you know what I think, Lea Fox? I think you've got a first class chip on your shoulder, lady, just because Roger Chung suggested my name to the Chief instead of yours. Come on, we're both in the same profession and need to help each other out. Haven't you learned the first rule of the brotherhood?"

"You said it," hissed Lea. "*Brothers*-in-arms; the little lady can just be classified as one of the secretarial staff."

Nick had the grace to redden slightly. He ran a lean hand through his dark, well-styled hair. "I *am* sorry, Ms. Fox. That was an unfortunate mistake; one I promise never to make again."

Lea stood, staring down at him for a full minute, and Nick felt uncomfortable under her scrutiny. Her purple eyes were slightly enlarged behind the black-rimmed glasses as she studied the nonchalant manner in which he sprawled in her brother's old chair. Restlessly, she moved towards the filing cabinet. A tidy office, Nick was reminded once again how messy and disorganized his own appeared. Of, course that was a misconception many made. *He* knew where everything was and could find it in an instant and while he'd been tempted to hire a secretary Nick enjoyed the solitude and chance to ponder his cases uninterrupted. He sorely needed that privacy considering his methods.

Lea's office, however, was so painfully neat it made him downright uncomfortable. Everything was labeled clearly and so excruciatingly ordered that he longed to toss a wad of paper upon the floor or disorganize those neat manila folders resting upon her wide desk.

Actually, Nick realized, as he stared at the desk, that it was a beaute; an antique made of rich maple and polished to an unlikely luster. It was at least six feet in length by three feet wide. A brand-spanking-new computer rested on the right-hand side of its brilliant surface, presenting the user with a large monitor that must have cost her a small fortune. A matching maple shelf organizer rested on the left-hand side of the immaculate desk, accompanied by a shiny black speakerphone-combination -fax on the far right. An embossed leather pad two feet square had been recessed into the desk, providing the perfect writing surface. If the lovely desk was any indication, Lea Fox was a real professional.

"Nice desk," he tried cordially.

Lea snorted. She had moved to another maple filing cabinet and yanked open a heavy drawer. "Wish my investigative talents could warrant as much attention as my father's old desk," returned the dowdy woman.

Nick sensed anger and something else he couldn't name behind the flippant words. Lea Fox briskly rustled through dozens of files, pulling out a few here and there before replacing them neatly, clearly not finding what she was searching for, or pretending not to, he suspected.

Nick took this time to study the petite woman more closely as she jerkily proceeded through the files. Her dark-rimmed glasses did nothing for her oval face and only managed to intensify her old schoolmarm appearance. A teacher from his youth, Sister Theresa, reminded him of Fox, and he rubbed his knuckles in remembrance of the sharp rap of her ruler freely administered when he wasn't paying attention. She was tiny, a full foot shorter than he, and her violet eyes were distorted under the concealing glasses with brows that could use a thorough plucking and cleaning.

Her lower lip was caught between her teeth as she valiantly searched through the endless files. She resembled an awkward teenager who hadn't learned how to make the best of what little she had. If he didn't know better, he'd swear she was hiding behind a uniform of dowdiness. She gave a small shriek of triumph and flung a big file atop the magnificent desk. Lea Fox shoved the heavy cabinet door closed with a bang. Her outdated tweed dress made her resemble some elderly misplaced Brit in the Big Valley. In fact, as he surveyed the small woman before him and the trappings of the too neat office, he noted that everything had a frayed, almost worn-out look that spoke of better days and richer times.

The desk, the faded Persian rug, the roller chairs—everything had the same antique appearance the woman reflected. She resembled some librarian or schoolteacher from the 40s or 50s who had passed her prime and was suddenly expected to function in the twenty-first century. His head jerked to attention, as he realized she'd noted him studying her.

"Not to your liking?" she stated abruptly.

He flinched. Nick had heard those words before, but they had been directed at him, and he remembered just how much he'd disliked them at the time.

"I'm not sure," he returned honestly. "Is there a quick mind enclosed behind that probing stare of yours or is it camouflaged behind blue plaid as well?"

She hesitated before firing back. "I guess that's for you to determine. I was *magna cum laude* at Harvard Law School, if that's what you need to determine whether or not I have the brains suitable for the job."

"Well, I guess that answers my question. So, you decided against practicing law?"

"The law decided against me," she returned. "I was too awkward, too unattractive, and too abrupt for the courtroom and their sitcom notions of what a woman should be. I decided to do my legal work behind the scenes and leave the courtroom battles to the '*Young and the Restless.*' It's a soap opera world. Didn't you know that, Mr. Thayne?"

Nick cocked a dark head at her. "I believe that some of us don't fit the expected notion of many Americans. Being half-Filipino isn't exactly mainstream, you know."

"You're still Hollywood beautiful. I'm sure they'd make an exception in the courtroom for a handsome half-breed like you."

"Don't call me that!" hissed Nick. Stunned, he was reminded suddenly of the hostess, Ann Peterson, from the British game show *The Weakest Link*, who always went out of her way to be insulting. He'd been vaguely amused by the

Brit's caustic nature; that was, until now. He immediately recalled Chief Rollins startled glance, one he'd discreetly directed elsewhere after discovering Nick wasn't the WASP he'd been expecting.

"Ah, sensitive are we? Well, tell me about it. My nickname in college was 'Clomper', dubbed such by my adoring roommate because of my limp. Not very conducive to promoting the comforting image of high-speed chases and TV show romances on our training course Bible, *Law and Order*. Those women are part Tomb Raider and Marie Curie all tied up in one. Brains and brawn. At least I have the brains, not like those waxen babes you're coupled with."

"Waxen babes." The image was so apt that Nick laughed. She was clearly as wounded as he. "Look, Ms. Fox. Let's quit the verbal sparring for now. I concede you're likely an expert on the Peebles case. I've been assigned to the Mayor's murder case, whether you like it or not, and all I know is that it bears a remarkable similarity to the Peebles murder. So, I'm asking you the only way I know how… can you help me out?"

"Are you getting a fee?" she asked abruptly.

"What? A fee?

"Is the Monroe Police Department paying you a fee for your services?"

"Well, yes, of course."

"Then I want half."

"Half?"

"That's right. You've taken at least fifty percent of my business in the region for over the past eighteen months, so I want some back. It's clear to me that you're in with the boys, and even though my father and brother had a great reputation with the MCPD, I need a chance to prove to the police department—and everyone else, for that matter—that I'm a competent investigator. If I help you, you have to help me. I need your endorsement and their business. If I work with you on this case while Roger is laid up, it could be beneficial for both of us." She paused significantly and eyed him disconcertingly. "I may even surprise you if you can get over your prejudices regarding my physical handicaps and womanly deficiencies."

Nick stared in amazement. Never in his life had he met a woman so blunt or seemingly callous about her own shortcomings. He suspected there was a lot more to Lea Fox then her superficial unattractiveness suggested. Suddenly, the great trait that made him one of the best detectives around surfaced as his curiosity overwhelmed him. He'd always suffered the acute need to *know* even as a child, and it was that one fatal flaw that had subsequently ruined his ordered and sequential life. He wanted to figure out this petite woman who stood so defiantly before him and determine just why she half-fascinated, half-repelled him. He rose from the creaky wooden chair and stuck out his hand while falling back on his old standby: the appropriate or inappropriate quote.

"*The only sure basis of an alliance is for each party to be equally afraid of the other.*"

"Okay," said Lea evenly. "You've stumped me. Who said it?"

"Thucydides, over 2000 years ago."

"I like the mutual fear part. It's probably the best way to start our alliance on this case because believe me, your charm is wasted on me."

Nick frowned. He'd have to keep a clear head around this woman. "Okay, Lea Fox. I'll agree to your terms, but you're not to forget I lead on this and answer directly to Roger Chung and Chief Rollins. You're to stay in the background."

They shook, Nick amazed by her strong grip.

"In the background," she agreed demurely between clenched teeth, her left hand hidden behind her back, the small fingers crossed. Nick Thayne had no idea what he was in for. If Nick Thayne thought she was simply going to hand him the folder and allow him to walk out to work on it that evening at Louise's Boarding House over a few cups of too-strong coffee and some leftover pizza, he was way off base. He wasn't getting one glance at the sacred files without Lea Fox right at his shoulder. Nick said nothing as he ran across the first set of photos, which were gruesome in their simplicity.

"They didn't locate her finger at first," stated Lea matter-of-factly.

"How'd they find the body?"

"A migrant worker suggested the girl had moved in with Luke or Deke. Upon searching their vehicle, they found blood in Deke's car. Both men swore they were innocent, though it was clear Ashley was involved with one or both of them. They later found a mass of blood all over the bathroom of the room the men shared—type AB. Deke's was O, and Luke's was A. Rather damning, I'd say."

A sudden frown crossed her face, and she moved to the filing cabinet again as he perused the file. "I'm certain I have photos of Deke and Luke somewhere. Anyway, the body was found purely by chance some two days later near the river, covered haphazardly by a thin layer of autumn leaves. The girl had been strangled and stabbed but not raped, but the coroner found an amazing detail. Ashley Peebles had given birth less than a week before her murder."

"Was the baby's body ever found?"

"Nope," said Lea, "but Richard Rollins—the inspector at the time—was certain he'd captured the culprits. The blood in Luke and Deke's bathroom matched Ashley's, so he figured they had to be the killers. Ah, here they are." She tossed two black-and-white photos upon the lovely desk.

Nick pushed aside the graphic photo of Ashley Peebles' scantily clad and bloodied body, concentrating instead on the young men's images. One was a handsome, dark-haired man by the name of Luke Cambridge, and the other a surly greasy-haired redneck named Deke Rhodes. No doubt about it—Jeremy Fox had been particularly meticulous about collecting every detail regarding the case. There were old newspaper cutouts and photographs, extensive coverage of the trial, and numerous photographs of the body. Both men had been convicted, and before Deke Rhodes had even come up for parole, he was killed in a laundry-room brawl.

"So, Luke Cambridge is still serving time?"

"Hasn't ever been granted parole, though he's has another hearing coming soon."

"No sexual assault?"

"No. While his fingerprints were found on bloody scissors in his bathroom, and Luke admitted to having been with the girl weeks before the murder, no assault was indicated. That's what bothered my father, since the court presented a love triangle as the reason for her murder. The deciding evidence was a pair of pantyhose found in the dash of Deke's car. It was ascertained the nylons were the murder weapon; that and the scissors. There was no doubt Luke knew the girl, and while he adamantly stated he hadn't killed her, there was powerful evidence he and Deke had murdered her and perhaps even the baby. The baby had most likely been born in their small flat, but no infant was ever found. No matter what their innocence or guilt, a jury found them guilty. Everyone accepted the verdict until my father received this over two years ago."

She handed him a tattered white envelope, and Nick pulled out the well-read letter, scanning it briefly. In it, Luke Cambridge begged Jeremy Fox to reconsider the evidence in the Ashley Peebles case. He swore that he was entirely innocent, and now that Jeremy Fox was a well-known private investigator, he urged him to reopen his case.

"So, did your father take on the case?"

"Of course he did. Both Lane and my father had a profound sense of justice, and my dad later told me that he'd always suspected Deke and Luke hadn't killed the girl."

"Your dad was police chief at the time of the murder, wasn't he?"

She nodded. "The chief investigator was Richard Rollins, who presently serves as police chief. Even to me, the evidence seemed a bit too pat. The two men were drifters who worked at the nearby Agrit-Empire harvesting potatoes, onions, and spinach. Apparently, Deke thought he was destined to be some sort of magnificent rodeo rider. The DA suggested they were short of cash and morals, and Ashley Peebles was a young girl looking for something to lift her out of her restrictive fundamentalist lifestyle. The case against Deke and Luke was weak on all counts. The defense lawyer proved that, while Ashley had delivered her baby in their bathroom, there was no indication she had met her end there. Luke testified that the pantyhose were indeed hers, but when she went into labor and they'd removed them to help facilitate the birth process. They stated she went into labor in their car."

"If the evidence was so flimsy, how were they convicted?" Nick watched Lea carefully. While it appeared she'd just pulled the file from the cabinet after his arrival, Lea had obviously familiarized herself with the case recently or simply had an incredible memory. He'd place his bets on the former.

"A fact arose that turned the tables on the two men. The DA insisted Ashley's murder was a crime of passion. Luke had mistakenly believed he was the father of Ashley's child and later discovered someone else had fathered her newborn baby. Luke was addicted to speed, and when arrested, was higher than a kite. No one could get a straight answer out of him, and Deke… Well, Deke was just plain vile. My father said he had never met a more foul-mouthed, hideously mannered man in his entire life. He admitted to sleeping with Ashley weeks before the murder, and Luke went berserk, nearly killing him right there before the jury. His inopportune fit of rage sealed his fate, and because of it, Luke has served about twenty-five years now for the crime I'm sure he didn't commit."

"How much more does he have to go?"

"He's serving twenty-five to life, though I believe there might be a good chance for him to get out on parole within the next couple of years. However, the Peebles campaign against that every time his parole hearings come up and have thwarted any chance he's had, though Luke's been a model prisoner. The family refers to him as the devil leading the innocent astray and all."

"The Peebles are still in town?"

"No, they moved out of the area shortly after her murder. Tyson Peebles worked for Anthony Montanari and the Agrit-Empire and felt he just couldn't stay in the area after the murder, so they took their son, Johnny, with them and left. I think Tyson owns some sort of cattle ranch east of Sacramento, but every time he hears about the hearing, the entire family trots down to Modesto and makes sure that Luke doesn't have a chance this side of hell of getting out."

"He wields that sort of power?"

"But of course," said Lea. "His uncle was State Controller for years, and his grandfather was a district judge. Tyson Peebles is a good ole boy, and all good ole boys look after one another." She nearly spat the words at him.

"You really have it in for the good old boy network, don't you?"

"I've seen it work its magic, and no woman, no matter how good she is, will ever break in. That's why you were hired when Roger went down, not me. And that's also why you could prove beneficial for my situation. You're already one of the good ole boys in spite of your ethnic peculiarities, and you're going to grant me access into the inner circles of the Monroe City Police Department."

"Ethnic peculiarities—now, that's an interesting term. So, why is it so crucial you infiltrate the inner circles?" asked Nick, half-amused.

Lea studied Nick Thayne's handsome visage. He was even better looking in person; the dailies didn't remotely do him justice. His lips, sensual and full, rested below eyes only slightly slanted and imbued with rich warm brown earth tones guaranteed to drive most women wild. His hair, cut in layers, allowed the thick black mane to surround his lean face dramatically. At 6'2", his well-toned body seemed uncomfortable in the overly stiff chair.

Lea was reminded of the exotic heritages of Keanu Reeves and Lou Diamond Phillips, though he was far better looking than either. His deep voice brilliantly managed to be soothing and sensual at the same time. He was the kind of man a woman could dreamily listen to for hours, that perfect blend of college professor and talk show host that gained your trust and weakened your defenses. She hated men like him because they were already half-way around the track before she'd even finished lacing up her running shoes.

"My dad never got to solve this case. He believed to the day he died that Luke Cambridge was innocent. I've vowed to continue the case and make sure I prove his innocence, even if it's been twenty-five years and I was only a girl of six when it happened. And now, the mayor's been murdered." She appeared almost gleeful.

"Ex-mayor," corrected Nick.

"Whatever; once a mayor, always a mayor. Thad's been murdered and his finger's been severed just like Ashley Peebles' was twenty-five years ago. A remarkable coincidence."

Nick pulled out the close-up of the picture of the missing finger from underneath the photos of the two convicted murderers. Lea reached into the top drawer of the antique desk and removed a small electronic gadget about 1 ½ times the size of a standard paperback. She whipped out a cord similar to a cell phone charger and plugged it in. Her thin fingers flew across a small keyboard.

"Indeed," said Nick. "Someone wanted us to find her ring. Someone who knew how she died and believed justice hadn't been served."

"Or is a serial killer taunting the people. But, that's a long space between kills."

"You have a photograph of the ring?" asked Nick.

"Yes, but unfortunately it's not a close-up. The silver ring was one that her great-grandmother had apparently passed down to the oldest girl child in the Peebles' family for several generations. It was a silver ring made of layers of braided rope, apparently quite unique." Lea pulled the photo from her desk drawer and pushed it across the desk. In it, a pretty Ashley Peebles, dressed in an elaborate Cleopatra Halloween outfit, smiled for the camera. Her jeweled arms crossed her chest and the ring in question glittered in the light provided by the camera's flash. Nick fished in his pocket and removed the Polaroid. The two rings were identical.

"Bingo," they uttered in unison.

Chapter 6

Fox had calmed down a bit about the ring and settled across the wide maple desk from him, removing her glasses to tiredly rub her eyes. She appeared far more attractive without the old lady spectacles, and her eyes were actually quite pretty. It was already 10:15 p.m. Because of her stubbornness, Nick read the files meticulously, occasionally stopping to write down a few notes. Every time he scribbled down something, Lea asked what he was doing and typed the details into her little box. He found her persistent questions annoying.

"Look, Ms. Fox, wouldn't it be a lot easier for both of us if I just took the files home?"

"Nope."

"We're partners remember."

"Partners? Hell, we're just working together. There's a difference; a partner is someone who adjusts to your working style."

"It's clear *you're* not making any adjustments, lady."

"Didn't realize I had to, since this isn't a long term deal," she shot back.

Nick closed the folder with a sigh. God, what a difficult woman! "We need to call Tyson Peebles and verify the ring found on Thad Fisher's finger is the one belonging to his daughter."

Lea gestured to the phone. "Then make the call."

Tyson Peebles spoke in a curiously dead voice, as if all the life had been sucked out of him. A dog whined piteously in the background against the drone of a Friday-night sitcom. He seemed startled when Nick indicated that the mayor had been murdered and a ring resembling Ashley's had been found on his finger. As Nick described the ring, Tyson Peebles emitted an excited breath.

"It sounds just like my little girl's! I'll meet you tomorrow morning at the police station, bright and early. I want to see that ring."

Nick hung up the phone with a look of victory. "Sounds like we're making some good progress. I'll meet him in the morning."

"*We'll* meet him in the morning," corrected Lea. "It's has been a long time since I've chatted with Chief Rollins. I wonder if he remembers me. I'm sure you need to scurry on home, as you probably have a date or something.

Nick gathered up his things and unwound himself from the uncomfortable chair.

"I'll see you at the station at 8 a.m. sharp, partner. " He strode out of the room, only missing the low doorframe by a mere two inches, thinking this could be a partnership made in hell. Unbeknownst to him, a paper wad smacked the office door as it closed behind him.

Saturday, 8 am, Monroe Police Department

Tyson Peebles, promptly at 7:55 am Saturday morning, waited impatiently outside the wide glass doors of the Monroe City Police Department as Nick drove up in his '68 Mustang. Lea frowned. The car sure suited the man.

"Wow," said Tyson. "That's some car!"

Time had treated Tyson Peebles poorly. Sparse hair, bleached pure white from stress and age, hung stingily around an unhealthy face, and his nose possessed that swollen, bulbous effect, which suggested he hit the bottle a bit too often. A flabby belly protruded over his doe-brown pants, and his pale blue shirt looked as if it had difficulty staying tucked in. In contrast to his disheveled appearance, he wore an enormous wooden cross around his neck like some sort of medieval priest hoping to ward off evil.

"Thanks. It's the original 390-cubic inch GT V-8 fastback with 335 horses. It can zip."

"The paint looks perfect."

"Had to have it redone, but they did a nice job. Matched the original color completely."

Tyson stuck out a pudgy hand to Nick Thayne, and they shook like old-time friends. Like most men, Mr. Peebles totally ignored Lea Fox. Since she was used to it, Lea said nothing and grimly followed the two men into the Monroe City Police Department. Just what *was* it about men and cars anyway?

Richard Rollins jerked when he saw her, but quickly plastered his meet-the-public smile upon his chubby face. He shook Nick's hand warmly and turned to the much-aged Tyson, holding Tyson Peebles' hand warmly by placing one paw another over the top of the aggrieved man's while murmuring condolences for the twenty-five-year-old murder. He didn't even bother to shake Lea's hand.

After Rollins released Tyson, Lea leaned forward and took Tyson's hand. He seemed surprised she was part of the team.

"I'm Investigator Fox and will be assisting Detective Thayne on this case."

"What are you doing here?" Richard growled under his breath as Tyson followed Nick into the station.

"Didn't Mr. Thayne tell you?" Lea responded sweetly.

"We're partners now working on the Peebles-Fisher case."

"The Peebles-Fisher case," he shot back before realizing Tyson Peebles stood not six feet from him. He stated more softly. "I didn't realize there was a connection. Please, everyone, come into my office and fill me in."

Nick gave Richard a measuring glance. Since Richard was originally the one who'd related the similarities between the severed ring fingers, he wondered just what the chief was trying to pull. The trio followed him into his good-sized office overlooking the wide grass lawn of the MCPD. The persistent hum of a lawnmower invaded the office interior and Richard closed the window. Beyond the green rectangle, one could glimpse the courthouse, and just behind that, the records center, all within walking distance. Monroe was a compact town, but well designed.

Richard sank behind his desk and steepled his fingers. "So?" he asked, making it a question.

"We have reason to believe," said Nick without preamble, "that the ring discovered on Thad Fisher's pinkie finger may very well have belonged to Ashley Peebles. Her ring's been missing over twenty-five years."

Richard quickly punched three numbers into the phone. "Dwayne, I want you to go retrieve the ring taken from Thad Fisher's finger, the silver one, you know, that was found on his pinkie. It's being stored in the evidence room."

Officer Dwayne Matthews returned within three

minutes, dropping the silver ring upon his chief's desk. Those minutes proved awkward, and Chief Rollins tried to fill it with pleasant conversation, asking Tyson how business was going and if he missed working for the Agrit-Empire. Tyson kept fiddling with his cross while Nick made a pretext of re-examining the files. Lea felt no need to be polite and studied Tyson Peebles openly.

The man obviously had a drinking problem, and his fingers, as they fiddled with the wooden cross, trembled. He had twice nicked himself shaving and his shirt was poorly pressed. Lea wondered if the negligent Mrs. Peebles perhaps spent more time on her house than her husband's attire. When the ring dropped before Richard Rollins, the chief didn't even have a chance to open the baggie before Tyson grabbed it off the table. Lea removed her mini-computer, her fingers poised over the keys.

"It's my little girl's! It's Ashley's ring. I never thought I would see it again!"

"You're certain?"

"Of course! It was designed by a Navajo silversmith and is nearly a hundred years old. My grandmother received it as a little girl and passed it down to my daughter on her 12th birthday." If Tyson Peebles' hands had been shaking before, they were absolutely quaking now.

"May I see the ring?" asked Nick politely and retrieved the now damp baggie from Tyson, who ran his hands nervously up and down the brown creases of his trousers.

"It's truly a unique ring, which indicates beyond a shadow of doubt that the murders of Ashley Peebles and Thad Fisher are related," stated Lea calmly. Chief Rollins frowned angrily at her.

"So, you mean," said Tyson, stammering, "that it wasn't that Cambridge boy or Deke Rhodes after all?"

"We can't totally rule that out," said Chief Rollins consolingly. He'd considered the outcome of the Peebles case to be one of his great successes. "It's certain they were involved in the murder. Perhaps there's a third party we were unaware of, or Ashley simply lost or had given the ring away. There could be any number of reasons this ring was found on Thad Fisher's finger."

"Such as?" asked Lea, eager to hear what her father's former subordinate had to say.

Richard turned it deftly around. "Well, I'm sure that you and Nick will find out what those reasons could be. But, until we've made all the connections, I don't think we have any more questions for you, Tyson. We just wanted you to identify the ring. You head home now, and we'll take it from here. As soon as possible, we'll return the ring to your family." Richard Rollins rose and extended a warm but dismissive handshake to the white-faced Peebles.

He suddenly appeared very eager to get Tyson Peebles out of his office, and Lea couldn't blame him. Chief Rollins thought he'd wrapped this old case up as neatly as a birthday present, complete with a daintily tied ribbon. Now his whole package was unraveling, and Lea almost chuckled out loud. She caught Nick's chastising glance and promptly set her small teeth together. Damn the man! There were so few chances for levity in her profession, and damn it if she didn't want to enjoy those moments, especially when dealing with a pompous ass like Chief Rollins.

Richard walked Tyson Peebles out, draping his arm across the man's shoulder and talking softly to him. Lea leaned over and, grabbing the file from Nick's lap, began squinting at the cramped type made to fit in too small a space.

"This coroner's report is really quite interesting," she said, ignoring Nick's hostile glance. "It states the mayor had beef stroganoff for dinner." Her fingers jabbed at her mini-laptop.

Nick folded his arms across his chest and frowned. "So, what happened to you? Drop out of finishing school?"

She stopped typing. "Never had the opportunity to attend such high class educational institutions during my formative years like you did, Silver Spoon. If you expect me to be Ms. Sweet Cakes, you've got the wrong gal. A man can get away saying whatever he wants, but a woman has always got to sweeten it up for it to be swallowed. Well, that's not me, mister, and if you'd been raised by my father and brother, you wouldn't have been all 'sugar and spice and everything nice,' either. So, you'd just better grin and bear it. And, a note to the wise, your Richard Rollins isn't too thrilled we've re-opened the Peebles' case. He thought he had that one all wrapped up, so expect him to put major roadblocks in our way."

"I can handle Chief Rollins," said Nick evenly, "but I don't want you to get him all defensive and riled up. He obviously doesn't like you, so why don't you leave the talking to me?"

"That's why we are going to make a great team, Harry. You can be all handsome and charming and sweet—buttering them up while I dissect the motive."

"My name is Nick, not Harry," he gritted.

"Harold Whitfield Thayne. I'm certain that's the name given to you in the *Times*. Nick is a *nick*name, I guess? Or—let me speculate—you read a bunch of crime novels and decided Nick was a hip name for a detective."

"Nick was my grandfather's name and preferable to Harry. Don't you forget, Lea."

"Whatever you want, big boy. You know, I think being called by one's last name is often preferable in working situations, don't you? It's a British tradition, after all, and some of the best detectives have been British. You know, Holmes and Watson, Poirot and Hastings, Nero Wolfe and Archie Goodwin, Inspector Morse and his Lewis. Tell you what. I'll be Fox, and you be Thayne. A great solution, since I think it keeps us separate but equal. A more modern type of segregation certain to prove highly effective and definitely more palatable. When you verbalize my last name you might even forget I'm a mere woman."

Distaste narrowed Nick's handsome face. "Where'd you hatch from?"

"My brother often asked my father that. It was one of the few pleasures of my Emily Dickinsonian-type life," she retorted, returning her attention to the coroner's report.

He sat and fumed. Damn those tabloids and their conscious violation of one's privacy. But what could he expect? They'd been after a story, and his break-up with his infamous father as well as his suspension and subsequent resignation from the SFPD had made news. The silver-spoon boy who'd turned his back on all that money and influence. Some had called him ungrateful; he'd called it downright brave. Nick now realized it would take his entire prowess to one-up Lea Fox. She was a formable foe who not only didn't give a shit about what he thought but also held a prejudiced opinion of him like so many others. Somehow, though, he suspected her opinion had nothing to do with race and everything to do with money, maleness, and power.

Nick dropped the baggie back upon the desk and returned his thoughts to the case. How on earth could a seventeen-year-old girl's ring have found its way onto the ex-mayor's finger? And where was the mayor's mistress, Connie Judson? In fact, the last anyone had seen of her was when little

Katie had spotted the decked out Connie emerging from the black limo at Chester Street. Nick was afraid the busty redhead had either flown the coop or would be found in a shallow grave not far from the mayor.

Chief Rollins huffed back into his office and slammed the door.

"Next time, I expect to have a little more information before someone like Tyson Peebles wanders into my office. Hell of a way to start off the morning! And just what is *she* doing here?"

Lea grinned sweetly at him. Aggravating Chief Rollins meant the day couldn't entirely be considered a waste, no matter what else happened.

Nick avoided the question. "I decided to look up Ashley Peebles' records as you directed," began Nick, "but they were missing."

"What?" roared Chief Rollins.

Nick spoke quietly, hoping to calm the irate chief. "They're absent from the country offices with no record of them ever being checked out for a good twenty-some years. Roger mentioned that Jeremy Fox had been working on the case with you, and I decided to look up Ms. Fox since she'd taken over her dad's business. Luckily, she had copies of all the files and has been *gracious* enough to share them with me." The word gracious and Lea Fox didn't mesh, and the chief was savvy enough to note it.

"*She* is not on contract with the Monroe City Police Department," bristled Richard Rollins. "Ms. Fox is not welcome here *ever* after her last public outburst. I'd fire you, Lea, but since you were *never* hired, you need to make yourself scarce!"

"I'll wait outside," said Lea as she rose and stuffed her mini-computer into her bag. "It's always such a pleasure walking around my father's old digs and the office he used to call his own. I'm sure you find his shoes difficult to fill, Chief Rollins. I'm sure that's why you're always so unsettled when I'm around since I remind you so much of him."

Today, Lea had dressed in a milky-blue suit textured in a knobby knit that appeared like it had been kept in mothballs for years and taken out just for this occasion. An unbecoming white blouse peeked from underneath the lumpy jacket whose oversized buttons looked like something Nick's grandmother might have worn. He had to admit, however, that her blue, serviceable shoes were a perfect shade to match the suit. God, where had she purchased them? The only thing missing from her assemble was the crutch from yesterday. Fox clumped off, slamming the door behind her.

Richard Rollins unleashed his full fury upon Nick Thayne.

"She is never to enter this office again! Do you understand?"

"You seem a bit too adamant about something that

really is relatively unimportant," returned Nick calmly, mustering up all his charm, fearing the chief was near cardiac arrest.

"Oh, yeah? Well, two years ago Lea Fox came slinking around here trying to re-dig up the Peebles case, saying there'd been some sloppy police work on the case. Well, if there had been, it was her own father's doing, since he was in charge of the blasted homicide. I only worked under him. Then she starts insinuating I may have been a bit slovenly in my job and should have done more to solve her father's murder case. Right then and there, I told the bitch to get out and stay out. I don't ever wanna see her face in this station again, do you hear? The only reason I didn't toss her out on her little crippled ass was everyone close to her had just been killed, and I'd been a personal friend of Jeremy's. Thought maybe she was going through some tough times."

It dawned on Nick that the chief didn't realize Lea's caustic nature was the norm, not the exception. "I didn't realize you'd had an uncomfortable encounter."

"I'm warning you, Nick, if you wish to stay on contract with us, you don't work with her."

"Okay, okay," said Nick, holding up his hands. "To tell you the truth, I don't like dealing with her either, but Fox won't grant me any access to the Peebles' files unless I allow her some input on the case. She has this notion that I've muscled my way into her territory and somehow owe it to her.

Don't you worry about it—she'll be kept in the background—usually at her office, doing computer follow-ups."

"She's lucky to have any business at all," grunted Richard, a half-smile crossing his lined face. A peculiar notion stuck Nick.

"I'll make sure she doesn't cross your doorstep again," promised Nick picking up the files on Thad Fisher. "I'll send you an update as soon as I can. I suggest you put that ring under lock and key. I wouldn't want to see anything else go walking."

Nick's back had only begun winding through the metal desks grouped in the central section of the police department before Chief Rollins was on the phone to Tony Montanari.

Fox waited outside, watching the rain birds sprinkle the police station's emerald green lawn. A couple of late robins hopped energetically, pecking at the shiny grass under the false rain. She was on her cell phone.

"Thanks, Susan. Please have Roger give me a call as soon as he's able." She stuffed the small Ericsson back into her hideous bag.

"Well, Fox, you sure have a way with people," said Thayne angrily.

"Let's just say that Richard and I have some unresolved *issues*. That is the favorite word of the Internet educated, isn't it?"

"Haven't you ever learned tact, lady? I get the distinct feeling that I'm not the real reason you lost a lot of business in this town. I believe the chief likely blacklisted you."

"You think that, do you, Thayne?" said Lea nonchalantly.

Suddenly, Nick recognized she'd known it all along.

"God damn it! You wanted to meet him so you could flaunt our association in his face because you knew my hands were tied in regards to those closely guarded files!"

She pretended to smile sweetly but failed. "How you misjudge me, Thayne. Of course I wouldn't do something like that being the innocent little debutante I am, graduating from the MRS University of Perpetual Happiness."

"Oh, shut up," said Nick forcefully. "I certainly understand now why you're not welcome at the station. Enough of your ridiculous playing around. I need to take a closer look at Dr. Koh's report, because there are a couple of things that don't add up. Let's stop at Millie's Coffee Shop so we can discuss it. I also need to update you on my chat with Philemon Jenkins, the gardener who found the body. He indicated that he'd been playing ball with a little kid he referred to as Bouncer and that the child steered him towards the magnolia tree. I think we need to interview this Bouncer character and find out what he knows."

"Whatever you say, partner," returned Lea.

Nick grimaced. Partner was not what he wanted to be

called by Lea Fox. In fact, he didn't want to be called anything by her at all.

Chapter 7

Saturday, 9:30 am

Twenty minutes later and immersed in the coroner's report at Millie's Coffee Shop, the strange report only generated more questions. They had ended up taking both their vehicles, since Fox refused to ride in his Mustang. It was for the best since it enabled Nick to blast Bruce Springsteen as he followed her little silver Mazda to the diner. Nick had already downed a double coffee laced with milk and sugar while the finicky Fox made poor Chastity go back three times to make sure that her hot chocolate was done just right. The first drink placed before her had obviously not been made with milk so it was sent back. On the second try, the milk wasn't hot enough, and Lea returned it as well; the comely waitress looking ready to spit nails. The third time, after the hot chocolate was slammed down in front of her, it spilled a bit of the hot milky liquid upon the table.

"There's too much whipped cream."

Nick blurted out, “Thank you so much, Chastity. That’s just lovely.”

The comely waitress whipped about, the white tails of her apron slapping across the rear of her well-filled out saffron uniform.

“She didn’t give me a spoon,” complained Lea.

“I’m surprised she didn’t dump it all over your head,” muttered Nick, hoping that Chastity would have calmed down a bit when he called her later. Lea growled under her breath, and grabbing Nick’s coffee spoon, stirred the whipped cream violently into the hot chocolate.

Nick read while she viciously stirred. “Dr. Koh must have stayed up all night for this. The contents of the ex-mayor’s stomach indicated that he’d consumed a culinary feast before his death. Not only was there the beef stroganoff but traces of brandy, vodka, and a French Bordeaux wine. Thad had also sampled chocolate mousse, some type of a green bean and almond salad with saffron rice and portabella mushrooms… and that was just for dinner. “

“He didn’t become beastly fat on salad, Thayne.” She’d removed the tiny computer and placed it upon the desk to take notes after vigorously wiping up Chastity’s spill with both their paper napkins.

“All right, Fox, my curiosity’s pricked. What is it?”

“I beg your pardon?”

Nick frowned. “That little contraption you always

whip out."

"Oh . . . that." She grinned, almost looking pretty. "It's my version of the detective's little black book. My dad had a small book where he wrote all his notes. The only problem was no one could decipher a line because of his hideous shorthand. So, I developed the Fox and Hound notebook." She thrust the little laptop towards him.

He studied the keys and laughed aloud. "This is unbelievable. You've got keys that state motive, witnesses, C/S . . . what's that?"

"Crime scene."

"That makes sense. Hum . . . evidence, suspects, numbers, priors. I get a sense of how this works, but explain it further to me."

"Okay. I designed it to give me shortcuts. If you press *Crime Scene*, I can draw the scene with my attached stylus here. There's a scale on top to make sure everything's accurate. I have a port to my digital camera and can take instant color photographs of whatever." She fished around her big bag and produced a tiny digital camera.

"Definitely a woman's toy. That thing's not much bigger than a micro-cassette."

"Serves the purpose. Now, when I punch in the category S*uspects*, this profile sheet comes up."

Nick gasped. A grainy photo popped up on the screen. "I can't believe it. That's . . ."

"Luke Cambridge, of course. Read the template."

Within sixty seconds, he'd read an abbreviated but complete rundown on the incarcerated felon.

"But this is even neater," she continued. Fox pressed the motive key. Several motives popped up with arrows leading to possible scenarios. "One of Luke's motives was jealousy." The arrows pointed to Deke, the grungy apartment where they lived, the car, etc. Lea pressed another key. The words 'Motive improbable' blinked while a paragraph explained why.

"How'd you get something as nifty as this?"

"It was my pet project in college. While others were skiing, I was making the perfect hand-held sidekick detective. Not sure even then I wanted a partner."

Thayne allowed that one to pass, so she continued undaunted. "It's cool as a one of a kind oddity. Can't see people wanting a hand held computer when they could just write on a tablet."

"That's where you're wrong—something like this is gonna be the rage in the future! Anyway, I was always interested in computers, and my brother was a tech whiz. Between us, we developed the Fox and Hound; our pet name for this pre-programmed mini-computer. Full-sized laptops were too cumbersome, but this was small enough to fit discreetly in a pocket or small handbag. Because of the preprogrammed prompts and scenarios, we were able to record and deduce things far sooner than before. I'm one who not only has to record the facts as they present themselves but also my impressions." She pressed a key marked IMP. "See, these are my impressions of the case. If I type in anything, it automatically records the date and time and links them to whatever aspect of the case I punch in."

"Sherlock Holmes would have loved this," Thayne said admiringly.

"Sherlock Holmes' mind worked like this. He wouldn't have needed a machine. Mine doesn't. I need time to digest all the information, and the computer prompts me in the right direction. For example . . ." She pressed a key, and Nick gasped. Chief Rollins' florid face, the size of a passport photo, appeared on the screen. "His profile is all here. You can see that, while I was waiting for you to finish with him, I punched in his statements and my reactions to them. Now, looking it over, my gut instinct says this."

She pressed the link key, and Nick shook his head slowly. "That's a far way to leap, Fox."

"Rollins wants to keep his position. He has to solve this case and *will* find a scapegoat. My guess is within three days. He's set to retire and doesn't need the headache. Also, I believe he's not only financially in trouble but his marriage is rocky." Nick squinted at the notes she'd typed.

"You're brutal."

"Perhaps, Thayne, but I prefer the terms clear-headed

and unprejudiced. And, if I'm correct about Chief Rollins, we don't have much time to solve this case and collect our checks."

"How do you type on those tiny keys?"

"I've learned to do a one-handed type. My brother had to use the attached pen. He was awfully slow."

"You miss him?"

"Who?"

"Your brother."

"I miss his mind and his energy," she admitted, "but not his foul mouth, womanizing, or drinking bouts. He was only thirty-six when he died, but already a confirmed alcoholic. We only got along because I listened well and had learned not to threaten his ego. He never viewed me as a woman, though that was probably to my advantage."

"And why's that?"

"Lane was my brother, but still had antiquated opinions about a woman's place. I managed to deal with him because he didn't view me as an equal or a threat. Other men, however, do feel threatened. My being unattractive at least removes their sexual motivations so I can get a lot further than my unfortunate sisters."

So her dowdy appearance *was* a kind of disguise, or perhaps more appropriately, a defense. "I'm not so sure about that," Nick said. "Men open up to sexy, attractive women."

"Not exactly. They *appear* to open up—but the woman is really their prey—thus any qualifications she has other than the possibility of a quick lay are considered a hindrance to any valid intellectual relationship. Once she has satiated him—he drops her and moves on. So much for her brains and beauty."

Nick took a long sip of his coffee. His wariness of Lea Fox went way up. Though she lacked in other attributes, she had a fine mind. Women were never to be trusted at the best of times, particularly those who thought too much, and Fox was particularly dangerous. He'd bet his *Playboy* subscription that a little dossier existed on the Fox and Hound regarding him. Nick could only imagine the contents.

"You're able to download from that?"

"Yup. Have the same program on my laptop and office computer. I *always* back up everything. So, you were asking?"

"About Mayor Fisher's build and eating habits," said Nick watching her fingers fly across the tiny keypad. "There were overly high traces of lead in his system. Not enough to be toxic but well above normal levels. It's the kind found in paint before it was regulated here in the States."

"So our ex-mayor was gnawing on a paint wall between courses from his funeral feast?"

"Very funny," said Nick. "Another interesting tidbit was that the hair around his wrists was almost totally absent."

"Hands probably bound with duct tape," said Lea

taking another sip of her hot chocolate.

Lea Fox was a quick study. "That sounds likely," he admitted.

"Have Dr. Koh check the mayor's wrist for duct tape gum. It usually leaves a bit of residue on anything it touches."

"I'll do that," said Nick, making a mental note. "He was gagged with his tie, which shows signs of saliva stains."

"Anything else?" said Lea.

"Yeah, it seems that his finger was snipped off with some sort of high-powered scissors. In fact, Dr. Koh suggests they might have been pruning shears, not scissors at all."

"Like a gardener's," mused Lea. "Anything else."

"Just that the man was missing his underwear."

"Missing his underwear?" mused Lea. "Hanky panky with his mistress while imprisoned? Her name is Connie, right?"

"Connie Judson. She's a telephone operator for AT&T."

"And what was that bit about the mayor's feet?"

"Rose thorns. Two were imbedded in the left heel and other lacerations on his ankles and legs were likely caused by rose bushes."

"Very interesting. Maybe Connie didn't like his flowers and whipped him with them."

"I thought you were the serious sort," mocked Nick, though he suspected this was the extent of Fox's sense of humor.

"Any follow-up on the wheel barrows?"

"Randy Phelps has impounded seven from the block. Dr. Koh's assistant is supposed to be analyzing them as we speak.

"Well then, it is clear what we have to do," said Lea, having drained all of her hot chocolate. It left two smudges on the corners of her mouth. Nick pointed a finger, and Fox picked up her napkin, giving her mouth a big swipe. "First, we have got to find out the whereabouts of Connie Judson. Second, we need to interview our ex-mayor's wife. What's her name?"

"Trish Fisher."

"And third, we have got to talk to the little boy, Bouncer, who told Philemon Jenkins about the magnolia. I'd lay odds Connie is either buried somewhere nearby or else basking in the South American sunshine."

"Whoa," said Nick. "Aren't you forgetting something?"

"And what's that?" said Lea.

"Luke Cambridge indicated he was not the murderer of Ashley Peebles. I'd like to hear what evidence he has to back up his assertion."

"That should be easy; we'll head down tomorrow towards Modesto and have a little chat with him at his state-provided digs. Are you through with your coffee?"

"Of course," said Nick. "I just need to make a pit stop. By the way, why did you dub it the Fox and Hound?"

"My brother actually named it."

"Because you're detectives and all?"

"No. That's what I thought at first as well until an acquaintance told me fox was to refer to my brother and hound to me."

"Never missing the scent?" He grinned. It seemed an apt description of Lea.

"Nope. My brother thought I was a real dog, so I got dubbed the hound. His own private joke. Unfortunately, I learned later he shared it with every man he met. It must have made a good conversation starter. And," continued Lea as if it didn't matter, "I see your little waitress friend signaling you. Maybe you should go sidle up to her and make a date or something."

Nick stared long and hard at her before throwing his napkin down upon the table. "I'll be right back." He approached the shapely waitress while Lea stared at the tiny computer so aptly named before dejectedly switching it off.

It took Nick a full ten minutes to convince Lea Fox of the futility of having both of them drive to the witnesses. She staunchly refused to ride in the vintage car until Nick mentioned that it was a waste of gas and money to take two cars. Since he was willing to drive, she should accept the favor.

"Alright, Thayne," she agreed suddenly and tossed her dowdy handbag into the back seat. "I prefer you drive."

"Of course, Fox. It will be my pleasure." She flinched as he gunned the motor, but her face remained expressionless. The F & H, as Nick decided to dub it, was soon in her small hands, and she typed furiously before nodding to herself as he cruised down the street.

"So, why did you acquiesce so easily? Certainly you can't be softening up?"

"Quite the contrary. I find it difficult to drive and type at the same time. Also, it will save gas, since money's quite tight right now. I suggest that on occasion, when we need to keep a low profile, we should take mine. However, no matter what the vehicle, you can always drive."

"Always?" He was surprised. He'd been positive Fox would never abdicate that position considering her stance on the male gender.

"Always. It makes a man feel in control when he's behind a big engine. This is a V-8 right? It all has something to do with penis size, I'm sure. However, since I don't give a damn about that—you can always drive; kinda like my chauffeur."

Nick slapped his hand on the wheel and snorted. "Remind me to give you the card of a friend of mine in Girard. He's a great psychiatrist. Maybe he can help you out."

"Did he help you?"

Nick swore so vehemently he nearly ran a stoplight. Fox chuckled delightedly to herself, and he suddenly saw the twisted humor in it all. Damn if she wasn't a pill.

Trish Fisher's house was on the way to Connie Judson's flat, so they stopped there first. The mayor had done very well for himself, though the two-story Victorian house seemed a bit of out of place amongst the Ranch and Mediterranean-styled houses lining his block. All had old trees and huge water bills and cost nothing less than two million bucks.

An expansive lawn slanted upwards toward the gabled entryway, which looked upon a huge circular fountain in which a naked cherub squirted water out of his mouth, barely missing the floating lilies under which bright goldfish dodged the artificial rain. When Nick lifted the heavy bass knocker, a black-clad maid politely answered after the second tap.

"My name is Inspector Nick Thayne," he said, "and this is Inspector Fox. We're wondering if Mrs. Fisher is available?"

"She's in mourning," said the maid hesitantly, her eyes just missing theirs. The Hispanic woman had been trained well.

"It's crucial we see her. I understand she's currently grieving, but need some information regarding her husband's last hours. Could you please ask her again?"

"Tell her if Mrs. Fisher doesn't speak to us now," blurted out Lea, "she'll be visiting us at the police station to explain her whereabouts over the past week."

"Good God, Fox," snarled Nick between clenched teeth. "She's not even a suspect yet. Jesus!"

The startled maid disappeared and returned less than two minutes later, gesturing for them to follow her. Lea smirked as Nick gritted his teeth.

"I get things done," she mouthed much to his chagrin.

The beautiful house's cluster of square-shaped panes let in glorious ribbons of light. Mrs. Fisher waited in a large music room near the rear of the house where a huge, ebony grand piano stately waited for competent hands. Lea instantly recognized it as an original Steinway, and her fingers itched to play chopsticks. Trish Fisher had draped herself in black. A lovely amber brooch bound the restrictive high-necked blouse at her throat. Elegance flowed from her like a rose's sweet scent. Lea instantly went on guard.

"Please, sit down, Detectives," the widow said stiffly. Mrs. Fisher had been quite a looker in her day, and even now, with her ash blonde hair swept up in a becoming chignon, she was still quite stunning. Her trim figure had just the right curves, and her tiny feet were clad in somber but stylish black pumps.

"I'm so sorry about your husband," said Nick quietly

and leaned forward to take her hands gently. Lea didn't bother to offer any condolences, choosing instead to watch Nick in action. The woman, like so many others before her, didn't even bother to acknowledge her.

"We're investigating your husband's case and have a couple of questions to ask you," began Nick. "I understand this might be painful, but it's necessary, since his murderer remains free."

The woman didn't ever bother to pretend. "You want to know where his trashy mistress is, don't you?"

Nick stiffened, but Lea instantly warmed to the woman's style. She said, as bluntly, "That's right, Mrs. Fisher. Do you have any idea where Connie Judson might be?"

"The last time I saw that bitch, she was having dinner at Di'Monicos with my husband. He had the nerve to call me and cancel our dinner engagement only 40 minutes earlier. Being hungry, I went out with a friend, and there he was, nestled in a back booth all cozy-like with her. I told him if that's how discreet he was going to be, he'd better not bother coming home."

"How long ago was that?" said Nick, marveling at the lovely woman's coldness.

"Over three weeks, and I haven't seen him since."

"You don't appear . . . regretful," stated Nick carefully.

"Why should I be? I'm going to enjoy my money and

hope his mistress is running fast because I know she did him in."

"How would you know that?" asked Lea.

"Because he had no money! You certainly don't think this is the first time Thad was fooling around do you? More like the umpteenth time, and after his second adultery, I told him that I didn't care what he did with his little trollops as long as I kept my money and he was discreet."

"Your money?" repeated Nick.

"That's right; *I* was the one with money. Do you think Thad had much when he married me? Oh, he had a fine scholarship education and lots of promise, and believe it or not, used to be quite handsome. He wouldn't have become mayor if it hadn't been for my dad's money opening doors for him. After I saw what a lying whoremonger he'd turned out to be, I made sure my sizeable dowry reverted to me. The brilliant man actually signed a prenup to marry me. And ten years ago, I took out a gigantic insurance policy on him. I actually didn't think was going to take this long to get back my initial investment since he was cruising for a heart attack or a jealous husband's bullet." She leaned forward. "But, you know what the best thing is? I no longer have to put up with all the behind-the-hands' gossip everywhere I go."

Nick squirmed at the woman's vituperative tone but continued gently. "I'm sorry about your marital problems. So, how did Thad get money?"

She sighed. "Our deal was that if he remained discreet, I'd make sure he had 10 grand a month deposited into his personal account. Three weeks ago, I froze that money. He had violated our agreement. His mistress had to know the gravy train was over. I'd check his accounts if I were you. I'd lay odds everything is gone! Thad also had a Rolex and a ring, which were worth at least twenty thousand. You might want to check the local pawnshop. Thad mentioned that he did some consulting or something—but I suspect that wasn't probably enough to keep his 'friend' in the lifestyle she desired."

Nick digested this information before continuing delicately. "I've just a couple more questions, Mrs. Fisher. Investigator Fox and I believe it is possible that whoever murdered your husband might have also been involved in the death of a young girl by the name of Ashley Peebles some twenty-five years ago. Certain aspects of the case are similar. Did you know her?"

"Ashley Peebles? I remember reading about the unfortunate incident in the papers just after I was married, but I'm afraid I know little more than that. I'm sure, however, that any similarities are a pure coincidence. It's clear my husband's mistress killed Thad. And unless that whore Connie was a murderer at age eight, there couldn't be any connection. "

"You and your husband have been married how long?"

"Twenty-nine years, which is about twenty-eight too long."

“Did your husband ever speak about the Peebles murder?” asked Lea.

“Not really. I remember him thinking it shocking that seventeen-year-old girl went missing and was murdered, but I don’t see how it bears any relevance to my husband’s death.”

“His finger was severed in precisely the same manner as hers. One of the unusual aspects of that case is that Ashley’s ring had been missing for over twenty-five years and was just found upon your husband’s little finger.”

For the first time, Mrs. Fisher paled. “Good God! I certainly *hope* he had nothing to do with that young girl’s death, but he always liked the pubescent ones, you know? The younger the better. Once he even propositioned our daughter’s friend from ninth grade right at the dinner table. Leaned over and whispered dirty nothings in her ear. She had the grace to turn red, and I ordered his fat, perverted ass from the table. So, who knows, maybe he *did* have something to do with that unfortunate girl’s death. Somehow, I wouldn’t put it past him. Good God. Wait until *this* hits the morning paper!”

Nick shifted smoothly. “The last time your husband was seen alive was at a home on Chester Street, not far from where his body was found. He was witnessed pulling up in a black limo at number 614. The owner’s name is Collins. The police haven’t managed to locate him. Do you know if Thad had any sort of business attachment to someone by that name?”

"My husband had many attachments, but whether for business or not is anyone's guess. I take it he was with *her*?"

"Yes, he was, madam."

"Well then he was probably having a wild bunny party."

"And you hadn't spoken during your separation?" interrupted Lea.

"Not even once, and we were barely speaking before that. I found it time to move past my husband's tawdry world. My father, who'd encouraged the marriage in the first place, died four months ago, so I felt I no longer had to make a pretense. It wasn't like Thad was mayor any longer. In fact, Thad resembled a leech in every way—that corpulent slug."

Nick pulled uncomfortably at his collar while Lea expertly typed in the information into the F & H. Mrs. Fisher's animosity hung so thickly towards the deceased it could be cut with a knife. Lea glanced up from her mini-computer.

"The time of death has been pinpointed to last Tuesday night, Mrs. Fisher. What were you doing that evening?" asked Lea, wondering just how painful plucking all but five or six of one's eyebrow hairs would be. Trish Fisher's brows were so sparse a forest the woman had to use eyeliner pencil to prove she had any at all.

"Every Tuesday night I attend our chapter's weekly Assistance League meetings. We help clothe and educate needy children in the valley. I was there from seven to ten, but you can certainly check the roster, as our secretary Thelma always takes attendance. Before that, I had dinner here, and my maid Carmen, who let you in, can attest to my whereabouts. Around 10:15 I arrived home, took a sleeping pill, and went straight to bed. On Wednesday, I play bridge with my group. We started at six p.m. at Charlise Ruskin's house, and I remained there until after eleven. Carmen may have noticed my arrival, though I doubt it. She normally retires at ten. Do I need to go further?"

"We'll double check those times with the maid," said Lea, not mincing words as usual.

Trish Fisher flashed topaz eyes at her, and Nick swore a glint of mutual respect passed between the two women.

"Thanks very much for your time, Mrs. Fisher. If there is anything that we can do for you, please give us a ring." Nick handed her his card, and before Trish Fisher had more than a chance to glance at it, Lea offered the black-clad woman hers as well.

"I'm available twenty-four hours a day, Mrs. Fisher, and if you come up with anything, just let me know. By the way, in the past few weeks has your husband been doing any painting around here? Perhaps whitewashing some walls?"

"No. Why do you ask?"

"Your husband apparently ingested some paint before his death. I just wondered if he had somehow swallowed some paint flakes by accident while sanding a wall."

“My husband perform *manual* labor? Surely you jest.”

Thayne interrupted. “Could we see your garden, Mrs. Fisher? Do you have a green thumb by chance?”

“Not really. I enjoy a lovely garden of course, but use a weekly service.”

“You don’t keep any tools?”

“A broom and rake perhaps. I really don’t know. It’s more a storage shed, though you’re welcome to check. Carmen will escort you out. Good day to you both, Detectives.

Chapter 8

Nick drummed his fingers on the steering wheel of his well-maintained Mustang as Lea limped to the car. She had taken a detour to check Mrs. Fisher's shed, so now he waited.

"Did you have to pick bright red?" she grumbled, lowering herself into the cramped front seat. That morning, she had discarded her crutch, and it was evident her injury bothered her. Her suit looked even more terrible in the harsh Saturday morning sunshine.

"It's my style," said Nick. "We *all* have a definite style, don't we? And it appears you have a soul mate. Mrs. Fisher's certainly not afraid to speak her mind."

"She didn't respect her husband much, did she? But I can understand that," said Lea. "Most men are swine anyway."

"Well, *thank* you," said Nick, noting how much Fox enjoyed making that statement. He started the Mustang's powerful engine and gunned it to see her squirm. He certainly didn't wish to dissuade her from her stupid opinion.

"Anyway," he said calmly. "I've asked Carmen to come down and present a statement at the station, and she agreed to take Mrs. Fisher with her at the same time. While it's clear that Trish Fisher hated her husband, I have sincere doubts she murdered him. There would have been no reason to."

"I'd have to agree, since it was clear the marriage was over and her money intact. No evidence of the usual gardening tools in their shed, just skis, brooms, and whatnot. And there's nary a rose bush in the entire garden. She prefers ferns and geraniums." Lea seemed mildly pleased. "She most likely got over her jealousy twenty years ago."

"She could have left," said Nick, "but wanted to stay for the money."

"It was her money after all," retorted Lea. "Why should a husband who is unfaithful get any of it?"

"She certainly forced him to stay in a miserable marriage."

"With all his floozies by his side to comfort him during his unbearable agony."

"I'd love to continue this discussion of Psychology 101, Fox, but we have another person to visit before lunchtime. Connie Judson resided in some ritzy condos down near Madrid Street."

Nick revved the engine, and Fox buckled up so hurriedly he had to laugh.

Unfortunately, the landlord didn't have much

information to give them. The last time the balding man had seen Connie Judson was over a week ago, though he indicated she'd mentioned embarking on some big trip.

"Said she was going down to Mexico to some pricey resort," said the stoop-shouldered landlord as he slowly shuffled some invoices.

"How long has Ms. Judson lived here?"

"About a year. I think her boyfriend bought this place for her."

"And would that boyfriend have been the ex-mayor?"

The skinny landlord shrugged his sagging shoulders. "I'm not supposed to notice things like that, but it sure appeared like he rewarded her with a nice little love nest. Always bringing her presents, he was. Of course, that didn't stop her from seeing the other gent."

"The other gent?" shot back Lea. "What other gent was that?"

"Some military guy from San Francisco assigned to the Presidio. Looked like maybe he was a
chief or colonel or something. Whatever his rank, he certainly had lots of fancy decorations on his uniform. Came here several times, always carrying flowers and chocolates, and she would throw her arms around him like some long-lost friend. Of course, he never arrived when the mayor did."

"*What tangled webs we weave*," Nick quoted. "You wouldn't by any chance have caught the name of the other guy?"

"No, but I do know what kind of car he drove. It was one of those black Toyota Land Cruisers, brand-spanking-new with all the extras, tinted windows, and luxury seats. Anyway, she stayed careful, and I don't think the mayor ever got wise to what she was doing,"

"Or maybe he or the second friend got real wise," murmured Lea under her breath.

"Could you open up the place for us?" asked Thayne.

The landlord seemed uncomfortable. "Don't you have to have a warrant or something?"

"Right here. Bless the chief's heart. He had them issue *me* two of these things. One for Connie's here, and one for the Jenkins'. Man's thinking ahead."

Lea flinched. Thayne was enjoying flaunting his influence with the chief in front of her.

"We're not going to find anything at the mistress's apartment, Thayne," she said smugly.

"Oh, really," said Nick, casting a glance at her as they followed the landlord through the beautiful grounds. A cascading scarlet bougainvillea brushed his sleeve, and potted ferns, azaleas, and dianthus peeked from every nook. A beautiful, flowering plum, its rich colored purple leaves casting brilliant shade over Connie's entryway, just cleared Thayne's head. "And just what makes you think that?"

"Connie was a smart girl, and while it's apparent she

was two-timing both men, there's no way she wanted to lose her meal ticket. If she was flashing a plane ticket around, it is very likely that Thad either never knew about it at all or he was the one who purchased it for her."

"And just what makes you so sure about what Connie may or may not have done? I wouldn't think your acquaintance with that type of woman would be that broad."

"I concede it's not as extensive as yours," she said. "But basically, all women are alike. You know what they really desire from a man?"

An evil grin crossed Nick's face. "I have an idea," he chuckled.

"Not that, you miscreant; that's what *men* want! Women desire security more than anything. You can call it anything you want; money, a home, a family, but it all boils down to one thing. Every woman seeks security, and Connie wasn't about to give up her secure lifestyle even if there was a more handsome hunk from the Presidio visiting her when Thad wasn't around. Unless Presido Boy was loaded, her officer wouldn't be able to provide for her like the ex-mayor."

Nick had known a lot of women, and he would swear security wasn't what *all* they wanted; in fact, he was positive about it, but then again, what did this frumpy private investigator really know about men, anyway?

"You think I'm way off base, don't you, Thayne," stated Lea as if she could read his mind. The skinny landlord fumbled with his keys before finding the right one to unlock Connie's door.

"Well, Fox, I think there is a lot about people you probably don't know. I think that maybe your experience has been somewhat limited, since you spent all your time studying at Harvard Law School and perfecting your gadgets. I can't imagine you getting out and playing much."

"I've done my share," said Lea vaguely. "But that's not the point. The point is that men and women have basic but diametrical needs. If you focus on what those needs really are, you'll discover the motive to most crimes."

"Exactly my point. So it wouldn't surprise me at all if Connie took off to be with her Presidio boyfriend. He gave her youth and that little something *extra* an older man can't provide."

"The door's open," voiced the landlord. He faced them, his lined face bland. "Wow, so this is real police work in action. Hypothesize all you want, madam, but that woman was bonking two men at the same time and accepting money and presents from both of them. She was just damn smart, I think. And if you took one look at that broad, you'd want to bonk her, too. No offense miss, but a man takes what he can get when he can get it. Just wish she'd looked my way—I'd have shown her a real good time. One thing I'll tell you, though, neither one of those guys lost out. Not one iota."

Nick smiled like the cat that'd swallowed the canary.

He withdrew his wallet and handed his card to the landlord.

"What's your name again, sir?"

"Marty. Marty Corelli."

"Well, Marty, if this *friend* from San Francisco shows up, you give us a call okay?"

"Sure. I'm *positive* he'd love to talk to you." Marty grinned and sauntered down the wide steps lined with brimming pots of gardenias.

"He should have been a bartender, since he knows so much," stated Lea grumpily. Nick made to enter the cool condominium.

"Wait, Thayne. Before you go inside, let's go over what we know for a minute. One. . . Thad Fisher is dead, and even though we know his wife despised him, she probably didn't kill him because of the money."

"Since it was her money in the first place?"

"Right. She stays married to the bum even though she's aware of his adulterous nature. That is, until he refused to stay discreet. Two . . . Connie the mistress was on the receiving end of Thad Fisher's meal ticket. I'd lay odds that we'll discover she owns more than forty pairs of shoes, her closet is loaded with expensive designer clothing, and she possesses a well-stocked jewelry box.

"On her answering machine, we'll hear messages from both Thad and the unknown army officer. Connie is not the killer because everything points towards her desire for security. There's no way she would have plugged him, simply because she needed him. I don't think Mrs. Fisher would have done her husband in, either, no matter how much she despised him. I get the sincere feeling that, while Mrs. Fisher didn't care for her marriage, she in many ways may have been thankful to Connie for providing services for her husband that she herself didn't want to perform anymore."

"The F & H conjured all that up?"

"The what?"

"The Fox & Hound. You touch a button and two suspects are exonerated just like that?"

"Nope. I just know. And, it may have been just one meeting with her, but there have been many women who have exactly the same story. If you think that all women begrudge their husbands keeping a mistress, think again. Some wives are downright grateful, and therefore I'd be inclined to believe that neither woman had anything to do with his death. They both had too much to lose."

Whatever Thayne's thoughts were, he kept them to himself and simply swung open the door. Lea followed his tall frame inside, limping slightly and confident Thayne would have to eat crow in about 15 minutes.

Nick had to admit he was a little more than put out by the time they'd finished examining Connie Judson's lovely condo. Lea's estimation that Connie would have hoards of shoes was right on target; in fact, it proved an underestimation, as she possessed over a hundred pairs. Her huge, theatre-like closet revealed an array of outfits extending from formal evening gowns to sleek daywear, all costly and sporting designer labels. Even Connie Judson's costume jewelry was exquisite, nestled alongside expensive pieces such as a pair of lovely emerald earrings and a matching pendant necklace. No woman in her right mind would have left those expensive trinkets behind. Three messages glowed on the answering machine. Lea listened carefully as Nick played back the recordings.

"This is Thad. Don't forget our date tonight, sugar," droned the nasal drawl of the ex-mayor. "I'll pick you up in the limo at five-thirty. Why don't you wear my favorite color?"

After the next beep came the professional tones of a travel agent. "This is Kathy from Taylor's Travels. Your tickets are ready and can be picked up any time after twelve noon today. If you have any questions, just give me a buzz."

A well-modulated voice spoke briskly, as if rushed. "I'll be in town on Sunday, Connie. I'd sure love a home-cooked meal from my favorite chef. Call me when you've got a chance."

"Now, isn't that interesting," said Lea, flipping open the plastic lid to retrieve the small tape and tuck it inside her oversized blue handbag. Nick glimpsed the metallic end of a small handgun before she zipped up the top.

"Nice kitchen," said Lea, strolling through the circular room. "I wonder what our chef's picked up at the local supermarket. It's amazing how a fridge reveals one's style." Fox wandered over to the shiny appliance and jerked open the door.

"Strawberries, even though they are out of season, with cream. A bottle of Brut Champagne cooling. Hmm, must be at least a hundred bucks a pop on this one. Filet mignon. Yuck. It's starting to turn. Sweet peas, caviar from Russia. This lady lived high on the hog. No wonder Trish Fisher was miffed."

Nick peered at the over-laden countertop. "And check out at all these gadgets."

He pointed across the immaculate granite. Everything from juice squeezers, a gigantic bread maker, to a state of the art food processor covered the iron gray surface.

"And lookie here," said Lea. She plucked something from off the magnet on the gleaming side of the immaculate refrigerator. "A graduate of Ethel Morton's School of Cookery. Why, our Connie really *is* an amateur chef. No wonder Mr. Fisher seemed a little bit too portly for his own good.

Uh-oh, her house plants are wilted."

"They are at that," agreed Nick. "This place is too clean."

"She must have a maid who just came or is the most

wonderful of housekeepers."

"Yeah, a real Martha Stewart slash Holly Homemaker. Every man's dream." Nick moved away from Fox's smug countenance and phoned Randy, instructing him to have the place dusted for prints. Lea met Nick back at the bright red Mustang after he returned the key and informed Marty an officer would be back later.

"So, I was right wasn't I?"

Thayne frowned. "What are you searching for, Fox? Validation that your hunches are correct? Well, you were right, *this time.* Thad wasn't killed here, and Connie was well taken care of. And I would agree that she likely didn't kill him."

"Because of her lavish meal ticket."

"No . . . because she loved him."

"What?"

Thayne tossed a letter onto her lap. She opened it carefully and then cleared her throat. "Not a bad poet." Nick added a couple additional syrupy cards and Lea bit her lip. "So, big deal—he was fond of her, too. I guess one should never underestimate the power of love."

Nick started the engine while adding disdainfully, "These cards practically gush with Thad declaring his undying devotion. So, that means both women are off our list."

"Maybe Connie is, but I think it makes Trish Fisher a more credible suspect. Most women will forgive an indiscretion or even a husband's habitual adultery, but a scorned wife, whose husband loves another, can become a lethal killer. Trish is back on my list."

"Women and all their damn emotions and moods."

"Inconvenient, aren't they?" she agreed as if she'd never held those noxious faults herself. Fox sat quietly upon the cream-covered leather of the '68 Mustang, lost in thought. She fussed over the F & H for a couple minutes before slapping shut the cover. "Where to next, Thayne?

"I want to check out the field. You haven't seen it yet, and I'd like your opinion. Who knows, maybe our Connie's pushing up the soil close by."

"And I need to need to talk to Philemon Jenkins," added Lea.

"About what?" asked Nick. "You think he might be withholding information?"

"Perhaps, or it may simply boil down to the fact he may not have known he was contributing to a crime." said Lea. "Dr. Koh suggests some sort of heavy instrument was responsible for the detachment of Thad Fisher's finger. Perhaps pruning shears might have done the trick and who better to supply that tool except for a gardener?"

"But he found the body by chance."

"It appears that way, but you have to remember the proximity rule."

"The proximity rule?" asked Nick.

"That's right. A person in the proximity may not be

directly responsible for a crime but might have unwittingly contributed to it, or worse, been motivated by circumstance. For example, if you wanted to get rid of someone, maybe you were in a garage and in that garage you grabbed something as a weapon, like a screwdriver. Later, wanting to remove the finger or an object upon that finger you grab another convenient object such as pruning shears. Philemon seems innocent, but we can't rule out his later robbery of that fancy ring Thad wore. I believe Mrs. Simms, Philemon's employer, has a gardening shed?"

"I'd believe she does."

"Then we need to have a chat."

Personally, Nick would lay money on an irate mistress or disgruntled other lover rather than an opportunistic gardener.

"So, how much did this put you back?" asked Lea as she fidgeted in the cramped front seat.

"I beg your pardon?"

"The Mustang. You told Tyson it was a '68?"

"Yup. I purchased it in mint condition. I managed to find one with a 4-speed manual, and though it cost a good chunk of money, it's worth every penny. About thirty grand at the time and in prime condition."

"You like cars I take it?"

"Yeah, I enjoy fiddling with them. Cars respond if you take good care of them. Give them a nice coat of wax and keep 'em tuned up, they'll be your best friend forever."

"Kinda like a mistress," mused Lea.

"Believe me, they're a whole lot cheaper and tons easier to deal with. We're coming onto Chester Street now."

Noontime, Saturday

The police had cordoned off the entire field adjoining the Simms and Collins houses on the cul-de-sac. Randy Phelps stood overseeing the meticulous analysis of the field.

"Any luck yet?" Nick asked the younger officer.

"Nothing. We found some rusted old cans to the north of the field near the river in an unsavory area where people have been walking their dogs, but other than that, except for the site directly under the Magnolia tree, nobody has disturbed more than a top inch of soil for a long time."

"No wayward finger?" asked Lea, though she hadn't expected them to find it.

"No, not at all," said Officer Phelps seriously, "but you'll be the first to know." He was a short, broad-shouldered man not much taller than 5'5" and one of the only officers to directly address Lea Fox.

She appreciated it.

"Thank you very much, Officer Phelps. I'll be speaking with you later."

"Friend of yours?" asked Nick. He wished he'd opted for his blue jeans instead of the gray suit. Comfort sometimes needed to override style. He glanced at Fox's awful outfit and shuddered. Hers was neither comfortable nor stylish. Jeez.

"No, just a man who knows how to be professional. I met him right after he'd hired onto the station. His older brother is a lawyer and was a friend of my brother Lane. So, this is the Simms property?"

"And across there is the Collins house. I'd like to try there first before we head to Mrs. Simms."

Lea stood for a long moment analyzing the fortress-like house and its ten-foot walls. The other houses on the block had low fences or none at all, their lovely gardens exposed to the wide street. A small child on a tricycle pedaled furiously in the hot afternoon sun, oblivious to the police activity or the heat.

"Let's see if anybody's home," said Lea marching up to the gate and ringing the intercom. Distantly, she could hear the bell chiming unanswered in the house. She lifted her bespectacled eyes upwards and scanned the second story of the sturdy house. Every window was draped in heavy curtains probably designed to block out the hot sun.

"Are the police planning to gain entry?" she asked Thayne who'd just finished cleaning his sunglasses. From the looks of it, they'd cost at least a couple hundred dollars.

"Chief Rollins is trying to contact the owner, Mr.

Collins. We'd prefer not to break the door down since the residence is equipped with a high-powered security system. Plus, we don't have a warrant yet. Not enough probable cause." He pointed to the camera.

"I would love to get inside that house," murmured Lea. "I just wonder . . . ?"

"What?" asked Nick, pushing his hands into trouser pockets and squinting against the bright early afternoon glare.

"It's strange. It appears more like a prison than a well-protected house. Hopefully we'll obtain the access code from the owner this afternoon. Meanwhile, let's go have our visit with Mrs. Simms."

Chapter 9

"Philemon Jenkins certainly does his job well," commented Nick a couple minutes later as he tried to hold a civil conversation with Fox, who seemed hell-bent on solving the case before nightfall.

They strolled up the beautifully cobbled sidewalk. The sweet scent of strong fragrant roses filled the afternoon air. While Nick couldn't name most of the hybrids lining the path, a couple near the house was familiar from his own mother's garden. He spotted a *Mr. Lincoln* and *Joseph's Coat* drooping against the relentless heat. Near the front porch, a lovely flowering plant called *Yesterday, Today and Tomorrow* bloomed magnificently even though it was late in the season. The tri-colored flowers sent out their own profuse, sweet scent in challenge to the heavy fragrance emitting from the roses.

Every inch of the ground was cultivated and well kept. The deep, dusty greens gave way to the sweet, fresh leaves of half a dozen pink and white camellias occasionally disrupted by a solitary blood-red hibiscus. Roses, geraniums, and irises vied for space as a golden butterfly, whose pointed tips were shot through with purple velvet, rested lightly upon a magenta geranium before airily lifting itself up over the slanted roof and disappearing beyond the great chimney. Nick lifted the heavy brass knocker after searching for an absent doorbell and heard the responding shuffle of slow moving feet.

Mrs. Simms opened the door feebly. In the bright fall sunlight, she appeared overly pale. Her make-up had been applied like armor, so caked and flaky it suggested she hadn't worn her glasses when smearing the cream over her lined face. Her jet-black wool dress, unseasonably warm, hung haphazardly upon her bony shoulders, but her hair, in contrast, was tidy while her legs, though painfully thin, were well shaped and free of spider veins. It was obvious she'd once been a pretty and vivacious woman, and even now, at her advanced age, the fine features of an aristocratic face broke through the layers of make-up. She cordially invited the two investigators into her spacious foyer.

"My name's Inspector Nick Thayne and this is a fellow investigator, Lea Fox. We're working with the MCPD in the investigation surrounding the murder of the ex-mayor, Thad Fisher. I hope we're not disturbing you too much, Mrs. Simms, but we need to ask you a few questions." His voice, so congenial and soothing, immediately disarmed the elderly woman.

"And oh, what a horror, a horror it is," she stated wringing her pale hands. "Please, please come in." She led them into her sitting room and sank down upon a lilac couch, her blue-veined hands trembling slightly. "Would you like some tea or coffee or something?"

"We're fine," declined Lea, watching the old woman intently.

"I just couldn't sleep a wink last night knowing that poor man had been dead and just lying there unnoticed in the lot bordering my home. I thought I was so safe and secure here, but now? Oh, how horrible, horrible it is. I could be murdered in my sleep."

"There, there," said Nick Thayne gently and reached over to take the elderly woman's hand. He patted the wrinkled surface.

"We have just a few questions for you and then a quick favor to ask."

"Of course, of course, anything." She tried valiantly to present a stout front, but presently, her face crumpled, the tears streaking her heavy make-up as her bony shoulders hunched pathetically.

While Thayne did his best to try and calm the old woman, Lea studied the lovely room. An immense painting, appearing so life-like it startled the on-looker, dominated the high wall of the huge brick fireplace. Above the enormous mantle, a woman held a violin nonchalantly in her left hand while her right languidly grasped a horsehair bow held against her vivid blue dress. Straight, raven-black hair winged her brow and settled in a cloud around her shoulders above a well-formed bust. Shapely legs and incredible high heels, which would have looked ridiculous on some and certainly on Lea, only enhanced the young woman's marvelous legs. Her straight, aristocratic nose flared slightly below snapping blue eyes.

The rest of the room was no less grand than the woman presiding over it. Herring bone parquet flooring partly covered by a huge circular Chinese rug woven in dusty blue and rose softened the spacious expanse of the expensive room. An enormous vase stuffed with an incredible array of silk flowers looked so lifelike that the gladiolas, baby's breath, and irises appeared to have been freshly picked from Mrs. Simms' garden.

The beautiful arched windows overlooking the rose garden spotlighted knick-knacks and souvenirs brilliantly displayed in a burnished, wood-framed glass case housing trinkets from all over the world. Lea noted that tiny, Russian-carved eggs, Swiss music boxes, and gleaming bronze figurines of Hindu Gods filled every recess of the huge glass cabinet as well as being accompanied by countless African carvings in ebony and teak. The woman before them had obviously lived a full and varied life.

A magnificent black Steinway nestled indiscreetly into

a far corner made the room seem too somber and cold without some accompanying music. Yet, Lea thought as her eyes scanned the tastefully decorated chamber, the room lacked something. Her brain, organized similarly to the filing cabinets she had searched the previous day, pondered what it might be before hitting on it. Except for the amazing life-like painting, no family photos graced any of the ornate tables. This woman was wealthy, but dismally alone. The elderly woman, starting to relax, straightened her sagging back.

"You are a dear, dear boy," she said sniffing into a dainty white handkerchief. "I'll do anything I can to help, though I'm sure Philemon would know much more than I."

"By the way, that portrait of you is absolutely stunning," Thayne said, glancing at the impressive painting.

Lea started. That was Mrs. Simms?

"I'm amazed you could recognize me, I've changed so much. But thank you, kind sir. That's one way to lift a woman's spirits." Did she actually blush under the layers of make-up?

"Could you just tell us what you know?" interrupted Lea. "We have to get a statement from everyone in the neighborhood."

"That's right," said Nick taking over. He didn't want Lea's abrupt nature to further rattle the already shaken woman. "Can you recall the ex-mayor visiting your neighbors across the street any time over the past couple weeks?'

"No," said the old woman running shaky fingers through her nearly white hair, "but I always retire early. I sleep so poorly now with my arthritis and all and head to bed fairly early because I'm up half the night."

Nick, about to continue in his sweet smooth tones winced at Fox's interruption.

"Then perhaps you heard last week's late-night disturbance at the Collins residence?"

"Disturbance?" repeated Mrs. Simms appearing vaguely confused.

Lea totally ignored Thayne's drooping mouth. "Yes. All the yelling, accusations, foul language? It happened sometime around midnight on Tuesday?"

"Goodness gracious, I didn't. Of course, I probably had the TV on. I enjoy the company the noise makes and always fall asleep never remembering just what I was watching. Of course, the quality of shows today is quite appalling. When my dear husband was alive, we had good shows, not this trash like *Jerry Springer*. Those idiotic people he has on as guests make any problems we might have seem minute. Of course, that was until now."

Nick glared at Lea. This was the first yelling he had heard about. Just what was she getting at?

"But it would have been quite distinct; since I'm positive the street is silent at that hour. Can't you remember anything at all, Mrs. Simms?"

The old lady frowned hard and then amazingly nodded. “Well, I can’t be sure, you know. I might have dozed off and heard the argument on the TV. That Jerry Springer is a putrid, putrid man.”

Nick bit his lip trying to stifle a laugh.

“He is putrid indeed,” asserted Lea, and Nick suspected she totally agreed with the elderly woman. “Just what exactly did you hear?”

Mrs. Simms totally ignored her, seemingly intent on giving a full commentary regarding her opinion of reality shows.

“There are just some things that shouldn’t be shown on TV. Why, the other night he had men on the show dressed as women and acted like it was an everyday occurrence. Well, I never!”

“Last Tuesday night, though?” restated Lea, intent on getting the woman back to the subject. It didn’t work.

“It wasn’t decent, I’m telling you, not fit for human ears. They were flinging around the ‘f’ word and ‘s’ word as if it was okay to utter those foul profanities. Believe me, the bleeping it out didn’t disguise what they were saying. I remember my younger brother Melvin having his mouth washed out for daring to say such things. The way young people act these days.”

“Yes, yes,” said Lea, “and they were arguing about *what*, Mrs. Simms?”

Mrs. Simms gave what could only be considered a ladylike snort.

"Money of course. It's always money. Spend, spend, spend! I was taught to save as a child, to try to earn a wage with an honest day's work, but now, if you don't have the money, you borrow. But believe me, missy, everything comes at a price, everything. There's no free ride. All those people who look like they have it made, well, don't begrudge them. They worked hard and sacrificed to get what they have. I sacrificed everything to have a good life, and many might say God has punished me for it. But those young hooligans! They make no sacrifices at all."

"I understand perfectly, Mrs. Simms," continued Nick smoothly. "So, what you're saying is that the yelling about money came from the house across the street last Tuesday night."

The old woman grimaced and looked down at her age-spotted hands. "I think it was Tuesday night, but, young man, I might be confused. It may have been Monday." At Nick's pained expression, she snapped. "Oh come on now, young man! At my age all days seem to merge into one. I'm lucky to remember what day Philemon is supposed to come and what to do, so I have to mark the calendar with a red dot and cross off the day just so I don't leave that poor sweet man standing upon my porch wondering where I am."

"Very considerate," mumbled Lea.

"How long have you known Philemon Jenkins?" asked Nick, relieved they had returned to more fertile ground.

"The man has worked for me for over three years. He received an excellent reference from my neighbor down the street, Eliza Carmichael. Unfortunately, she passed away fourteen months ago and before that was in a nursing home, so I kind of inherited Philemon from her. He's an excellent gardener. His wife sings at the Southern Baptist Church on Cherry Avenue. Such a good man. I've never had one moment's dissatisfaction with him." Suddenly, the skinny Ms. Simms straightened up and glared at Nick. "You don't think that he had anything to do with this monstrous affair?" she accused.

"Not really, madam. I'm just asking questions. We have to formulate a solid picture of the workings of the neighborhood before we can move further in the case. Philemon Jenkins found the body, therefore we need to ask questions about him and anyone else who may have had contact with the ex-mayor."

"Well, if I find you giving that poor man a hard time in any way, you'll have me to answer to."

Lea barely stifled a laugh. The little lady couldn't have been more than ninety-five pounds and looked like a strong breeze would bowl her over.

"Philemon Jenkins is not a suspect at the present time. We just need to note how long he's worked for you and establish where he was on the probable night of the murder just as we need to know your whereabouts."

"Well, I'm glad to hear it," said Mrs. Simms huffily. "I told you. I was sleeping. And Philemon has a lovely wife who I'm sure can vouch for him."

Nick held his hands up in defeat and tactfully changed the subject. "Do you have a garden shed, by any chance?" he asked.

"Why, yes I do. Philemon keeps it nice and tidy. It's more than a shed, actually; it's really a greenhouse. That nice young officer came and took my wheelbarrow this morning. There were at least eight or nine of them being hauled into a truck." Her eyes sparkled with excitement. "Was the murder done with a wheelbarrow?"

Nick smiled. "No, we just need to check all the neighborhood wheelbarrows out. Don't worry—you'll get yours back soon."

"Oh, that will be nice. My greenhouse. Would you like to see it?" A note of pride crept into her brittle voice.

The case for her was simply forgotten, and only delight remained. Nick and Lea followed Mrs. Simms through the stately house and out to the expansive backyard. A huge rectangular greenhouse with glass sides and a slanted, transparent roof sat at the outer edge of the finely manicured garden. The cobbled walkways meandered between various arrays of flowers, and to the right, a huge koi pond benefited from a gushing waterfall under which swam ten to twelve languid gold and white fish.

"This is my pride and joy," said Mrs. Simms, leading the pair into the overly warm enclosure. The hot house measured at least thirty feet by ten feet and was equipped with long wooden counters lining both sides.

"It's as big as my first apartment," muttered Lea studying the incredible variety of orchids.

"What's that you say, dear?"

"It's very large."

"It has to be," said Mrs. Simms turning around and spreading her arm, "for these are my children."

What lovely children they were indeed. One orchid, the palest pink and lightly veined with violet, stretched out its long, delicate neck towards Nick.

"The temperature must be kept between 72-80 degrees," Mrs. Simms explained. "Orchids thrive in humidity and light, so I have a high-intensity sodium vapor system. I prefer an intermediate or warm house."

"I beg your pardon?" asked Nick wondering just how much this layout cost.

"My greenhouse caters to those orchids preferring intermediate or warm temperatures. Without consistent temperatures, the orchid will not bloom."

"And Philemon understands all this?"

"He's learning quickly. He looked as bewildered as

you, my boy, when he first started, but now is nearly as knowledgeable about the plants as I. And that's saying a great deal, young man." Her glowering stare indicated neither detective dare even suspect her Philemon.

"Every day, I come out to see how these most perfect of flowers are progressing." She marched down the wide aisle, calling out the names of the various orchid species while Nick struggled to stay focused.

"My favorites are *Vanda* and *Cattleya*, though I also experiment with many *Paphiopedilum* and *Dendrobium*. Ah, here's one of my favorites, *Cattleya Bicolor*. Isn't he beautiful?"

The small white and mauve orchid looked like it possessed a tongue sticking out of a brilliant green mouth.

"Very nice," mumbled Thayne, and Lea glared at him.

Mrs. Simms chortled on as the two detectives studied the huge greenhouse, whose flooring consisted of interlocking red brick. A shiny, deep basin near a potting trough separated a long wooden shelf upon which dozens of healthy orchids rested.

"This is some display of flowers, madam. More than a hobby I take it?"

Mrs. Simms paused before a long stemmed orchid she referred to as *Cymbidium Giganteum*. "Flowers and beauty are my life. If one can make this world a lovelier place, if one can nurture the perfection of flowers, I believe we add to the world's harmony." Her Buddhist-like philosophy was not wasted on Lea.

"What a magnificent collection," breathed Lea, and Nick thought that, for once, she was genuinely impressed.

"Oh, really?" said Nick involuntarily. A strange, long-necked orchid in flecked crimson strangely resembled a spider in appearance.

"That's a *Masdevallia Bella.* Quite difficult to achieve a bloom, and I need to be careful since it likes a cooler room. I usually keep it in my bedroom window and just brought it out to fertilize today. While not suiting some, its strange shape and coloration gratify me somehow. So imperfect to some, but perfect to me. Philemon has such a way with my orchids, as if he can almost coax them into bloom. I can tell, young woman, that you harbor a similar gift and love for plants."

"Yes, but mostly for violets and roses. I've never had the time and patience for orchids."

Mrs. Simms grasped Lea's arm with amazing strength and pulled her towards a collection of yellow orchids reaching for the artificial light. Nick gratefully watched them head away before scouring the greenhouse.

It was furnished with an enormous built-in fan and cooling system, and even a novice such as himself could recognize the system's high quality. Mrs. Simms clearly loved and nurtured her orchids. It was amazing how fragile and delicate the various plants appeared with their fairly thin green stems holding up the lovely slender necks of the flowers.

"Where do you keep your gardening tools?" asked Nick as Fox leaned over a pearly white stem. While no great flower lover, he knew never to insult someone's grand passion.

"Over there," Mrs. Simms hobbled to the end of the greenhouse and opened a small wooden door leading into a six-foot by six-foot square room. She flicked on the overhead light bulb, and hanging on the walls were various tools, picks, hoes, and rakes. In a neat row, four pairs of various-sized pruning shears dangled from long nails.

"Mrs. Simms, would you mind an officer taking a look at this room?" asked Nick, seemingly noncommittal.

Mrs. Simms twitched, and her veined hand grasped the wooden shelf for support. "Why? Is something missing?"

"Nothing at all. Only your gardener, Mr. Jenkins, uses these tools?" asked Thayne.

"No, I use some of them as well. I trim the orchids myself and repot them when necessary. It's very tiring work for me, but the rewards are great. When the need arises, I use some of the smaller hand tools over there."

Two stainless steel hand clippers rested upon the counter next to a blue-handled trowel.

"What's in the large red box?" said Lea pointing to a rectangular metal box faded with age.

"That's my late husband's tool box. I keep all sorts of odds and ends in there. Screwdrivers, pliers, and whatnot.

Would you like me to open it?"

Mrs. Simms lifted the lid, revealing a neat little pocket in the top of the metal cabinet loaded with various screws and nails. Underneath, Phillips and flat-bladed screwdrivers, as well as wrenches and pliers, were haphazardly tossed onto the main tool bed.

"Do you use these very often?"

"Oh, once in a while, but it's really Philemon who uses them. If I need to hang a picture or something comes loose, he fixes it right away. I used to be so spry in my younger days, but now it takes so much effort to even climb up on a step stool. I'd be lost without my Philemon!" She glanced fearfully at Nick and Lea.

Thayne raised a hand reassuringly. "Don't worry, Mrs. Simms. We're doing a search of all the neighboring houses. We're not here to implicate your gardener. We understand how much you rely on Mr. Jenkins."

"Well, that's a relief," sighed Mrs. Simms. "Is there anything else?" and before Nick could retrieve his own embossed business card, Fox handed her drab one to Mrs. Simms.

"Please feel free to give me a call anytime, Mrs. Simms."

They followed the feeble old lady back through the house, admiring the high vaulted ceilings with its beautiful wooden beams and diamond-shaped Tudor windows slanting lovely bursts of sunshine into the spacious and welcoming rooms.

"You know," said Mrs. Simms hopefully, right before they reached the front foyer. "If you'd like to come for tea sometime, it would be lovely. I could show you more of my orchids."

"If we have time, we'll certainly do so," said Nick pleasantly and shook her cold, palsied hand.

Fox clucked under her tongue as she followed Nick down the lovely cobbled pathway. "Well, Thayne, I have to hand it to you; you have a definite way with women. If you can charm a sixty-five-year-old woman, imagine what thirty-year-olds must do when you appear in their vicinity. Do you they simply fall down and beckon you to come hither as they acquiesce to your mighty charm, or do you ever have to work at it?"

"Here's something to plug into the F & H? *Everyone* wants to be treated like they matter, Fox, even little old women."

Chapter 10

Thayne crossed to the other side of the street. There was something to be said about good manners, which was something Lea's father, no matter how great a police officer he'd been, had failed to instill in his daughter. While animosity tinged every emotion Nick felt about his parents, at least the pair had managed to instill some sense of propriety in him. Nick briefly detailed instructions to Officer Phelps before joining the other officers in the field to survey the two white-clad men using metal detectors to scour every inch of the empty field.

Lea shrugged, watching the busy proceedings in the vacant field. My, but he was touchy. She knew damn good and well that if a male colleague had stated what she just had, he would have been slapped on the back with all-encompassing camaraderie. It didn't bother her much, since she was used to being the odd woman out, and left his tall, handsome form to shoot the breeze with the officers. She paused before 614 Chester Street, surveying the sharp spikes jutting from the tall white fence. Such a peculiar house with its vast cast iron gate and menacing appearance; a house full of secrets.

Upon impulse, she rang the intercom buzzer again. The loud peal of the bell rang through the house, but again no answer. Lea was about to turn away when she heard the slight crackle of underbrush.

She leaned against the fence, her keen ears picking out the rustle of leaves. Could this be the elusive Bouncer Philemon had reported? As if in answer, a ginger cat sprang to the fence and hissed at her.

"Jeez," she said, sorely disappointed. She meandered around the fence, searching for something, anything that could have been missed. The neighbor's house to the left had a wide expanse of yard with jasmine bordering a well-maintained lawn. Lea wandered into the Crawford's' yard, and using her foot, lifted the heaving foliage up from the drooping bottom leaves of the fragrant plant, searching for anything unusual. Suddenly, she spied a small red rubber ball nestled against the wall, halfway into the yard. Jubilant, Lea picked it up, hurrying back to 614 as quickly as her limping gait would allow. Philemon hadn't lied. The ball existed. Now, if she could just find its owner.

Lea leaned once more to the intercom and rang the buzzer again and again, to no avail. She spoke into the metal mouthpiece.

"I found your ball. Why don't you open up the gate

and let me in so I can return it to you." Silence dictated its staunch refusal.

She tried repeatedly until finally giving up in defeat. When Thayne's voice called out to her, Lea immediately thrust the red rubber ball into the wide pocket of her tweed blazer. One thing was for certain, while no one answered the bell at 614 Chester Street, someone or something definitely lived there. They needed to gain access.

A voice drifted across the empty lot from under the magnolia tree. "Hey, Fox! Could you open my trunk and bring me the small flashlight in the crate next to the first aid kit? We may have found something!"

Fox headed to the driver's side and flipped the trunk opener.

"What an appallingly small trunk," she said to no one in particular. A small crate, 18 inches square, was squirreled up into the left of the tiny trunk and in no time, Lea found the flashlight. An artist's sketchbook leaned against the opposite side and without an ounce of remorse, she opened it. She only managed to flip through three of the sketches before Thayne's voice rang out again.

"Fox! Bring the flashlight!"

She slammed the lid and headed towards the big tree. "What is it?" she asked.

Thayne peered up into a branch about seven feet above the earth at the rear of the magnolia. "Give me," he ordered.

Flipping on the powerful beam, he pinpointed some thin scratches at right above his head. “Look.”

The single word *Phile* was freshly carved into the aged trunk.

“Jeez,” said Fox.

They stood beside the curb, waiting for the chief. Within minutes, his metallic blue sedan slid to a stop by them. Chief Rollins rolled down the Ford’s electric window exposing his florid face. It was obvious he wasn’t thrilled to be called out on a Saturday afternoon, murder or no murder.

“What is it?” he barked.

Nick handed him the Polaroid of the tree carving.

“Phile?” he said. “Philly Cheesecake? Philadelphia?”

“Or perhaps a nickname,” returned Thayne quietly. “It had been freshly carved at the rear of the tree. In the first flurry of activity, we were all focused at the base of the tree.”

“Hmm,” pondered the Chief. “I’ll have Dwayne run this through the system. Maybe he’ll come up with something. Oh, finally managed to get through to Collins’ office. Collins is in New York, but his secretary says you can search the entire premises. Apparently, no one lives in the house; it’s kept as a training and conference retreat for some of the high-ups in his company. I don’t want to hear from either of you until Monday unless something else important breaks or you’ve solved this case. If I don’t attend my wife’s high school reunion this evening, I'm dead meat. You can reach me on my cell if it's an emergency, but at no other time." The chief's mobile tinkled. "Rollins," he barked. "Oh hi, Hon."

"*Hell hath no fury like a woman's scorn*," quoted Nick smoothly.

"Oh, pleez," grumbled Lea. "If you're going to quote something at least get it right!"

"That's not right?"

"No. It states *Nor Hell a fury, like a Woman scorn'd.* William Congreve. My father was a quote-aholic as well. Between him and being an English minor in college . . . I sense a fraud at work."

"And did it work on the women? Your father's quotes?"

"Well, my mother still married him."

"Probably impressed by his wit and intelligence."

"Knocked up with my brother. And I think the more appropriate word is *tolerate*," said Lea icily.

Chief Rollins flipped shut his phone and rolled his eyes wearily before handing them a file with a post-it on top indicating the house's security codes. "And another present for you from the good doctor with some *interesting* tidbits."

"Such as?" asked Nick.

"An analysis of the paint particles found under Thad Fisher's fingers. It makes damn good reading, but it's the other stuff that I'm sure would fascinate the likes of a pair of world-class private investigators such as yourselves. After you read it, you'll understand how close we are to making an arrest!"

He snickered and drove off without uttering one word to Lea, pulling his vehicle around the bulb end of the cul-de-sac without so much as a goodbye.

"And a good day to you as well," she stated to the rear end of the blue Ford. "What does he mean, an arrest?"

"You're right, Fox. He wants this wrapped up and pronto. So, what do you want to do first?" asked Nick handing her the code. "Read the addendum to the report or enter the premises now?"

Lea said idly. "How did you know where to find the word carved into the magnolia?"

Thayne's eyes flicked to hers before languidly studying the liquid amber trees swaying gently before the beautiful, gabled, charcoal-slate roof of Mrs. Simms' house.

"I didn't *know* anything, Fox. I just thought the crew might have missed something."

"Definitely not partners," mumbled Lea and turned abruptly towards the Collins house. "Now that we've got the warrant, let's see what delights it has to show us. We'll check out Steven's report later."

Nick's eyes narrowed. "Okay. Could you wait just a moment while I return my flashlight?" He strode briskly to the Mustang and popped its trunk, remaining a long moment behind the shielding hood before slamming it down harder than it warranted.

"Been nosy, Fox? Why do I feel like my privacy's been compromised?"

"I'm a P.I., Thayne. That stands for *Privacy invaded.* You coming or do you plan on glaring at me all day?"

The heavy black gate swung open with a mighty echoing creak. Thayne had called Officer Phelps to join them, not because he felt Randy's assistance was necessary, but to serve as a buffer between him and Fox. He seethed inside, and it wasn't until a putrid smell assailed their nostrils that he came out of his preoccupation.

The smell reminded Lea of unclean toilets and rarely used campgrounds where repulsive deeds were inflicted upon the innocent in the dark. Fox saw Thayne's mahogany eyes crinkle in disgust.

"Good God, that's rank," hissed Nick, searching his pocket for a wadded-up handkerchief.

He held it to his nose as they headed up the concrete walkway edged in red brick to match the house. The beautifully designed house reminded Lea of houses constructed during the colonial days, the bright red brick indicating a stout but classily built house. Cascading gables and a charming balcony jutted off two of the upper story windows. A huge, sheltered entryway led to a two-story foyer where twin brick chimneys thrust from the sharply slanted roof.

"Nice looking joint," said Officer Phelps, who Lea noticed, was chewing gum. Trim, young, and energetic, though a bit on the stocky side, his pleasant face still possessed the eagerness 18 months on the force hadn't yet dampened. "So where to now, Inspector Thayne?" he asked the tall detective.

"Let's check the front yard out first." The three wandered through the pleasing garden. "That's interesting," said Lea. "It's a row of *Prunus Laurocerasus*."

"And what's that?" said Nick, barely polite.

"English Laurel. They've covered the entire length of the brick wall in the shrub. The typical English Laurel can reach at least ten feet high, but this has been trimmed down to only about four feet." She hobbled over and plucked one of its purplish-black fruit. "Some people call this a Cherry Laurel. While not very common here on the West Coast, it makes a perfect shrub if well trained and watered as this has been. It's strange, though; most people use Laurel as a fence, not a hedge planted against an already existing wall. Mostly used in English gardens. You can see it's been severely pruned and mighty recently, at that."

She touched one of the light green stalks devoid of leaves at the top. "It will be full of pretty cream-colored flowers in the spring."

"You sure know a lot about plants, Inspector Fox," said Officer Phelps.

"I do. It was my mother's passion. You might say she was a frustrated landscape artist."

In a very thin strip along the walkway, *Weigela* flowered in a pale white-pink. The rest of the yard was covered in rich green dichondra grass.

"This part of the yard is not used by children," announced Fox. "Dichondra doesn't take wear and tear well, and it's a tough grass to keep nice in this climate." Two huge eucalyptuses towered from the middle of the vast emerald green lawn

"Strange," said Thayne at her shoulder. "It's clear that the lawn has been mown quite recently and someone has to take care of that incredible hedge here as well as this little border of flowers, but everyone indicates no one is ever seen at house, that is, except for last Tuesday."

"Maybe the gardener resides here," suggested Lea. "But why wouldn't they answer the door? Have you noticed, Thayne, the lack of trees close to the house?"

He merely grunted.

"Some nice rose bushes, though," said Randy Phelps awkwardly, noticing the two detective's tension.

"Yes, whoever's the gardener here at least shares Mrs. Simms' love of flowers. Ah, here's one of my favorites!" Lea pointed to a brilliant pink flower. "This one's called *Duet*. See its dusty color?" She moved a little closer. "A true rose lover designed this garden. Do you notice how they've alternated pink and red roses with white ones? All hybrid teas; there's not a floribunda in the bunch."

"Is that important?" asked Randy. Thayne continued staring at the roof, a frown upon his handsome face.

"They take a lot more work, so someone has to live here because the garden needs more than an occasional gardener. Dichondra is a tough lawn to take care of, since it's subject to weeds. English Laurel must be constantly trimmed and the dead flowers removed so it continues to bloom. Roses need lots of fertilizer and are hard work to maintain at this standard. The dead blooms must be removed and constantly fed systemic to repel aphids and fungus. None of these roses have a trace of rust, and I haven't spied an aphid anywhere. Here's *First Love*, *Electron,* and one of my favorite roses, *Honor,* just to name a few. And nary a dead petal anywhere. So why is this house considered vacant?"

"Could just be the neighbors not noticing," said Randy.

"What do you mean?" asked Nick, totally ignoring Fox.

"It's like where I live. No one pays any attention to the neighbors unless they're too loud or there's a dog barking or something. Shoot, my neighbor works the night shift, so I've only met him once."

"That's a valid point. One side of the house borders the empty field, and the other has a good thirty feet before the side fence begins at the Crawford's'."

Lea punched their findings into the F & H before summarizing, "So, it's obvious this garden is doted on and serviced often, perhaps even yesterday. That means someone likely *was* here when Philemon Jenkins found the body. And," stated Lea, "remember how Philemon insisted a child played ball with him?" She reached into her pocket and pulled out the red rubber ball. "This was under some bushes along the outer fence in the Crawford's yard."

Thayne returned to her side and removed the ball from her thin hand. His face became shadowed, and he rubbed his forehead before handing back the ball. "Philemon was telling the truth. Let's check out the backyard, then. The child has to be there."

Two large Mexican pots of incredible circumference held enormous cycads near the entryway. Thayne knocked loudly upon the door, which echoed hollowly. Not a peep from the huge house.

"Just what I expected," reflected Nick.

Officer Phelps and Fox followed his determined figure around the side of the house. The driveway curved abruptly, revealing a two-car garage angled discreetly along the side of the house. A narrow pathway, once again edged in red brick, led to a low gate separating the backyard from the front. A huge silver padlock hung from the black wrought iron gate. Nick wasted no time.

"Randy, I need you to head around the other side of the house and see if there's another route into the backyard without us having to bust this lock."

Randy returned in less than two minutes. "No. The other side is padlocked as well. I guess this means I've got to fetch my kit." He grinned and trotted down the driveway.

Lea once again surveyed the yard as they waited, noting the well-trimmed eucalyptuses, which remain an on-going challenge since the huge trees are known to be rapid growers and constantly shed limbs and bark. Nothing crowded the house or the high, white fence. The fact somehow bothered her.

"I don't like this house," stated Thayne, suddenly lifting his head and sniffing. Once again, the putrid smell of sewage assaulted his nose.

"I know," said Lea, "how could so beautiful a place seem so . . ."

"Vile?" Nick finished for her.

"Indeed." She stood a long while in thought, rubbing her aching hip absently.

"A penny for your thoughts?" he asked finally.

"I visited a prison once with my father when he had to interview an inmate. They had trees centered inside the prison yard and far removed from any structures. Somehow, this house and yard reminds me of that prison with its steep slant of roof and low hedges making the wall inaccessible. And nothing, *nothing* grows close this house except for the rose bushes armed with *thorns*." The lift of the wind brought the awful smell of the sewer back again, and she scrunched up her unattractive face.

Randy arrived at a dead run. Using heavy-duty metal cutters he hacked through the expensive padlock, and the now-useless pieces fell to the ground with a clang. The passageway down the south side of the house was narrow and the high wall felt too close. Between the house and this fence, only a mere four feet separated the prison-like wall from the dusty red brick of the colonial house. The stench gradually increased until Nick finally halted and grabbed his nose, his stomach churning.

The passage way widened out to open into a huge back yard and while the smell remained overwhelming, the backyard revealed a child's paradise with a massive wooden play set equipped with slides, swing, and sandbox. A small hut had been built into the side of the swing set and opened onto an enormous sandbox, big enough for any school playground. Two large eucalyptus trees shaded the massive garden, but once again, were centered directly away from the house and surrounding fence.

Lea followed her nose with Nick and Officer Phelps reluctantly following. A long distance away from the play set and near the back fence bordering the length of the vacant field, a huge pile of leaves lay undisturbed except for copious amount of dung drying in the shade. This area had clearly been used as an outdoor toilet, but by whom or what?

Chapter 11

Saturday Afternoon

"Jeez," said Randy Phelps holding his nose and trying not to look disgusted. "You would think that a mansion like this could afford indoor plumbing."

"Yes, you would," agreed Nick softly. He backed away from the offensive pile and moved toward the well-built playground.

"No money has been spared here," he observed.

He stooped to allow the small doorframe to accommodate his height and entered the child-sized hut. Lea didn't follow, leaving Officer Phelps to examine the play area. She moved towards a large, round stake situated a distance away from the play set. Lea squatted and studied it. A rusty metal loop had been welded onto the top of the stake and the entire area around the driven wood, some ten feet in circumference, was trampled down.

No grass grew within the circular limits as if some

animal had been tied to the stake and had run countless circles around it. The dung pile distantly bordered the beaten area, and nearby, a discarded ceramic water bowl, the kind used for a dog, sat empty, clumps of dirt clinging to its side. What kind of animal had paced impatiently here; perhaps a tame pig, or even a chimp or baboon? The latter would explain the humanlike feces.

"Officer Phelps," called Lea rising. "Would you take a photo of this stake, the playground, and the dung pile? Also collect a sample of the feces. While a large dog makes sense, I suspect a more exotic type of animal was chained here; perhaps something rare or endangered."

Randy grimaced. One thing remained certain about being the junior officer on the squad; you were always assigned the most disgusting jobs. He headed sourly to his baking squad car for some plastic bags. Lea moved to the hut, and unlike Nick, did not have to stoop to survey the inside. The simple square structure had a plank floor upon which rested a brimming wooden box piled high with rusty play cars and dump trucks. Tiny damaged miniature cars spread across the rough flooring as if the child had suddenly been jerked away in the midst of his game. Very few plants lined the back wall. In fact, except for an abundance of some reddish-orange bamboo cut low, the dichondra grass ran right up to the back fence.

"The entire plot must cover at least an acre," stated

Lea. "I wonder if all the houses on the block have such huge yards? What's on the other side of this back wall?"

Nick leaned out of the hut and shaded his eyes against the sun. "Just the fields of the Agrit-Empire. I believe someone mentioned lettuce, potato, and spinach plots. Would you and Officer Phelps like to check out the other side?"

"I would," said Lea. "Ashley Peebles was supposedly killed by two farm workers, isn't that correct?"

"It is, indeed," returned Nick.

"If this is the furthermost edge of the suburbs with nothing in between except for vacant land and the fields where farm workers toil, who knows what sort of characters may have traipsed over to the cul-de-sac. The fence around the vacant lot isn't very high, at least compared to this: perhaps three feet max. Any child could scale over it. Shall we enter the house?"

Randy had returned and rapidly shot several photos of the huge yard before screwing up his face as he picked up some of the dung. Nick stifled a grin. The trio headed to the back door.

Nick rapped. "Is anyone home? We're the Monroe City Police Department. Please open up. We have a search warrant for the facilities."

Though they waited several minutes before heading around the huge house again and lifting the heavy brass knocker of the front door, he rapped several times before turning to Randy Phelps, “I believe that covers our civic duty to knock. The keypad is located on the left wall of the foyer. You’ll only have around twenty seconds until all hell breaks loose. It’s all yours, Randy. Have fun.”

It took him less than thirty seconds to pry open the door. Lea gasped and gazed into the mischievous eyes of the rookie.

“If you’re free sometime, Randy, I’d like you to come and check the locks on my house. What you just did makes me extremely nervous.”

Randy punched in the code before leading them into the lovely portico. Beautifully tiled in the softest cream, it opened into an elegant foyer. A towering staircase fronted them, separating an expansive library on one side and a formal living room on the other. Nick moved directly into the living room, shouting out their identity once again.

Randy whistled appreciatively at the impressive design. The sunken room eventually opened into a Chinese-partitioned formal dining room with an octagonal trace ceiling. Sprawling, hand-knotted wool and silk rugs were strewn across the floor as if they cost no more than a K-Mart blue-light special. The dark and expensive built-in wood was polished to a dull luster. Nick pointed to some of the artwork.

“There’s a bunch of Gothic-American stuff. That painting alone is probably worth a police officer’s entire month’s salary, and the furniture is all heavy mahogany. This setup must have cost a mint."

An incredibly beautiful wall unit with recessed lighting illuminating adjustable glass cells had been filled with tiny brass and glass figurines. A huge mahogany table decorated with a creamy, knotted table covering dominated the dining room, and upon it sat a vase bursting with roses from the garden. Lea moved close and sniffed. They'd been cut recently.

The living room delighted with a mass of two-toned leather couches, large Persian rugs, and bronze light fixtures. The massive brick fireplace had been laid with logs, though the season was still too hot for such luxuries. The floor-to-ceiling windows let in ample light and revealed the large backyard.

The trio wandered into the stainless steel kitchen, noting the granite countertops and gigantic stainless steel refrigerator, the dual oven, and large dishwasher; all were spotless and incredibly expensive, but barely made a dent in the kitchen's spaciousness.

"No one's used this kitchen for a while," said Lea.

"Maybe. But look at that."

Thayne pointed to a small pile of dirt near the pantry.

Lea knelt down painfully. "Possible the maid tracked in some dirt on her shoes. She'd get fired in Trish Fisher's house for this kind of negligence. Officer Phelps, bag some of the soil please."

That proved the only blemish upon the entire house,

yet the elegant structure just didn't feel right. The long countertops were too vacant, the appliances too new. The center island, while containing a food processor, blender, and an incredible array of kitchen knives, had been designed for looks, not convenience. Nick and Lea visited the library with its full bookshelves surrounded by comfortable leather couches and reading chairs. Dainty Victorian lights strategically illuminated the room, but once again, this room appeared unused, the impressive collection unread.

Nick made his way upstairs and observed the spacious rooms. The masculine master bedroom on the right came equipped with its own fireplace and spacious en-suite bathroom. The vaulted ceilings towered twelve feet high, and the room was supplied with a luxurious gray-tiled bathing area, which included a separate tub and shower as well as a Jacuzzi.

The next two rooms were also equipped with en-suite bathrooms, and while lighter in color, had obviously been decorated by the same hand. Pale silk flowers broke up the monotony of the house's white walls, and fresh yellow throw pillows livened up the beige bedspreads.

Officer Phelps had trotted up the stairs and now peeked into the second of the two guest bedrooms.

"What are your perceptions about this home, Officer?" asked Nick, once again avoiding Lea's gaze.

"I don't like it," said Randy shortly. "Not only does it stink outside but this house seems sterile; like some expensive hotel nobody but the snooty can afford. It may be nicely decorated with all these high ceilings and expensive furniture and stuff, but it's the kind of house you'd be afraid to sit down on the couch and have a coke or something because you might spill it. It's just like my grandma's house—she's got plastic on the couches and only removes it on Sundays when we come to dinner. Me, I like houses where you can go put your feet on the furniture and spill some popcorn on the floor knowing your dog will clean it up."

Nick smiled. "My perceptions exactly. Seems like there's only a couple more rooms."

The next room served as the office. It housed a miniature library full of engineering and bio-tech books, an elaborate computer station including an adding machine and fax and what appeared to be a drafting table. Still, the well-equipped desk seemed little utilized.

The final room proved a different story altogether. Nick stopped short, his heart in his throat. Bathed in light with pale blue walls, its creamy curtains were dotted with rising red, blue, and yellow balloons. A bright wallpaper border hugged the ceiling, and made the chamber appear merry and cheerful. On one side, an enormous crib was situated below an enormous hot air balloon headed for a distant snow-capped mountain. A low table, with a caddy crammed full of crayons and markers centered on it red surface, was scratched and marked with mindless doodles. Lea flung startled eyes at Nick as he let out his breath slowly. Randy opened the empty closet. Like the other three bedrooms, it held only the memory of occupation. Lea covertly took out her own small camera and snapped a shot.

A sharp pain just behind his Nick's eyes momentarily blinded him. This was not the right place.

Lea crossed her arms and thought hard. "I would say that this house is kept in waiting, unused until the owner decides to visit."

"Makes sense," said Nick awkwardly. "That would explain the sterile feel. They probably employ a maid and gardener to keep the place in readiness."

"Think this house could have a basement?" asked Lea abruptly.

"Maybe," said Officer Phelps, "but most houses in this region don't bother. It's not like we get tornadoes or anything, and from the size of this place, they're sure not lacking for space."

"I know," said Lea, "but it would be interesting to see if we could find a cellar where the owners store their personal belongings."

The trio spent the next twenty minutes searching the downstairs, but every door they opened led either into a pantry, closet, or ample storage space, but little in regards to personal items.

"There's just something about this place that strikes

me all wrong, Fox. If little Katie's correct and there was a big party here last week, there must have been some mighty fine cleanup. I suggest we let Randy and the team loose to scour this place with a fine-toothed comb. Maybe we'll get lucky."

"Perhaps," said Lea. "Let's check out Steven's report and find out what Chief Rollins was so merry about."

Chapter 12

Nick watched the other officers headed by the energetic Randy Phelps scurry through the Collins' house with photographic and dusting equipment. He felt tired, and the fare at the diner ordered nearly four hours ago had long ceased to stave off his hunger pangs. He could sure use a long, cold drink, preferably one that frothed and boasted a magnificent head.

"Let's return to my office," offered Lea generously. If the truth were to be known, her crippled leg was killing her as it always did whenever she'd stood on it for too long. She could use a break as well, and her stomach was beginning to rumble.

Nick remembered her too-neat office and shook his dark head. "No, I need a beer and distance from this block." Fox followed his eyes to the Mustang's trunk.

"Drop me off at my office, then," she said suddenly.

"Why? Need to do some research?" he asked tersely.

"That, and I need to speak with someone."

"And who would that be? Thought you worked *alone?"* he said sarcastically. He knew damn well what she was up too.

"I have a boyfriend, you know."

"You do?" his eyes widened in shock.

"And some people say *I'm* rude, Thayne." A flicker of hurt briefly clouded her violet eyes.

"Guess that *was* insensitive," he said non-contritely. "What I meant to say was I'm surprised he'd let you wander around on a Saturday, since that's usually everyone's day off. He'd probably want to go . . . *bowling* or something."

Lea stared long and hard at his unrepentant face, and Nick wished irrelevantly he could give her some helpful tips on how to maximize her appearance. Fox wouldn't look half bad if she just worked on it. Not half good, either, but anything could be improved; even her.

"Bernard understands my life's demands and gives me space."

"Oh, really? And just what does this *Bernard* do for a living?"

"None of your business."

"Ooh," scoffed Nick as he opened the door of his cherry-red Mustang. "A bit sensitive, aren't we?"

"Not at all. It is just that my personal life is to remain my personal life, no matter how curious my partner might be about it."

"So, we're partners now. And I can totally understand feeling a *violation of privacy*.

Fox lifted her head. "I just reckon you have more to *offer* this partnership than I previously suspected." Lea fiddled in her purse for sunglasses and finally hooked clip-ons over the atrocious black wire-rimmed spectacles. She sank down beside him and straightened the awful skirt over her bony knees. She now looked worse, if that was possible. He'd always thought only little old ladies who drove Thunderbirds and muscled their way through supermarket parking lots leaving nicks on other people's cars wore those kinds of shades.

"You're a good artist," she said abruptly. "How do you pick your subjects?"

Lea thought he wasn't going to answer. Finally he uttered, "They pick me."

After a long poignant silence she said shakily. "I see. One shouldn't scoff at one's gifts. You willing to let me look at more?"

"Maybe," he said and started the car. They'd driven for a full five minutes before he added, "If they seem relevant." And then, many minutes later, as if what had been said didn't matter, he said, "So, what happened to your leg?"

She glanced over at him, her small hands clenched as if dealing with some strong emotion. "I mentioned my brother drank?"

"You did."

"At the start of my ninth grade year, he had to pick me up after school. I could smell the alcohol on his breath, but didn't have the guts to get out of the car and walk. It's quite foggy here in autumn. Anyway, we ended up wrapped around a tree near the onion fields. My brother walked away with nary a scratch—I've heard that drunks often do because they're so relaxed—and I spent the next five weeks in the hospital as they pieced together the bones in my left leg and hip. My dad and brother blamed the foggy conditions, of course. Dad could never see any sort of fault in Lane."

"You're bitter?"

"Of course. Wouldn't you be? Because of *everything*, I don't drink and I don't lie, particularly to myself. I am what I am, and if someone doesn't like it, they can stuff it."

"Indeed," he said. "I like your attitude. Here's your office. I'll pick up some food. Give me an hour, and then we'll see what Dr. Koh's come up with."

Ninety minutes later, Thayne showed up. He carried two aluminum cans of soda in one hand and three fast food bags in the other with his sketchbook tucked under his arm. He'd clearly stopped by the boarding house to don worn blue jeans and a red-checked, short-sleeved cotton shirt. He politely offered her a vegetarian sub, and Fox hesitantly took the foot-long sandwich and diet soda, watching him wade through Steven's report as they ate.

"The paint shards found inside Thad Fisher's intestinal track are the kind found in cheap furniture bought across the border or in items that predates our current stiff regulations regarding lead content," she said, squinting at her F & H.

"That's right," said Nick wolfing down three fries at a time and licking his fingers.

"We can assume one is still able to purchase items in Mexico, where the regulations are not as stringent."

"You can get anything down in Mexico."

"So therefore, Thad Fisher," she continued, "ingested paint flakes from something purchased down south or made a trip to Mexico in recent weeks."

"He hadn't traveled," said Nick taking a hefty bite of his meatball sub. "Maybe he consumed the paint particles without knowing it. I've heard pots imported from Mexico and used for cooking leak out lead and toxins into food without the victim even knowing it."

"But it wasn't leaked into his system," said Lea picking up the report and pointing to one interesting sentence. "He had particles in his teeth, almost as if he'd been gnawing at something. And what about the two good-sized rose thorns embedded in his feet?"

"Interesting, but unfortunately there are lots of roses in Monroe County," said Thayne. "The town hall alone must have fifty or more. And, of the yards I checked on Chester Street, 60 percent of them, including the Simms and Collins' houses had roses."

"True."

"Are you going to finish that?" Nick pointed to her half-eaten sub. She ate like a bird.

"Go ahead. So Thad was seen last alive at Chester Street." She gazed at the F & H and read from the possible scenario section she'd punched up. "Visualize this. Thad Fisher tried to escape and plunged through rose bushes in his haste. If you combine that with the fact that Thad lost his finger by the probable use of garden clippers, it would make sense to suspect he was killed at Chester Street. Every house should have their gardening equipment checked. I'd bet your Mustang one of them has the tool that was used to sever the mayor's finger. Plus, the word on the tree—*Phile.*" She pressed a button on the F & H and cocked an unplucked eyebrow at him.

"You know who you're implicating with this logic?"

"Yes," said Lea squinting across at him through her too prominent glasses. She held up the tiny screen for him to see the name illuminated there.

"Philemon Jenkins," read Nick.

"I personally believe Mr. Jenkins didn't murder Thad Fisher. The fact that he led the police to the body plus the simplicity of his story reeks of the truth."

"I'd have to agree," said Nick. "But even a challenged individual like the chief will put two and two together. Unless we find something concrete to lead us away from a garden scenario for the murder, I have a feeling that our Mr. Jenkins is in for some real trouble."

"May I see the sketch again?" asked Lea politely.

Nick sighed and wiped his mouth. "Here you go."

The drawing pad was thin. Nick had obviously removed what he considered irrelevant. He tapped a well-manicured finger on the first. "I drew this on Wednesday morning—around 3 a.m. I'd been drinking—booze seems to 'increase' my artistic abilities."

The magnolia tree trunk hung heavy with foliage under a full moon. A small, red ball, exactly like the one Lea had discovered earlier that day, lay on the unsettled ground near grossly upturned fingers. Fox squinted at him. "You 'saw' it just like this?"

"Exactly. It's an image I can't hold onto unless I draw it. You can see there's nothing place descriptive. No identifier or street sign anywhere. I have to 'hope' the crime will find its way to me."

"I don't understand."

Nick leaned forward. "I have these 'visions' or whatever—usually propelled by the use of alcohol. I have no idea where they come from and what they relate to. I do know that, usually, there is some connection to my life or someone I know. I believe that my friendship with Roger was my connection—though I had no way to know he'd succumb to appendicitis and I'd be called in. But, that's how it works. There's a connection, but damned if I know what the connection is. Sometimes I can figure it out. Other times, I never do."

"You're clairvoyant!" said Lea, half marveling, half repelled.

"Whatever."

"You got more of these?" she asked excitedly.

"Dozens. But many have nothing to do with this case—or so I think. I figure if weeks pass and I haven't figured out the connection to a drawing . . . then I missed the boat. Here's three of the most recent, so these most likely have some relevance to the case." He shoved the drawing of the tree limb with the word *Phile* on it towards her.

Fox cleared her throat. "I've . . . ah . . . seen this."

"Figured. You goddamned snoop. And this."

It was a picture of a crib with a large balloon and fluffy clouds. Lea didn't tell him she'd also glimpsed this one in his trunk. "It's not the same room, but the crib is familiar." She punched her F & H and turned the screen towards him. "See, yours has clouds. This room doesn't. Crib is similar, but not an exact match. At least now we know the crib is important."

"And here."

"The putrid playground. Lucky we can't smell it. Any more?"

"Not that I'm willing to share at the present time. You amaze me, Fox. I felt you were so grounded in reality, but you accepting these 'drawings'. . Wow. I'm shocked, to say the least."

"I'm a shocking woman," was all she returned. "I'll meet you here at 8 a.m. sharp tomorrow morning," stated Lea, rising from her father's chair. The food was finished, and she had some research to do and needed to get away from Thayne's claustrophobic presence.

Nick untangled his long frame from her brother's chair. "Alright. Maybe I'll show the rose thorns around to some local nurseries and get a possible ID on the type of bush. I'd also like to head back to Connie's. Maybe someone caught a glimpse of our Presidio boy or his car. I'd sure like to know his name and where he is now. I'll also check on the wheelbarrow angle. It's probably too soon to learn whether the feces are human or not, though our Dr. Koh is like some sort of forensics Superman. If I hear anything earth shattering, I'll give you a ring."

"I'll wait breathlessly," purred Lea. "Also, I'd suggest you serve yourself up a salad for later. If you keep eating fast food, the cholesterol and salt will likely result in high blood pressure, hardening of the arteries, and possible heart disease, just to name a few. You must treat your body as a temple, and if you do, it will serve you well."

"You're full of shit," returned Thayne, tossing his

crumpled fast food bag into the bin in an effortless arch. For a moment, he'd almost forgotten what a pain in the ass she was. If *her* body was a temple, he'd sprint to KFC.

After several hours of work at home, Lea spoke to Bernard for a while before fixing a simple late supper of soup and sourdough bread. Her tabby cat jumped up on her lap and Lea scratched his ears absently. After all her research, she was more in a quandary than before. Until Connie Judson was located, even with Thayne's 'gift', they were stumped. She'd researched Thayne's days at the SFPD, but none of the articles came right out and stated he was a psychic; they only hinted at his 'spooky' methods. Could she accept his 'gift' and somehow allow it to steer their investigation? Lea couldn't believe how readily she had accepted what he was. Maybe his peculiarity made him more similar to the outcast she was. Lea ladled her minestrone soup from the copper cookware she preferred and sprinkled some Parmesan cheese on the top. The cat jumped down in disdain.

She loved this house, and as she wandered into the cozy nook straddling the kitchen, she wondered how long she could afford to keep it. Her cash flow nearly non-existent, Lea knew if she didn't come up with some real money soon, the house would be forfeited to the mortgage company. Lea was intensely private by nature and if not peculiar in her habits at least particular. Plodding and methodical, she disliked—if not dreaded—hectic big cities like Los Angeles and San Francisco. Unfortunately, that was where the work was, and she had no delusions that without widening her work sphere, bankruptcy was inevitable.

A niggling feeling lurked in the back of her mind that Thayne, even with his classic, bright red Mustang and expensive suits, was probably in the same boat as she. Somehow, she had to finagle her way into the Monroe Country Police Department's good graces and be taken on as a permanent consultant. Maybe between that and the independent jobs she hoped a good reputation might generate, she could make it financially. But, did Thayne have the clout she hoped would propel her out of this jobless purgatory perpetuated by Monroe's malevolent police chief?

Thayne rang at 9:00 p.m. "I've had a bit of luck. Mr. McKinney at Rose World is positive thorns from a bush rose called *Mr. Lincoln* are similar to the ones extracted from Thad Fisher's feet. Unfortunately, that rose is found in nearly everyone's garden."

"Let's check again at Chester Street for *Mr. Lincoln* roses tomorrow morning. I'll meet you around nine a.m."

"No problem. I will also have you know that our Presideo lover is balding, thin, wears an officer's uniform, whistles when he walks, and drives a 2002 Land Cruiser, the color black."

"Jeez. Another 'drawing'?"

"Nope. A legitimate source. And you?"

"Soaked in the tub, removed the fur balls from my cat's throat, and whipped up some minestrone soup. Now I'm just watching reruns of the *Joe Millionaire*. Maybe I'll get lucky and find a hunk as cute as you."

Thayne slammed down the receiver, and Lea grinned. He'd been hoping for a compliment. Wait until he saw what she'd dug up.

Sunday morning

The shrill jarring of her bedside phone awakened her at nearly two a.m. It was the ever-pleasant Chief Rollins.

"I wouldn't have called you," said the Police Chief nastily, "but I can't get hold of Nick Thayne and thought you might know where he could be."

"And . . . ?" she said letting the word dangle.

"We received a tip-off and found Connie Judson's body twenty minutes ago, and it isn't a pretty sight. I need Nick to meet me off of Highway 106 as it heads towards the Agrit-Empire's potato fields and turn right at the first dirt road. We're waiting about a quarter of a mile down. We've got a dual homicide on our hands, and unfortunately one of our best suspects has just been found pushing up some rock. You don't need to bother showing up, as it would probably make you sick."

"I doubt it. I've lived with men," returned Lea. "We'll be there as soon as possible." She hung up before he could retort. While Lea suspected Nick's whereabouts, she didn't have the number of the young woman from the diner, so she called his cell phone and left an urgent message.

Lea parked her Mazda under a huge oak tree and walked towards the group of grim-faced men standing over a shallow grave. A large spotlight slanting downwards from a makeshift pole revealed the cordoned-off area. Fox forced herself to study the deceased woman, whose auburn hair shifted slightly in the breeze. While no blood or physical wounds were superficially evident, a horrible grimace contorted Connie Judson's heavily made-up face.

The woman lay perfectly rigid in a shallow grave, her high-heeled red shoes standing daintily beside her as if she'd been asked to remove them. Her slender arms were duct-taped to the bright crimson dress distastefully stained by dirt and struggle. Her legs, bound together at the knees by the fabric tape, were clad in expensive stockings that were savagely ripped and shredded. One small piece of duct tape covered her mouth but hadn't managed to conceal the horrible grimace twisting her features. Her wide-open, jade-colored eyes glittered eerily in the unforgiving spotlight.

"Where's Nick?" rumbled the chief.

"Coming. How did you find her way out here?" asked Lea.

Randy Phelps had also been obviously roused from his bed. His haggard face glowed greenish-white in the harsh lamplight around which a hundred moths fluttered.

Officer Phelps answered for the chief, who hesitated. “We received an anonymous phone call around 1 a.m. from someone who said they’d discovered what looked like a body in the field but didn’t wish to get involved. The guy had a Hispanic accent and is likely some wetback afraid he’ll be shipped back down south if we learn who he is.”

“How did she die?” asked Lea.

Randy seemed unable to answer, so the chief did it for him. “At first, we thought maybe she’d been strangled, but there are no contusions around her throat. Whatever it was caused her a great deal agony, if her facial contortions are any indication.”

Chief Rollins pointed a pudgy finger at Connie’s left hand. “They left the same calling card as the mayor.” Her slim ring finger had been removed.

Lea quietly studied the still corpse for a long while. If the horrible sight disturbed her, she gave no outward indication, and that fact alone irked the chief to no end

“You may find this interesting, girlie.” Chief Rollins bent down and pointed to a baggie Lea hadn’t noticed before clutched in Connie’s other hand. Inside, a hairy male finger still wore its huge gold nugget band. He paused for effect. “Gruesome, isn’t it?”

“Interesting, I’d say,” was her only response.

The roar of a well-tuned engine slid up the dirt road,

and out of the red Mustang stepped Nick Thayne, his hair tousled and shirt askew. He swayed slightly.

"I guess this is one way to get out of a high school reunion," he slurred mildly to the chief, who only frowned.

"Glad you made it so Miss Whodunit can get back to her knitting."

"So, this is Connie."

"Yep. Used to be quite a looker."

Nick spotted the baggie and knelt down. "Talk about orchestrated by the killer. Jeez. How'd you find her?"

"Anonymous tip."

"Any tire tracks?"

"We've isolated some over there and already took some plaster of Paris castings, but they watered the field tonight so the imprints have run. Hard to tell if they're from a picker's truck or car. From the looks of her, she's been here at least two days. Hey, Fox, get away from that body! Jesus, can't you keep her on a leash?"

Lea's fingers froze while lifting Connie's red hair at the chief's bark.

"The coroner coming?" asked Nick seeking to distract the irate Rollins.

"Should be here any minute."

"May I see those tracks?" Nick asked.

Lea rose as Chief Rollins pulled Nick over to examine the tire treads. As soon as they'd moved out of earshot, she called to Randy Phelps.

"Do you have a rubber glove, Officer Phelps?"

"Of course," he said, fumbling in his pocket.

Lea pulled it over her slim hand and lifted up Connie's hair, frowning intensely.

"Does that look like a piece of paper tucked atop her ear, Officer Phelps?"

He squatted beside her. "Why, it sure does."

She carefully tugged at the dirty paper less than three inches long and folded in half. Lea squinted in the glaring light and read the simple words aloud.

"*The red-nosed reindeer is next. Unless* . . ." She peered across at Randy. "Unless what?"

"That can't make any sense. It's nowhere near Christmas time."

"Give me the baggie." She ordered and slipped the soiled paper inside.

Lea examined the bottom of Connie's feet for several seconds before noticing a scratch and puncture on the right hand side of the slain woman's trim ankle. She'd bet her eyeteeth the wound had been caused by rose thorns. Lea took out her mini digital camera and snapped several flash photos before leaning over the corpse.

"What's that awful smell?" Randy Phelps shook his head, unable to identify the pungent odor.

"I'm not sure, but I've smelled it before. You okay,

Officer?"

"I'm fine Inspector Fox." He suddenly lurched away from the scene and vomited at the dark perimeter of the crime scene. "Sorry, sorry," the young rookie gasped.

"Stand away for a while and get control of yourself, Randy." Lea sniffed again. The odd pungent odor permeated the woman and Lea leaned closer to the dead woman's lips and sniffed again. "It almost smells like ammonia."

"What are you up to, Ms. Fox?" snapped the chief placing his hands on his beefy hips.

Lea glanced up at the belligerent man. "This woman has been poisoned, and in a particularly gruesome way. Our killer left us a Christmas card. I sure hope Dr. Koh doesn't mind an early wake-up call."

Chapter 13

As it happened, he didn't. Dr. Koh organized the careful bagging of the once-beautiful woman under Nick's watchful eyes. Lea observed the proceedings silently, keeping her distance from Chief Rollins.

"You still here?" he snapped, glimpsing her in the shadows. Lea's baggy green sweat pants hung so loosely they threatened to fall off at any moment, and she wore a faded blue t-shirt and worn trainers without socks. Her tangled nutmeg hair hadn't been combed, and her glasses needed a good cleaning.

"Sorry to disappoint you, Chief."

"You can take off any time. Things are well under control."

"Are you positive about that?"

Rollins growled and cornered Thayne away from the glare of the spotlight. Steven Koh removed his thin rubber gloves and watched his assistant push Connie towards the ambulance.

"Hello, Lea," he said gently. "Haven't seen you around for a while."

"Been steering clear of homicide. It's bad for my mental health. I'm particularly not fond of the insects it attracts." She pointedly glanced towards the chief.

Dr. Koh's assistant, Daniel, deposited Connie inside the coroner's van and signaled to Steven he was ready to head out.

"Meet me at my office. I have something I need to speak with you about." Dr. Koh motioned to Daniel he was ready and swung his thin frame into the passenger seat.

Nick indicated he had a few loose ends to wrap up, so Lea trailed Dr. Koh's white van to the County Coroner's. She watched silently as he and his groggy assistant prepped the body. It didn't take Steven long to find out the cause of death.

"See the severe inflammation of her upper torso?" Mottled scarlet patches covered Connie's ample chest. "If you tap here, you can hear the fluid. But not just any fluid. Check out her tongue." Connie's normally small, pink tongue was swollen and bright red. His stoic assistant snapped a photo.

"I've never seen anything like this," said David.

"I haven't seen anything like it since med school. We used to work on cadavers, many of them pickled in formaldehyde. From the smell, combined with the swelling and odd color of her tongue and chest, I'd suggest she may have been forced to ingest the preservative."

Lea shook herself. It was hard to imagine the agony Connie must have felt in her last moments.

"Why don't you go type up your notes in my office, Lea, while I examine the corpse more closely?" Kindness was evident in his tired voice.

"Before I retreat, you had something to tell me?"

"Daniel, if you'll give us a moment." His sandy-haired assistant moved silently beyond hearing range.

Steven's eyes shone coal black in the florescent glare. He removed his glasses and stared at them for a while as if reluctant to continue. "I've heard something about Nick Thayne that disturbs me."

"Go on."

"Either he's been sleeping with the enemy or is involved in something else because he always seems to have the inside scoop. He was fired because of suspected collusion and possible receipt of bribes."

"I know that."

"And you still agreed to work with him?"

"*Work* is the key word. I don't have much, remember?" She plucked at her wrinkled t-shirt dejectedly.

"Because of Rollins," he surmised.

"And my own endearing personality."

"I don't think you're so bad."

"Then you're the only one. As for Thayne, don't you worry about me. I know who I'm dealing with." She eyed the sanctuary of his office. For some reason, his close proximity made her nervous. “I noticed a scratch on Connie’s ankle, Dr. Koh. Thought maybe she had a close encounter with a rose bush like Thad Fisher.” She normally called him Steven.

“I’ll check into it, Lea, and forward the results to you as soon as possible.”

Nick scuttled in just as she departed, and Steven Koh sighed after her retreating figure.

Nick stared at the once-beautiful Connie; she was now ghostly pale and puffy, her scarlet fingernails hideous in their mockery.

“Just getting started?”

Steven Koh ignored the question. “So, you’re working with Lea Fox, Inspector Thayne?”

“Just for now. And please, call me Nick. Fox had some information on the Peebles’ case I needed. It’s a relationship bred by necessity.”

Dr. Koh picked up the baggie and felt the severed male finger through the plastic. “Her father had reopened that particular case just before he was murdered. Has she . . . spoken at all about her father’s death?”

“Not much. I know both her father and brother were murdered and hanged from a tree about 50 miles from here.”

“That partially correct. Actually three men were killed and two by hanging. The other, their assistant, John Weinberg, was shot as he waited in the car. The case, technically outside the jurisdiction of Monroe County, remains unsolved to this day. Lea had to identify the bodies. Being there and know how excruciatingly painful it was for her. Everyone she loved was murdered that night, and since then, she's retreated into a bitter shell. Lea's still astute and prickly like always, but definitely changed. I suggest you tread gently with her and if you ever get a chance, see if she'll talk about it."

"Hell, I'm no psychiatrist. Shit, I can't even come to terms with my own personal hang-ups."

"Well, believe me—you're probably relatively healthy compared to her. She's a top notch detective but tough; too tough. She'll help you solve this case if you'll only let her. No matter what Lea says that's personally inhospitable or downright rude to you, just ignore it. Don't rise to the occasion, and for God's sake don't let your male ego intervene in any way. She hates men on principle—perhaps justifiably so—and you're a man's man, which in her mind is akin to a bad virus."

"At least I don't seem to hold the top position for her rancor. That honor belongs to Chief Rollins."

Dr. Steven Koh sighed as he studied the handsome Eurasian face before him. "He couldn't or wouldn't help solve either of the crimes that interested her most. I'll have this report to you as quickly as possible."

"Send it to Fox. She can plug it into her little gizmo." Nick nodded towards the corpse. "So, you're going to work on her now?"

"I think our Connie deserves prompt attention, don't you?"

Nick's cell phone screamed at seven a.m.

"Formaldehyde," repeated Nick, grimacing as he listened to Fox's unemotional voice. "So Dr.
Koh verified it. It must have fried her from the inside out."

"It did. Traces of blood were found in her urine and feces indicating she didn't die at once. Dr. Koh says it probably took about 15 minutes. The bizarre thing is that she must have been forced to ingest the chemical via a straw since her mouth and lips were not burned."

"No wonder her eyes displayed such horror." This was Freddie Kruger type cruelty.

Lea agreed. "Someone wanted her to die a painful death, but for what reason? Could it have been a wife's jealous rage, or some diabolical serial murderer who removes the finger of one victim and places it in the hand of another?"

"Either could be right, Fox," said Nick, "and my gut instinct screams that Trish Fisher had nothing to do with this murder."

"She certainly had enough anger and motive," mused Lea, "but I'm inclined to agree with you. Both murders reek of purpose, suggesting a serial or ritualistic killer. And let's face it. Serial killers don't harbor remorse after a murder, they just pick up the pace. This community won't handle the idea of a possible serial killer on the loose well. And the note is a distinct threat. It promises more to come."

Nick agreed. "I sincerely hope Chief Rollins can keep it out of the papers."

The dailies served it up with breakfast.

At 10:00 a.m., Lea waited impatiently in her office for Nick, and by ten-thirty was thoroughly disgruntled by his tardiness. She made herself a strong cup of tea and opened the Sunday *Times* for her ritual review. Hand jerking, she spilled some of her Darjeeling tea right across the aggressive front page. Thad Fisher's pudgy face, in all his mayoral glory, grinned back at her. Beside him, in a complete foil to his soft corpulence, Trish Fisher tilted a perfectly coiffed head. The headline screamed: *Mayor's Wife Implicated in Murder—Steamy Love Triangle Revealed.*

"Good God!" burst out Lea to the empty walls of her wood paneled office. "You would think this were a London tabloid, not a sleepy newspaper from some Podunk town. And how did the paper get this info so fast? It had to be Rollins!"

The article would have been hilarious if it weren't so pathetic. Much of the story was simply he said/she said gibberish, which completely misguided the entire piece and was clearly written for effect not substance. Lea threw the paper down in disgust. One particularly nauseating paragraph suggested Trish Fisher had hired a private hit man through the mob to rub out her husband. It, of course, was followed with the clichéd disclaimer of 'from a refusing to be named source.'

The phone jarred her from her less-than-ladylike thoughts, and she grabbed up the black receiver.

"Sorry I'm late, Fox, but I've got some bad news for you. Philemon Jenkins was arrested early this morning. I'm down at the police station. When can you get down here?"

"Now."

Thayne waited solemnly at the station, his head and fingers throbbing, partially from too much drink coupled with too little sleep, but mostly from the 'gift' he so despised. The precinct was livelier this Monday morning than it had been in years as Fox entered through the swinging glass door. Nick grabbed her before she had time to so much as say good morning to the plump dispatcher, who was dusted with sugar powder from the massive donut she was consuming, and dragged her into a vacant conference room.

"There's something bizarre going on here. Philemon Jenkins was arrested at home before 8:00 a.m., read his rights, handcuffed, and dragged to the station after being accused of first-degree murder. I'm positive there's something Phil *forgot* to share with us."

Lea handed him the paper and he scowled, growling, "Goddamn dailies. This is a fine kettle of fish."

"My feelings exactly. You sick? You look like hell."

"Thanks. I see you dressed up for the occasion." Her mind-altering green outfit made him want to shudder. Unfortunately, his head throbbed too much to allow himself that pleasure.

"Thanks, it's one of my favorites."

Jesus! "Do you drink soda, Fox?"

"I never touch the stuff. All sugar. Did you know that teeth decays 250 times more quickly in soda than in water?" She hesitated in her condemnation of soft drinks. "That's a mighty strange question."

Thayne looked strangely disconcerted and shrugged his shoulders awkwardly. "Just thought you just might prefer cream soda or something. It's nothing. So, here it is; the key reason for Philemon's arrest was those hand clippers found in Mrs. Simms' shed. A speck of blood has been discovered on them, which bodes ill for our gardener friend."

"Wow, and all this *just after* the morning paper hit the street. This was preplanned, Thayne. I wonder how long before the mayor gives her prepared speech thanking the department for their speedy work. But why all the rush?"

"Chief Rollins wants this case wrapped up and us out of the picture before we stumble on something he prefers remains buried. He's waiting for us now in his office."

Chief Rollins looked like he'd slept in his clothes, and his icy blue eyes were red-rimmed with fatigue.

"Sit down," he ordered, slapping down a thin manila

folder before the pair. "I would have thought you'd have done your homework a sight better than this, Thayne. To tell you the truth, I'm quite disappointed in you. Disappointed, but not surprised, considering the company you keep."

Nick ignored his tirade and scanned the first page, his almond eyes widening. He pushed the file closer to Lea.

"A convicted felon," blurted out the Chief, "living and working here right under our noses. Not only that, he's been connected to the Marcelli Mob in Detroit, and while the cops were never able to nab him, it's suspected he was one of Teddy Marcelli's elite hit men for the last twenty-five years."

Chief Rollins reeked smugness.

"Mr. Jenkins said he worked for a major auto company," said Nick quietly. "And I believe him."

"Oh, he did, he did," returned the Chief. "But that was just his cover, and a perfect one, at that. I'm amazed you didn't at least run his fingerprints after taking his statement."

"I agree. We *should* run the prints of anyone African-American. Just on principle, you know," countered Nick sarcastically, the hairs on the back of his neck bristling.

"Wise ass, ain't ya? And I don't need a civil rights lecture from you. You missed an important fact, and luckily for us, I was smart enough to check the gardener out!"

"You're right," admitted Nick tiredly. "How could one know Philemon was not who or what he said he was." It was a lie. An image of Philemon standing over a dead corpse muscled its way into his brain.

Lea wasn't so quick to acquiesce. "Don't you think you're adding up the numbers a little bit wrong, Chief Rollins?" said Lea as sweetly as her slightly gruff voice would allow.

The pea green linen suit would have looked out of fashion in her mother's day and was already horribly wrinkled. Where on earth did she get her clothes? Goodwill?

"Just because Philemon had mob connections in Detroit doesn't mean he isn't retired from all that now."

"Oh, really," mocked the Chief. "Then perhaps I should share an interesting tidbit of information with you. Did you know that one of the telltale characteristics of the Marcelli Gang was to hack off body parts, as mementos of their hits, and bury them beside their next victim as a warning to others not to mess with the mob?"

Nick suddenly visualized that all-so-important check dissipating under Chief Rollins' cold eyes.

"As I recall," said Lea evenly, "the Marcelli Gang preferred ears and male genitalia, not fingers."

Nick marveled as to how Lea got her information, but as usual the chief ignored her.

"One pair of hand clippers hanging in Mrs. Simms' tool shed shows traces of human blood. We're waiting for the final results now. If it's a match to Thad Fisher, this case is shut tighter than a virgin's door."

"You're not certain the blood is Thad Fisher's? You jailed Philemon Jenkins just because you *think* Thad Fisher's blood *might* be on the clippers?" accused Lea.

Chief Rollins pointed to the door. "That and the 'word' your spooky partner found engraved in that blasted magnolia just happen to be the first five letters of Mr. Jenkins' name. *Phile!* Why don't you go powder your nose, Ms. Fox? I'll wrap things up with your *partner* here. And don't you worry your pretty little head; both of you will get a check for three full days' work. I'm feeling generous."

"Right. If I were the murderer, then by all means, I'd carve my name into the tree right at the site. Like freeway tagging, you know. Aren't you forgetting something?" asked Lea, refusing to budge from her chair. It was dangerous to call her pretty when she never deluded herself.

"Like what?" snorted the Chief

"Like a motive."

"I beg your pardon?"

"If Philemon is the murderer, a paid assassin as you have suggested, then who employed him?" She tossed the morning *Times* on the table and pointed to the highlighted sentence speculating Mrs. Fisher had hired a hit man to rub out her adulterous husband.

"This is entirely ludicrous!" snorted Richard Rollins, who'd obviously not had time to scan the morning papers.

"It seems, if you've done your math correctly, and two

plus two *really* does equal five, you should arrest her as well."

Chief Rollins swore long and loudly. "Trish Fisher is no more guilty than my dog. I've known her for years. This accusation from our flawed local paper is absolutely ridiculous. I'll be demanding a retraction as soon as you two vacate the premises."

"I'm sure that's precisely what Philemon Jenkins's wife thought as they dragged her innocent husband away, and besides," said Lea. "While I don't agree with *any* of your logic, I have to concede that poison is a women's choice, after all, and Connie was forced to swallow formaldehyde, of all things. Pretty lethal and cruel, if I do say so myself, and cruelty like that reeks of a wronged woman. The *only* wronged woman I'm aware of in this whole tawdry mess is Trish Fisher."

"I oughta toss the both of you out on your misguided asses."

"You're just upset because you know Fox *is* right," said Nick. "I'd suggest you research your facts better before you brand a local black man as the killer," said Nick, inciting Chief Rollins to swear again, this time even more loudly and foully.

"You'd better watch your step, Thayne. I'm not releasing Philemon. The law states I can hold him for twenty-four hours, and by that time the blood samples will prove his clippers were used to take off Thad's finger."

Thayne straightened his shoulders. "If you fire us, no

one will be around to prove that Trish Fisher *didn't* hire Mr. Jenkins. And I refuse to condone his arrest or bail you out simply because you knew my father. If the papers interview me, I'll tell them I believe this office has a racist mandate."

"Why you . . ." growled the chief.

Nick glanced out the office's window into the active main room. "I sure don't see any African-Americans on the staff here. I wonder why?" Nick lifted himself from the cheap office chair. "Come on, Fox. Let's go find the reporters." Lea obediently rose, enjoying Nick's laconic tone, which only hinted at the wrath he so obviously felt.

Chief Rollin's watery blue eyes held Nick's for a full minute. His florid face flushed even redder before he lowered his eyes under Nick's forceful gaze.

"Now, hold on, hold on. Don't be hasty. Sit down." His eyes stabbed at Lea as she sank down as gracefully as her wrinkled green suit and unresponsive foot would let her. Nick remained standing, towering over the portly police chief.

"Goddamn it! Sit down, man. My neck ain't like no flamingo's. You have to agree the gardener's arrest was justified. He was a Mafia hit man, for God's sake!"

"You're probably right," said Lea mildly. "Philemon is such a good assassin that he stabbed the mayor with a screwdriver in one hand while clipping off his finger with the other, just to save time, you know. I know his type. Black and bad. Synonyms really, aren't they?"

"You know what you are, lady?"

"A Capricorn?"

"An unemployed bitch as soon as the lab report comes back. You believe someone else did it, then find out who *really* hired Jenkins. You have 24 hours. And you, Thayne, keep a leash on her!"

Lea grinned, totally unfazed as Nick followed the awful green suit out the door. She paused by the water cooler and smoothed her skirt, looking quite amused for one so verbally abused.

Nick didn't share her humor. "Not only a racist bastard, but a sexist one as well. How does Roger put up with him?"

"What I want to know is what's his connection to Trish Fisher?"

"You got your antenna up, Fox?" He leaned against the wall.

"Yup, and I'd say he's mighty sensitive about the woman; his ears were burning red when I suggested that she too should be picked up for hiring Philemon Jenkins as a hit man. It's time I spoke to this Mr. Jenkins myself. Since Chief Rollins has placed the personal stamp of disapproval on him, I'm sure I'll like him."

Chapter 14

Sunday, 11:30 am

Philemon looked like the life had been punched out of him, but rose politely when Nick and Lea were led into his cramped cell.

"How you do, ma'am," he said genteelly. His grizzled head dipped as he extended a calloused hand first to her and then to Nick. His glasses were spotted and a nasty stain marked his green t-shirt.

"Glad to meet you, Mr. Jenkins. I'm Lea Fox and I'm working with Inspector Thayne here. Do you mind if I ask you some questions?"

The dignified gardener dropped heavily upon the county-issued mattress and ran a weary hand through his wiry hair. He lifted dark eyes to the petite woman and studied her with a face neither filled with recriminations nor excuses. The slightly blurred walnut eyes, red-rimmed from fatigue, were sharp with subdued intelligence. This man had played second fiddle all his life, but not anymore. He had learned, just like most women, to hide his sharp mind behind what appeared like submissiveness. Lea suspected it wasn't racism that caused this pretended intellectual indifference. He had once worked for men of few scruples and twisted intellect and managed to walk away from Detroit still intact in body and soul. Lea instantly admired Philemon. He was the type of man she'd befriend if his circumstances weren't so desperate.

"Not at all. I ain't going anywhere. How are you, Mr. Thayne?"

"Not very good since I didn't expect to find you here."

"You and me both. They say I'm in here for killing the mayor and that mistress of his. I don't even know her name. This morning passed like a blur when they slapped the cuffs on me and dragged me away, my woman weeping and clinging to me like her heart would break. Please, can you look after my Darcy? Her heart won't take the strain. I'm nothing without my Darcy."

"We'll stop by and see her right after lunch, Mr. Jenkins," Nick promised.

"Please, call me Philemon. Less formal than Mr. Jenkins. So, what did you want to ask me, Ms. Fox?"

"Are you a born-again Christian?"

Both Nick and Philemon jerked. This was not the question either had been expecting.

"Why, yes. Yes, I am."

"And when did this conversion take place?"

"It's been over five years since I pledged my soul to the Lord."

"And were you a hit man in Detroit, as Chief Rollins states?"

Philemon gripped the gray-striped mattress with taut fingers. "I enjoy being a gardener, Ms. Fox. I never imagined a job more fulfilling than the cultivation of plants. Every day, I notice something in Mrs. Simms' garden that fills me with awe. Sometimes it's a rosebud that's just opened, or a piece of ivy that's finally reached the eaves of the house. The bees are alive and on a quest. Bumblebees, honeybees, and little black striped bees I don't even know the name of. And then there are the birds. The pyracantha found in her garden is full of orange-red berries, and the leaves are so shiny and smooth that the robins, with their fat round bellies, love 'em. God bless the beasts and the children. You know no sparrow drops without God's knowledge?"

Lea nodded. This man's faith gave him joy.

"Mrs. Simms desires color and harmony and respects my opinion. She said to me once, 'Philemon, you sure have such a way with living things.' So I spend my days nurturing the perfect and thoughtless—the plants and flowers and wild birds—just like I did when I was a boy in Georgia. And when I do that, it nourishes my soul and replenishes it. My poor, *tarnished* soul. I've done many things in my life I regret, Ms. Fox. Just what those things were are now only between God and me. I answer to no man, or woman for that matter, only to our sweet merciful Jesus. *He* knows who the real killer is and will reveal it when the time is right. The guilty are always punished unless they repent."

Lea sighed and pulled out her mini-computer, her fingers rapidly entering his response.

"Unfortunately, you may have to answer to a jury, Mr. Jenkins, whether you wish to or not," she stated. Philemon's ample Adam's apple twitched, but he remained silent. "You didn't kill Thad Fisher, did you, Philemon?" she added more gently.

"I swear on the sweet baby Jesus that saved me I never killed him or that woman," he drawled, the accent from his childhood days never having left him even though he'd lived elsewhere for 45 years.

"Any notion who did?" asked Lea not missing a beat.

Philemon looked up in surprise. "You asking *me*?"

"Of course. You've been sitting here for a good three hours and have probably been thinking about nothing else. What does your gut tell you?"

Philemon glanced at Nick and then slowly smiled. "Well, girl, since you asked. I've been pondering little else as I set here in the fine accommodations afforded me by our local authorities. It ain't an accident that I found the body, you know. God demands justice and has used me as a vehicle to make sure it's obtained. He didn't leave me helpless, you know. He gave me a clue. You need to ask that child, Bouncer. He's the key. I'd bet my life on it."

Lea studied him for a long moment before shutting down her F & H. "What's your favorite Christmas tune, Mr. Jenkins?"

He stared blankly at her. "Christmas tune?" He rubbed his thumb and forefinger over his lean chin. "I'm partial to two, really. *Jingle Bells* and *White Christmas*. I must admit, I do miss Detroit's white Christmases. Why do you ask?"

"No reason, really. You've been very helpful, Mr. Jenkins, and when this is all over and you're released, give me a call. I have a garden that needs tending as well." She flipped a card at him, which he caught in one graceful swoop.

"I'll be eager to survey your garden, ma'am, or give you insights in other areas. You seem to lack one thing in this business, miss."

"And what's that?"

"An excess of sin. Your partner knows what I'm talking about. I could certainly help you understand the components of sin if you'd like me to."

Lea peered at the older man for a long quiet moment. "I'll keep that in mind . . . *when* you're released.

"We'll stay in contact," promised Nick, as he followed his stiff shouldered partner out of the county jail.

"We're heading to my house," stated Lea. "If you'll

just follow me."

"Your house?" said Nick amazed. He imagined a sterile, box-like house painted in a ghastly lime green to match her nauseating suit, its dust-free environment equipped with large computer screens dominating every chilly room.

"I need to be somewhere clean and organized to sort all this out. Are you coming?"

"Do I have any choice?"

"None in the least." She paused before finally adding, "And Philemon isn't totally correct, Thayne. Sin follows me around and mocks me for my naiveté."

Nick was amazed to find himself sitting upon a circular pine bench in a well-designed breakfast nook sipping a monstrous combination of something that tasted like a cross between tomato juice and motor oil. Good God, what was it?

"What's in this?" he sputtered after a particularly revolting gag.

"My father's secret cure."

"Which is?"

"It wouldn't be his secret cure if I told you. So, you had fun with Trixie last night?"

"Her name *is* Chastity. And it was great fun until your phone call. I'll have to remember to turn off the beeper on my cell phone. If I'm working with you, I have the noxious feeling you're going to be calling at all sorts of ungodly hours."

"It is hardly unlikely you'd turn off your mobile phone, because your natural curiosity would never allow you to totally disconnect with the world, no matter what the circumstance. You're too afraid you might miss something. While assuredly uncomfortable in the middle of bath or during an intimate moment, it's what makes us good detectives. And I bet her name is highly inappropriate now, if it wasn't already."

"Oh, really," scoffed Nick. "So, you're an expert on male/female relations are you? And what you're saying is that I'm a good detective because I can't keep my goddamned nose out of other people's business?" Why did she have to be so fricking annoying?

"Admit it, Thayne. As a kid, you rummaged through your father's desk, didn't you?"

A horribly vivid memory sprang to the forefront of his mind—a memory he'd struggled to keep quarantined back in the furthermost recesses of his mind. He swallowed as she continued her relentless analysis, oblivious to his regret.

"You won't stop until you know the whole truth. That's why you instinctively recognized
Chief Rollins' premise about Philemon as a big load of crap."

Nick took another ghastly swallow and managed to sputter out, "Did your father ever appreciate you, Fox?"

"What?"

"Did he appreciate your instincts, your intellect, and perpetually revolting mind?"

"No, he only denigrated those faults, though he did seem to enjoy my cooking." Lea removed the rose thorns from the baggie Thayne had given her and set them upon the table, squinting fiercely. Removing her F & H, she booted it up and nodded to herself over the slight hum.

"Well?" asked Nick, shivering as the last of the dreadful concoction slid down his protesting throat.

"It's clear Thad Fisher sought to escape his captor. I believe a reasonable conclusion is to surmise that he tried to escape by leaping through a window, and landed in a rose garden below. He was found shoeless, which would explain the embedded *Mr. Lincoln* thorns in his feet. You have any 'premonitions' about roses?"

Nick leaned back and rubbed his forehead, hoping to encourage his throbbing headache to disappear. "Nary a one," he said thickly. "But both Mrs. Simms and the Collins' properties have gardens brimming with roses."

"True, but we mustn't forget there are also wild bushes in the areas located between Chester Street and the Agrit-Empire's fields, plus several other houses on the block favor the flower."

"How could you know that?" asked Nick

"I woke up early this morning and drove around. There are some wild patches of *Belinda* and *Belendar* roses growing in huge clumps throughout the field about three hundred meters from the vacant lot. However, their thorns are smaller, and since they're patchy, they're less likely to be the culprits. Since it was probably dark when the mayor bolted, there's a slim chance he ran through the field from the other side, climbed the short wall, and was murdered near the magnolia tree. That's only vague speculation, though. He could just as well have been a prisoner in either the Collins or the Simms' houses, or perhaps even another on the block. The only thing we know for certain is that he and Connie visited the Collins' house last Tuesday and haven't been seen alive since."

"And the note?"

"Oh that's easy. It's from *Rudolph the Red Nosed Reindeer.*"

"I got *that.* I was hoping you might know what it refers to."

"Not a clue. *Yet.*"

"Where's the toilet?" interrupted Nick abruptly.

"You mean the bathroom."

"Whatever."

"Civilized men do not say toilet; they say bathroom or men's room or restroom."

"Whatever, Guinevere. I need to *rest* badly and now!"

"It's down the hall and to the left," stated Lea disdainfully. "Put the seat down when you're finished and make sure you flush."

"Yes, Mom."

The bathroom, of course, was spotlessly clean and painted in fresh shades of cream and the palest yellow. He fingered a tiny ceramic rose bowl crammed with sweet smelling soaps. While he preferred masculine colors, he had to admit her place had a homey feel. He *did* flush and remembered at the last minute to replace the toilet seat.

He paused in the hall, after observing Fox with her head bent over her mini-computer, to examine the cluster of photographs on the wall. A happy-looking family posed casually in the first, and an easily identifiable young Lea, not more than seven or eight, smiled eagerly back at him. A frilly dress of pink and white ruffles smothered her small frame, but her pleasant-looking mother wore a sky-blue dress with a low bodice. Mother Fox was handsome, but not beautiful. Father and son looked amazingly alike with homely, intelligent faces.

Lane, at six to eight years older than his sister, was already a lanky teenager with a bad case of acne. The next photo, however, set an amazingly different tone. Lea appeared remote and dull. Her father's worn face glowered aggressively, and her brother's reflected an insolent or even abusive nature. Mother Fox must have been dead for quite some time, and Lea appeared no more than thirteen or fourteen, her eyes hidden behind large spectacles. No trace of a smile softened her face, and her mouth looked pinched and unhappy.

"Stop checking out the family treasures," said Fox from the nook table.

"You must have eyes in the back of your head," returned Nick, refusing to be embarrassed.

"No, just sensing an invasion of my privacy."

"What's fair is fair, sister. Besides, photos hanging upon walls are not private. And *one picture is worth a thousand words."*

"Fred Bernard was not talking about photographs, he was referring to ads."

"Same difference. So, you own this house?" he asked, his stomach still churning from the witch's brew, though it did appear his headache might be easing somewhat.

"Yes. I sold my father's after he died and moved here."

"Nice place, though there's a few too many growing things."

"My dad hated plants and preferred that heavy mahogany wood, which reeks of male dominance and needs every-other-day dusting. My brother, on the other hand, loved techno-mod furniture; all metal and glass and geometric shapes, with glaring lights and plastic cushions. I was comfortable in neither."

Nick suddenly had an insight into the continually belligerent woman. Lea had never been allowed to be herself, and this little dream home was probably the best glimpse he'd ever get of the defensive woman. The golden pine kitchen exuded warmth and comfort, its country design practical and spacious with wide counters and the inviting nook. The furniture, though sparse, gave a pleasant effect. The beige and mauve couch fronted a small brick fireplace loaded with wood and waiting for the turn of season.

A broad oak entertainment center, equipped with stereo and CD player, a large TV and DVD player, as well as a glass cabinet revealing an eclectic mixture of movie classics, mysteries, and kids' films, covered half the living room wall. *Shrek* sat next to *Murder by the Numbers* and *Gunga Din.* One of his favorite series, *Twin Peaks,* rested atop her DVD player. The top shelf held a wide variety of painted eggs.

"You collect eggs?"

"Sorta. My mother did, and I inherited them from her. That blue one is from Russia, the gold one with the silvery face from New Orleans, and the huge carved ostrich egg from Kenya. My father gave it to Mom as a honeymoon gift. Those rather garish orange and red ones are from a trip I took to Mexico. I'd like to get more—but right now, travel is out of the question."

He wondered what the rest of the house would reveal about the prickly Lea Fox when a 5 by 7 photograph, positioned reverently inside the bookcase, arrested his attention. A young man with nondescript brown hair, dark-rimmed glasses, and a prominent nose rested his arm around the Fox's willing shoulders. Her relaxed head half-leaned against the man's chest, lips curving in a wide smile as she responded to something he'd just uttered. Lea's dress was feminine and actually pretty, glimmering in lilac flowers. Much longer hair cascaded over her shoulders, and a complimentary heart-shaped silver locket nestled around her small neck. He'd never before seen her happy or half-way pretty.

"This your boyfriend?" he asked impishly.

"Stop snooping, Thayne. You're trespassing."

"It's what I'm paid for." It had to be Bernard. Nick returned to the round table covered with a spotless white tablecloth. The phone shrilled, and Fox jerked it up.

"This is Fox. Really? Is he there now with the chief?" One hand clenched the functional black phone while the other rapidly typed into the F & H. She frowned. "And the other's a dead end, then. Drat. Thanks so much. Keep me posted."

Nick raised an eyebrow. "Well?"

"That was Randy Phelps. I asked him to give me a buzz if anything unusual happened. Apparently, none of the eight commandeered wheelbarrows have anything other than dirt clinging to them. They'll be returned to their owners early tomorrow."

"I'm not surprised."

"Neither am I. The Christmas note lacks fingerprints and is typed in simple courier font, size 18. Anyone with a computer could have whipped it out. The paper is the local stationary store's brand—nothing unusual, so, except for its unique content, the note's origin is a dead end. But get this. Mr. Anthony Montanari of the Agrit-Empire has apparently been closeted with the chief for over an hour. He wants permission to survey the bodies before burial, supposedly to give a private farewell. He says he was good friends with both Thad Fisher and Connie Judson."

Nick seemed puzzled. "Now, that's an association I was unaware of," he stated.

"It's not surprising, though. Anyone who'd run for mayor in this town would have needed to obtain the financial support of the Montanari family if they hoped to earn any votes from the agricultural sector."

"But why would he want to view the bodies?" asked Nick looping his hands over one knee.

"Let's check him out." Nick rose heavily and followed his petite partner into a small study. She powered up the state of the art computer.

"Nice technology," he said, glancing at the small room. Several computer manuals lined the shelves and upon the opposite shelf stood a huge collection of baseball trophies.

"Your dad's?" he asked, pointing.

"No, my brother's. Didn't have the heart to give 'em away. The computer was my dad's though. He said a properly programmed PC was almost as helpful as a good snitch. He kept this unit at home, and it contained the dossiers of most of the influential people in the area. I'm certain he did his homework on the Montanari's, if I know my Dad.

Within minutes, the lined, flawed face of Anthony Montanari filled the screen.

“Anthony Montanari Sr. was married in 1951 to someone called Ruth Peroni,” began Lea. She gave birth to their oldest son, Anthony Jr. in December 1952. He had—whoa, count them—six children with Ruth. That’s what you call a fertile Catholic family. Anthony Sr. inherited his land and money from his Italian born dad, Fabio Montanari, who’d bought land in the northern part of the Big Valley when Anthony was about ten and started growing potatoes, lettuce, and cucumbers. This blossomed into the Agrit-Empire, which Anthony took over in the late-seventies. Fabio Montanari long since retired to Florida and died about eight years ago.

“Boy, our Tony’s life certainly wasn’t totally fortuitous,” said Thayne, leaning over the glimmering screen. “His two oldest boys were both killed in Vietnam, just before the US pullout, and he was left with three daughters and a small son. Not a great deal of information on them. I wonder what Anthony’s real connection to the deceased is.”

“We could do some nosing around,” Fox suggested, looking like a little girl who’s just been offered forbidden chocolate.

“Hmm. Guys like Montanari hire illegals to broaden their profit margin,” said Nick. “It’s almost a California tradition.”

"Just a minute," spouted Lea. She leaped up as fast as her bad leg allowed and scurried into the front room, returning several minutes later with a beaten-up old briefcase. The tattered leather of the stained satchel seemed so unlike her that Nick lifted his eyes in enquiry.

"It was my dad's as well. You might say I have a sentimental attachment to it." She clicked open the flaking brass latches and removed the Peebles file.

"Let's see. If I remember correctly, Ashley Peebles was discovered in the middle of a potato field just like Connie, and both are owned by the Agrit-Empire. That reminds me of something else." She flipped open another thin file and smiled. "Here's the last letter from Luke Cambridge my Dad received. Read me the second to last paragraph."

Nick rubbed his blurry eyes and laboriously read aloud.

"I implore you, Mr. Fox, to reconsider my case. As I stated to Inspector Rollins, I swore that I saw Mr. Montanari's Buick driving down the dirt road where Ashley's body was found. He was speeding as if running away from something and didn't see me standing under a large avocado tree. No one investigated this lead to my knowledge, and I'm hoping that if you reopen the case you might do so."

Nick scanned the rest. "It just goes on to say he loved Ashley and didn't kill her. It's signed, Luke Cambridge, March 3, 2000. Sounds mighty articulate for a drifter and farm worker," stated Nick, refolding the letter before passing it back to Fox.

"That's exactly what my dad thought. Apparently, Luke educated himself, passing his high school equivalency exam while serving his sentence. He is also, from what I've heard, a first-rate mechanic who services many state vehicles at the prison."

"So, your dad followed up on Luke's assertion that he saw Montanari's vehicle in the vicinity around the time of the murder?"

"He did. I remember him conferring extensively with my brother about it. I wasn't working fulltime for my dad at that time, mostly just evenings and weekends because I already had a job at the District Attorney's office. Unfortunately, I didn't pay as much attention as I should have to their progress, and then they were murdered less than three weeks later. I know Dad collected extensive notes, and my brother boasted they were about to crack the case wide open. Dad spent long hours typing up his reflections on his office computer, but when I took over after my father's death the computer's hard drive had been damaged. 50 percent of the data was irretrievable."

"Someone tampered with the computer?"

"I'll never know. The technician stated the computer had suffered an electrical overload, similar to a lightning strike. I've managed to salvage many of his files, just not his notes on the Peebles case. To think I actually read some of his insights while retyping my Dad's shorthand irks me to no end. Fool that I was, I didn't read them thoroughly enough or have a strong enough point of reference to interpret them correctly at the time."

"So that file you have there is just the copy of the original you obtained from the police department?"

"That's right."

"You know, Fox," said Nick slowly, rubbing his narrow chin. "Potatoes fields, three bodies, and stray fingers. These two cases are connected, and the chief doesn't want us to find out how or why. I need to speak with Luke Cambridge today."

Chapter 15

Sunday Afternoon

Thayne decided to drive south to where Luke was incarcerated. Lea needed the time for research, so she cheerfully suggested to Thayne she would see him later that evening.

"Do you mind?" he asked of the coroner's report. Nick needed to digest the results of the autopsies a little at a time since his head still pounded.

"Not at all," said Lea, feeling quite generous, handing him the original after making a copy for her reference. It tickled her to see him looking so pale and out of sorts. Many men believed they could handle their liquor and work as competently as they would without it, but she knew that to be an illusion. Her brother had certainly proven that.

"Ah, Fox, you might, um, want to check the field just below the lot. I have a feeling the slipshod Monroe PD may have missed something. That is, if you've got some spare time. If not, we'll check it out tomorrow morning together," he said in a peculiar tone.

Fox glanced up, and he gave a tiny nod. “I’ll do that,” she promised.

As soon as Thayne had gone, Lea sat for the next two hours, searching every available source on the Internet. She printed out a few pages, distressed by what she’d read about Philemon Jenkins, almost hoping Thayne would find out something seedy about Connie’s military boyfriend. Her hopes were shattered less than thirty minutes later.

Her cell phone jangled and Nick’s breezy voice filled the airways. “Bad news, Fox. Our Presido boy has contacted Chief Rollins. Guess what? He’s no offshore boy toy for our deceased Connie. He’s her cousin of all things. Arriving tonight to set up burial proceedings. Name’s Lieutenant Mark Bales. I spoke to him briefly on the phone, and he’s making a statement to Officer Stevens at the station as we speak. Apparently, he wasn’t even in California last week, having traveled with some fellow officers to Florida to receive some training. Alibi looks airtight, and his distress regarding his cousin sounds genuine.”

“There goes one of our best leads,” sighed Lea.

“He might still have some insights,” remarked Thayne, trying to be positive.

“We can only hope since Philemon has six priors. One for grand-theft auto.”

“Good God.”

"Actually, God was good. Philemon's wife was in labor and his engine blew a gasket. He hot-wired his neighbor's Impala and drove her to the maternity ward. He was arrested ten minutes after the birth of his second son. Only served community service on that one. Neighbor was understanding but not amused."

Nick laughed. "Anything more incriminating than that?"

"One DUI, one driving with a revoked license after the DUI, two trespassing, and one assault upon a neighbor's barking dog."

"Hmm. I bet the trespassing ones are the most interesting, and I *completely* understand the dog situation. Not surprised there's nothing more concrete than that. Our Philemon was a professional and left no tracks. I'm just pulling into the prison's parking lot now. I'll let you know how the interview with Luke goes."

He hung up abruptly. It seemed they were moving backwards instead of forwards. The wind blew briskly, and a chill had crept from the north, indicating fall was finally on its way. Since she wasn't making any progress here, Lea decided to take Thayne's advice and check out Chester Street and the fields nearby once again. Fox slipped into a pair of baggy jeans, her worn trainers, and a mud-brown sweatshirt with oil stains on it. She'd never figured out how to remove the spots after changing the Mazda's oil filter. Before leaving her house, she picked up the red rubber ball retrieved from Philemon's play with Bouncer and stuck it into her coat pocket, planning to ring the Collins doorbell one more time. Maybe she'd get lucky.

Lea drove slowly down Chester Street, sighing at the lovely neighborhood. Wide sidewalks lined the beautifully landscaped avenue, with huge mature elm and maple trees giving the neighborhood that high-class feel only old trees can bestow. The cul-de-sac had little traffic this Monday afternoon, and only a few shorts-clad girls jumped rope in the street, politely shifting to one side as she glided her silver Mazda towards the bowl-shaped end.

Lea strolled the wide sidewalks and studied the stately street again. The broad overhang of shady elms produced such a lovely image of peace and tranquility. Everyone's lawns were expertly trimmed, and sparrows sang amongst the leafy branches. She noted several houses maintained both hybrid tea and floribunda rose bushes. It was conceivable Thad Fisher had been imprisoned in any of them, though she didn't believe it likely.

She returned to the Simms house, analyzing the lovely exterior for several minutes. The Tudor house was tastefully designed with high white stucco walls covered in the typical dark criss- cross patterns distinctive to their unique style. Its left-hand side was covered in ivy, and across the top story, the beautiful slate lines dove in dramatic lines.

One particular second floor room boasted a lovely, pale stained-glass window depicting the rays of the sun slanting off a vivid peacock strutting amongst slender orchids. Mrs. Simms sure had taste, alright.

Lea noted the rose bushes lining the pathway up to the house and adorning the wide front porch. Needing to take a closer look and hoping the elderly woman wouldn't mind, she limped up the curling cobblestone to study the thorny plants lining the front porch. The orange-red *Mr. Lincoln* vied for space with its more dominant cousin, the crimson *Oklahoma.* Her nose puckered at the lavish scent of *Perfumed Delight*, while her senses appreciated the stately grace of *Duet*.

Lea's sharp eyes analyzed the thorn-incrusted stalks, any one of which could have played havoc with a man's feet. No plant looked damaged, all blooming in perfect, heavy-blossomed radiance; the rose connoisseur's idea of heaven. Reluctantly, she left the beautiful Simms garden and headed towards the vacant field bordered by bright police tape.

Memory of Nick's quiet voice reminded Lea of his request to recheck the lot and field. She awkwardly lifted her pants-clad leg over the restrictive, sticky barrier, finally succeeding in hobbling into the quiet field as she headed towards the majestic magnolia. Another smaller expanse of tape surrounded the actual murder site situated at the base of the elderly tree where Thad Fisher's body had been discovered by Philemon Jenkins. The tree bloomed heavily, its thick white blooms stretching towards the afternoon sun.

Lea surveyed the turned soil under the magnolia's heavy canopy where Thad had been unearthed, the white chalk outline insulting the earth. She lurched around the vacant lot, noting that the area saw a great deal of foot traffic since it was obviously a place people let their unleashed animals roam, if the fairly frequent piles of dog droppings were any indication. A little boy on a small bike waved at her from the sidewalk. She waved back.

She studied Mrs. Simms' short wall, which barely topped five feet high. Anyone could have scrambled over the heavy block fence. Lea searched around, and finding an old cinderblock, dragged it to the fence and climbing atop, teetered clumsily. Now finally tall enough to gaze over the wall, she surveyed the lovely garden. The impressive greenhouse dominated the large backyard, and Lea noted how roses fought for space with camellias, azaleas, and hyacinths. Directly hugging the inside wall where she perched, a scarlet hibiscus attracted bees, which zoomed noisily past her ears. Roses lined the house's façade, but no more than any of the other half a dozen homes on the block.

She hopped awkwardly off the broken block and headed towards the ten-foot high brick wall that surrounded the north side of the Collins residence. No trailing vines or disobedient shrubs dared cling to these walls. She crinkled her nose, the smell of dung still strong, but less pronounced than the previous day. A faint rustle sounded, and Lea swore she heard a faint snarling sound as if an animal protested against its boundaries.

"Hello," she called tentatively. The frenzied snarling increased for a second before suddenly diminishing to a low, moaning growl. She fervently searched for something high enough to elevate her short statute enough to peer over the ten-foot wall, but found nothing to accommodate her. Anyone who wanted to peer into this protected yard would need a good-sized ladder.

Thoroughly agitated by her short height and inability to conquer her surroundings, Lea clumped back to the sidewalk and spent the next 90 minutes interviewing families from the eight houses further down the block. After accepting strong green tea from the Chun family, tasting Mrs. Borman's apricot cake, and bouncing the Kurgan tot upon her knee, she was now even more convinced than ever that the homicide had not taken place at any of these residences, though several had *Mr. Lincoln* and other similar roses in their well-kept gardens. Her mind kept returning to the Collins' fortress-like home at the end of the cul-de-sac.

Now at nearly 6:00 p.m., the impatient sun began to melt behind the tops of the aged trees. In frustration, Lea finally stood peering over the edge of the wedge shaped lot into the rocky ravine. A short rock wall standing less than three feet high separated the vacant field and its elite neighborhood from the tangle of brush that dotted the open land. She lifted up her heavy feet, and hoisting her bottom upon the low fence, swung her legs over the crumbling stone.

Lea half-slid, half-careened down the short incline, brambles and yellowish dry grass pulling at her walking shoes and trousers. A small sparrow the color of dust flew near her feet while a mockingbird's endless chatter filled the afternoon air. The sky surrounded her like a ceramic Mexican bowl, not a cloud disrupting its perfect blue hue. Bees hummed near a snarled riot of wild roses, and a few wild dandelions thrust their bitter stalks towards the sinking sun.

Lea slowly and methodically searched the area, convinced Chief Rollins' haphazard crew must have missed something. The field bordered a dry wash enthusiastically named the Monroe River, which only filled after the winter rains. Dust puffed up from the dry dirt, revealing little but irritating her allergies. Fox had nearly given up after thirty minutes of brushing the annoying flies away and flinching at the indignant crows who circled too closely above her. She paused under a scraggly scrub oak, barely tall enough to afford decent shade. A glimmer near the dirt road separating the tract from the start of the lettuce fields owned by Agrit-Empire had her moving as quickly as her damaged leg would allow.

Lea squatted by a pile of fresh, corrosion-free soda cans as a flock of five crows hopped in the distance cawing angrily at her disruption. Bees still hummed around the sticky sides of the empty containers, which had probably been dumped by teenagers who'd parked on the outskirts of the fields to smoke dope or make out. She was about to rise when a glob of gooey crimson caused her to start. Lea bent, and removing a long, dusty twig from the littered ground, shifted the can slightly.

The dislodgement revealed the stained bottom of a cream soda can tarnished a faded crimson. Something niggled at the edge of her brain. Lea moved the stick again and suddenly flinched as the can tilted slightly, allowing the contents within to slide partially out of the tab opening. No amount of experience could have stopped the involuntary recoil at the ghastly sight of the bloody end of a finger protruding out of the opening. The bitter bile rose in her throat as Connie's slender finger, still adorned by a huge diamond, slid grotesquely towards her.

Lea stumbled backwards, her hands reaching for support as she slammed hard against an old river boulder. Dirt clods clung to its rocky side and dissolved under her trembling fingers. She leaned against it, her lungs fighting for breath and calm.

"Thought you might prefer cream soda," echoed Thayne's melodious voice as she quickly punched in his number. He answered it on the second ring.

"Where are you, Thayne?" she croaked.

"Just pulling into Burger City. I finished my interview with Luke and visited Philemon again. He's remembered something about the Collins house that might be a lead. I—"

"I need you to come to Chester Street right now," she stammered, cutting him off. "I found the finger."

"The what?" he asked.

"I think I found Connie's finger. It's in the can."

"The . . . can?" he repeated.

It was only then that she realized how ludicrous her statement sounded. "In a soda can near the lettuce fields not far from where Thad's body was discovered."

His voice altered, taking on a harsh edge. "I want you to stay put, Fox, and call 911 and Chief Rollins. Don't touch the can!"

A wave of protest emitted from her. "No," said Lea stubbornly. "I want you to examine it first without any interference from the police." There was a long pause as Thayne contemplated her request.

"All right," he agreed slowly. "I'll be there as soon as possible."

The phone went dead in her hand. A daring crow hopped closer, and Lea backed away, searching for rocks to ward off its approach. She hurdled a fist-sized stone as hard as she could, missing the bird completely, but dispersing the flock for a while. The next fifteen minutes were spent guarding the small pile of cream soda cans from the persistent birds and battling her nausea. A wave of relief washed over her when Thayne arrived in a cloud of dust, the chrome from the highly polished car nearly blinding her.

The fire-engine-red Mustang succeeded in dispersing the persistent crows much better than her awkward rock throwing had. Thayne appeared much recovered from his drinking bout from the night before but still managed to turn pale at the sight of the protruding, enamel-accented finger.

"This is recent," he said after a moment's examination. "The soda can hasn't dried out yet in the heat."

"The blood and soda are still tacky, almost as if they were dumped after the fact." Fox stood as far removed from the pile as possible, her tacky outfit stained with dirt and perspiration.

Thayne sat back on his haunches "I believe this pile of cans was probably deposited here early this morning or last night at the latest. The question is why?"

"Perhaps whoever did this killing thought the area wouldn't be examined again after Friday's police convention? You and I both witnessed the police scouring the field fairly thoroughly as well as the Simms and Collins residences, but this area only got a cursory check. What better place to dump incriminating evidence than in a place that has already been searched?"

Nick voiced quietly, "Perhaps, but why not use a distant trash bin?" He studied her small tight face dwarfed by the overly large glasses. "I'm inclined to believe the murderer wished us to find it."

"Those are serial killer tactics. I find it hard to believe that's what this is."

Nick straightened. "Maybe we're on the wrong track, and this is a serial killing and not a passion killing after all. There are three bodies now, even though one is twenty-five years old. Who knows what other vagrants or drifters might have had met a similar end out here and were just never found. They might have been deposited in the rugged foothills, and with all the coyotes and buzzards about, not much would be left after a few days."

"It's not a serial killer," asserted Lea.

"You sound so certain."

"I'd stake my minimal reputation there's only been these three killings. This isn't random or impulsive; it's thought-out and methodical and has a connection between the mayor and Ashley Peebles. The killer is very, very smart and loves taunting us. He wanted us to find the note, and now, Connie's finger."

"While I'm inclined to agree with you, how would the killer know we'd search this area again?"

"I don't know, since the only reason I searched it was because you told me to. Did you draw something?"

The silence was deafening. He finally said, "Yes."

"Let's see it."

Thayne's Adam's apple worked as she analyzed the simple sketch. "It's just a pile of cream soda cans."

Thayne gave a helpless shrug. "I need to talk to Roger."

Fox remained silent way too long. "You trust him?" she said finally.

"Implicitly. Roger goes by the book. In fact, I think he probably wrote the book, but he has a heart, which is something Rollins lacks entirely. That, and tenacity. You, ah . . . wouldn't happen to have any hidden forensics skills, would you?

"Na, I flunked science in college. Any plastic bags in your car?"

Nick's head jerked, his deep brown eyes narrowing. "Just what are you suggesting, Fox?"

"Dr. Koh works for the police department, and if we have him examine the finger, we're following policy. Plus, he's a friend of mine and will help us out."

"That's circumventing the correct channels a bit, wouldn't you say, Fox?"

"Rollins is clearly not our friend, and I for one, won't hand him this finger to later get lost in some bureaucratic shuffle while Philemon Jenkins is indicted. I swear, Thayne, if you give Steven Koh two hours, he'll come up with something. As long as we take photos of the scene, don't taint the evidence, and deliver it to the proper authorities, what's wrong with that? *Besides*, we've been hired to find the killer while Roger is incapacitated. That's all the authorization we need."

"So why does it feel a bit immoral to me?"

"Immoral? I never suspected you bought into morality, Thayne. And just who states this code of morality? Is it George W. Bush, Jimmy Swaggart, my deceased father, or perhaps even Chief Rollins?

"You understand morals better than anybody, Fox. I'd stake my career on it."

"Then you'd be wrong. Morals are merely the stepping-stones to attaining what you need. You remember our pledge to Philemon? If I follow the mandates of Chief Rollins and roll over, he'll be arraigned for Thad's and Connie's murders faster than you can say *Murder One*. I have my own set of morals and values to follow, and I refuse to submit to any of that bozo's stipulations. If I do, we can kiss this case goodbye."

"No wonder you're not welcome at the police station. At least Gandhi would have agreed with you. He said, *True morality consists in not following the beaten track, but in finding out the true path for ourselves and fearlessly following it.*"

"Touché for Gandhi. Just remember, they didn't want me in the Girl Scouts, either, because I questioned the validity of earning those ridiculous homemaking badges. And, I believe I'm inclined to enjoy your quotes, but only when they support my intentions." A sudden thought struck Lea. "I almost forgot something important after the shock of finding Connie's finger. I swear I heard something moving behind the Collins wall, Thayne. It sounded like some sort of chained animal."

"You're positive?"

"Absolutely. The snarling and growling was clearly confined and distant as if the animal was restricted to a box or a kennel, or," she added, "in a basement we weren't able to locate. Of course, the blasted ten-foot wall hampered my determining exactly what it was."

"Thank God for small favors," Nick mumbled. All they needed now was a blasted trespassing charge. He remembered his grandmother once describing her irascible husband as a little bandy-rooster, always scratching for a fight. That term aptly described Lea Fox.

"Okay," he acquiesced. "Let's check out my trunk for bags and stash our newfound treasure before it gets cold."

Chapter 16

Fortunately, Nick had had a couple of decently clean grocery bags stashed inside the Mustang's small trunk. After snapping several photos using her tiny digital camera, Lea picked up the aluminum cream soda can using two dusty sticks as Nick held the bag for her. Not a word passed between the pair. Fortunately, the finger slid back inside the can as Fox lowered it into the bag. Thayne made quick work of picking up the remaining five cans and placing them in yet another supermarket bag for transport.

"Where's your car?" he asked emotionlessly.

"I left it in the cul-de-sac. I guess I'll have to ride in your hot rod again."

"Well, at least we'll arrive at our destination a great deal faster than in your Mazda. How old is that thing? Twenty years?"

"Eight, and at least it's paid for," she snapped back.

He licked his pointer finger and held it up. "Touché, little lady, but at least this baby is worth the shackles of debt."

Lea buckled up as he headed down the dirt road, leaving a trail of dust behind him. At the main highway, he opened the throttle.

"So, you think Dr. Koh's at home?"

"Probably; it's nearly 6:30."

They headed towards a modern section of town where clusters of well-designed condominiums lined the beautifully landscaped street.

"New part of town?" he asked as if searching for something valid to say.

"About ten years, as you can tell from the size of the trees. Turn left on Craven Street. He's in the second complex on the left."

A single-storied, sprawling complex designed in Spanish Mediterranean style with red tile roofs and clinging bougainvilleas pleasured the eye. At the second door on the right, Lea stopped and rang the intercom. Each unit had a private entryway and reasonably sized patio. Dr. Koh's was filled with beautifully nurtured bushes and hanging plants surrounding a melodious fountain that dripped lazily into a pool where naiads dipped their marble hands. A heavy wrought-iron table, with a beautiful blooming pink fuchsia centered upon its surface, enticed the visitor to sit down and relax.

"Good afternoon," came Dr. Koh's voice through the

speaker. "May I help you?"

"We certainly hope so, Steven. We've got some homework for you."

"Ah, Lea Fox. Why am I not surprised? I'll buzz you in."

The beautiful flat glowed in oiled teak, Spanish pavers, and hand-woven throw rugs. A small pot-bellied Buddha squatted in the corner, surrounded by a shrine of houseplants. An enormous TV leaned towards a nut-brown leather couch strewn with the two latest issues of *Sports Illustrated* and a grisly forensics magazine. Upon the rectangular glass coffee table, a single light beer and some dry-roasted peanuts sat next to one of those ingenious little sandboxes complete with miniature rake. The hanging art was colorful and modern, but not too garish. The large windows let in the late afternoon sun, and Nick instantly liked the place. A man could stretch out his legs here.

Thayne deposited the plastic bag right in front of Steven Koh before moving aside as the Asian-American opened the bag with long slim fingers.

He scolded. "What have you been up to, Lea?"

"Not much, Steven, really. Thayne and I were just taking a Monday evening drive and discovered a can with a human finger by a field. Thought we'd bring it to you for examination."

Thayne winced at the blatant lie.

"And I'm Mary Poppins. What a coincidence! I just happen to have two bodies missing fingers cooling right now at my office. *Lea!* Shame on you, girl." He sighed heavily.

Nick got the impression he'd dealt with Fox's antics before.

"Since I don't want to contaminate either bag here, would you two be good enough to follow me?"

Steven Koh turned right down a thickly carpeted hall and flipped on a low switch at the second door. The interior resembled a doctor's office with low metal tables, wide counters, and a deep utility sink. Dr. Koh scrubbed his hands after setting the grocery bags upon an examination table.

"Pretty nifty having a lab in your own home," exclaimed Nick, noting the sterile but well-equipped room.

"Believe me, it's a real turn on for the girls. Actually, it's my hobby that motivated me to build the laboratory." He pointed to the wall. There, a dozen beautifully framed shadow boxes displaying countless butterflies and other bugs lined the distant wall.

"I originally planned to be an entomologist," he stated matter-of-factly. "But after taking a forensics course, I realized I was destined to follow in my father's footsteps. I have a real way with the dead. Lea, would you hand me that tray?" He opened a metal drawer and pulled out a pair of thin latex gloves, easing them over his artistic hands.

"And that one there," he added.

Lea handed him the tray like a professional nurse. It was stocked with tweezers, scalpels, and other instruments more suitable in a medieval torture chamber.

"Don't look so startled, Mr. Thayne. I'm no Jeffrey Dahmer; I really only dissect bugs unless otherwise instructed by my guests. Unless you're dead or have six legs, you hold no interest for me." He pulled out the aluminum can holding the finger and set it upon a stainless steel tray.

"Grab me a slide, Lea," he requested, and Fox immediately passed him a slender glass plate. Dr. Koh scraped the side of the can and placed the bloody gum upon the thin glass plane. "While I'm positive this is human blood, I'll know for certain in just a moment."

Nick observed the pair. Dr. Koh conversed little with Lea, but she seemed to know instinctively what he wanted. Using the precipitin test, he examined the blood under the microscope, afterwards placing it into a small flask to which he added a pale chemical. He then painstakingly struggled to remove the defiant finger. After three minutes of exasperated persistence, he finally managed to pull it out of the can with long-handled tweezers.

"Severed, just like the mayor's," he observed studying the clean cut. Steven Koh was incredibly thorough. He not only took a tissue sample of the fingernail with its accompanying nail polish but checked the severed finger for hanging or foreign fibers. He scrutinized the hair on top of the finger before examining the lovely ring. It was the ring that interested him most.

"Not a robbery, for sure. No thief in their right mind would have abandoned this trinket. It's got to be at least a full carat." He squinted at it with a small black eyepiece, appearing more like a jeweler than a coroner. "Nearly flawless." He replaced the ring in a small metal container and moved to the severed end of the waxen finger, which appeared rubber-like under the glaring florescent light.

"It's very clean. See, there's very little splintering of the bone. Do you notice the grayish, mottled hue? I would say it has been removed from the hand at least five days ago, if not more. That would coincide with the death estimate for Connie's body. My preliminary suspicion is that it was removed after her death, but not long after, considering the constriction of the blood vessels. Your report said Connie was last seen alive Tuesday night?"

"That's right," confirmed Lea. "A little girl down the street named Katie saw Thad and his girlfriend cruise up the street in a limo just around dusk."

"Does Chief Rollins know about this… ah… find?"

"Well," maneuvered Nick, "he definitively knows the finger's missing and instructed the entire force to be on the lookout for it." It was the first time he'd seen Fox grin.

"We're just following orders," smirked Fox.

"Good God, you're infuriating, Lea. They used to give

lobotomies to women like you in the 19th century in an effort to try and control their impulsive natures. When will you ever learn that you have to follow the proper channels? That's what got you in trouble before, and now I'm party to this. Jesus!" He tossed his stained gloves upon the squeaky clean table and glared at Lea. "Come back at 8:00 a.m. Now, get out of here and let me work."

Thayne made for the door, but Lea paused. "I, um, forgot to tell Steven something." Thayne continued through to the front room. She turned to the annoyed coroner.

"I'm sorry, Steven. I . . . ah . . . well . . . you're right about us not finding the finger by accident. Actually, Thayne was asking me about cream soda earlier . . . whether I drank it or not and then asked me to scour the murder scene again. It was not far from there that I discovered a pile of cream soda cans. Later, after I called him, he showed me a sketch of a similar can, including the finger, sticking out in the trunk of his car."

Steven froze, able to surmise the most important part of her rambling, nearly incoherent statement. "You suspect him of being party to this murder?" he croaked.

"No."

"Did he draw the picture?"

"Yes."

Steven digested this information slowly. A man of science he was being presented with something that was unpalatable, though he'd heard the rumors. "That's how he got the name the spook." It wasn't a question.

"Yes," she said, verifying what they had both researched.

Steven grunted. "I trust your judgment, Lea. Do what you believe is right. You're a pragmatic woman. Don't let his 'methods' sway you from where good detective work leads you."

"His 'gift' led me to the cans."

Steven removed his glasses and rubbed his tired eyes. "Play it safe and legal, Lea. Have evidence for everything and go by the book. Not like this. Not skirting the rules and procedures. You understand me. Thayne is the flash, you're the elbow grease. Don't forget it. Tell him I need to speak to him."

Thayne sat drumming his fingers upon the steering wheel while the Eagles eerily sang *Hotel California*.

"Dr. Koh wants to speak with you privately," Lea stated gruffly.

"Surprise, surprise," he stated, slamming the car door grumpily.

Steven Koh sat upon a metal stool in his home laboratory, gazing sightlessly at the severed finger. Its scarlet nail polish made the bodiless finger appear even more grotesque.

"Is there something you wanted to speak with me about, Dr. Koh?"

"The name's *Steven.* It lets me pretend I have a palatable job and that people really give a shit about me as a person." He turned his dark eyes towards Nick and studied him.

"I've heard things about you, Thayne. Roger once told me that you get "notions" about cases that invariably prove themselves correct. Said he wasn't sure where these "notions" come from, but mentioned they called you a spook in detective school."

"Soap opera stuff. I'm just a regular guy with a partner from hell."

Steven tapped the sticky can. "Lea has a right to be a bit *spooked.* You have to admit that it's strange that you mentioned cream soda to Lea earlier and encouraged her to search the area again. And lo and behold, not only does she find what is probably Connie's finger but, later, you share with her a sketch of the can complete with the aforementioned finger."

"A coincidence, I guess."

"And you're full of shit. Roger told me about some of your escapades. But it's not important that *I* understand your spooky notions or where they come from. It's only important Lea feels comfortable enough to work with you and trust you."

"That's the whole problem," protested Nick. "You

see, Fox, she's the Holmes type, all evidence and hard work and tapping out possible scenarios on that little handheld contraption of hers. I wouldn't dare bust her bubble." Both men stared long and hard at each other.

"Did you draw that sketch?"

"Yes."

"Did you ever know Thad Fisher or Connie Judson?"

"Not while living."

Finally Steven shrugged. "You're right about Lea loving her facts, so here's another one she can punch into her mini-computer. The formaldehyde used to murder Connie Judson had traces of human DNA not related to Connie in its composition."

Nick swallowed uneasily. "That means . . ."

"Another person's remains had been floating around in the formaldehyde before Connie was forced to ingest it. This is a serial killer, Nick. Serial killers have no conscience and no mercy. They only possess an insatiable hunger for eliciting that addictive expression of terror upon their victim's paralyzed faces. Both Connie and Thad's faces bespoke of incomprehensible horror as well as something else."

"And what was that?"

"It was disbelief. Disbelief that they were really being killed by whoever murdered them. The killer doesn't look like a killer, doesn't act like a killer, and therefore is all the more deadly. Lea's storming ahead as if these are straight-forward murders. I'm not sure she's capable of handling this."

"She seems pretty tough," countered Nick.

"Does she? Well, I was witness to that tough bravado during her family's funeral. Did you know that both her father's and brother's tongues were cut out before they were hanged? Their severed members stuffed inside their coat pockets along with the message, *The past is now buried.*"

Nick swallowed heavily. "That wasn't in the papers."

"Even Chief Rollins has some vestige of mercy, though he despises her."

"And *why* does he hate her so?"

Steven Koh turned his thin face towards Nick. His oriental eyes were much narrower and more darkly shadowed than Nick's. Nick recognized it took a great deal for this intensely private man to confide in a near stranger.

"It's because she's not only smarter than him but also that Rollins knows he did her a gross injustice by not ensuring the culprits were apprehended. Lea was positive that, while the Russian Mob might have been involved in her family's murder, her father had stumbled upon something so big, so incriminating that he and Lane were rubbed out. Then, to further stifle her investigation, Rollins blacklisted her in this town so she could barely make a living, because she dared speak her mind. I've sent some cases her way and would help her more, but her pride is as great as Rollins' animosity. To add insult to injury, he belittled her femininity and sexuality by suggesting any man who had been or would be interested in her must have a screw loose. Not that he's any great shakes himself in that department."

"I see," whispered Nick guiltily.

"So, do me a favor. Make sure she carries her gun and level with her if you can. Lea needs someone like you to monitor her impulsive nature and tell her the flat truth regarding her rogue methods. And she doesn't need someone around who doesn't have her work ethic. She's the most hard-working, down-to-earth person I know. So much so she pisses off any man in his right mind."

"And you're not in your right mind, I take it? But what about her boyfriend? Doesn't he have any impact or influence on her behavior?"

"Boyfriend? *Bernard*? She *told* you about him?"

"Only a little. She's intensely reserved regarding the subject. Thought she would chew my head off when I dared comment on that cozy photograph of them in her hallway."

Steven's head snapped up. "Lea let you in her house?" A strange expression passed over his face, and if Nick hadn't known better, he'd swear it was awe. Whatever caused his intense reaction, Steven didn't elaborate.

"She did. It's kinda nice, but too much like a jungle for my taste. You know Bernard?"

Steven straightened his tools needlessly upon their spotless metal tray and didn't answer the question directly, saying instead, “I believe everyone has a right to privacy, and regarding Bernard, I have no right to comment one way or another. Just tread softly and keep her away from Rollins. I’ll do what I can on this end to facilitate a quick and successful end to this case.”

“Alright,” said Nick cautiously. Something didn’t add up. Why didn’t Steven Koh just spill the beans and say what needed to be said? He had the uncomfortable feeling that Dr. Koh was protecting Fox. But from whom or what?

Chapter 17

Sunday Evening

Fox fiddled restlessly with the adjustment for the Mustang's bucket seats. Much too self-conscious, Nick immediately suspected she'd been going through his glove compartment.

"Watch out for the Glock .45. It's loaded and dangerous," he scolded, flicking an undisguised rebuke.

"Nice pistol, but I prefer the Glock .40. The large double-stacks on the .45 are just too big for my hand. I need the versatility and comfort of a sub-compact." She pulled a small pistol out of her oversized handbag. It fit like a glove in her hand, and she held absolutely no feminine remorse about toting so lethal a weapon.

"Should have guessed. Just promise me you'll leave my firearms alone. You have a permit for that thing, I take it?"

"Of course. I'm by-the-book Fox, you know."

"Right." He started the engine.

"While we're waiting for Steven's results, why don't we return to my house and fiddle around with the Internet. I want to find out more about the owner of the Collins house. Have you discovered anything about the Montanari's?"

"I asked Randy to work on it, but I have to say he's much better in the field than on the computer."

"And what about Roger? Have you heard from him?"

"I spoke to Susan this morning. He's recovering nicely. We need him, Fox, if we're going to be allowed to solve this case. He has credibility and a working relationship with the chief. Plus, Susan is Steven Koh's brother."

"Of course. You can see the family resemblance."

"He's worried about you."

"Steven is always worried about something. That's why he has all those attractive stress lines in the middle of his forehead."

"He cares about you and believes this is a serial killer."

"Oh, fiddlesticks! He just thinks I'm going to meet my father's fate and will have to unzip me from a black bag."

"Aren't you a morbid one. And you're wrong. This person is one you'd least expect to be a killer."

"Hmm. Steven's advice is never to be ignored, and because of that, I'll research everything I know about trophy collector serial killers tonight. But I'd have to disagree with him. We're missing something, Thayne, something smack-dab front of our noses."

Nick glanced at his steel watch.

"Am I keeping you from something?" she asked.

"Just a phone call that is a sight more pleasant than all this skullduggery."

"A serious girlfriend for once?"

"Nope. And I absolutely refuse to take women seriously; that's what gets a man in trouble every time. I suspect our poor mayor would echo my sentiments, if only he could."

Fox seemed uncomfortable with the banter. "You interviewed Luke Cambridge?"

"Yeah, I did. He reached into the console and handed her a small micro-cassette. "I recorded the conversation so you could hear it verbatim and use the F & H to record your findings. Take your time enjoying it. He's made some interesting points."

"You saw Philemon?"

"Just for a few minutes. He seems in good spirits. Was reading the Bible with his wife when I arrived. I asked him about the smell coming from the Collins house, and he stated a mild stench has surrounded that house as long as he's worked there. It's rarely noticeable, and usually only on hot, breezeless days like we've been having recently. Mrs. Simms indicted she'd actually called the city regarding the odor. They speculated it was probably a septic tank too close to the surface or a faulty sewer pipe. I didn't inform him about the dung pile."

"And his status?"

"He's been charged with both murders, and apparently, Mrs. Fisher was called to the station to give a statement. Not sure what turn that's going to take. Also, met Connie's cousin on my way out. There certainly wasn't much of a family resemblance. He's tall, thin, and balding; rather nondescript, actually. It's been verified he was in Florida with several other officers all last week. Presidio Boy was planning to have dinner with Connie on Saturday and learned of her death instead. He's arranging the services for next Friday and will go through her things as soon as the chief releases the premises. Rollins had Officer Steele there bagging up a ton of stuff this afternoon."

"He's barking up the wrong tree. Connie was killed because of the company she was keeping. I doubt if it was premeditated. I'll be sure to buy the *Times* tomorrow for the next update."

They pulled up in front of her pretty little yard. A couple sparrows dove from her feeder, which hung off a mulberry branch, disturbed by Thayne's bright red car.

"I'll meet you inside. I have to place my call," Nick stated.

Ten minutes passed before Thayne entered the house,

an expression suggesting only guilt upon his lean face. Lea suspected he had given his mother his ritualistic Sunday evening call. It prompted her to ask.

"So, why do you hate your dad so much?"

She was seated by her computer in the small neat office. The abruptness of the question and tone startled him. And he'd thought he was getting used to her by now.

"None of your business," Nick growled.

"Oh, come now, I need to know why you have such volatile moods and have lost yourself in Girard instead of flaunting your wares in San Francisco where they would be much more appreciated. Besides, no one would understand domestic problems better than I."

She'd powered up the computer and waited patiently as Windows loaded.

"Ah, shit," he murmured finally. "Knowing you, you probably have a complete dossier on me as well."

She actually did, but was not about to admit it. Besides, it was filled with way too many holes and speculations.

"My dad is a first rate bastard, and I only found out his true nature about four years ago." He sank down upon the comfortable window seat and watched her small hands type in a password and wait for Internet access.

"I'm quite familiar with men who are bastards," she said softly.

He was certain she was.

Her home phone jangled and he politely picked it up and handed it to her. It was Roger Chung.

"Hello, Roger," she said as sweetly as her gruff voice would allow. Fox listened for a moment before raising a finger at Nick. "Roger needs to have you call Chief Rollins right away. Could you use your cell outside—this is the only line I have."

"Is he gone?" asked Roger a minute later.

"Yes. How you doing?"

"I feel like some fool doctor's been messing with my insides, but other than that, I'm just hunky dory."

Lea gave a hoarse laugh. "So, I guess I have you to thank for Nick Thayne showing up on my doorstep." It was half-accusation.

"You could do worse."

"Perhaps. You're his friend, right?"

Roger gave a short laugh. "If that means I put up with his shit, then yes."

"What can you tell me about him? He's like a clam."

"Look who's talking. So, what do you want to know?"

"Just two little things. Why does he hate his father and why was he kicked off the force?"

"So, you want to know everything do ya?"

"You bet. Thayne has shared with me sketches relating to our crime scenes. Tell me all you know."

After a long pause Roger said. “Alright, but I’m warning you Lea. You need him. No matter what his methods, he’s the best there is, and you’ve got to trust him.”

“Prove it.”

“A real doubting Thomas, aren’t ya. Okay. Here’s one story the dailies won’t ever know. Nick was born just outside of Subic Bay in the Philippines. It was the usual story of a seventeen-year-old girl getting involved with a young naval officer. In most Asian countries, half-breed children, especially the offspring of US troops, are particularly scorned by the native populous.”

“That happened in Vietnam and Korea,” stated Lea. “So. the grand protector America isn’t as beloved as George W. would like us to believe?”

“Please don’t get me started on politics,” Roger snorted before continuing. “Thayne’s mother was tiny and had difficulty delivering her oversized half-Caucasian baby. She bled severely after a long labor at a Catholic home for unmarried girls before finally succumbing to infection. The orphanage was run by the Dominican Sisters of Mercy, who immediately took in another blessing America had bestowed upon one of their unfortunate daughters. His mother Constance is buried in a small graveyard behind the orphanage.”

“Does he have a photo of her or anything?” Lea asked.

“Well, kinda. I’ll get to that. Nick remained in the orphanage until age three, when one day, a man and his wife showed up at the orphanage. The childless couple took one look at Nick and started the wheels in motion for adoption.

"Charming even then, I take it. His mother must have been thrilled to finally have a child."

"Oh, she was, believe it or not." He chuckled to himself. "Nick was quiet and well-mannered even then. The sisters, you see, were quite generous with the switch when passing on their concept of perfect obedience."

The Montanari birth records popped up and she pressed the print button. Roger paused his narrative, and she could hear him ingesting some fluids nosily. He wasn't the type of man who took being laid up well, and she grinned to herself.

"So, what happened between him and his dad?"

"Impatient little broad, aren't you. I'm getting to that. Martin Thayne is a powerful man, and as you probably know, holds a seat on the State Water Commission."

Lea understood only too well the power of that particular committee in this water-strained state. "I managed to dig that up."

"I'm not surprised, you little ferret. From what Nick has told me, it appeared Martin Thayne's sole goal in life was to please his father. Thus, Martin joined the naval academy, served as an ensign, and married his high school sweetheart at age twenty-two, who of course, is Thayne's adopted mother.

"After giving back his time to the Navy, Martin took

over as top engineer for the California Aqueduct Project and finally ran for office, serving as the Water Commissioner in the Sacramento Valley while Nick was sent off to Stanford. Thayne wanted to be a lawyer, but Martin insisted he pursue engineering or business administration." He chuckled, and Lea wondered what was so funny.

"Unbeknownst to Martin, Nick, who was always ornery, studied for the law school entrance exam and passed." He paused significantly.

"And . . . ?" she prompted.

"At law school, he met a young Filipino woman who'd also been adopted by an American family. She'd managed, with the help of the military of all organizations, to locate her natural parents and urged Nick to do the same. So, Nick took some of that Thayne wealth and made a trip to his homeland." Roger hesitated and Lea heard a small dog barking in the background and the rattle of something falling near the phone.

While she waited for Roger to continue, she began scanning what she'd pulled up on Connie Judson. The thirty-four-year-old woman had been married twice and pursued careers in modeling, retail, and telephone marketing. That was before she'd struck it rich by becoming Thad Fisher's squeeze. Her cousin, Mark, was her only living relative and Lea felt momentarily sad, knowing few would grieve the voluptuous redhead's demise.

"Sorry, Lea, that damn dog came in here and broke a

plate. Thank God it wasn't one from Susan's treasured wedding set. Where was I?"

"Thayne visited his homeland."

As he returned to his recital, Lea typed in Edith Simms' name, address, and phone number and hoped that her search engine would discover facts regarding the elderly woman's family. Roger's voice took on a strange quality, and Lea realized that what came next was very important if she was to understand Nick Thayne.

"After Thayne traveled to the orphanage, the nuns informed him that his grandmother was still alive and living in Manila. In disbelief, he journeyed to the crowded dirty city to enter a small apartment resembling more a shack than a flat with its dirt-packed floor and swarming flies.

Nick told me that he expected her to reject him outright. After all, he was living evidence of her teenage daughter's fall from grace. Instead, the old woman welcomed him with open arms and cried her eyes out, hugging Nick and repeating over and over how he was the exact image of his mother, yet resembled his father as well in size and build. Nick discovered his biological father had been a constant guest to her tiny home. He'd made her great promises including the biggest, vowing to wed Constance.

"Grandma Silva was a bit of a legend in her neighborhood, supposedly having the *gift of sight*." He paused again.

"Oh," said Lea a cold shiver stiffening her spine.

"Yeah. Well, she indicated she'd always known Nick would be a successful man and began thrusting photos of Constance, his deceased grandfather, and other countless relatives into his hands. And then she handed him one last photo. It was of his father."

Lea hunched her shoulders in anticipation of what was coming.

"It was his adopted father, Martin Thayne. You have to hand it to him. Though in acute shock, Nick managed to keep his shock and despair from the fragile old woman, who died a few months later. She never knew that Nick's biological father had adopted his own bastard son; that he had lied to his wife, the orphanage, everyone, because of some warped concept obtained from his grandfather regarding his own natural superiority.

"You see, fortunately or unfortunately, Martin Thayne believed blood is thicker than water, and it was his own overwhelming curiosity that finally overcame his guilt. The moment he laid eyes upon Nick, he saw the suggestion of his own face and thus allowed his childless wife, who he was married to even while promising the world to a naïve Filipino girl, adopt his bastard son.

"Are his parents aware that he knows?" ventured Lea.

"His father, yes. Nick stated his father slapped him on the back and said, 'Boys will be boys, you know. Besides, how can you resist a woman who offers you anything?'"

Lea swallowed heavily, feeling half sorry for Thayne.

"You've heard of his temper?" queried Roger.

"Yeah. He lost his job with the SFPD because of it." Her concise little dossier referred to his problem temper, which always blasted at the wrong time. That and his drinking.

"It's still a little vague if he quit the force or was asked him to leave. I don't think I want to know. As far is his father is concerned, Nick's completely severed ties. Has contact with his mom though." Roger sighed. "Does that give you a better picture?"

"It does indeed. Thanks, Roger. I appreciate your honesty."

The information on Edith Simms had printed out, and Lea moved on to Philemon Jenkins. This was no means the end of the story, and she wasn't one to give up on any unsolved mystery, even Nick Thayne's. Thayne rattled the front door on returning, his eyes narrowing.

"You've sure been on the phone a long time."

"So have you. I think Roger wants to talk to you."

Thayne grabbed the phone while Fox made a pretense of scanning the file on Edith Simms, who had retired as a librarian nearly five years earlier.

"What's up Roger? So, it will be another week before you can officially come back. How am I holding up?" He snorted. "I'm working with a gentle goddess, and I just spent the last ten minutes placating your boss. Believe me; I count my blessings every night before I go to bed." He rolled his eyes at Fox, who glared back.

"Swine," mumbled Lea, returning her eyes to the screen.

"I'll be in contact." Nick dropped the receiver into its cradle and watched her.

"What were you talking with Roger about?"

"Your temper, your drinking, and your unspecified methods."

Nick narrowed his dark eyes at her. "I drink how I want to drink. We all have our crutches, Fox. Mine just isn't as obvious as yours."

His beautifully slanted eyes focused on the metal half-crutch leaning against the wall. She had gone without it recently but suspected she'd need it again soon. Nick would not apologize for any weakness, just as he knew Fox wouldn't make excuses for her lameness. The pages on Philemon printed out, and Nick grabbed them.

"Shit," he summarized.

"I believe men who swear have low vocabularies. I'm convinced Eddie Murphy and Eminem are barbarians, regardless of their money. And yes, this provides ample fodder for our Chief Rollins."

He growled, appearing ready to take her head off. She ignored him.

"And look at this," She pointed her finger at the lighted screen. "Believe it or not, it looks like a nutrition company has ownership of the house. Collins is the name of their manager."

Nick squinted, "Leroy Collins of Mother Earth Industries. He gives his address as Sacramento, California."

"Here's his number, as well. Let's give him a ring," she said, handing the number to him. "Men usually deal better with other men on the phone. Let's hear some of that famous Thayne charm now. I'll put on the speaker phone and maybe some will rub off on me."

Thayne grabbed the receiver. Charm, his eye. If she'd just learn some goddamned manners, she'd get a lot further. Leroy Collins was amazingly pleasant.

"Oh yes," he said, "sometimes we have officials that work with the Agrit-Empire visit Monroe, and we put them up in the house."

"You're owned by the Agrit-Empire?" Thayne saw Fox stifle a gasp.

"We're actually an affiliate, but yes, you could say that we're under the umbrella of the mother company. Many of their products go into our food supplements as well as a natural line of produce where we take the wheat, lettuce, and potatoes and sell them to the public indicating they are not chemically altered in anyway."

"The Agrit-Empire has an entire section of their fields

that uses no pesticides?"

"That's right, and we're mighty proud of it."

"So, the house on Chester Street is actually used only to house executives from your company?"

"Not just my company, though my name's on the purchase form. We bought it for all three companies: Agrit Empire, Mother Earth, and Corporal Building Products."

"Corporal Building Products? Montanari is more diversified than I expected."

"Of course. Many of the major building projects in the Big Valley have actually been supplied by Montanari's Corporal Building Products Company. In this day and age, most corporations have to diversify to stay in business in this unstable economy."

"Does anyone live there now?" asked Nick, tapping his pencil on the pad where Lea had written down the number.

"No, I don't believe so. Two months ago, Cheryl Haines and Rod Sturgis stayed for about five days to solidify the canning and packinghouse deal with Tri-Pack. I believe Al Crispen and his team from Corporal Building Products are slated for next weekend."

"Does the house have a guard dog, by any chance?"

"No, but I'd have to say I'm not a real authority, since I've only been at the house once since it was purchased for the corporation. At that time, I met with Ruth Montanari who was the one who actually furnished the entire house and had the alarm system put in. I guess it's a hobby of hers, since she comes across as a frustrated interior designer. I have to admit that Mrs. Montanari did a wonderful job, but I was only there for about fifteen minutes to take a walk through."

"I appreciate your time, Mr. Collins. You've been most helpful."

"So, the Montanari's actually own that property," mused Lea after Thayne hung up the phone. "And now Anthony wants a private viewing of the body. I wonder if Mr. Montanari was present at the 'dinner' for Thad and his mistress?"

Thayne grinned. "I do believe, Inspector Fox, that we have another suspect."

Chapter 18

Papers were strewn everywhere as Thayne began scrutinizing the Montanari family tree at Fox's oval dining room table. Lea had moved the computer in and started a family tree with Anthony Montanari and his wife Ruth next to him.

"There are three daughters and three sons of Anthony Montanari, who was married in October, 1950," began Thayne. "His wife, Ruth, started young—only 17, while the elderly Anthony was 20."

"Catholics have to marry young so they don't commit the sin of fornication."

"Really," said Nick, mystified. He'd never personally felt fornication was that big a deal. "Their daughters are probably married. Nope, I take that back. Julia, the second oldest daughter, is a Dominican nun and lives in some convent in New Mexico." He paused, and Lea tapped her pencil impatiently. "Wow," he said, "for so many Montanari's in the family, there sure aren't many in the way of grandchildren. Randy and Anthony Jr.—Anthony's oldest sons—were both killed in Vietnam in January 1972, within—get this, Fox—two weeks of one another. Randy was caught in machine gun fire, and a firebomb destroyed Tony's bunker.

"Their sister, Julia, joined a convent at age seventeen within weeks of their death and the oldest daughter, Rose—Randy's twin—ran off with a Jewish IRS agent. She lives in New York and doesn't have any children. Rudy's not married, of course, and is set to inherit everything. He's thirty-one years old, will be thirty-two in late November, and was born in 1970, a full nine years younger than Maria, the last sister, who's a professor."

"What did you say his name is?" interrupted Fox.

"Rudy, short for Rudolph."

"Like the red-nosed reindeer?"

Nick set the paper down very carefully. "Yeah, just like the song."

"He's next."

Thayne's eyes widened. "Then we've got to give him a call and warn him."

Lea held a hand up. "No, the warning would be meaningless to him. It was meant for someone who cares for him."

"Like Anthony Montanari?"

Lea stood up and scanned the paper over his shoulder.

"Maybe. But it could anybody; Anthony or Ruth—or even one of his sisters or maybe a girlfriend or friend. And the youngest sister?"

"Maria is unmarried, but the information on her seems a little vague." He lifted a sheet, searching for a marriage or more information.

"Oh, I remember. She's a lesbian," stated Lea. "Heard it while I was in school. So, there's a real dearth of boys, unless Ruth has another child at age 69. I think that would mean real problems for the Montanari family."

"And you think these sorts of things still matter in a Catholic family?" asked Nick.

Fox cocked a thick eyebrow.

"You're right," he sighed.

Fox pushed the society section of the *Monroe County Press* across the table to him and Thayne clucked under his breath as he read. "So, Rudy is thinking about marriage to one Beatrice Schuster. Pretty thing. I'm sure that's a relief to his parents."

"Or a threat to someone who doesn't want him to marry." Fox returned to her seat and sat down with a sigh. "Let's allow that delightful tidbit to ferment for a while in the F & H and get back to the Peebles connection. Rudy was only seven when Ashley Peebles was murdered," said Lea, looking at the family tree she'd designed.

"That's right."

"So he was only two or so when his brothers were killed?"

"Let me check," Nick rustled the papers. "That's right. Anthony Jr., the oldest son, was almost 21, and Randy just 19. What a bloody shame."

"I wonder what the two boys were like?" pondered Lea. Her landline rang shrilly. It was Officer Phelps. She listened intently and then smiled. "You're a pip," she said.

"What's up?" Nick asked.

"Guess who's heading for the morgue as we speak?"

"Anthony Montanari!"

She grinned, pushing her glasses up. "Time for a road trip, Thayne, and bring the copy of the note found with Connie's body. I think Anthony just might be interested."

Lea despised mortuaries almost as much as hospitals. The only reason she didn't hate them more than hospitals was because they, at least, didn't try to delude the family that a person might get better. Hospitals seemed to generate pain, and if they made a goof, this is where you ended up.

A line of mourners drifted out of the mortuary, their cars moving sullenly through the parking lot. Every adult used a pair of concealing sunglasses to disguise their grief, and the somber black outfits looked depressive and dismal in the waning sunshine. Lea felt sad just looking at them. Montanari's Buick, black and sleek and costing a small fortune, was already parked under a palm tree. His vehicle was hard to miss, since the license plate read '*Taterman'*

Thayne followed the limping Fox into the foyer. Its bright stained glass gave the interior a churchlike feel. Nick hesitated, not sure which way to head.

"They keep the bodies ready for viewing in the small chapel to the right." Fox's eyes were way too bright and her hands shook. Of course, she would know *exactly* where the caskets were located.

Thayne pushed open the swinging door to find Anthony leaning over the corpse. He lifted Thad's right hand, revealing the missing finger. "Just like the other," he muttered to himself. He replaced the mayor's hand and gasped upon noticing the pair observing him intently.

"What are you doing here?" he barked, not even trying to be cordial.

"We just wanted to say goodbye to the mayor since we will be probably be working during his actual funeral," stated Nick, smiling. "My name is Inspector Nick Thayne and this . . ."

"I know who you are. You're the snoops Rollins was forced to hire while Chung recuperates!"

Thayne ignored his rudeness. "So, I guess you couldn't make the funeral later this week, either? That's why you're here?"

"He was a good friend," said Anthony stiffly.

Lea had not seen him in years, and the interim had not been kind. Fifty pounds overweight, his once-black hair was almost totally gray. Lea noted his fingernails were bitten to the quick and a huge gold nugget ring glimmered on his pinky finger. His clothes, though expensive, hung poorly on his portly frame.

"So, you were in school with Thad?" asked Nick.

"No, but I supported his campaign twelve years ago when he was running for mayor."

"Supported it well, I take it?" commented Lea.

Anthony Montanari frowned. Women who didn't know their place deserved a sharp slap. "Political campaign donations aren't made common knowledge. It's Ms. Fox, isn't it?"

"That's my name."

"Jeremy Fox's kid?"

"That's right.

Anthony was a blunt as she. "He was whacked a couple years ago, wasn't he? Made for interesting reading on an otherwise boring Sunday morning. Did Clements Mortuary handle the services for you, as well?"

Thayne wasn't sure he had witnessed such cruelty in the flesh before and understood Trish Fisher's hatred of the man much more clearly.

Fox swallowed stiffly, but as usual, wasn't to be outdone. "The note, Thayne."

Nick actually enjoyed handing it to her.

"What do you make of this, Mr. Montanari?" she said icily.

Anthony Montanari's face blanched and his hands trembled. "Where did you get this?" he demanded.

Lea moved closer to the casket. "Tucked in Connie Fisher's ear so it couldn't be missed. You have a son named Rudolph, don't you?"

"Yeah, I do, but what of it?"

Lea seemed the picture of innocence, but Thayne knew her by now. "Just thought the *red-nosed reindeer* might somehow be a warning to you?"

"That's a load of crap." Anthony leaned over the body, which was set out upon royal blue velvet in the most exquisite silver and wood casket. Thad Fisher's face appeared smooth and expressionless, his wrinkles having disappeared. A smart blue suit, red power tie, and expensive leather shoes gave the impression that the ex-mayor was somehow in control. It was amazing how genie morticians can work magic.

"So, when will Chung recover?" snapped Montanari, distancing himself from the casket and the two detectives.

"Soon, I'm sure," said Nick mildly, intensely disliking the older man. "I'll let him know you're concerned with his health."

"So, you found a ring on Thad's finger, didn't you?"

"Now, how would you know that?" said Nick,

watching the agricultural giant's face carefully.

"Let's just say a friend told me, and I have *lots* of friends." The implication was clear.

"In the police department?" chirped Lea.

"Maybe. Let's just say that Chief Rollins is a buddy of mine, so what he told me in casual conversation is not a crime."

"Maybe not a crime, but it's a little unusual for you to have access to that information, since it wasn't released to the papers," stated Lea. She had totally regained her composure and stared Anthony Sr. right back in the face.

"Ashley Peebles was killed on my property, as were Thad and his girlfriend. It seems to me that I have a *right* to know."

"So, you knew Ashley then?" declared Fox.

"Rollins was right when he said you were a first-class bitch. Let's just say I knew who she was. She wore really short skirts and liked *all* the boys, if you catch my drift. And at least she was a looker." He sneered at Fox.

Nick interrupted whatever retort Lea had ready. "Have any idea who might have killed the mayor?"

"Yeah. It was that Negro hit man. And I know why. Even Roger Chung was aware that Thad loved to gamble. He flew to Vegas at least a couple times a month and liked to live high on the hog. I'd say he got behind on some debts and paid the big price to the lenders."

“Did Thad know Ashley?” asked Thayne.

“Now, that I don’t know, but Thad sure liked the women—that *everyone* knew, even his poor wife. I’ve seen enough.”

A somberly dressed woman with a strange, still face stepped into the viewing hall.

“I didn’t realize Mr. Fisher had visitors.” She slammed the casket’s half lid down before continuing primly. “It’s customary for guests to check at the reception desk before viewing the deceased.” Her pin indicated her name as Helen Clyde.

“Don’t worry.” Anthony hitched a finger at the deceased. “Thad here didn’t mind the visit.” He pushed by the irritated woman. Mrs. Clyde had no choice but to turn her attentions to Fox and Thayne.

“We apologize,” said Nick quickly. “We didn’t mean to disturb the sanctity of this place.”

The middle-aged woman nodded curtly and motioned them towards the exit.

Lea followed Thayne out to his shiny Mustang and Nick waited until she was strapped in. “Don’t you find it a little strange he visited the corpse when it was clear he really didn’t want to say goodbye.”

“He was checking out the missing finger.”

“But why?”

“What if the missing fingers weren’t trophies like

Steven suspects?" said Fox. "Serial killers often take souvenirs, but if this *isn't* a serial killer—as I believe—then what is the use of cutting off the fingers?"

"As a warning?" speculated Thayne.

"That's it. The killer wants someone to take heed and know they meant business. They added the letter just to make sure the intended got the message."

"The intended as in Anthony Montanari?"

"Makes sense to me."

Nick started the engine, which purred like the kitten it was. "I wonder if Dr. Koh has finished his examination of Connie's finger. You mind heading over there, Fox?"

"Not at all." Lea suddenly witnessed the strangest expression pass over Nick's face.

"Déjà vu?"

"Something like that. You got any photos of Montanari's three boys?"

"Of course."

"Good. Meanwhile, let's see what Steven's been up to."

"So, what have you got, Doc?" asked Nick.

"There is nothing unusual about the finger, though it is clearly Connie's. Tissue type is an exact match. The finger has been detached at least five days. As you can see, the capillaries have dried up, but none of that is very interesting."

"It isn't?" asked Lea, watching Steven poke the gray finger with a steel instrument.

"Nope. It's the can that's interesting. A light coat of lip-gloss surrounds the tab. Connie's lipstick was scarlet, just like her fingernails. I believe the killer or perhaps even killers drank from the can before depositing the finger inside.

"So the killer's a woman?" asked Nick.

"Not necessarily. This isn't your normal, everyday brand of lip-gloss."

"It isn't?" asked Lea, not being very familiar with cosmetics.

"Normal lipstick is basically a waxy solidifier to which various chemical tints are added, but this particular one has Octyl Methoxycinnamate usually found in lip balms containing sun block."

"Connie was redheaded and redheads burn easily. Maybe it was hers?" suggested Nick.

"I don't think so. Connie's lips held a trace of bright red lipstick lacking any SPF ingredients. She was into color, not protection. Give me a little time, and I can find out the exact brand."

Thayne interrupted. "Let's have Randy check out Philemon's house and see if he, by any chance, used some sort of lip protection. I'll give him a call in a couple minutes."

"You do that. Meanwhile, I'm going to store this baby safely in the refrigerator."

"So, what's for dinner?" asked Lea as she watched Steven Koh nonchalantly place the plastic-bagged finger beside a carton of low fat yogurt.

"Very funny."

"Her blood type?" asked Lea.

"Our Connie was Type O, Thad, B. Neither of their blood types was found on any of the wheelbarrows we checked. Still waiting on the results of the snippers."

"And Philemon?"

"He's type B as well. Rollins had ordered a DNA analysis. I expect he's determined to link the gardener to any crimes if possible." Steven's face remained impassive.

"Like a backup—in case Philemon didn't do this murder. Maybe he can nail him for something else." The whole idea pissed Lea off.

"Our dear chief does seem to have an agenda. I believe Rollins would be content to serve up calumny with breakfast if it served his purpose," Nick said wryly.

"Great quote. Who'd you steal it from?" scoffed Fox, looking up for her F & H, where she now recorded the blood types.

Nick stroked his chin, pretending to look affronted. "I don't know. Of course, I could have had an original thought. It's crucial we get Roger to fend off the Chief to allow us enough time to find the real murderer."

"Roger's home now," stated Lea. "I called Susan, and

he was released to her care just after lunch. Susan indicated he wasn't the greatest hospital guest."

"I'm not surprised." Nick grinned.

"Why don't you stop by to see him while I listen to your taped conversation with Luke? I'll see you tomorrow bright and early. That means 8:00 a.m., Thayne, in my office. If you're a good boy, I might even purchase you some doughnuts."

"You think I still long to be a cop?" said Nick, watching her face.

Dr. Koh didn't see the humor. "Donuts have got to be one of the worst foods on earth. They're deep-fried and then loaded with sugar. And Americans wonder why they're overweight. I hope you're jesting, Lea."

"Men," snorted Lea giving Steven a shove. But if the truth was to be known, she felt far more comfortable with them than women.

Lea fixed herself a strong cup of chamomile tea after Nick dropped her off and sat staring at the Montanari files. Lea spent the next hour probing every connection to Montanari and Thad Fisher she could but found few references other than old society pages and a mayoral presentation to the farm workers at Agrit-Empire several years ago.

Lea placed the deceased Montanari brothers'

graduation photos before her. They greatly resembled their father, though slimmer and taller. The elder's expression was far from calming. She'd seen his kind before—arrogant and rich. The world was their oyster, even if that meant stealing from someone else. Both were handsome, but Randy seemed more vulnerable, with something akin to sadness softening his eyes.

Lea scrutinized the downloaded photo of the entire family. All had inherited Montanari Sr.'s nose and dark eyes, and while Anthony Jr. was the spitting image of his father, Randy appeared restless and wild, though handsome in the crisp uniform he'd donned before shipping off to Vietnam. Lea requested police records on the pair through the MCPD database and jerked violently when Randy's handsome face appeared, defiant before the police camera. She scanned the charges. Driving under the influence, possession of a stolen vehicle, and worse yet, sexual assault. All the charges had been dropped just before Randy and his older brother enlisted three weeks later.

Instinctively, Lea realized this was important. She shifted through the details, but no name was given for the victim of the assault because she'd been a minor. Why had the charges been dropped? Had Anthony Montanari Sr. bought the family off? He certainly had the money and resources to do so. Still, what could this possibly have to do with Thad's and his mistress' murders, or the tragic death of Ashley Peebles? Lea slouched in her most comfortable armchair and pondered the facts, occasionally rubbing her always-aching leg.

Fifteen minutes later, she switched to Edith Simms' file. Lea had learned long ago, that whenever stumped, she had to move on to another project until her ever-active subconscious could push an answer to the surface. So she read. Edith had been a widow for over thirty years and had only had one daughter, a girl named Delilah, who'd died in childbirth in the early 70s. The records revealed her newborn son hadn't survived. No wonder Mrs. Simms knocked around that huge house growing beautiful roses and orchids and overpaying her gardener while she searched for companionship.

Lea wondered if that was how she was going to end up, perhaps widowed and alone, or worse yet, never married at all and doting on some little dog, or growing exotic orchids only she could appreciate. Edith had lived on Chester Street for over five years and before that resided in Cameron, where she'd retired as a librarian. The information on Mrs. Simms also indicated she'd been a bit of a traveler and had written several articles for her local newspaper about trips to Thailand, China, what was then the Soviet Union, and Africa. She'd even canoed down the Amazon. Mrs. Simms may have lost her husband, but not her zest for living. Nothing much else seemed interesting about Mrs. Simms. If Lea did the math correctly, Mrs. Simms was 66, though she appeared much older and feebler than that.

So, that left Philemon Jenkins. There was no question in her mind that the gardener was a retired killer. The key word was *retired.* And what about the child Bouncer? Lea reached over on the table where she'd set the red rubber ball earlier and rolled it between her fingers. Finally, she poured herself another cup of tea and sank down into her flowered mauve recliner, lifting the footrest so her poor throbbing leg could ease somewhat. She pressed the remote to her CD player until the strands of Pachelbel's *Canon in D Major* drifted through the air. Its beautiful rise and fall of music, sounding just like a waterfall, washed over her, and Lea half-shut her eyes, allowing herself to drift off into a semi-trance hoping she'd discover how the murders of Ashley Peebles, Thad Fisher, and Connie Judson were somehow connected.

Chapter 19

One of Lea's biggest flaws, or perhaps virtues, was her tenacity and desire to figure out the truth about everything. A man now rotted in jail for a young woman's murder of twenty-five years ago and another sat in the Monroe County jail, innocent, at least this time. Finally relaxed after thirty minutes of classical music and tea, she allowed herself to listen to Thayne's interview with Luke Cambridge. Nick's rich, tenor voice filled the tape, questioning the gruff convict.

"Mr. Cambridge, two years ago you sent an initial letter to Jeremy Fox regarding the Ashley Peebles murder, and I wondered if you would be willing to talk to me now about the case?"

Luke snorted. "I don't know why I'd help you. He dumped me flat after indicating he had a lead that could probably prove my innocence. After Fox found out I didn't have any money, he dropped my case faster than you can say *new little Porsche*."

"Now, what would make you think that, Mr.

Cambridge?"

"His secretary called, one Maria Jennings. I remember she had the sweetest voice in the universe, but nothing she said made me feel good. She stated her boss didn't feel my appeal was winnable because the evidence was too circumstantial. She suggested that I might want to try Walters Investigative Services in Modesto as if I had the money to consult that pricey firm."

Lea's finger slammed down the stop button. Secretary? The only secretary her father had ever possessed was first her mother, and later, her. Her dad had hated secretaries, convinced they messed with his things and broke confidences. So who in the hell was this Maria Jennings? She steadied herself and pressed the button again

"I'm sorry to hear that," soothed Nick's voice. Of course, he couldn't know the secretary was bogus.

"Then I heard that him and his son were murdered not three weeks after I contacted them."

"Their murderers were never apprehended, and it was believed they were wiped out by the mob," verified Nick.

"Oh well," snorted Luke. "Couldn't happen to a nicer pair."

Lea winced. She'd had her own personal grievances with her family, but it still hurt to hear others berate them.

"So, why are *you* here?"

"I'm reopening your case, because the ex-mayor of

Monroe and his mistress were killed in a manner similar to Ashley Peebles."

"The ex-mayor? You mean Thad Fisher?"

"You knew him?"

"Sure. We all *knew* him."

"And just what do you mean by that?"

"Thad Fisher really liked the girls, particularly the young, eager Hispanic ones who were looking out for a handout or an easy ride. He used to visit the encampment near Pike's Creek to see a couple of the girls. They were only teens, most of them, some as young as fifteen, but for him the younger the better. I heard he bought them some real fancy stuff if they pleased him. Pig." Luke spat distinctly enough for Lea to imagine the splat.

"Now, this would be ten years before he was mayor. He was elected nearly thirteen years after the Ashley Peebles murder," stated Nick, his voice giving no indication how he felt about Luke's information.

"Yeah, but he got elected anyway, didn't he." Luke didn't bother to hide his disdain. "Guess his wife never found out or just didn't care."

Lea remembered the venom in Mrs. Fisher's voice and understood it better. Fifteen-year-old girls. How pathetic.

"And what about your boss, Mr. Montanari? Did he know about Mr. Fisher's conquests?" asked Nick.

"Of course he did. In fact, he encouraged the girls. Said

everyone had to look after themselves and find their own way; that they had a right to make money any way they chose. He was suspected of visiting a couple of girls himself." That interesting tidbit of information made Lea want to dance a jig. Too bad her leg was killing her.

"Was Ashley Peebles a regular at Pike's and perhaps a special friend of the ex-mayor's?"

There was a long pause until Luke said tersely. "Maybe. Ashley itched to get away from her fundamentalist parents; said they were stifling her. She wanted things. You know . . . like pretty trinkets, the kind her parents wouldn't allow her. I was going to marry her when I got some cash, and I would have, too, if Deke hadn't gotten in the way."

"You're suggesting that Deke ruined her plans?"

"And mine as well. Deke kind of . . . Well, he pandered some of the girls and recruited them for Thad Fisher and a couple of head honchos; you know, the well-respected men of the community with money. When Ashley started coming to the camp to seek a piece of the action, well . . ."

"Well what?"

"She swore to me she didn't, that the baby was mine, but Deke, he said she'd slept with that jerk. He was soft and flabby like a baby, always flashing his money around because he had a rich wife. Thought he had a right to prowl the camp because he and the Montanari boys had been friends."

"Thad was friends with the Montanari boys?"

"Yeah, but I guess even their dad couldn't buy them out of Nam, and like so many others, fifty thousand, I guess, they kicked the bucket. Their old man must have liked Thad Fisher real well because he treated him like some kind of royalty. I always thought that it was strange, the way he would drive him around, showing Fisher the fields and calling the girls over to the car."

"Most of the people who lived in the Pike's Creek camp were Hispanic, weren't they?"

"Of course. Most migrant workers are."

"So, why were you and Deke there? Neither of you were Hispanic."

"I was an artist, still am, for that matter, but it's hard to get anyone to show your work in this area. I was just doing some summer work to help pay the bills. Anthony Montanari didn't pay well, but he paid regular."

"So, why do you think the court found you guilty of murder?"

"It was mostly on his word."

"You mean Anthony Montanari or Thad Fisher's?"

"It was Montanari Sr., that bastard. Said that Deke and I killed her after she ran off and had some wetback's baby. That was ridiculous. Everyone knew I loved her even though Deke said the baby was Thad Fisher's. And then . . . "he snorted. "And then Deke said he'd slept with her, too!"

"And you attacked him in court?"

"Yeah. Cooked my own goose."

"Did Jeremy Fox know all this information you're relaying to me now?"

Lea tensed.

"Why, sure. I mailed him all the stuff and told him to contact the authorities regarding the car."

"The Buick near the murder scene?"

"That's right. I'd told the police, but they brushed it off. I saw Montanari's car on that gravel road, not a quarter of a mile from where my Ashley was killed."

"So Ashley had her baby?"

Luke's voice noticeably changed. "Yeah, but it died. She said the poor little guy was premature.

She still had about six weeks to go, and at the very end of her pregnancy, was acting awful strange. Ashley said she had to provide for the future and figured she knew how. I swore I'd take care of her and offered to marry her. I wanted to take her to Seattle. I had a lead at a graphic art firm where my second cousin was employed, but Ashley wanted everything right away. She laughed and said she figured I couldn't even take care of myself. I never killed her, Mr. Thayne. I loved her and still miss her."

A long silence ensued. Finally, Luke asked, in a voice not much louder than a whisper. "You believe me?"

"Yes."

The tape ended abruptly, and Lea had to agree with

Nick. She believed him. So, Thad Fisher had been friends with both the Montanari boys and their dad. Very interesting. She glanced at the flowerpot clock hanging beside her refrigerator. 9:25 p.m. Not too late to pay a visit to the grieving widow, was it?

The visits of the ex-mayor to the Pike's Creek Camp and the fact that Mayor Fisher had been friends with the Montanari boys filled her mind as she drove cautiously through the well-lit streets to Trish Fisher's house. It seemed strange to her that Anthony Montanari had remained such close friends with Thad after his own children were deceased. Anthony Montanari must be at least 15 years Thad Fisher's senior, so what was the basis of their friendship? Using her cell, she dialed the expensive residence. A crisp male voice answered the phone, and Lea paused momentarily, taken back.

"I'd like to speak with Mrs. Fisher, please."

"May I say who is calling?"

Lea made a sincere effort to rein in her abrupt and impulsive nature and began as pleasantly as she could. "This is Lea Fox. Inspector Nick Thayne and I are currently working on her late husband's case, and I was wondering if I could speak to her."

"I see," the voice somehow sounded vaguely familiar but Lea couldn't place it. A muffled sound indicated the man had placed his hand over the receiver to shield his conversation though Lea could vaguely decipher the higher tones of a woman and his garbled response. The connection cleared, and Mrs. Fisher's carefully modulated voice answered.

"Ah, Ms. Fox, how good of you to call. I've been expecting you'd have more questions for me about now."

"I'm not sure how appropriate it is to speak over the phone, Mrs. Fisher, and wondered if I could drop by?"

Lea peered out her windshield. A breeze lifted the high eucalyptus tree branches to her left. She'd parked no more than a block from the widow's house.

"It's quite late. But, of course, Ms. Fox. Come right over."

An unfamiliar sports car squatted before Thad Fisher's spacious and elegant home, a sleek Mercedes convertible. Lea automatically memorized the unusual license plate—RRM DOLL. She knocked on the wide door, and the same placid maid answered, her face a model of discretion as Lea was lead into the library.

Trish Fisher rose, rustling in black mourning silk, her blonde hair smoothed perfectly above pearl teardrop studs. A matching coil of lustrous pearls surrounded her pale neck, and her hand, extended to take Lea's small one, felt stiff and cold.

"That was quick. So, where's your counterpart?" she asked, a touch of venom in her voice. If Lea didn't know any better, she'd think the lady resented Thayne's absence. Nick had that effect on women.

"I gave him the night off." Her snippy answer obviously perturbed the lady, but she had the good manners not to retort. Lea, in her typical manner, took that opportunity to jump right in. She removed her F & H and launched her attack.

"I ran into Anthony Montanari Sr. at the mortuary. He apparently wanted to say goodbye to your husband before the funeral next week."

Trish blanched, her ramrod straight back jerking. "Indeed. He's no friend of ours."

"Oh, really? I'm positive I heard otherwise, since he financed your husband's bid for mayor years ago."

Trish swallowed painfully and sank down on the expensive black leather couch that matched the Japanese end tables perfectly. She retorted stiffly.

"Let me put it another way. He's no friend of mine. The man's crude, uncultured, and totally lacking in scruples. He might be the wealthiest man in Monroe, but certainly lacks class. He remains on the outer fringe of our social group, his money always welcome, his obnoxious behavior not."

"Was your husband viewed in the same way?"

"Believe it or not, Ms. Fox, my husband was a graduate of UCLA with a degree in business administration. Thad actually had a fine brain until he let his dick determine his destiny. You've heard of sexual addicts, of course. My textbook-case husband couldn't get enough variety *or* satisfaction."

Lea led her back to the subject of the Montanari's. "And are Anthony Montanari's wife and family considered on the 'fringe' of the upper strata?"

Trish's aristocratic face softened. "No. Ruth Montanari is a fine woman; her charitable works are not only well known in Monroe but throughout the Big Valley."

"So, you work with her?"

"We both belong to the Monroe Assistance League. She spearheaded a fundraiser that clothed over two hundred migrant workers' children. I believe that achievement is exceptional in itself. Her kind, generous nature is the sort that rubs off on you. I know it certainly has on me."

"But you have no sympathy or liking for her husband?" Mrs. Fisher's exquisite dress had probably cost her more than Lea's monthly house payment.

"Even a woman such as you knows that women of our class are often forced to marry men our fathers choose. Ruth was no exception. She was beautiful and intelligent, but had no control over her own destiny. Obediently, she married the man her father chose for her, and in turn, gave him six children in nineteen years. She unfortunately seems committed to staying with a man who blames her because he has no grandsons at the present time." Again, that disturbing, reoccurring theme regarding the importance of carrying on the male line reared its head.

"Couldn't Anthony possible obtain some of those precious grandsons from his remaining son or daughters?"

"That is highly doubtful. In fact," she mocked, "it's *inconceivable*."

"And what do you mean by that?"

"Let's just say that Anthony's children dislike him so much that they all refuse to grant him what he desires most—a grandson. You reap what you sow."

"Just what is it about Anthony, besides his bad manners, you dislike so much?"

"How much time do you have, Ms. Fox? To start with he is a bore, a womanizer, and a child and wife abuser. He's never given a cent to anyone in need even though he has money coming out of his ears. He needs Ruth to soften his rough edges, but abuses her because of her generous nature. No wonder every one of his daughters ran away from him and his sons joined the military to escape."

"They weren't drafted?"

"No, both boys joined the military though certain they'd be sent to Vietnam."

"You knew his older sons?"

"By reputation only. They were wild and uncouth—just like their father. The daughters and youngest boy took more after their mother. I believe Anthony luckily neglected them except for his routine verbal and physical abuse."

"His abuse caused the three sisters to leave town?"

asked Lea.

"The town? You mean the state! They moved as far away as they could to get out of his control. One even became a nun to prevent him controlling her unborn children. He's a tyrant, Ms. Fox, and that's why I despise him as well as my husband, who, while a man of many faults, knew just what kind of man he was dealing with."

"So, you're saying Thad snapped at the hand that fed him?"

Trish Fisher bristled. "I beg your pardon! My husband accepted donations for his campaigns, but Anthony Montanari never controlled him or influenced any of his decisions. In fact, I believe it was more the other way around, like Thad held some sort of sway over Anthony."

"Were they business partners?" Lea's fingers flew over the keys of the F & H.

"They may have had some investments together. Though God knows how legal. Thad always seemed to have enough money."

"And what about Anthony's last remaining son?"

"Rudolph." Mrs. Fisher swallowed. "He deals with his controlling father the best way he can, I suspect."

"And he's never married."

"No, but that's no crime, Ms. Fox. You're not married, either, I take it, or ever shall be?" Lea ignored the barb. "And besides, what connection does all this have to my husband's murder?"

"Did Anthony know Connie?"

"You mean that trollop of my husband's mistress?"

"Her body was *discovered* in one of his fields."

Mrs. Fisher crossed one slender leg over the other. "That means nothing. The Montanari's own thousands of prime acreage around here. Their property borders every side of this town. Go five feet in any one direction, and you'll run into one of their stinking fields."

"I just thought it was interesting to note that Ashley Peebles' body was also found on their property. Did your husband know her?"

The muscles worked in her throat, and Trish Fisher's voice turned cold. "I believe he might have known *of* her, and I'm certain he was acquainted with her murderers. He used to visit the farm workers on insurance business."

"Insurance business?"

"Yes, he was an insurance broker before he became mayor. Thad was a Jack of all trades."

"And were you aware of your husband's infidelities even then?"

No hint of a blush tinted the hardened woman's face. "No, I only became aware of them just before he became mayor. I had the misfortune to walk in on one of his *campaign briefings*; he was missing his *briefs* while *briefing* his secretary."

"I'm sorry to hear that."

"I wasn't, and it made it quite easy for me to never again feel obligated to perform my wifely duties. Besides, I didn't want to *catch* anything."

"One other question, Mrs. Fisher. Do you really believe Philemon Jenkins murdered your husband?"

Trish stiffened and smoothed the fine fabric of her expensive dress. "I have my suspicions he may have."

"Why?"

"This is something I didn't really want people to know, but now . . . My husband had a gambling problem. I've tried to keep that information out of the newspapers, but since I'm certain everything will come out in the papers tomorrow, and Richard Rollins can't shield me much longer, I might as well tell you. I believe that when my husband fell behind on payments to bookies, I'm afraid they may have hired a professional to take care of their *little* problem."

So, at least Anthony and Trish had their stories straight.

"But I thought you said Thad always had enough money. Now you indicate he couldn't pay his debts."

"I believe he was *generally* lucky in his gambling, but this once, perhaps fell behind."

"Hmm. I'm a bit confused—it all seems so *drastic*. The loan sharks certainly wouldn't receive any payback if he were dead. And why have a hit man kill the mistress as well? It doesn't make any sense."

“I’m not sure they meant to kill him. From what I can ascertain about my husband’s demise, I believe they tortured him and his girlfriend in hopes of gaining information about how to access his funds. In fact, I’m positive about it.”

“And how could you be so sure?” asked Lea, leaning forward.

“Because cutting off a finger is an oriental threat. I was raised in San Francisco and that particular calling card was often left as a warning to those who didn’t pay their bills. I’m sure that Thad and his mistress were persuasively warned and when they refused to pay up, things got out of hand. Philemon Jenkins was a hit man in Chicago. He was hired by the Asian loan sharks and did his job.”

Lea sighed. “Everyone sure knows a great deal about information that’s generally kept from the public. I wonder how that can be?”

“I have friends,” snapped Mrs. Fisher.

“Your Chief Rollins certainly agrees with you about Philemon’s role.”

“I don’t know if that’s what Chief Rollins believes, but after I told him all I knew about Thad’s gambling problem, he found evidence to support my assertion.”

“So, *you* where the one who told him about Philemon?”

“Not exactly. The gardener’s name and previous occupation were mentioned when I gave my statement, and it all seemed to fit.”

Lea changed tactics. She had been right about Chief Rollins and Trish Fisher, but there was nothing to be gained by indicating she knew about their relationship

"Whose car is that outside, Mrs. Fisher?"

"Just a friend trying to help me through hard times," she answered stiffly.

"Oh?" Lea let the monosyllable dangle.

"The vehicle belongs to Rudolph Montanari. He brings his family's condolences."

"I see."

Trish Fisher made an exaggerated yawn. "Do you have any more questions for me, Mrs. Fox? It's late, and I need to obtain some rest, since I know some rather unsavory information will be exhibited in the paper tomorrow. Unfortunately, a woman is always judged by her husband's actions, so I need to prepare myself."

The maid materialized from nowhere, and Lea found herself led out. The Mercedes coupe had disappeared.

She'd barely strapped herself in when her cell phone sounded with Beethoven's fifth.

"I have a piece of information for you, Lea." said Steven. "Connie Judson died from formaldehyde poisoning just like everyone expected, but there's something else that's even more interesting. During the examination, I noticed that Connie has a nasty bite on her upper arm."

The snarling animal from the Collins house

immediately sprung to Lea's mind.

"Just what kind of bite?" she asked excitedly.

"Human. Most likely an adult male, since the jaw and teeth show mature development. I swabbed the wound and hope for some DNA from the culprit's saliva—but that's a long shot. I have Philemon Jenkins' DNA just in case."

How dreadful Thad and Connie's last hours must have been. This revelation pointed more and more towards some cannibalistic serial killer on the loose.

"Thanks, Steven."

"Um, Lea. Where's Thayne?"

"Running around just like me, trying to solve this case before Chief Rollins tosses us out."

"I don't like that you're wandering around on your own, he scolded. "Don't forget to pack your gun. And promise me you won't interview any of your suspects alone. This killer's as dangerous as a tiger in a kitten's suit."

"Oh, come on. You know how much I love cats. I'll be talking to ya, Steven."

Chapter 20

"You're looking loads better," observed Nick.

"You're full of shit, but thanks anyway." Roger shifted in the giant king-sized bed and frowned at the broth Susan had strategically placed on the wicker side table.

"So, any insights about this case, Roger?"

"Just that I need to get out of this bed before you and your partner kill each other."

"She's not my partner!" Nick retorted.

"Oh, really? You could have fooled me. Rollins may not have called her in because he hates her, but I'm glad you've teamed up. Lea Fox has a first-class brain."

"And a first-class attitude."

"Had a tough life. Just like you. The tougher the life, the better the investigator. That's why the two of you are better than me. I've got it too good."

"Now, *who's* full of crap?"

"Well, I'd like to be *full* of something. Susan's damn near going to starve me! I want something edible to eat, not this stinking broth!" He shouted it loud enough for his patient wife to hear in the nearby kitchen.

"I'll sneak you in a greasy burger piled high with chili and onions, just like you like it."

"It would likely probably kill me." He leaned over and took the bowl, slurping loudly. "Not bad for broth. So, let me get this straight. Philemon's in jail charged with Thad's and Connie's murders. He's most likely an ex-hit man. You can't figure out the connection between the murders except that both Thad's and Connie's fingers were severed and Ashley's ring was found on Thad's finger. The word *Phile* was carved on a tree. Anthony Montanari has some connection to all this, and Connie's cousin is the only one we know didn't do it. Oh, and there's some kid creeping around the Collins' yard who likes to play ball, and something about Christmas carols. Have I got it all?"

"A stinking pile of dung in the Collins back yard, and Philemon didn't do it."

"How can you be so sure?"

A strange expression passed over Nick's face before he answered. "I'm positive he's retired and reformed. Fox thinks it's true, as well."

"So you *are* listening to her."

"Only between fits of rage."

Roger laughed and suddenly clutched his side. "Yowzer that hurts! Jeez, I feel like a million years old."

“You look it, too.

“And some say you’re charming. You and Lea get over to Chester Street first thing in the morning and wrap up this Bouncer connection. And interview Mrs. Simms again. Maybe she witnessed Philemon doing something suspicious. Footwork, Nick. That’s the key. Anything else?”

“Yeah. What have you heard about the oldest Montanari boys?”

“Just that they were real pricks. Anthony Jr. was the worst, though Randy was almost as bad. Dad must have rescued them a dozen times from messes they got in. It’s a shame they were killed in Nam, though. Don’t know much else.”

“They were both dead when Ashley was killed right?”

“By at least five years.”

Nick squinted and thought hard. “And Ashley’s son was never found, though Deke swore the baby was buried outside the encampment.”

Roger thought for a moment. “Lots of animals, coyotes, and whatnot. Baby could have been dug up and dragged away.”

“There’s something about the baby that bothers me.”

“You having one of your *premonitions* again? I just wanted you to know that I never bought that shit about your mob connections or the payoffs. Your gift rescued that little girl.”

"It's not a gift."

"Denial's good. It's the cornerstone of my existence. . So, if the baby bugs you, do your thing. There don't seem to be many other leads in this blasted case besides the possible identification of the reindeer as Rudolph Montanari. Rollins will have Jenkins nailed to the cross for this if you don't come up with something quick—and that just ain't right. How you doing with Lea?"

"One thing I can say is that Fox doesn't mince words. She doesn't have the manners God gave a chipmunk."

"Sharp as a tack, though," chuckled Roger.

"Pisses me off and enjoys doing it."

"It's because she doesn't care what you think," said Roger. "Lea doesn't give a hoot if you
believe she's smart or attractive or brusque. She is who she is, and if a man doesn't like it, tough shit. That's what I like about her. Lea gets results. And *that's* what you really need in a partner."

"She's not my partner or *going* to be my partner."

"Well, she's the closest thing to a partner you're gonna get while I'm strapped to this bed. What's Lea up to now?"

"Listening to Luke's tape and going over the files on everybody. She's has this nifty little contraption she calls the F & H with the tiniest little keyboard. Has motives, crime scenerios, everything."

"Her *real* partner. Well, I have a sweet fact for her to put into her little gadget. Rumor has it that about 12 years ago, Richard Rollins had a little fling with Trish Fisher."

"You're positive about that?"

"As positive as a good rumor mill can be. Have Lea punch it in. Maybe she'll pick something up. Steven Koh helping you out?"

"Yeah, but he's an odd one."

"Don't let Susan hear you say that, though I'd have to agree. Steven's a hard one to fathom, but a first-class coroner. Susan told me once that he followed us out here to Monroe from the Coast because his heart was broken when his best friend won the girl he loved. He's pretty close-mouthed about it. Keeps to himself mostly. You seen his *lab*?"

"Talk about home entertainment centers."

Roger chuckled weakly. "Gave me a framed Brazilian butterfly once for my birthday. Kinda pretty, but odd, you know. Not sure where to hang it."

"Just one more thing, Roger. What can you tell me about Bernard?"

"Bernard?"

"Fox's *boy*friend?"

Roger seemed confused. "So, she has a boyfriend. Actually, I think Steven mentioned him once. Glad to hear it, though he must be a tough nut to put up with her."

Susan appeared at the door. "It's late, Nick. Roger's

got to get some rest."

"I'll be in touch."

"Good. Oh, and Nick. Take your vitamins. You'll need them if you're going to spend much time with Lea Fox." He gave what could only be called a giggle and Nick itched to clobber him.

Monday Morning

The phone rang shrilly at exactly 5:55 a.m. the next morning. It had been a wild night, and Nick searched vainly for the phone amid the chaos of his room as the bitter sound refused to go away. Chastity, the curvy blonde, purred and handed him the phone.

"You are a popular man," she said in a throaty whisper and slinked from the bed in her all-together. The Moral Right had it all wrong. Barbie girls really did exist, even if it took liposuctions, tummy tucks, and a boob job to get it.

He growled into the phone, "This'd better be good."

"It's Fox. Get your lazy butt out of bed and down to my office. We've been summoned by Chief Rollins to his office at eight, and we need to synchronize our stories."

"You're kidding. He called you this early?"

"No, actually, it was about twenty minutes ago, but I decided to be nice and let you sleep until six."

"Then your watch is fast," he snapped as Chastity

glided back to the bed. This was going to be hard to explain to the amazingly energetic blonde. The waitress glinted blue-gray eyes at him, and suddenly Nick was glad for the opportunity to leave. She appeared the clingy type.

"I'll be right there," he responded, making sure he gave a pained expression for Chastity's benefit. It was clear she wasn't a natural blonde.

"I can hardly wait," chirped Fox and hung up.

Nick gave his best little boy grimace and hang-dog face; it worked nine times out of ten. By the time he was done explaining his unwelcome duties to the comely waitress, she was offering to whip him up a quick something to fortify him for his grueling morning.

Nick *was* late. He strolled in at seven-fifteen, satiated in all ways. Lea had observed that expression on her brother's face a hundred times before and had little patience for it today.

"You're tardy," she growled.

"It just couldn't be helped. I had to have some breakfast. I need nourishment."

"Yeah, and I'm Pope Paul. So, are you religious by any chance, Thayne? Do you go to Mass regularly to confess your sins?"

"I used to, but since it only made me feel better once, I gave it up as a waste of time."

"You swine," she said, meaning it.

"Only you would think that. My lady friends get what

they expect and are satisfied. Are you satisfied with your life, Lea Fox?"

"Only when my mortgage and car are paid off. I *need* this check."

"Like it's *me* who has the problem with Chief Rollins. So, what's up?"

For fifteen minutes Lea relayed everything down to the last detail, the F & H clicking slightly. Finally, finished with her task, she added the punch lines.

"The chief was screaming on the phone this morning. Said Trish Fisher wasn't impressed by my manners. And . . ." she paused significantly. "Philemon uses a lip product called *Solar Gel*, and a smeared fingerprint on the Cream Soda connects him directly to Connie's finger. The blood on the snippers was found to be Philemon's. Said he remembered getting a scratch when he was planting some rose starts, but I'm doubtful that's gonna help him. Thus, our summons to Rollins' office at eight sharp."

"The chief knows you visited her?" Nick screwed up his face. Why didn't Fox just let him do the interviewing? Her abrasive approach was going to get them nowhere fast.

"Yup. Indicated I was harassing Thad's widow and should apologize to her. He's downright smug about the lip balm. Things don't look great for poor Philemon. He mentioned I'll have lots of free time later in the day to catch up on my knitting."

Nick peered out her very clean office window at the two heavily laden shelves of African Violets and what looked like a couple of hot pink geraniums leaning towards the sun. "Fox," he mused as she collected her F & H. "You know how to avoid getting fired, don't you?"

"How?" grunted Lea. Today she was dressed in a teal paisley pants suit that made her look figureless and dumpy and twenty years older than he knew her to be. Heavy-duty black pumps that reminded him of the kind worn by the sinister Sister Agnes at his primary school encased her small feet. Nick, in contrast, wore a sharp gray blazer over a spotless white shirt tucked into smoky trousers.

"You don't show up."

Fox peered thoughtfully at him through her thick glasses before nodding. She plucked up her mobile phone and switched it off. "I'm currently unavailable."

Nick grinned, flashing his perfect white teeth and following her around the office as she brewed her coffee-black tea.

"There's one common denominator in all three murders besides the severed fingers."

"Every person murdered knew Montanari," she responded, dunking her tea bag a few more times.

"That's right."

"So, where does Bouncer fit in?"

"I'm not sure," said Nick watching her squeeze the

last drops of water out of her spent teabag. “But we’re not going to find out by sitting here.”

Chester Street was peaceful as usual when they arrived at the cul-de-sac at exactly 8:00 a.m. Lea could visualize Chief Rollins sitting in his crammed office waiting futilely to chew them out before booting them off the case. She, for one, wasn’t ready to be axed just yet. Nick punched in the code supplied by Mr. Collins and waited for the wrought iron gates to swing open. The expansive lawn gleamed in the early morning air as he pulled Lea’s Mazda inside. It had been a major argument as to whose car they should use. They’d finally come to an agreement that they would alternate vehicles, with Nick as the designated driver. He’d had to scoot the seat all the way back just to accommodate his long legs.

The lawn sparkled from its early morning watering and the mauve roses glimmered beautifully against the reflection of the recently cleaned windows. Nick parked the car around the side nearest the garage and emerged from the small car with difficulty. A strange snarling sound issuing from the backyard caused both Lea and Nick to freeze in their tracks.

“Did you hear that?” he whispered.

“Yes,” breathed Fox.

She led the way, limping badly, and pushed open the side gate, which luckily was still unlatched. It opened without a squeak, and the pair tiptoed quietly down the walkway.

Unfortunately, Lea's uneven pace didn't allow for a very silent advance, and she scuffed the brick walkway.

"Shush," Nick hissed.

Lea resisted the urge to slap him. Mr. Buff couldn't possibly understand an injury like hers. The smell of feces once again assailed her nose as they paused below a low bottlebrush shrub at the entrance of the rear garden and stared in stupefied horror.

The metal stake Lea had noted earlier now held a heavy metal chain to which was leashed a snarling creature. Clothed in a loose brown robe, it ran frantically to the end of its tether, tossing a stick into the air and trying to catch it between claws and teeth. An elderly, balding man nodded in a plastic patio chair, his bristled chin sunk upon his chest, which rose and fell in deep sleep. Nick grabbed her arm, holding her back. The chained creature was no beast but a child!

The boy or girl, or whatever it was, instantly stopped its play, having somehow recognized their approach. As it turned towards her, Lea could not contain a gasp of horror. A dwarfish creature, whose giant, misshapen head was covered in bristling red hair cut obscenely short, stared back. The dwarf was so obese that his eyes were simply slits inside great rolls of flesh. His panting mouth hung open, the drool staining the brown cotton material of his formless gown.

The dwarf's legs were short and stumpy, but that didn't seem to hinder quick movement. The creature issued a blubbering sound, his fickle moods changing in an instant. He suddenly barked like a dog, and the old man jerked violently, his head snapping up. The seated man fastened light-green eyes made blurry by alcohol and age upon them.

"Christ," he shrieked. "You're . . . you're trespassing!" He clutched the white plastic chair and rose feebly. "I'm calling the police," he announced shakily.

Nick made a start as if to move forward, but Lea restrained his arm.

"Wait," she ordered quietly. She reached inside her awful paisley jacket and pulled out the red rubber ball. The slits obscuring the boy's eyes widened, appearing surprisingly coherent.

"We're with the police," stated Nick and pulled out the warrant from yesterday's entry. The old man, apparently more nimble than he first appeared, lunged for the boy and yanked at his chain.

"I swear I only chain him up when I sleep. If I don't, he destroys everything or tries to escape. You can see he lacks the ability to take care of himself." He quickly unlatched the chain from the collar now apparent upon the dwarf's neck and backed away, fearful of how the situation appeared to the detectives. The freed child/man instantly scurried to the high wall, making small useless jumps to escape just like a dog would.

"Bouncer," called out Nick tentatively, remembering

Philemon's term for his hidden ball partner. The dwarf stopped his frantic pawing of the fence and cocked his over-sized head to listen intently. So obese he appeared to lack a neck, his collar, barely recognizable between the folds of fat and the loose fitting cotton robe became apparent.

"How do you know his nickname?" sputtered the elderly man, who was as thin as the dwarf was fat. He moved quickly towards the drooling, disheveled creature, and suddenly, Bouncer lunged, hugging the old man's legs and nearly toppling him over.

"Philemon, the gardener from next door, told us about him," said Nick cocking his head at Lea. "Toss him the ball."

Bouncer's tiny eyes watched them through narrow slits. Lea tossed the ball high and the dwarf leaped, catching the ball in teeth which appeared more pointed than blunt. A chuckle, almost normal sounding, rose up as drool slathered the red ball.

"It's not what you think," said the old man straightening. He appeared very tall, though his actual height was hard to determine next to the dwarf. "You need to understand that Bouncer is simple-minded and unfortunately can harm others as well as himself. He behaves like an animal and isn't even house-broken. We just couldn't bear to put him in a home. I'm an old man, and I can hardly take care of him or myself anymore." The last was a plea.

Lea noted that at least four of the creature's fingers

were loaded with thick golden rings. “What’s his real name?”

The scarecrow man blanched. “His name is Charles, or Charlie, but he never responds to that. We’ve played ball for years and have talked so often about the toy bouncing that one day he pointed to himself and said Bouncer, so Bouncer he is.”

“He talks?” asked Nick in disbelief. The creature’s IQ couldn’t be very high.

“Only a little, much like a three year old. He mostly points, and after all this time I know instinctively what he wants.”

“Why is he hidden here?” said Nick, suddenly disgusted by the whole scene.

“I would like you to imagine that you’d given birth to a child such as this. His parents were embarrassed,” said the old man, who suddenly looked incredibly proud. “His family depends on me to take care of him, and I cater to all his needs and make sure that he is kept safe. We all felt it was a better option than putting him into some institution.”

“Are you related to him?” asked Nick, trying to see if there were any facial similarities, but could recognize none in the rolls of fat. Bouncer was now licking the ball.

“Distantly,” said the old man evasively.

“And what’s your name?”

“Murdoch. Eddie Murdoch, or Edward, for your records. So, you gonna arrest me?” he straightened even taller and for a man so thin and frail he suddenly looked as gallant as a soldier who's done their duty unashamedly.

"I don't know," asked Nick. "Should I?"

He watched the elderly man's anxious face intently, but before Edward Murdoch could answer, the ball suddenly sailed into the air. Nick reached up a quick hand and caught it as expertly as a professional baseball player. The dwarf shuffled forward on stubbly legs and giggled obscenely, stretching out short arms equipped with oversized hands. Nick tossed it back to him, and once again the man, who Thayne realized was far older than a child but who still possessed the eternal youth of the mentally handicapped, caught the ball in his teeth. Though clearly his coordination was poor, Bouncer could still catch the sphere like a faithful retriever. The trio watched as he laboriously retrieved the ball with his left hand and threw it up into the air again.

"Good," said Nick, catching the ball nimbly. He tossed it further this time and Bouncer rushed to capture the ball using his hands much like an ape might. It had rolled near the dung heap and the proximity of the putrid pile must have compelled Bouncer, for suddenly he squatted, a yellow stream running amongst the stained leaves. Lea fought her nausea and embarrassment. Nick however, was not remotely embarrassed, only angry.

"I believe that the Child Welfare Department would not appreciate the situation here. I also strongly suspect that you may be a witness to a double murder and have chosen not to report it."

"I witnessed nothing," said Eddie Murdoch between clenched teeth stained yellow from years of cigarette smoking.

"So . . . can you explain the limo?" said Fox.

Eddie Murdoch straightened his bony shoulders. "I'm not saying anything without a lawyer." He hobbled back to the white patio chair and sank down, folding his hands across his lap. Bouncer waddled over and squatted beside him, bouncing the ball up and down. Nick flipped open his cell phone and activated the line. There were six messages, all from the police station, but he didn't even bother to retrieve them, instead directly dialing Chief Rollins. Even *he* couldn't ignore this new development.

Chapter 21

Pure chaos erupted at the Collins residence as the police, and later Social Services, converged upon the house. Eddie confessed that Bouncer had been housed in a basement accessible through the broom closet, but refused to say much more. Lea let Thayne deal with all of it in his smooth, efficient way, deciding it was much better to leave the still-irate chief to him. Bouncer remained passive enough until the African-American social worker decided to try and lure him into the waiting vehicle using a candy bar as an enticement. Without warning, he lunged at the social worker, imbedding his teeth in the shoulder of her cream-colored suit.

She shrieked as two policemen wrestled the dwarf away from the stricken government worker.

"Stop it," shouted Eddie at the top of his lungs. "You're hurting him!" He shoved Officer Guzman to the ground, and grabbing the dwarf, shoved Bouncer safely behind him.

"Get away or I'll kill you!"

“Take it easy,” said Dwayne Matthews, the most senior of Chief Rollins’ force. “We’re not going to hurt him.”

“You touch him, and I’ll smash your face in. Don’t come near us. I’m warning you.”

The social worker held a hand to her bleeding shoulder. “He’s like an animal,” she cried. “Look what he did to me!”

“Just take it easy. Randy, you get behind Mr. Murdock. Use the candy bar as bait.”

Officer Phelps did as he was instructed. “Here you go,” he coaxed, holding the chocolate nut bar in plain view of the dwarf. Charlie began to inch away from his protective caregiver.

“Nooo!” screamed Eddie. “Leave my boy alone! Come any closer and I’ll kill you with my bare hands. Nobody’s gonna take either of us away. This is our home. Back off! Back off, I tell you, or I’ll break your neck! Pigs, pigs! All of you! Leave us alone!” So intent was he on facing off Officer’s Phelps and Matthews that he didn’t see Enrique Guzman rise from the sidewalk and maneuver himself behind the irate man. The solid police officer pushed Charlie to the side where he cowered sniveling and shaking, and finally managed to grab the older man in a bear hug. Handcuffs flashed and suddenly Eddie was a prisoner.

An irate Eddie continued his verbal abuse of Monroe’s finest as the bleeding woman sought medical care and Charlie was restrained with handcuffs as well. Bouncer sent up a howling chorus that eerily split the morning calm.

Chief Rollins froze, listening intently to Eddie Murdock's diatribe as Lea watched the chief study the strange child/man with the oddest expression flitting over his florid face.

Thayne sidled up to her. "Katie, the little girl down the street, mentioned a light in the second story and a ghost with wild hair howling at the moon. I thought it only a child's fantasy."

"But it wasn't. After that little scene with the social worker, it's clear where Connie's tooth marks came from."

"It places Thad's mistress here, alright. Our chief appears about ready to explode. I don't think things are going his way." The police crew was snapping countless photos of the chain and dung pile. Nick tapped Lea's arm as the chief approached. "Why don't you take this opportunity to wander off and find where our little friend was housed? I'll deal with him."

Lea made her way back into the house. Once again inside the beautifully designed house, she recognized that all the expensive trimmings were just superficial trappings in a house designed as a prison. She headed towards the broom closet under the stairwell, and after searching diligently, finally discovered how the carefully designed door handle could have fooled the casual observer. Fox jerked the door open, revealing a short flight of steps.

Lea didn't know what she had expected; a dungeon, perhaps, equipped with a grim metal cot complete with chains or a cell to house the animalistic dwarf. Instead, surprise transformed her face, as she realized the huge room below stairs had been converted into a castle, painstakingly designed for its inmate's comfort. Bouncer obviously loved balls because there were piles and cartons of them everywhere. Little metal cars littered the plush carpet, and she recalled the box of toy cars in the playhouse. A huge track, complete with an elevated bridge and realistic river, skirted the playroom, and many little trains and cars were positioned upon it.

The most interesting piece of equipment had to be the large, plastic cube structure similar to one found at a fast food restaurant and bulging with hundreds of little plastic balls. A curved, heavy-duty slide had been thoughtfully constructed so the mentally handicapped man wouldn't get hurt during his wild rides. Boxes of adult-sized diapers peeked out from behind a curtain displaying colorful tropical fish skimming a coral reef.

Near the back wall, a crib the size of a double bed but with extremely high bars, sat vacant. Upon inspection, it was clear that one side of the bars dropped downwards while a discreet upper gate section had the ability to swing closed over the top, totally imprisoning the dwarf. The prisoner had fought the metal bars, for they were clearly marked and scratched by his continual gnawing. A tiny kitchenette, complete with mini-refrigerator and double hotplates as well as a kettle and toaster, sat within five feet of the crib; a container of chocolate milk leaked onto the marble countertop.

On the other side of the room and distant from the jail-like crib, a partition stood. A queen-sized bed with a nondescript beige bedspread and two fluffy pillows sat next to an antique nightstand equipped with reading lamp and telephone. A brightly colored Picasso print hung above, sharing space with several faded blue and red ribbons, indicating success in collegiate wrestling. Directly across from the bed, a lovely ornate chest of drawers held a large TV set and DVD player. Sharing the comfortable space, a well-stocked bookshelf and an elaborate stereo system housed an eclectic collection of reading and DVDs. The partition totally enclosed Eddie Murdock's space, providing his small retreat a needed sense of privacy.

What a horrible living arrangement this was. Lea moved to the only remaining door and frowned. Inside, a huge bathroom with a low step down tub and huge drain in the middle reminded her of a sterile hospital. A portable showerhead with a large coiled pipe was obviously used to hose down the simpleton. The whole washroom smelled of strong disinfectant and the lingering odor of feces. More packages of adult diapers were neatly stacked inside a wicker stand. On the opposite side, a lovely bath and shower combination, along with dual sinks and lovely cabinets, gleamed tiled in a calming powder gray.

Whoever had built this place had built it with not only the comfort of the caretaker in mind, but also had recognized the difficulties of housing and maintaining a creature like Bouncer. Charlie may have been a prisoner, but he was well taken care of and painfully overfed, evidenced by the Twinkie wrappers and a half-eaten bag of potato chips lying crumpled next to a discarded apple core. Likely, eating, bouncing balls, and playing with childish cars made up Bouncer's entire existence. Lea heard a voice echo from the top of the stairs.

"Are you down there, Fox?" called Thayne, and she answered in the affirmative, beckoning him to venture down the steps. He stood for a long moment, surveying the room and absorbing its implications.

"Well," said Nick finally. "I'm not sure we've solved our case, but have certainly uncovered, if not a crime, a gross mismanagement of a handicapped person."

"It's not the crib from your sketch."

"No," sighed Thayne.

"What are they going to do with Edward Murdock and the dwarf?"

"Take them away. Bouncer to a better facility, and Eddie, I just don't know. His ranting and raving about killing everyone certainly places him in a precarious position."

"Didn't Philemon say that Bouncer repeated the word

'magnolia' to him?"

"That's right," responded Nick. "It's in the report."

"I wonder if we could get him to say the word again. That would suggest he knew something about the murder. And look at this." She clumped over to the crib and pointed. "Teeth marks. While they're probably from Bouncer, maybe someone else was kept a prisoner here as well."

"I'll get the boys to gather paint flakes off the crib and any hair or other samples. If they match the flakes found inside Thad Fisher, then we'll know the mayor and Connie were restrained here against their wills."

Lea added unemotionally. "I guess this means that Eddie Murdock is most likely the murderer?"

"I don't know. What would be his motive?"

"Blackmail most likely. I suspect that Bouncer is Thad's child and he was being blackmailed by the boy's caretaker, Eddie. When the mayor decided to finally stop paying, Eddie sought to convince him and his girlfriend over a nice dinner that halting payments was a bad idea. When they wouldn't cooperate, Eddie finished them off." Fox watched Thayne's face carefully. While she didn't believe the scenario she'd just spun, Lea wanted to test his reaction.

He finally said, "So, you're suggesting that Bouncer is to be viewed like some sort of obscene Calibus—the offspring of the mayor and Ashley Peebles? I don't agree. And, unless Eddie is insane, why would he choose formaldehyde, of all things?"

"It makes as much sense as anything else, I guess."

"Then where does Anthony Montanari fit in, and Philemon? His lip balm was found on the can containing Connie's finger, after all. That's mighty incriminating."

"Maybe it's not just Rollins who has something against the gardener," said Lea.

"I wondered that myself. But, as far as motive, blackmail seems the most reasonable." He suddenly shook his head violently. "No. It's all wrong, but I just can't make the connection."

"Maybe Bouncer killed Connie and the mayor."

Nick cocked his head thinking hard. "He's certainly strong enough, if he got hold of a screwdriver. Who knows? Perhaps Eddie Murdock was into more morbid behavior than it appears. I'll have the crew search this room. Who knows? Maybe there's another room that leads into Eddie's little shop of horrors. Um . . . Fox . . . have you considered that maybe Ashley wasn't as . . . *willing* as everyone has suggested?"

His strange meandering from the clues at hand made Fox's head jerk straight up. Thayne's dark eyes were hazy, and Lea had the notion he'd drifted far away.

"I hadn't pondered that possibility, but it's worth some contemplation."

A voice shouted from above, and Thayne gave himself a mental shake before heading up the stairs with Fox following painfully behind. Bouncer was gently being led away by a different social worker, who, this time, was large and male. The capable bald man patted him on the arm and spoke in low tones. Bouncer suddenly stopped abruptly and began to wail, refusing to budge an inch.

The social worker searched his pocket and handed the dwarf a small metal car. Instantly, the wailing ceased as Bouncer's beefy hand closed over the small toy. His heavy head lifted, and the small slits of his eyes widened as he peered out the gate. Its gaping presence seemed to terrify him, and the dwarf froze and pointed, suddenly shrieking again. No matter how the social worker tried to comfort the handicapped young man, Bouncer wouldn't stop his high-pitched cries.

"I think he's afraid of the street." The stout government employee patted the dwarf on the shoulder and tried once again to lead him outside.

"Mag. . . mag… nol . . .lia," he suddenly shrieked, pointing a chubby finger at what appeared to be the second floor of Mrs. Simms' house. But then again, it could be just about anything, for a flock of crows were frantically cawing and circling the field. Liquid ambers swayed in the stiffening wind at the front of Mrs. Simms' yard as a ginger cat crouched upon a neighbor's wall, her back arched as the feline eyed the noisy crowd approaching the gate.

Anything could have set the dwarf off. Bouncer suddenly began to caw like the crows and now clearly pointed to where the solitary magnolia stood in silent testament to murder. Finally, the sobbing child-man, clutching his toy in one hand and pointing hysterically with the other handcuffed hand, was eased gently into the waiting sedan of the social worker. Thayne moved to where Chief Rollins watched the whole proceedings in undisguised disgust before stalking to the backyard.

Lea realized she didn't have much time, and suddenly making up her mind, scurried into the spacious kitchen. Ignoring the sleek appliances and long, gleaming counters of the oversized kitchen, she headed towards the pantry, gently parting the white doors and slipping inside. Just as the swinging doors stopped rocking, she heard Thayne's voice calling her name and Chief Rollins bellowing.

"I need to talk to Fox!"

"She headed off with the social worker."

"We believe Charlie, or Bouncer as he is nicknamed, may have been witness to the murder, since human teeth marks were found on Connie Judson's upper arm. You witnessed Charlie's attack on the social worker. We think he was there at the crime scene. Maybe Fox can coax the truth out of him."

"Is that right?" scoffed Chief Rollins. Fox could just barely discern his heavy form moving about the kitchen through the wooden slats. "We'll see if she can charm the truth out of an idiot. Let her follow that wild goose chase. What we have is a simple case of child abuse, nothing more. Philemon

Jenkins is our man. His fingerprints and lip balm are on the soda can housing the finger. He was a hit man hired to get rid of a man who didn't pay his debts. Case closed."

Randy Phelps suddenly appeared at Chief Rollins' shoulder. "We've got the samples from the crib and took several photographs."

Chief Rollins grimaced. "God damned crib. There are a bunch of sickos out there, and I for one have had about enough of this whole mess. Check the rest of the house and garage for gardening tools." The young man scurried off.

Thayne turned back to the chief. "You're dead wrong about Philemon."

"Yeah? Is that what your unladylike partner told you? Well, here's a word of advice. Part company with that broad. I'll keep you on the case and pay her off for the three days she's worked. If you don't split with her, you're released as well. You understand me?'

Nick stared long and hard at the angry chief. "You can't ignore this new evidence. If I didn't know better, I'd think you already knew about Charlie."

Rollins's facial hair bristled. He bellowed, "Listen, you fricking asshole. It's only because of Roger I'm letting you remain on this case at all. Now, if you did some real investigative footwork instead of that moodoo voodoo you're famous for, you might realize that Philemon is the killer, hired by Eddie Murdock to do in the Mayor when he wouldn't pay up his child support."

"Now, that's a switch. We've gone from gambling debts and the mob to child support? Frankly, that makes much more sense since both Fox and I are convinced blackmail is indeed involved. I need to see Ashley's death report and the murder book. I have a sneaking suspicion she was raped and Charlie is her child!"

"Of all the goddamned notions! You have *got* to be kidding. That girl was more willing than a child in a Santa Claus line. I don't need some of your Asian 'intuitions' muddling up this case."

That was the final straw. Nick began quietly and deadly, "Then maybe your relationship with Trish Fisher needs to be further investigated. Since you had an affair with her years ago, perhaps you just got fed up with waiting for Trish to become free of Thad and popped off her husband! Or maybe Bouncer's a relative of *yours*?"

"Of all the goddamn nerve! That's it! You're fired! Get the hell out of here before I have you thrown out!"

"Are you threatening me, Chief? Such an over-reaction. The way I see it, no one would respond the way you do unless they have something to hide. And believe me, my forte is finding out even the most reluctant's hidden secrets and sharing them with the world. You've heard of my 'gift', boss? Well, I 'see' an envelope with your name on it, bulging with cash. There's a sleeping, oblivious wife, and a car easing down a driveway, silent and sinister. Should I go on? I have a word of advice for you, bucko. Back off and let me do my job. And you better have the key to Philemon's cell ready—because you know as well as I do that he's innocent. So, be ready, Chief, be ready." Thayne's voice had taken on a tone Lea had never heard before, and it frightened her. It must have startled the chief as well, because he took a step back.

"Get out of Monroe," Rollins squeaked weakly.

"When I'm good and ready, and not a minute before. I want this entire house turned upside down for Philemon's prints, which I can guarantee you aren't going to find. But who knows, maybe yours are spattered about, or perhaps even Trish Fisher's. And do mold of Charlie's jaw, because I'm positive the bite mark on Connie Judson's arm is a perfect match, which puts this case in an entirely different light. And, if I hear a peep of contention from you or any effort to derail the proper investigation of this case, I'll head to the current mayor faster than you can say *Obstruction of Justice*. Do I make myself clear?"

The chief didn't respond for the longest time. Finally he said in just above a whisper, "Then go do your goddamned job, you half-breed bastard."

"That's a given. I'll be updating Roger regarding our *conversation*." Thayne turned on his heel, the kitchen door banging shut behind him.

His diminishing footsteps echoed upon the tile, and

Lea noted Chief Rollins' face had become ashen. He sat down shakily upon one of the dinette chairs and removed his handkerchief, first mopping his brow before mindlessly wadding and unwadding the crumpled square of white linen. The chief remained that way for a full twenty minutes, staring into space, as the overworked police unit went about their business. Lea painfully remained dead still, her injured leg at first only aching until finally turning numb.

Randy Phelps finally appeared in the doorway. "We're finished, Chief."

"And Thayne?"

"Took off a couple minutes ago. Said he was heading for Dr. Koh's."

"Well, it's almost all over then. You guys go on and head out. I'll lock the place up."

The rookie hesitated. "You alright, Chief?"

"Yeah, yeah. This case is just taking it out of me. As soon as those paints flakes from the crib are analyzed, I want to be notified immediately. Have Koh call me."

"Of course, sir." Officer Phelps backed away. The chief didn't look so good.

As soon as the junior officer left, Richard Rollins rushed over to the beautiful porcelain sink and turned on the tap. He ducked his head underneath and drank like a child from the gushing flow. Cupping his hands, he splashed water over his pallid face before grabbing a blue-checked dishtowel to mop his pasty cheeks. It took several minutes before he finally gained control. Finally, he pulled out his cell phone and punched in a single number. He waited a long time for a response.

"Hello," he said. "It's me. I know, I know. I'm not supposed to call you at home, but there's something I need verified . Was Thad aware of the dwarf being babysat here at the Collins place? Now, don't go and get all hysterical on me. I just want to know if you knew anything about it. Please calm down, honey. Nobody's pointing a finger at you. It looks like the kid was probably held prisoner here, and frankly, there's gonna be a lot of questions. I'm not sure if I can ward them off or if I even want to anymore. A part of me believes that, after all this time, everything should come out in the open. There, there now. Come on, sweetie; everything is going to be fine. Let's meet tonight and talk about it. It's been so long since we've talked." A short pause made the chief even more agitated.

"What do you mean you're not free? You used to be free all the time." Chief Rollins rubbed his balding head fiercely. "That's better. Okay. Seven p.m. Let's meet at *The Range*? I need some answers and no more excuses, babe. Do you understand? You've been putting me off for far too long, and now look at this damn mess. I swear Thayne knows. Tonight then." He abruptly disconnected the line and sighed heavily, his broad face sad but determined. He whispered to the empty kitchen, “You owe me, girlie. It’s my right to know. I’ve rolled over and played dead for long enough.”

Chief Rollins strode resolutely out of the kitchen and through the open doors of the house, which slammed hollowly. The key turned in the lock, and finally, Lea heard the rev of his engine followed by the creaking of the metal gate. Lea waited until the roar of his Ford had fully diminished before leaving her retreat, limping badly as she tried to rub some life back into her stiff limb. She waited in the immaculate kitchen and listened for a long while. Finally satisfied, she wandered about the first floor.

Try as she could, though, Fox could find nothing after fifteen minutes of fruitless searching. She then headed back upstairs to the cozy and lavish bedrooms so clearly unused and sat on one of the lovely beds thinking long and hard, before finally whipping open her cell.

“May I speak to Daniel, please?”

It took only a few moments for the assistant coroner’s deep voice to answer. “Daniel Scott.”

“This is Inspector Fox. I had Officer Phelps bag up some dirt found in the kitchen of the Collins residence a couple days ago and wanted to know if you’ve had any time to analyze it.” Daniel Scott had been Steven Koh’s assistant for the past three years and was more of a general science expert than a coroner.

“I’m just writing up the report now.”

“Could you give me a thumbnail sketch?”

“Of course. The soil is a subterranean mixture of 24 percent river clay, fairly sodic, mixed with unmetamorphosed sandstone and likely having low permeability.”

“And now for the translation?”

Daniel laughed in his nerdy way. “What it means is that this is deep soil, not loamy—which means it lacks plant matter. It maybe came from a well or manmade cave or something.”

“How’d you know that?”

“Okay, I cheated. My brother’s a geologist who contracts out to the Agrit-Empire’s Soil Management Department.”

“Figures. Thanks a lot Daniel.”

“No problem. Next time give me something really hard!” You had to love a scientific zealot.

It was all beginning to make sense, and after a couple minutes, Lea ended back in the tasteful kitchen staring at the lovely granite countertops. A small metal wine rack sat next to a food processor. She leaned forward and removed the single bottle, her eyes widening at the year; a 1993 *Heitz Cabernet Sauvignon.* Even *she* knew this was an expensive bottle of wine. On the sloped shoulder of the bottle sat a fine layer of dust.

Dust? It came to her like a bolt of lightning. Of course! A house like this had to have a wine cellar, and if there was a cellar, maybe . . .

"Wine has to stay cool," she murmured to herself looking around. Hadn't Thad Fisher ingested not only good food but fine wine? And where would you stash a wine cellar? Where those dirt piles had been discovered, of course! Fox clumped to the pantry and flipped on the overhead light. Moving aside a small footstool, an ironing board, and several brooms, she discovered a heavily stocked white shelving unit with jams and relish lining its dusty planks.

She yanked forcefully at the whitewashed panels, and the shelf swung open without a sound.

The metal door's knob was slightly tarnished. Lea smiled and pulled, revealing a set of steep wooden steps and a light switch on the whitewashed wall. One flick and the plunging stairs were fully illuminated as a cold draught spiraled upwards. Fox held onto the metal railing and descended carefully. The large, square room smelled musty and damp, and Lea marveled at the vast collection of varied vintages.

Reds, whites, and rosés crammed the dusty racks. She grasped a dark bottle and read its peeling gold label. 1979. Another said 1978, and lay next to countless others in dusty rows. One ledge had such an accumulation of dust Lea had to scrap away the dirt, revealing a dozen bottles dated from 1965. Good God, there was a fortune housed here! In fact, as she scanned the amazing contents, Lea realized there must be hundreds of bottles of wine stocked in the chilly cave.

French, Chilean, South African, Californian, Italian, you name it, had all somehow found its way here. Chardonnay and Riesling, Rose and Merlot, Pinotage and Chenin Blanc. Heavy, foiled labels of dessert wines rested next to southern Spanish Sherries and there was even the strong, sweet Port her father had so often consumed after dinner.

This place was a wine connoisseur's wet dream, but Lea remained oblivious to the dusty fortune shifting beneath her frenzied hands. She tugged and yanked at every appendage, seeking the catch to a hidden door she was positive must be secreted within the cellar. Finally, situated between towering racks of dusty vintage and behind several empty boxes, a metal door protected by an oversized padlock gleamed dustily before her. Lea prayed and pulled, jerking at the silver lock. Unfortunately, her feeble efforts proved useless; the rusty door stayed securely bolted, and without a key or Randy's unparalleled expertise, it would stay that way.

She hesitated, wondering if it was worth the effort. This door might simply lead to an exclusive wine chamber housing even more expensive wines. She'd heard of rich men hoarding wines that were fifty, sixty, even a hundred years old and worth thousands of dollars apiece. Yet, she argued against herself; this had to be the secret passage leading out of the house. How else was Bouncer transported here unseen, the neighbors never realizing a mentally handicapped dwarf was kept on the premises? How else did Eddie Murdock slip in and out to obtain his groceries and cash, all the blocks' nearest residents—including Mrs. Simms—oblivious to the house's occupation? Only once had activity disrupted the calm façade of the house, and that was when the little girl Katie witnessed the big limo's arrival.

Eddie Murdock probably had his car parked at a neighboring house. The home directly to the left of the Collins mansion belonged to the older couple named Crawford. While highly unlikely, it wasn't impossible. Directly across the street, the Shaw family with three teenaged children and two huge Rottweilers lived and squabbled. Then there was Katie's house and the many others Fox had visited. Lea couldn't imagine Bouncer behaving himself around children or dogs and the closest four houses except for the Crawford's' and Simms' housed an ample number of each.

Lea remembered Mrs. Simms' comments about never seeing anyone in residence before another possibility struck her. If it wasn't one of the neighboring houses then perhaps a passageway led either into the vacant lot between the Simms and Collins houses or the scrub oak field behind it. That had to be it! That would explain how the cream soda cans with the finger and Philemon's incriminating fingerprints were deposited.

The chill of the wine cellar numbed Lea's fingers, and she decided to ascend and search for the key. Clearly, Eddie Murdock had not expected their arrival after the MCPD's previous search. If he had, he'd certainly have scuttled the dwarf down into the cellar until any possibility of any encounter with unwanted visitors had disappeared. Thus, the most likely spot for his keys was the subterranean basement where Bouncer was lodged.

It was behind the high partition where Eddie Murdock slept that Lea began a tentative search through his drawers, roughly moving aside his plain white boxers and socks. So intent was she on riffling the drawers that she almost missed the extremely expensive *Cartier* watch sitting on a gaudy orange Mexican plate. This was no imitation; its circular face housed twelve decently sized diamonds. One thing was certain; whoever was paying Ed Murdock rewarded him well. There, in plain view next to the watch, sat his keys. It was hard to fathom having so many keys. Lea's own brass keychain, emblazoned with her three initials, simply consisted of keys for the front door, garage door, office, and car. She snatched the keys up and scurried back to the hidden door.

She cursed in frustration after countless futile insertions of a dozen or more keys. Murphy's Law guaranteed it was the second to the last that finally opened the padlock. Placing the heavy lock gingerly on the rough wooden floorboard of the cold wine cellar she creaked opened the narrow door.

At first, in the dim light, the second chamber appeared a twin of the other cellar with its high racks filled with dusty bottles of wine. However, as Lea flipped on a light switch to her left she saw a long hallway reinforced with heavy timbers that held up the ceiling. The narrow passageway reminded her of a mine tour that she'd once taken at *Knott's Berry Farm.* The long shaft proceeded fairly straight for what appeared about twenty feet before taking an abrupt left. She knelt and fingered the soil. It felt identical to the small pile found earlier in front of the pantry doors.

Lea flipped out her cell phone and punched in Nick's number but only static answered. She'd have to ascend the steps one more time to get hold of him. At the top of the stairwell, she keyed his number again.

"Thayne," she said.

"Where the hell are you?"

"I'm still at the Collins house. Didn't you see my car parked here?"

"Of course, but I thought you hitched a ride with Randy or one of the other officers. Chief Rollins will be a little PO'd to find you remained on the premises after he locked up."

"So, big whoopdeedo! Look, I need you to buy me some time."

"Fox . . . what are you up to?"

"Rollins is covering up for someone. I heard him say as much on the phone while I hid in the pantry."

"Hid in the panty?" returned Nick's annoyed voice. "Now, why doesn't that surprise me?"

"Just shut up and listen. Rollins indicated that he was

going to meet someone, a woman, at seven o'clock at some place called *The Range*. From what I could glean from the one-sided conversation, she was mighty hysterical about the discovery of the child. I want you to find out what and where *The Range* is while I nose around here some more. Something stinks in Denmark, and I've going to find out what it is."

"Oh, come on . . . you're the computer whiz. You head back here and do it yourself. I'm following up on the crib particles with Steven Koh, as well as the measurements of the bite mark, and don't have time for this."

"I'm too busy. You do it! I spoke to Daniel, and I've discovered a—"

He interrupted. "I'm not going to drop everything and play your gopher."

"I've left a key under the office door mat for emergencies."

"Didn't you hear a word I said? And a key under the mat?" he sputtered. "How original! I've got a *feeling* about Ashley Peebles and need to follow it up."

"Look, since I can't be in two places at one time you're just gonna have to do what I ask. And I prefer *facts* not *feelings* mister."

He swore under his breath. "You're the biggest—"

"Ah, shut up already! It's already settled that you're a swine and I'm a bitch. Life goes on. I heard you tell the chief you knew he was having an affair on the side?"

“He was, with Trish Fisher. Roger told me last night.”

“So, why didn’t you tell me?”

“I forgot in all the turmoil. Anything else?” he hissed. God, she pissed him off.

“Yeah. Check if any of Anthony Montanari’s family was ever involved with a Murdock. I’ll call you back in an hour.”

“Rightio,” he said sarcastically before hanging up before she could think of any other chores to add.

Deciding she didn’t want to carry her handbag, Lea tucked her cell phone into her jacket pocket and took out her revolver. For all her bravado with Thayne, she honestly had never shot it except at the firing range. It felt warm and comfortable as she dropped it into her left-hand pocket along with the small penlight attached to her key chain. Fox flung her purse onto the chair inside the kitchen nook and headed back down the steep steps of the pantry into the shadowy wine cellar. The humid dampness assaulted her nostrils and she resisted an obligatory sneeze.

Moving quickly to the now-open passageway door Lea stood for a moment, contemplating her choices. Perhaps she should hurry back up the stairs and call Thayne again asking him to accompany her, but her stubborn, practical nature resisted. It was too crucial for Thayne to discover if a connection really existed between Eddie Murdock, Charlie, and Chief Rollins. And the *feeling* he had about Ashley

Peebles had to be significant. There was just too much at stake here for her to wait until Thayne arrived. Her mind made up, she left the door open a crack and started down the long passageway.

The first few paces were covered by rough wooden boards but soon gave way to a rocky, beaten path. The man-made tunnel measured only five feet across at its widest point and was a mere six feet tall. The claustrophobic passageway was built for utility, not looks, the rough earth muffling the tedious clump of her limping stride. Lea proceeded twenty feet before making an abrupt left. She paused for a moment, seeking to determine her whereabouts in the neighborhood.

If the path continued straight, as it looked like it might, Lea figured it would head right into the empty field. Maybe the base of the magnolia hid more than a body. She picked up the pace, appreciative of the single glaring bulbs above her, which cast enough light so that the path could safely be trodden. Lea continued another twenty-five paces or so when the tunnel took another sharp turn. She stopped, momentarily confused and studied her feet. Not two paces from where she stood, a rusty blue midget car lay discarded in the dust. Fox scooped up the toy, her pulse quickening.

With only a moment's hesitation, Lea turned and followed the path, which had narrowed drastically until a steep flight of earthy steps appeared in front of her. She felt so turned around. Was she near the magnolia tree or deep inside the rough scrub oak forest behind Chester Street? Or, worse yet, had she ended up at one of the nearby houses? Lea ascended the rough-hewn stairs at the end of the passageway. A nondescript wooden door equipped only with a metal latch was all that lay between her and the answer.

Fox lifted the catch and the rickety door immediately swung open. Directly behind, a more modern door painted bright green with sturdy metal hinges and utility handle beckoned. She jerked it sharply and the door swung it open. An incredibly sweet dampness assailed her nose, so cloying it made her cough uncontrollably.

Lea stepped into a hot, humid paradise, her violet eyes widening behind her rapidly steaming glasses. She never saw her attacker, nor had the ability to fathom what struck her. The only memory was a flash of black so complete that Lea crashed like a fallen tree at the feet of someone clearly as amazed as she.

Chapter 22

Monday Afternoon

Steven was remarkably understanding when Nick explained why he had to leave.

"So, duty summons," he said wryly, having overheard Nick's end of the conversation with Lea. "Don't worry about it. I need to head over to Social Services and examine Charlie anyway. I'll get back with you as soon as possible. Any prints from the house?"

"Lots. Now we just have to match 'em. Wouldn't want to be the one taking Bouncer's fingerprints. He's got a real stubborn streak and a nasty bite. I guess it's a moot point to note the feces are human, now that we've discovered Charlie Murdock."

"And to think I analyzed that smelly stuff for nothing. I can hardly wait to take his jaw mold. As soon as I determine whether the impression matches the dimensions of Connie's bite, I'll phone you. Daniel will start on crib paint analysis immediately." Steven lifted a hand as Nick let himself out of the coroner's office.

Nick wasted no time dallying in Lea's well-organized office. He powered up the computer and took the opportunity as it booted up to go through her unlocked filing cabinets. He quickly found the folder entitled Luke Cambridge and then, curiosity overwhelming him, scanned many of the others. One particularly caught his eyes. Entitled *Buffy* he saw to his amusement it contained a clever wanted poster for a white toy poodle announcing in bold letters, *Reward, Lost Dog.* Business must really be bad if Fox was reduced to searching for lost animals.

The computer appeared to have stalled. "Damn, she's got a password, and I didn't think to ask what it is."

He whipped out his cell phone and listened impatiently while the phone rang and rang before a recorded tinny voice said, "*The subscriber you have contacted is not available. Please leave a message after the tone.*"

"Fox, this is Thayne. I need your computer password. Call me back as soon as possible either using your office phone or my cell."

Knowing Fox, it was likely she'd only get back to him when she damn well pleased. He smiled. He'd be hard put to find a woman he couldn't figure out and generally passwords were easy. You just had to discover who or what the female loved or desired most. Thayne cracked his knuckles and began to type.

He started off with her family. Sometimes people's passwords are as simple as their first name so Nick typed in Lea and then Leah. That doesn't work. Her father's name—Jeremy. No luck. Brother—Lane. Strike.

Nick deposited himself in Lea's beautiful swivel chair and leaning back, laced his fingers together. He turned his earthen colored eyes to the ceiling and began to talk softly to himself.

"Hmm. Unmarried woman in her early thirties. Ah-ha. Maybe her boyfriend." He typed in Bernard, but once again, access was refused.

"Maybe Bernard has a nickname? Bernie. Nope. Did she possess a pet?" There was that cat he'd caught a glimpse of at her house, but damn if he knew its name. His almond eyes scanned the office. She sure had a lot of plants. The window and its shelves were filled with healthy philodendrons and African Violets. Maybe those were considered her pets.

He was striking out royally. What could her damn password be? Suddenly an image of Fox thumbing her nose at every man around filled his mind's eye and a single descriptive word leaped to the forefront.

He typed in the five letters slowly and the computer beeped its greeting. *Hello, Lea.* No wonder she remained unfazed when referred to as *bitch.*

Nick typed in Murdock first. There were about 16,000

of them in California alone. He narrowed the search with the name Edward and paused. Eddie Murdock was probably born in the thirties. He punched a range of ten years and waited, drumming his fingers upon the beautiful maple desk. No luck.

He then looked up Montanari's daughters to see if any of them had been married or involved with a man named Murdock. Strike four.

He dialed Roger, hoping he was conscious. His friend's voice sounded strong.

"I need some help, buddy." He relayed all they'd discovered at the Collins house and his search for connections to the Montanari's and Chief Rollins. Officer Phelps had already forwarded most of the details to Roger's home computer. That rookie had potential!

"You on her computer?"

"Yup."

"Look in Child Welfare."

"I did. Hey, Roger. Do you think this Charlie could be as young as twenty-five?"

"Why do you ask?" asked Roger shifting on the plush beige couch as he stared at the digital photo Randy had snapped of Bouncer. He had managed to convince Susan he'd die and atrophy if he stayed in bed much longer and she'd obligingly made up the couch all comfortable-like with the mandatory pillows, chips, and remote. Almost heaven. Now, if he could just get to work before the chief had a nervous breakdown and fired the whole damn office.

"You remember how Ashley Peebles had a baby, and it supposedly died? What if it didn't die, Roger, but was hidden because it was abnormal? What if she was raped and had Charlie?"

"Raped?" asked Roger. "Actually, that would make some kind of convoluted sense in this bizarre case."

"If Ashley Peebles was killed twenty-five years ago, then I'm positive Bouncer must be that old. In fact, I'm willing to bet that Anthony Montanari bought that house under the name of Collins to hide the existence of his illegitimate son, who is Charlie Murdock. And maybe our Ashley wasn't as willing as everyone likes to insinuate."

"The child's the result of rape?" asked Roger, thrilled his brain finally functioned. "You would have thought that if Anthony had somehow impregnated a seventeen-year-old girl, he'd have quickly paid for her to have an abortion."

"But he's Catholic, after all, and fairly devout from what I've heard."

"Devout my eye," scoffed Roger over the phone. "Screwing around or maybe even molesting a teenaged girl is not what I call a religious man."

"Okay, maybe just religious in tradition. So let's assume we're correct. If Charlie really is Anthony Montanari's child, then what does that have to do with the mayor and his murder?"

"Well," said Roger thinking hard, "it's a long shot . . . but . . ."

"But what?" queried Nick impatiently.

"Don't you think it's a little peculiar Anthony Montanari would pay his respects to Thad Fisher when it was clear they really didn't like each other much; that is, if Trish Fisher is to be believed. So, what's the real association between Montanari and Thad Fisher?"

"Luke Cambridge mentioned Thad Fisher was actually a friend of the Montanari boys. He was only about six or so years older than them while Anthony is almost his father's age. Maybe that's the connection?"

"Wait a minute. What if Thad Fisher knew Anthony Montanari was the father of Ashley Peebles' child?"

"Blackmail," said Nick his dark head springing up and his eyes narrowing. "Hmm. But it makes a lot more sense if it was Eddie Murdock blackmailing the mayor."

"But what if Thad Fisher was blackmailing Anthony because he knew the child was a Montanari? Anthony got tired of it all and decided to rid himself of Thad Fisher and his expensive mistress," suggested Roger, almost feeling himself again.

"I don't know," said Nick rubbing his head and leaning back wearily; a horrifying image refused to dislodge itself from his brain. "If what you're surmising is correct, then Anthony Montanari was the killer all along. It could make sense that he killed Ashley Peebles to silence her about bearing a child with him out of wedlock—a child that could destroy his marriage. If the boy was handicapped, then he'd have to have someone take care of it and that's where Eddie Murdock comes in. Eddie Murdock, therefore, must have some special connection to Anthony Montanari."

Roger felt his brain defrosting. He jumped on the bandwagon. "Okay. Let's pretend that Thad Fisher, who was known to be quite a ladies man even back in those days, needed some extra cash, but his wife refused not only to divorce him but also threatened to cut off his funds if Thad's adulteries were exposed. Our poor mayor didn't make enough as an insurance salesman to fund his campaign *or* pay for the expensive tastes of his girlfriends, so what does he do? He blackmails the richest man in the neighborhood, who doesn't want his own wife or any of his remaining four children to find out."

"I like where this is heading," smiled Nick at the receiver. "Let's continue with the assumption Anthony did have an affair with Ashley Peebles or raped her. She threatens to squeal about the rape or child so our Potato Prince kills her and Anthony frames Deke and Luke for her murder. Luke Cambridge sees Anthony Montanari's car not far from where Ashley Peebles' body was found, but with all the blood found in the pair's room—no one believed him."

"Poor bastard. Since Ashley Peebles' son was not

only mentally handicapped but a dwarf, Anthony knew that he couldn't place him in a normal children's home, so he has to hire someone to take care of him. Someone who has some sort of attachment to the boy, and that would be Eddie Murdock."

"When Jeremy Fox makes noise about opening the case again, Chief Rollins makes sure the records disappear from the County Clerk's office," added Nick.

"So, we're bringing in my boss?"

"He's definitely got something to hide. Fox overheard Rollins talking on the phone, and she thinks it's likely he knew about the boy already. Fox had mentioned—more than once—that the good ole boy network is strong here, and I'm inclined to believe it."

"Unbelievable," was all Roger said.

Nick continued. "If all this speculation is valid, then we can surmise that when Thad Fisher and Connie Judson came to visit, our Eddie was probably witness to the murder, as was Bouncer. Anthony had to be there!"

Roger sucked on his apple juice straw before answering. "I wonder if Anthony can verify his whereabouts on Tuesday of last week."

"Still," said Nick, his mind already powering ahead. "I remember Anthony at the morgue. He was checking Thad's missing finger. Fox is inclined to believe that Thad had been killed as a warning to Anthony and that the note left with Connie was warning Montanari that his son was next if certain demands weren't met." He pulled open the right-hand drawer of the beautiful desk and rummaged through Fox's fancy paper clips. Damn if they weren't color-coordinated. The woman needed serious help.

"Rudolph Montanari," said Roger. "But what about Philemon's lip balm?"

Nick hugged the phone to his ear to free his hands and started linking a paper clip chain—first blue, then pink, then green—guaranteed to drive Fox insane when she found them.

"Philemon might have drunk some soda and left it lying about, and Anthony grabbed the can—knowing whoever had drunk from it would be connected falsely to the murder. You'd think Rollins might have the brains to recognize that possibility."

"Do I hear a hint of animosity towards my fine superior?" twanged Roger.

"Guy's an asshole. Treats Fox like shit."

"Some would say she deserves it."

Nick sighed. "Hey, speaking of Fox . . . It's been over an hour."

Sounds of shifting and groaning indicated Roger struggled to get comfortable. "I hope you're wrong about Chief Rollins."

"Let's see if Fox's baby can discover what *The Range* refers to."

Nick quickly punched in Chief Rollins' name, but after

many minutes of futile searching, found nothing to shed a glimmer of light upon the case. “I can’t find the connection,” said Nick. “I’d sure like to run this by Fox. She seems to have a better mind for quirky facts. You know what Rudyard Kipling said. *A woman's guess is much more accurate than a man's certainty*.”

“Not another of your damned quotes,” said Roger.

“Hey, you got a yellow pages handy, Roger? Maybe *The Range* is a nightclub or restaurant or something.”

Roger laboriously flipped to the restaurant section and scanned all the eateries in Monroe and the neighboring cities. None remotely fit the description. He sighed loudly, fatigue evident.

“I wonder . . .” said Nick.

Roger suddenly snorted. “These drugs must be warping my mind! *The Range*! Of course. You know where Chief Rollins goes every Sunday afternoon?”

“We’re not that close,” quipped Nick.

“He goes golfing. Richard keeps a bag of clubs in the trunk of his car. When things are slow at the station he heads to the range, the *driving* range. It’s at the edge of town, and Fox says he has a date at 7:00 p.m.? I’ll meet you there.”

“Like hell!”

“Susan has her Book of the Month Club at 6:30, and she’s meeting some friends in a few minutes for an early dinner. Says I’m driving her crazy and has got to get out of the house before she loses her mind. She'll never know I'm gone."

"Susan will kill me if I you drive yourself anywhere."

"You're right. So pick me up in an hour."

"Roger!"

"Have mercy, man. I'm going stir-crazy here, and this damn incision itches like hell. Besides, your partner is AWOL, and you need me."

"She's not my partner!"

"Wedding bells are gonna chime."

"You shit. I'll be there in 60 minutes. Maybe I'll get lucky, and your stitches will bust wide open." He slammed down the phone.

Nick had some time to kill before he picked up Roger. He shuffled through the printouts Fox had organized, each in its own separate file, complete with color-coded label. Likely OCD. He sat for a long while staring at the Montanari brothers' faces made slightly blurry by the distortion of the computer printout. Both boys resembled their father significantly. The phone jangled, and he snatched it up, expecting Fox's husky voice.

"It's Roger again. Charlie has been detained at the Waterford Children's agency, but they plan to move him. Apparently, from Eddie Murdock's testimony, Bouncer is over 30 years old."

"No! Any way we can verify that?"

"Not until we get the birth records. Murdock refuses to tell us much more except that the boy is an orphan and his birth certificate is lost."

"Lost my eye."

"Precisely. I also just chatted with Anthony. He was in Vegas from Monday morning to Thursday around noon, meeting with some of his distributors and taking some R & R. Will drop all the hotel and business receipts at the station. Uh-oh," he whispered. "Susan's coming. See you in 30." The line went dead.

So, Anthony had an alibi. Somehow, Nick wasn't surprised. He picked up Ashley Peebles' file and stared at the fresh-faced picture of the 17-year-old killed in 1978. The girl's hair was dark and wavy, and he wondered if she'd ever dyed it red. The image wouldn't leave his brain, and he finally gave in and headed to his Mustang, lifting his portfolio out of the trunk. Once inside, he removed the sketch and studied it. No matter had he angled the photo, the girl in the picture was not the one in his drawing.

Nick closed his eyes and relaxed, letting his mind foliate. Finally, he flipped open a new page in his pad and began to draw. Within 15 minutes, the pencil sketch was complete, but he felt more disturbed than ever. The unknown man with dark hair had his back to Nick as the struggling couple battled by a sluggish stream. The girl's face, turned towards him in terror, seemed familiar somehow—so pretty and intelligent, but definitely not Ashley Peebles. He needed to talk to Roger right away.

Roger sat slumped in Fox's squeaky office chair, a blue polyester pillow scrunched behind his back. Nick had avoided Susan by a good 15 minutes, and getting Roger out of the house had been a snap, since the kids were at their cousin's. Roger came armed with a liter of bottled water, pain pills, a brown bag, and the navy blue pillow. He wore faded black jeans and a well-worn, long sleeved t-shirt proclaiming UC Berkley's prowess as a football team. His slip-on sandals didn't quite go with the outfit, but Nick suspected they were all Roger could force on his feet.

Roger winced.

"You okay, old man?"

"Just hunky dory. The fresh air is doing me good."

Nick tossed the first sketch into Roger's hands, followed by the second he had drawn earlier in Lea's office.

"That's Charlie's mother, and she isn't Ashley Peebles."

Roger sighed heavily, shaken by the second picture. "This is nasty. So, how do you know it's Bouncer's mom?"

"I just do."

"Damn it, man, can't you just level with me. You drew these right?"

"Yeah."

"Well, you're a damn good artist. Has Fox seen 'em?"

"Nope. I'm actually a little concerned. She failed to call me like promised."

"Wonders never cease. Nick Thayne concerned about a woman."

"Fox is a woman?"

"Very funny," chortled Roger.

Nick said more seriously. "I was just recalling something your brother-in-law said—that the murderer is someone you'd least suspect—and knowing Fox, she'd rush in where fools fear to tread."

"Lea can take care of herself. She's a dead shot." Roger dropped the unbearable sketch face down on the carpet.

"I saw her weapon. Jeez, remind me not to make her mad. Do you by any chance recognize the woman?"

"Not in the least. You got any ideas?"

"It's either someone I've met or . . .

A brisk knock sounded upon the door and a handsome young man with sleek brown hair and 500 dollar sunglasses stepped into the office. "You Nick Thayne?" he asked extending a hand.

"I am," returned Nick quickly rising and grasping the young man's hand. "I'm afraid I haven't had the pleasure."

"Rudolph Montanari, but you can call me Rudy. I thought I'd stop by because I'm a little concerned with the direction Thad's case is taking, and I wanted to make sure that

Trish Fisher was in no way implicated. I've heard through the grapevine that certain people in the police department, especially your chief, believe she might have hired a hit man." He cocked an eye at Roger as if he was the purveyor of such lies.

"This is Roger Chung. I'm helping him on the case after his surgery."

"Ah, yes. *The* Detective Chung. Where's the Fox woman?"

"I'm not sure."

"Probably best that way. Trish wasn't impressed with her style or her manners. As I was saying, the papers state that the MCPD believes the Jenkins man held in custody was hired by Mrs. Fisher. Trish would never do a thing like that. Much as she disliked her cheating scum of a husband, she's no killer."

"And how would you know that?" asked Nick, eyeing the man dressed in an elegant, beige three-piece suit. His rig must have cost four or five thousand dollars.

"I know because I love her."

"*You* and Trish Fisher?" Would wonders never cease?

"That's right. She and I have been seeing each other for over 18 months since meeting at a charity function. I'd gone there to assist my mother, and believe it or not, she actually introduced us.

I couldn't believe what an elegant and intelligent women Trish was. We started conversing about art as well as her involvement with the Guide Dog Association of Monroe County, and I was amazed at her depth. Here was a rich woman who could remain idle and waste time improving her tan, but instead chose to help out other people, whether at a children's home or volunteering money and time to juveniles stricken with leukemia.

"I quickly discovered that I liked a lot of things about Trish Fisher, and it didn't matter that she was seventeen years older than me. She had something I needed—a quality I admire in my own mother, which is as simple as compassion. I know she might appear harsh, but you have to realize her back is against the wall. Trish doesn't know what you guys think and is afraid she might be implicated in a murder she had nothing to do with. That's why I have asked her to come and speak to you, but she refused. She's afraid her reputation will become further tarnished if the public finds out she's dating a younger man. Of course, after her husband's behavior, how could it become more damaged than it is?"

Nick noted that Rudy Montanari was as large as his father in stature, but trim and fit; only his sideburns showed the faintest hint of gray. He would be thirty-two or so remembered Nick; just a small boy when Ashley Peebles was murdered.

"Do you suspect my father?"

"What makes you think I might believe your dad is a murderer?" asked Nick quietly.

"If you're a good P.I., you'd have to suspect him. Is that bourbon in there?" Nick's eyes flicked over the desk as Rudy opened the maple cupboard. Did that outstanding bottle of seven-year-old bourbon really sit on Fox's shelf?

"Please, help yourself," he said and wasn't surprised when the younger Montanari poured himself a stiff drink. Roger glanced at Nick, a pained expression on his face. His current medications and alcohol didn't mix.

"It needs ice," Rudolph said, "but this will have to do. I have some information for you that will prove Trish Fisher is as totally innocent as my scumbag father."

Roger leaned forward painfully. "You have proof?"

The youngest Montanari took a hardy swig of his strong liquor and nodded. Nick would have to remember where Fox kept her alcohol.

"The police discovered Charlie Murdock at the Collins house, didn't they?"

"This morning. It's a very interesting situation."

"And they learned Eddie Murdock was his caretaker?"

"That's right. So, you know about him?"

"Of course I do, as does Trish and my mother."

"Your mother knew about Charlie Murdock? Your father's illegitimate child?"

Randy started, spilling some of the expensive liquor. "What do you mean my father's illegitimate child?"

"Isn't Charlie Murdock the son of Ashley Peebles and

your father?"

Rudy Montanari looked bewildered. He violently shook his head. "Of course he isn't."

Roger threw out, "But Charlie *is* related to you, isn't he?"

Rudy flinched again and took the remaining swig of the alcohol.

"You can have more if you want," said Nick. The young man poured himself another stiff portion.

"I don't know if I'm really related to him, but I'm positive that my father isn't Charlie's dad."

"How can you be so sure?" asked Roger, vicariously enjoying every sip the younger man partook of the amber inebriant.

"Because when I was 18 years old, I overheard a conversation between my parents regarding Charlie's welfare. My mother begged for the child to be raised with loving care, as it was obvious he would never be a threat to the family's integrity. She never pointed a finger at my father or accused him of fathering Charlie. Instead, it seemed as if . . ."

"As *if* what?" said Nick leaning forward. Roger's color had heightened.

"It seemed as if my father had taken on the responsibility of Charlie because of the something else. I remember my mother putting her arm around my father, and for the first time, I saw true affection between them. Up until then, all I did was pray and wait for a divorce, never realizing my Catholic parents would *never* divorce. My mother would go on being who she was; sweet, loving, and giving, and my father would go on being a demanding and overbearing jerk. My three sisters all ran off, and my two brothers . . . Well, they enlisted and headed to Nam. That should tell you a lot about my dad."

"So, you believe that the child is somehow related to you but don't know the real connection?"

"Maybe . . ." He shuffled his feet, appearing highly uncomfortable. "Trish said her husband knew the whole truth and was blackmailing my father."

Nick wanted to chortle with glee. "So, Thad Fisher knew the child's origin and had become a blackmailer."

"I think so."

"You *think* so?"

"Well, I can't be sure if he was blackmailing my father about Charlie or something else, but I know for certain he was blackmailing my father. Once, when my father was gone on a business trip, I went through his papers. I must have been about twenty at the time, and I discovered a dozen or so checks made out to Thad Fisher."

"Checks in what amount?" asked Nick.

"Five thousand or ten thousand at a pop, dated every two to three months. My dad was keeping Thad Fisher, and most likely, his many mistresses as well."

"That's one of the things that attracted you to Trish Fisher, wasn't it? You viewed her as a scorned and betrayed woman, so you reached out for her." Roger's voice sounded kind.

"It's true," said Rudy, turning his gaze to Roger, who sat humped in the chair, the pillow billowing around him. "My father's just learned about my relationship with Trish and is livid. He had my wife all picked out. I've informed him that if Trish and I marry, we won't have any children."

Nick remembered the tabloid and Rudolph's supposed fiancée. "And the Montanari line will die out," said Nick. "You'll be the last surviving male Montanari."

"That's right," said Randy. "And that's not such a bad idea. Bad blood runs in my family—at least in the male side. I'm praying I've sidestepped that genetic flaw. You've surmised my father isn't the most noble of creatures, especially since he started having some financial difficulties, which he won't explain to either my mother or me. He bought the house on Chester Street under the company's umbrella and put up Eddie and Charlie Murdock there."

"And that's bankrupting him?"

"Not that. It's because my father was being blackmailed by both Thad Fisher and someone else. I found this in his desk two weeks before Thad was murdered."

Nick grasped the envelope extended towards him. A message written in a strange, cramped scrawl went straight to the point. Nick read it out loud for Roger to hear, suspecting Rudy Montanari already knew it by heart.

"*How dare you, Anthony Montanari,*" he read, "*indicate that you will no longer take responsibility for your family's sins! She was defiled, I say, defiled, and if you want me to expose all the sordid details to the police, you had better pay up and keep paying just like you have always done. If you even consider breaking our covenant, you will receive a most brutal sign from God. I will rid you of that leech who drains your funds, your youth, and your health. I will help you, but by doing so, you must never break our pact. It is a mere penance for his sins; a further chance to buy his soul out of purgatory. You will meet your obligations as I have always met mine.*"

There was no signature, just the small crabbed handwriting so odd and contorted that Nick wondered if someone had written it with an old feather pen; the kind you dipped into the inkwell and scratched upon protesting paper.

"It's obvious this is a threat," said Nick. "Fox remained positive the fingers were a warning. You might have saved Thad's life if you'd shared this with the police."

"I know. The least I can do is let you keep the letter. I expect Trish or my father can't leave town?"

"We already know Anthony was out of town when Thad and Connie were murdered and verified Trish was busy those nights as well," said Roger carefully.

"So I've wasted my time."

"Telling the truth is never a waste of time. This letter may be the key we're looking for."

Rudy tipped his glass and gulped the last the bit of bourbon. "Thanks for that, at least."

He set down the drink upon the cluttered desk and shook Nick's hand somberly. "No, don't get up," he said to Roger, who struggled to rise, and leaned down to shake the detective's hand. Rudy jerked back as if burned. "Where did you get that?"

Roger seemed momentarily confused. "I beg your pardon?"

Rudolph snatched up the sketch of the young woman with the bronze hair. "That's just like the photo."

"You know her?" exclaimed Nick.

"No. I mean, I know of her. My mom organized a scholarship fund in her memory."

"You're positive about that?"

"Yes—I remember specifically. Mom set up a science fund for disadvantaged girls in the county. It's been ongoing for several years now. I attended the banquet last year where five scholarships were handed out. They call the fund the Miss Delly Science award and her photo was on the program. She was quite pretty with beautiful red hair. I'm afraid I don't know her last name."

"How did she die?" burst out Roger.

"I believe my mom said it was some unique disease

causing her to pass away in her senior year of high school. She'd been accepted to UCLA, but never made it."

"Were your brothers acquainted with her?" asked Nick, watching Rudy's slackening face. The alcohol was taking effect.

"I don't know. Maybe. I'm sorry I don't remember any more. Is she involved in all this?"

Nick smiled. "Hard to say. Thanks, Rudy; you've been a big help."

"I love Trish Fisher, Inspector, and would protect her with my life, and I swear on my brothers' graves she was never involved in any part of her husband's murder."

Rudy teetered his way out the door and down the hall, his footsteps shuffling in the hall.

"We're fortunate he didn't see this one." Roger scooped the other sketch from the floor, the brutal rape screaming for revenge. "The woman's real, then. So how did *you* come up with this?"

"Images come and images go. If I draw them, they stay."

Roger whistled. "No wonder they call you a spook. Fox is mighty unsettled about your *little* gift."

"It's the nature of the beast," dismissed Nick. The phone jangled.

"Thayne, this is Officer Phelps. Eddie Murdock is being booked on suspicion of murder. Dr. Koh just phoned.

Charlie Murdock's teeth marks are a definite match to the bite on Connie Judson's shoulder."

"And the kid?"

"Under surveillance. No one can get an intelligible word out of him."

"You're a pip," said Nick, suddenly straightening. "Come on Roger. I need you to look at something else before we play tag with Chief Rollins."

Chapter 23

There are cold dark places that no one should ever wake up to. They smell of formaldehyde and dust and death. They have shelves loaded with everyday things intermingled with the vile and hideous. Lea gasped at the seemingly innocent face before her as the truth settled into place, her nostrils flaring before a prick in her arm sent her into a dreamless void. The killer wondered if it was necessary to remove the P.I.'s finger after death. But hey, why break with tradition?

Louise's Boarding House was fairly, quiet except for an obnoxious poodle that kept yapping and sniffing at Roger's sandals as Nick unlocked his room.

"Get away, you putrid beast," growled Roger at the pretentiously groomed white fluff ball.

"Not a dog lover, Roger?"

"I like 'em well enough if they have a dignified bark and some flesh on their bones. God save me from a toy poodle."

"Come on in, buddy. You'd better find a chair before you redesign your face on my carpet."

Roger sank gratefully in the overstuffed chair positioned in front of the large TV screen. "This is where you stayed before—last time you were here on that missing person's case."

"That's right. I'd break ole Louise's heart if I dared go elsewhere. Can I get you something to drink?"

"Yeah, some of Fox's bourbon," Roger grumbled.

"Humph. A diet coke for you." The can hissed before finding its way into Roger's tired hand. He took a sip and smiled.

"God bless caffeine. So, why did you drag me here?"

"I need you to look at something; something you have to promise you'll share with no one else."

Roger balked. "I share *everything* with Susan. She's my right-hand man."

"Not this time, buddy. You've got to promise me."

Roger thought long and hard. "Alright," he said finally. Why did it feel like a betrayal of his marriage vows?

Nick unearthed his portfolio from the bottom drawer of the pale chest of drawers and handed it to his friend. Roger unwound the string, and within seconds, let out a long whistle.

"You're quite the artist."

"Yeah, right."

Roger squinted at the first drawing. The gangster's t-shirt stated *Big Rapper* in slasher-style letters across the front. A dead body lay ominously still at the teen's feet.

"It was his shirt that enabled Rick and I to finger Mendez. The search warrant revealed the discarded top in the clothes bin and the rival gang victim's shirt held traces of Julio's blood. He was tried as an adult. It didn't hurt that Mendez confessed.

"And this one? It's just of a building."

"The place where the Wiederitz twins were being held. Luckily, my partner Rick was familiar with the area and recognized the coffee shop on the corner. The kidnapper was a pedophile who dealt in child trafficking. He was the biggest sicko I've ever met."

"So, how does it work?"

Nick cracked his neck, the sound unnaturally loud in the otherwise quiet room, and sank down at Roger's feet. "I don't know, it's sorta like . . . I absorb scenes or information that is unvoiced and it in turn ends up on the paper. When I go about my daily work, I meet lots of people; people who may or may not be criminals or victims. Usually, when I'm working on one case, I can pinpoint the sketches' origins, but sometimes—like at the precinct—I run in to so many people with so many pasts that I have no clue as to who or what the sketch refers to. That's why there's a ton of drawings in my portfolio that have no point of origin. I can't make heads or tails of them."

"Freaky. So you're like a sponge, absorbing significant images, but not always able to decipher how they're important. But, what sparks your impulse to produce the pictures?"

The truth was embarrassing. "It usually happens when I drink. Something flows out of me and the pencil flies across the paper and images appear. I always use pencil, but sometimes, like here . . . a color is so vivid I have to put it in." A little girl's face peered fearfully at Roger. She sat on a rickety bed clutching a threadbare stuffed dog, the bright blue ribbon in her hair the only startling color within the entire drawing.

"This was another kidnap victim?"

"Yeah. I call the gift *the flow* because it seems to flow out of my brain into my fingers and onto the page. Thank God I was working on that case, or I wouldn't have known how to reference the picture."

"So that's the real reason you quit the SFPD?"

"For the most part. Every night after a few beers, I'd produce 4 or 5 of these. Imagine me the next morning, trying to wade through their meanings and relevance. It was driving me crazy. Plus, I lived too close to my dad. Another unfortunate incident motivated me to leave the force; I connected a flow with someone I truly believed was innocent. It became too much of a bitter pill for me to swallow when I learned the truth."

"I see. Mind if I examine the rest of these?"

"Not at all, if you have the stomach for it."

It was an exhausting 30 minutes for both of them. Roger was thorough, studying every sketch and occasionally breaking the silence by asking pointed questions.

"I take it the ones with the star to the right remain unsolved?"

"Yeah, nearly two-thirds of them. Some crime-solver, huh?"

Suddenly, Roger drew in a sharp breath. He had examined over 100 sketches and was nearing the end of the hefty pile. The last few drawings were encased in a top folding sketchpad, the dates scribbled on the lower right hand corner indicating they were current.

"Good God!"

Nick leaned forward and sighed. "Yeah, that's a beaute isn't it?"

Lane and Jeremy Fox hung from a huge oak tree skirting a potato field. On the periphery of the horrific scene, an obese man dressed a three-piece suit, his back to the viewer, impassively smoked a large stogie.

"This is one image never released to the papers. And of course, the mystery man was never in the original photograph. I wonder who he is? Fox would kill you if she knew you'd drawn this. When did you do it?" Roger shuddered slightly. He'd helped cut the bodies down.

"The other night after a royal binge. I completed the next one as well."

A man's head rested against the steering wheel, the gunshot wound to the back of his head oozing black-penciled blood. "Shit," burst out Roger.

"You know who he is?"

"That's John Weinberg, the third man killed that night. Worked for Fox and was popped off as he waited in the car. Christ, man. It's like you photographed these but from a different angle and perspective."

"It's almost enough to make me stop drinking," snorted Thayne. He wished he could take a long, cool drink right now.

"The soda can with the finger and the two of the girl—that's all you can link to this case?"

"Nope, there's this last one, but I've already identified the subject."

Roger made a sharp noise. "The oldest Montanari boy?"

"Yup, Anthony Jr., army uniform and all."

"Show me the other two—the ones of the girl."

Nick rose and wandered to the dinette where he'd tossed the plastic bag housing the three sketches. He tossed them onto Roger's lap. "What do you think?"

Roger tapped his finger on the pretty redhead's face; her locks were the only part of the picture with color. "So, we at least know her name's Miss Delly."

"Yup. And in the second frame, she's being raped by a dark-haired man. God, look at the terror on her face." He cleared his throat. "I'm inclined to believe it's Montanari Jr."

"Maybe—or the senior. It's hard to tell from your sketch."

Nick sighed. "So what's the use of the damn gift if I can't figure out the most important facts?"

Roger leaned back against the pillow and scratched his stitches absently. "I take it you inherited this special *gift* from your maternal grandmother? You referred to her once as a 'seer.'" He sighed deeply. "You know, Nick, gifts are gifts, and you've got to learn how to use them to your advantage without letting them destroy you."

"Kinda like Spidy, huh? But how credible would it be to show the sketches to a suspect?"

"Now, now, you can't expect to have complete acuity regarding the *flow* can you? You know, there are a few simple things we can do, like run this sketch all discreet-like through the system and see if there's a match. The key, in my opinion, is finding someone who can link you to the meaning of the drawing."

"Like Fox, who has all the details of her family's murders?"

"Yeah, or me perhaps. What happened, as far as I can surmise, is while you were around Fox, the images surrounding the unsolved murder of her relations crowded into your subconscious. I'm sure the reality of that triple murder never really quits her mind. Those images, sparked by Fox's passion to find her family's murderer, flowed out later during your binge. Because you'd heard of the case, you were able to make the conscious connection to the Fox murders. But the tantalizing question is where did the figure of the fat man come from?" He lifted a finger, his dark eyes intense. "That's the challenge, my friend."

"That's why I'm a spook."

Roger laughed. "That you are! So, be cautious with whom you share the magnitude of your gift. The advantage is you're not on a force anymore. You can work alone—or get yourself a team who accepts the gift for what it is: a useful tool."

Nick scoffed. "So, I find a few compatriots who are willing to work with a freak?"

"Freak is a relative term. I prefer *uncomfortably gifted.* Imagine the unstoppable force you could become as a detective."

"And just where do I find these compatriots? In Fox?"

"Yeah, our bitchy Ms. Fox would be a fine foil to your methods."

"Oh, give me a break. She's so pragmatic they could dedicate a *Dragnet* episode to her."

Roger chuckled and then immediately clutched at his

painful stitches. "*Just the facts madam—just the facts,*" he quoted. "I can see what you mean. But you've made a start by sharing with me. I can help and most definitely keep a secret. Susan would divorce me if she knew I'd held out on some of our past escapades."

Nick grinned evilly. "Speaking about topics for blackmail . . ."

Roger rose heavily. "Drive me over to the station and I'll run this through."

Thayne ran his damp fingers over the front of his perfect trousers. "You don't find all of this a little bit odd?"

Roger nodded. "Of course I do—you're a first class wacko—but then again, I always knew something else was up with you besides just being a plain old pain in the ass. And, if you knew some of the weird relatives I have . . . your little *gift* is almost mundane. My cousin May Ling swears trees and plants protest to her about the agonies of pruning. My uncle Titus only goes trout fishing stark naked, and my brother-in-law is a *coroner*, for God's sake. Talk about weird. You should witness our dinner conversation whenever Steven visits. Moo Goo Gai Pan combined with discussions of hypoxia and vagal inhibition can really stimulate the salivary glands, I tell you. I least now I *understand* you. Now, run me to the station and I'll put this through."

Randy Phelps was bucking for an award as the world's

best junior officer. Not only did he accept the sketch unquestionably, but promised to call Ruth Montanari to see if she remembered Miss Delly's last name.

A familiar, deep baritone voice greeted them. The face was welcome.

"Well, hello, Inspector Thayne. And you, Detective. Ain't you supposed to be in bed?" This Philemon directed to Roger, who was hanging onto the counter while Randy assisted Nick.

"They sprung you?" smiled Nick, genuine relief on his face. Philemon looked no worse for wear, but hugged his Bible against his chest like a shield. His clothes might be rumpled, but his spirits were high.

"You bet they did. I just had time to call Darcy to come pick me up—when they handed me back my wallet and watch and whatnot—and presto, here I am—a free man. Between the facts that I was at choir rehearsal every night last week practicing for our Fall Festival and they've pulled in someone else as a suspect, I guess they just couldn't keep me." He beamed, his dark eyes turning misty behind his glasses.

"I'm happy to hear it. So, now what?"

"They say I'm not to leave town. That poor young woman's finger was found in a soda can I'd drunk from, so I'm still not totally off the hook. I explained that cream soda is my downfall—I must chug a six-pack a day, and I have a tendency to leave the cans everywhere. I just hope all comes right. Meanwhile, I'll see if Mrs. Simms wants me tomorrow. I can't imagine that little old lady is able to cope with that garden of hers. I long to be among the flowers and trees again. Ain't a lot of 'em here."

Roger agreed. "That's for certain."

Nick edged close to Philemon. "It you ever get tired of cutting grass, why don't you give me a ring." A tasteful business card was pressed into the older man's hand. "Not certain I could pay you much more than you make gardening, but I sure could use someone with your kind of savvy around."

"You're aware of what I've been?"

"Never convicted, were you? All hearsay, I'd say. And I know you work hard—that's one mighty fine garden on Chester Street."

Darcy burst into the station, bypassing the understanding receptionist.

"Phil, Phil! You alright honey?" She gripped the slight man stoutly, pressing him forcefully against her plump bosom. She smelled of vanilla and cinnamon and children's laughter.

"Don't cry, missy, I'm coming home. There, there." He patted her gently; nodding to the two detectives over his wife's shaking shoulders. Finally, in hopes of calming the distraught woman he asked, "What's for dinner? I'm hungry."

Darcy Jenkins pulled away and sniffed, searching for a crumpled handkerchief in the recesses of her large black handbag. "Bless you, Philemon. You can eat the entire backside of a horse and still be hungry. It's meat loaf, with my special homemade gravy."

"Better than that truck they serve up here." Philemon took her hand firmly, and waving the Bible at the pair, proudly escorted his wife through the wide glass doors of the station.

"What about the sketch?" asked Roger pointedly.

One of the many drawings in Nick's portfolio had depicted Philemon standing over a still corpse, a silencer in his experienced hand.

"That was long ago. He wasn't wearing glasses and sported more hair. And who am I to mistrust the reviving and forgiving power of Jesus? We've gotta go. Thanks, Randy. Keep in contact."

The freckled rookie nodded while feeding a copy of the mystery girl's sketch into the fax machine.

It was a quarter to seven, and after tucking Roger into the cramped bucket seat of the Mustang, Nick scooted to the golf range to wait for Chief Rollins.

Just like clockwork, Richard Rollins showed up at seven on the nose. He parked his car in front of *The Range* and maneuvered his heavy body out of the sedan; his face was drawn and pale. He didn't bother to wait near his car, but immediately scuttled through the wire gate where golfers would line up to tee off. Nick and Roger followed him discreetly, partially hiding themselves behind the equipment shed. Chief Rollins paced and kicked at the dirt. It was mostly empty at this hour, the nearest golfer a hundred yards away at the other end of the driving range. Pretty soon the purr of an expensive car, followed by the clatter of high heels filled the evening calm. Nick wasn't remotely surprised to see Trish Fisher.

"Hello, Trish," said Chief Rollins, reaching out his arms to enfold her. She gracefully pushed him away, keeping her distance. Mrs. Fisher was still dressed in black, but this time, had draped an expensive fox stole around her shoulders, animal rights clearly not one of her charity priorities.

"It's all going to come out now," said Trish abruptly. "And if you don't come clean, your job may be forfeit. I have that much clout with the mayor, Richard. She has a personal hatred of bastards who lie."

"I know," said Richard heavily. Clearly this interview wasn't going how he planned. "I've been thinking about retiring anyway and taking Nancy away somewhere. All this is weighing too heavily on my shoulders. I should never have made that stupid promise to Anthony."

"This town is full of secrets," said Trish. "Too many secrets, in my opinion. And I, for one, have had enough of them. You know that gardener Philemon Jenkins didn't do it just as you know I never hired him. The man is retired, for heaven's sake. He's practically purchased the new steeple of the Southern Baptist Church single-handedly with his tithings.

God, I hate born-agains!"

"I released him just before I came here."

"It's high time you did *something* right."

"Anthony must have finally snapped," said Richard heavily. "I never really believed he'd pop off Thad."

"I never thought it would come to this. While I can't say I'm sorry the bastard's dead, it must have been an awful way to die. I appreciate you trying to protect me, but you can't shield me any longer. Thad was a horribly flawed man, and Anthony must have finally had enough. And Richard, dear, you've got to come to terms with the fact that our relationship was over years ago."

"We could have made it, Trish, if you'd just given it a chance. I always thought . . . hoped . . . that maybe we could get back together if my wife and I got divorced. It's not too late."

Trish Fisher was a strong woman and used her incredible fortitude now. "I was wrong to cheat on my husband with you, Richard. At that time, I didn't care because he was out with any woman whose skirt he could lift. But that's all in the past. I've found a new man now, and I'm going to start over as soon as this all dies down"

"It doesn't have to come out."

"Oh, pleez! Use the brains God gave you!" she said sharply. "Blackmail always returns to bite the blackmailer in the butt. You know it, and I know it. My husband had a black heart and hung around the Montanari boys a little too much in the old days and became just like them. Sooner or later, the truth's coming out. That Fox woman is a tenacious one—if she doesn't already know the truth, she'll ferret it out; that I can guarantee you."

"Goddamn Fox. Every time she comes into the picture, my life gets screwed up."

"Answer me truly, Richard. Did you want the wrong man convicted of the crime?"

Richard hung his head. He had always been one to seek the easiest way out. "No," he mumbled.

"You know, Richard, I always suspected Thad killed that poor girl Ashley years ago, and after that he was out of my heart and my bed. I may have done him an injustice, but I still know he was somehow involved in her death. I need the truth to finally come out—all of it!"

"What a goddamn mess!"

"Now that Charlie's been found, you've got to force Anthony to come clean as well, because if he doesn't, I *will.*"

"I'll call him tonight," said Richard heavily.

"I'm leaving this town as soon as everything is settled. You might think about relocating as well, since our days are finished here. We need to pass the reins over to a new generation." Trish Fisher straightened her stole. She hesitated before leaving, giving Richard Rollins a soft peck on the cheek. "I'm sorry if I've hurt you, Richard, but you haven't done well by anyone by protecting Anthony."

"Please, Trish."

"Don't phone me again, Richard. Nancy never found out. I'd like to keep it that way."

She scurried off, leaving Richard standing forlornly as the moths and night insects fluttered furiously around the street lamp. Finally, he straightened his tired back and headed towards his car. As he passed their hiding place, Richard turned his head towards the darkening sky slowly becoming encrusted with pinpricks of light that gave just enough illumination to reveal the single tear trickling down the police chief's cheek.

Nick and Roger waited until the chief's car took off.

"So, now what?" asked Roger tiredly.

They sat in the cherry-red Mustang indecisively until Nick's cell sounded.

"Inspector Thayne, this is Randy Phelps." The rookies' voice rang high and light, as if he were in an excited whirl.

"What is it, Phelps?"

"It's about Charlie."

"Charlie—you mean Bouncer."

"Yeah, the dwarf. Mrs. Neil from Waterford called. They managed to settle him down, and he was playing with some cars and all. I guess Mrs. Neil started asking him his name, and you know what he said?"

The kid was a master of suspense. "Well what?"

"Bouncer. Bouncer *Cimey*. He started chanting it over and over again. Mrs. Waterford called, sounding confused because she was under the perception his last name was Murdock. So I went to the holding pen to see Mr. Murdock, and he refused to verify it one way or another, so I think it must be true."

"You've been a big help, Randy. No trace on the girl?"

"None, sir, but I'll keep trying. Ruth Montanari is in San Diego at some sort of interior designer's convention and doesn't answer her cell phone."

"Keep trying with Mrs. Montanari and look up Cimey in the state birth records, and call me as soon as you find something." He disconnected and peered at Roger. "Let's head to Chester Street. I'm worried about Fox, and I'd like to take another look at both the Collins and Simms houses; there's something that bothers me about the whole setup. So, Bouncer's last name is not Murdock. This is the key, Roger."

Roger squinted at this wristwatch. "Oh, go ahead. I'll be up shit creek already once Susan discovers I'm not home. I might as well bury myself in the stuff."

"I like your attitude, Chung!"

"Just wait til you get married, you heartless bastard."

Chapter 24

Nick screeched up in front of the Collins house. Fox's car was gone.

"I guess she's taken off—and without calling. How typical. Well, since we're here, I'd like to speak with Mrs. Simms again."

Nick strode up the cobbled, well-lit pathway to her front door, Roger lagging behind. Even for all Nick's pounding, it took several long minutes for the shuffling feet of Mrs. Simms to open the door. She peered at them behind her small spectacles.

"May I help you, gentleman? Oh, Inspector Thayne. How nice to see you again. And who are you?" She adjusted her glasses and peered intently at him.

"I'm Roger Chung from the Monroe PD."

"You're the one who had that terrible attack."

"Yes, of appendicitis."

"And does your family know you're out gallivanting around in your condition?"

"Um . . . yes." Roger lied. "I'm perfectly fine now."

"Hum. You could use some chamomile tea. That'll put you back into sorts. Come in, come in."

The pair followed the scarecrow-thin senior citizen into the impressive foyer. Roger whistled admiringly as Mrs. Simms beamed.

"We were wondering if Inspector Fox paid you a visit this afternoon?" asked Nick, more concerned about Fox than Mrs. Simms' lovely home.

"Your young crippled partner? Yes, she was here. In such a hurry, though. Didn't want any tea." Mrs. Simms appeared indignant.

"About what time was that?" asked Nick

"Maybe four or five. It was still afternoon—not dusk. Maybe five-thirty. Oh, I just don't remember." She appeared momentarily confused. Nick noticed a lovely pale salmon orchid setting on a low oriental table with beautifully carved legs. "I just brought that in today," said Mrs. Simms proudly, noting the direction of his gaze. "Isn't it lovely? Yesterday, it was just a bud and now it's bloomed."

The flower's stamen, resembling a small tongue, edged out of the interior of the delicate blossom. Nick and Roger followed Mrs. Simms into the elaborate living room, the high ceilings of which emphasized the chamber's pleasant use of space and style.

"Detective Fox asked you some questions, I take it?"

"She certainly did. She was very interested in my greenhouse. Said there was some connection between the greenhouse and Philemon."

"Philemon Jenkins?" asked Roger, leaning down to sniff the flower.

"It doesn't have a scent, Officer. Yes, my gardener." Mrs. Simms led them into a beautiful sitting room whose ebony grand piano sat dustless and quiet. "Please sit down, gentlemen. I don't get much company." Roger sank down gratefully upon the plush blue couch and unashamedly hoisted his feet up on the matching ottoman.

"Did she mention what the connection was?" Thayne wasn't about to mention that Philemon had been released earlier that evening.

"Ms. Fox was certain now that my gardener—though I find this very difficult to believe—had actually killed the ex-mayor. I told her I didn't believe it even though the police had confiscated some tools that they said had Philemon's fingerprints. I told her, just like I told that sweet young officer on Saturday, that of course his fingerprints were on it. He's my gardener, after all, and a wonderful gardener at that."

"Does Philemon ever do any work inside your greenhouse?"

"Only sometimes. The orchids in there are my own personal pets, but he's quite interested, and a quick learner. Philemon is a whiz in the garden. He does a wonderful job of taking care of my hydrangeas." Mrs. Simms leaned closer as if sharing a trade secret. "He sprinkles just enough acid fertilizer on the roots to insure the deepest purple blooms possible. I've never had that great luck of with them until Philemon started work. I told Ms. Fox that she was entirely incorrect about him."

"Did she relate the events from this morning at the house across the street?"

"Events?"

"A young retarded man, who is also extremely handicapped, was discovered living there with his caretaker."

"She didn't say a thing! Why, that's impossible. I've lived here for years, and I'd swear on a stack of Bibles that *no one* resides there."

"But didn't you report a sewage problem earlier this year?"

"Why, yes. Philemon said there was often an awful stench coming from the rear of the house. The city indicated it was probably a broken sewage line."

"And you didn't hear the commotion this morning?"

She tapped her ear. "My hearing isn't what it used to be. Oh, and I went out for some groceries mid-morning. I must have missed it."

"I'm surprised she didn't relate the incident to you."

Mrs. Simms held up a thin hand. "Ms. Fox was probably going to tell me but got a phone call right in the midst of our conversation."

She teetered daintily upon the corner of an East Africa pili-pili bed covered by a rich burgundy Afghan rug. The room was amazing in how it blended warm Western couches with more exotic pieces from all around the world. Next to her sat several Polynesian woodcarvings of sea turtles, which Nick knew represented good luck.

"I see," he said. "Do you know who initiated the call?"

"Ah, let me think. Yes I believe she said, 'Hello, Mr. Cambridge. Are you holding fast?'"

"Luke Cambridge," repeated Nick under his breath. "So, what did she do then?"

"Well, she left so abruptly, saying he had some crucial information for her. I think she said she was going to drive down to Modesto. But it was going to be dark soon. Driving at night is such a strain on the eyes, and I told her so. And she didn't even look at the greenhouse. I have a *Coelogyne rhodeana* that just came into bloom and wanted to show it to her."

"She mentioned nothing else?"

"Oh, she did. Just as she was leaving, Ms. Fox actually mentioned that you might stop by, and then it happened." Mrs. Simms appeared genuinely reluctant to continue.

Roger's ears pricked up. "And what was that?"

"She was in such a hurry that, well, she slipped on the tiles and fell. I was so dreadfully appalled, but when I tried to help her up she seemed rather . . . indignant."

"She slipped and fell?" exclaimed Roger. "Was she hurt?"

"Oh, I think it might just have been her pride—you know, because of her foot and all—but anyway, her cell phone fell and broke into five or six pieces. I helped her pick it up, but she was swearing under her breath. So unladylike."

Roger bit his lip to keep from smiling. Somehow that didn't surprise him at all.

Nick seemed less amused. "So, you're certain she got a phone call from someone named Cambridge and then took off?"

"Yes. I watched her walk right out the door and get into her car. It was a little Mazda."

"That's very interesting."

"You know, I suggested that she take her phone into the mobile repair center right near the mall. I've heard some fine things about those people. As she was leaving, I told her she was all wrong about Philemon, and that I was thinking of posting his bail. I know he's innocent."

"That's very kind of you," said Nick vaguely. "I was wondering if Detective Chung and I could check out your greenhouse?"

Mrs. Simms looked mildly surprised before brightening. "Of course. I have some lovely flowers in bloom. Please, come along, but do watch your step as it's gotten quite dark."

They followed the elderly woman into the brightly lit greenhouse where a couple dozen orchids bloomed exotically. Mrs. Simms pointed to some of the tools hanging on the wall. The shovel looked clean and bright.

"I remember now why she wanted to visit my greenhouse. Ms. Fox said she wanted to see this shovel. Said something about the curvature of this end part here, that she suspected it might have been used by Philemon to cut off the ex-mayor's ring finger. I told her she was absolutely barking up the wrong tree, that she had her facts all mixed up. It was all so peculiar. She's an odd one, she is."

"You can say that again," murmured Nick. Mrs. Simms turned, obviously expecting Roger and Nick to follow her. Roger did so obediently, but Nick lingered, looking along the broad benches of the spacious greenhouse. At the far end, a broken pot littered the wooden slat floor.

"Did you have an accident, Mrs. Simms?"

Mrs. Simms turned around. "What's that, young man?"

"I notice you have a broken pot down here."

"Oh, I dropped it. It's my rheumatism." She held up stubby fingers to show him. "I'm finding it harder and harder to take care of my orchids." She led the pair away from the humid greenhouse and down a pathway made of circular steppingstones. "I just hope I don't have to get rid of them, but

I have to face facts. This old house, the orchids, and plants are all just too much for me. I dread moving into a smaller place or accepting that nonsense they call assisted living. I won't let that happen to me."

Roger nodded half-heartedly, his mind elsewhere. Mrs. Simms was offended. "Don't scoff, young man. It can happen to you. Before you know it, you're in your sixties and poof, the body refuses to cooperate with the mind. You start falling apart."

"These are indeed lovely roses," Nick said, hoping to calm her. It worked.

"Oh, yes. While my orchids of course are my pride and joy, my other favorite flowers are roses. That's a *Mr. Lincoln*. Though you can't really see the hybrid teas well in this light, they bloom a bright, crimson red and are quite fragrant. You should come back sometime during daylight and visit me for tea. Bring Ms. Fox back when she isn't in such a hurry. I do enjoy having company so."

Nick smiled and leaned towards the rose bush, taking a deep whiff of the pungent blooms.

"I love your garden," stated Roger, nearly out of breath.

Mrs. Simms shook an arthritic finger at him. "Thank you, but you need to be in bed, young man." She shifted her gaze to Thayne. "I suggest you take him home right now."

Nick straightened and turned abruptly. "You're

absolutely right Mrs. Simms. Come on, Roger, let's go. You've played hooky from your sick bed long enough for one evening. I'll drop you off, and if I'm lucky, catch Fox on her way down to Modesto. Thank you so much for your time, Mrs. Simms." Instead of returning through the house, the senior citizen led them through a side gate.

"Please come back and visit. I'll make you some of my famous toffee."

"Will do," said Nick pleasantly and headed towards his car. The gate clanged shut, the shuffle of Mrs. Simms' retreating feet echoing in the cooling night air. They were nearly to his Mustang when
Thayne's cell phone vibrated. It was Officer Phelps, who was breathless as usual.

"I think I found the connection. Listen to this, Inspector Thayne. Edward Lawrence Murdock is the youngest son of Jane and Stanley Murdock, who had three children. His two older sisters' names are Edith and Margaret. Margaret is deceased but Edith . . . Edith married a man by the name of John *Simms*. Her daughter's name was Delilah Simms, and she died in childbirth in 1972."

"So, Mrs. Simms is Murdock's older sister?"

"I'd lay odds on it," Randy continued. "You know, about that Charlie. He was really hard to understand, so I got to thinking and I called Mrs. Neil again, asking if he might have meant Simms, not Cimey. She said it was likely, considering his lack of mature vocalization, as she called it."

"That's it!" cried Nick. "Charlie is Delilah Simms' son; the child of her rape. You get Anthony Montanari on the horn right now and ask him what he knows about a Miss Delly and her relationship to his sons."

"Will do," said Randy, disconnecting.

"I need fluid," said Roger leaning against the car and breathing heavily. He opened the door and grabbed his water bottle out of the passenger seat, fumbling for his medication. He took two tablets in loud gulps.

Nick watched his friend for a long time. Roger was sweating even though it wasn't that hot. Finally he spoke so quietly Roger could barely discern his whisper,

"Steven Koh suggested the murderer was someone you would least suspect. Who, in their right mind, would be wary of a feeble old lady like Mrs. Simms?"

Roger straightened. "Do you have the number of the Modesto Penitentiary?"

Less than five minutes later, Roger disconnected his cell. "Luke Cambridge never phoned Lea."

"Then I was right. Take a look at this, Roger." Nick reached into his coat pocket and produced a worn, red rubber ball.

"That's exactly like the ball Philemon said he used to play with Bouncer. Where'd you get it?"

"I just found it in Mrs. Simms' yard, near the rose

bush. When I leaned down to smell the flowers, I retrieved the toy and placed it into my pocket while you were chatting with her. At the time, I just suspected maybe it was one Philemon had dropped accidentally."

"So, you think that Mrs. Simms had something to do with all of this?"

"I'm positive. How would *she* know it was Thad Fisher's ring finger that was missing?"

"That means . . ."

"Of course. And there's something else. Did you notice the shattered pot in the far corner of the greenhouse?"

"I did. I figured Mrs. Simms had dropped a pot while she was planting."

"Maybe, but I remember something Fox said to me about the proximity rule. Sometimes a weapon is chosen because it is nearby. That's why a screwdriver killed Thad."

Roger swallowed. "You think Lea was there . . . in the greenhouse?"

"Yes, and I don't believe that nonsense about the shovel for an instant. And isn't that just like Fox, gallivanting off on her own without notifying backup?" His voice was half-angry, half-admiring.

"She's worked alone for the past three years. She doesn't ask for help or think she needs any."

"Well," said Nick gruffly. "I'd lay odds she needs some now."

The basement where Charlie Simms had been imprisoned felt cool, the lack of windows and the thick walls keeping the heat at bay.

Nick spoke softly. “Little Katie down the street witnessed a limo bringing two people to this house. No one ever saw them leave.”

“Because they were dead?”

“Maybe, but they weren’t killed here. This place’s as clean as a compulsive’s kitchen. But I suspect they didn’t go far.”

“If no one ever saw anyone enter or exit the Collins house, except for that limo the one night, then there must have been another way. It’s not like there’s a helipad on the roof.” Roger took out his handkerchief and mopped his forehead even though the basement was cool.

“Mrs. Simms is a proud woman. She loved her grandson, but he lacked the two things she wanted most in a grandchild.”

“And they were?”

“Beauty and intelligence. What a blow it must have been to a woman so obsessed with the visual perfection we find in her garden. And poor Charlie certainly offered her no intellectual stimulus. So she hid him and made those she felt responsible for his gross deficiencies pay. But she had to see him, being a grandmother, even though improvement was hopeless. So, it's got to be here somewhere."

"What's got to be here?"

"The way in and out of this house without using the road. There's no additional way out here. Let's look upstairs."

Roger progressed very slowly up the stairs and Nick immediately felt concerned.

"You alright, buddy?"

"Just gonna get some water in the kitchen. You search for that secret door. We know from experience the builders were fantastic at hiding 'em."

A few moments later a shout erupted from the kitchen. "Nick!"

Thayne bolted into the kitchen. Roger pointed to the breakfast nook where Fox's dowdy bag dangled on one of the mauve chairs.

"Is her gun inside?"

Roger dumped the contents on the Formica table. A wallet, chewing gum, a small ring of keys, a business-like comb, a Spanish-English dictionary, the F & H, and a half-empty bottle of water made up the entirety of the contents in her oversized purse.

"Not here, so she went armed. But to where?"

"I have an idea," returned Thayne. "I just hope we aren't too late."

It took them nearly 20 minutes to locate the wine cellar. The huge metal door opening to the tunnel had been left slightly ajar.

Roger's cheeks were overly flushed. "She was here."

"Goddamn, Fox. Guess she didn't believe this little passageway was significant enough to mention to me. You brought your service revolver, Roger?"

"Never leave home without it."

"Then come on." They followed the well-designed passageway under the stark glare of the carefully spread out light bulbs. They were rewarded at the end of the meandering tunnel with a set of earthen steps. The heavy wooden door at the top was firmly shut, obviously padlocked from the inside.

"Now what?" panted Roger.

"I think this is where the valiant police inspector takes out his gun and fires at the lock fearing that a young woman's life may be in danger. I do believe that's your cameo role in all this, Mr. Chung."

Roger grinned, his straight, white teeth flashing. "Always saw myself as the hero. Stand back," he ordered and aimed his pistol at the brass fixture, blowing it to smithereens.

"Clint Eastwood would be impressed," mocked Nick gently. It was just as he'd suspected—the wide wooden door opened up into the humid greenhouse. The broken pot had been swept up and discarded in the circular green trash bin. Roger leaned over and salvaged a large piece.

"Does that look like blood to you?" he asked, angling the jagged piece so Nick could inspect the stained surface.

"I think this is where you call backup," stated Nick grimly and Roger nodded. "Let's just hope Connie Judson's fate hasn't happened to Fox." He remembered almost pleasantly her petite form, straight back, god-awful clothes, and determined chin. Though it galled him to admit the fact, it was highly likely Lea had Mrs. Simms figured out way before he did.

The back door was unlocked, enabling Nick and Roger to step cautiously into a country kitchen furnished in sweet pine and modern appliances. A loaf of delicious-smelling banana bread cooled on a wooden cutting board, and white soup with large chunks of potato simmered gently on a gas-burning stove. Nick raised his fingers to his lips and silently pushed open the swinging door. A large, raftered dining room whose oval cherry wood table was decorated with a massive Chinese vase crammed with pink and white roses remained still and inviting, the fragrance from the cut blooms nearly overpowering.

Nick gestured cautiously to Roger, indicating he should search the left wing of the house while he took the right. The serviceable scullery situated next to an ample-sized utility and pantry yielded nothing. The adjoining library was deserted, its huge stone fireplace seasonally decorated with huge pinecones and facing wide shelves crammed with books. A wine-colored recliner complete with discarded knitting needles and a pale yellow and white, two-inch strip of yarn gave the room a homey, satisfying feel. Mrs. Simms appeared the epitome of the gentle old grandmother puttering around her large house and lamenting the advent of old age. A silver-framed photo rested on a small writing desk.

"Bingo," whispered Nick.

Delilah Simms had indeed been lovely; a testament to innocence and beauty. The screaming, contorted face of his sketch barely resembled the tranquil stillness of the redheaded teenager in the photo. Roger appeared at the doorway, and Nick pointed to the picture. Roger shook his head. The horror of it all was becoming way too clear.

"Nothing down here. Let's try the upstairs."

Roger followed his friend as they moved soundlessly up the richly carpeted staircase. An impressive landing opened onto a wide hall. The first bedroom on the left held a king-sized bed adorned in soft mauve colors and appeared to be Mrs. Simms' room. The other two bedrooms produced nothing out of the ordinary, but the third housed a large crib similar to the one found in the basement of the Collins house. In the corner, a small pile of little metal cars and trucks lay scattered, along with a few red and yellow balls similar to the one in Nick's pocket.

"Clouds," said Nick, gazing at the wallpaper. This was the place.

Further examination of the crib revealed peeling flakes of paint as if someone had gnawed at its metal sides.

"Look," hissed Roger. Clear scratch marks marred the crib's side—marks that could have easily been made by handcuffs or chains. Had Thad Fisher been drugged and chained to this crib? This room faced the rear of the house, so neighbors wouldn't ever hear the screams of the incarcerated. Nick approached the Tudor window and swung it open. Directly below, a trellis, upon which a lovely *Joseph's Coat* crawled, tilted at a crazy angle. At least a dozen other species of rose bushes filled the planter. Two of them had deep red petals; just like Mr. Lincoln hybrid tea roses.

"Thad tried to escape by jumping from this window. I'm positive he landed in the roses, the thorns from the Mr. Lincoln's there imbedding his bare feet."

Roger edged closer. "I bet he made for the green house, knowing about the passageway."

"And she was there, halting his escape with a well-placed screwdriver."

Roger disappeared, only to return a few moments later. "There's only a large bathroom at the end of the hall, but it's worth checking out."

This bath/shower combination mirrored its huge twin in the basement of the Collins house. A large drain, centered within the tile stalls, indicated that Charlie had used this facility often.

"I'd like to wait for backup, but we've got to find Fox. Time may be running out. Where the hell is she?"

Roger speculated for a long moment. “It’s clear she’s not in the main house. There’s got to be a basement; somewhere Mrs. Simms could stash the boy while Philemon or anyone else for that matter was around.”

Nick snapped his fingers. “The broom closet! I’d bet we’ll find a similar door to the one in the Collins house that led to Bouncer and Eddie’s bedrooms. Come on, Roger!”

Chapter 25

The hearty soup still bubbled on the unattended stove as a persistent fly's blue metallic body buzzed near the perfectly browned crust of the banana bread. Nick pointed to the broom closet door near the rear entryway. "Does that look familiar to you, Roger?"

"It does indeed," agreed the older detective.

The staircase was amazingly steep, its steps formed from roughly cut, thick wood. Even so, a plank near the bottom creaked loudly at their descent.

A pleasant voice drifted towards them. "If you move another step closer, I'm afraid your partner will never understand what really happened to her after she entered my greenhouse."

Mrs. Simms sat prettily in, of all things, a grandmotherly rocking chair. The *Kahr K9* resting in her dainty hand, however, was not grandmotherly in the least. Edith Simms shook the solid little pistol confidently at Roger.

"I'd place your service revolver on the floor there, or

I'll have to have to demonstrate what years of practice at the firing range have achieved for me. You've seen someone shot at close range, of course, officer? The blood can splatter most horribly and I really do hate messes."

Roger tossed his revolver on the wooden floor, but Nick was hesitant to follow. Mrs. Simms leveled the gun at him.

"Do you know why I like this pistol, Detective? It's so simple to use. Nothing fancy to mar the singular purpose of a gun, which is to kill. There's just this simple trigger, slide lever, and magazine release button. Oh, and of course two seven-round magazines, in case I miss you after my first attempt."

"Okay," said Nick dropping his Glock beside Roger's service revolver.

Edith Simms smiled pleasantly and began to rock gently. Nick's eyes finally located Fox in the dim light cast by the pretty table lamp. Small hands tied with green plant tape, her small pixie face was marred by rivets of blood from the blow she'd sustained earlier that day. She rested uncomfortably upon a narrow cot, though Mrs. Simms had covered the young woman with a blue-crocheted blanket.

The room was clearly designed as a huge playroom similar to the one found in the Collins house. Another large crib hugged the corner, and a frighteningly large metal loop was bolted into the wall. In addition, a small utility kitchen, an easel, a playhouse, and once again the hordes of toy cars and bouncing balls, filled the echoing spaces. But it was the shelf behind Mrs. Simms' rocking chair that arrested Nick's vision. Shelf upon shelves of glass bottles lined the whitewashed wall. This was not only a play center but a laboratory storage room for a biologist.

Mrs. Simms followed his eyes. "Most were my husband's you know. He was a professor at the University, and every time we embarked upon a trip, he brought back specimens of the numerous animals and insects he'd observed. He pickled them in formaldehyde, the first step in his quest to understand how they had developed and were formed. John swore everything living on this earth was beautiful, whether they be plants, animals, or human beings. He never found the negative in anyone's actions or motivation. That is what I kept trying to understand, you know." She looked sadly at Thayne, the pistol trembling slightly in her aged hand.

Nick started uncontrollably. There, in a large canning jar near her head floated the bodies of baby birds, featherless and revoltingly naked. Another housed a miniature elephant embryo, complete with tiny perfect trunk. And the third . . . Nick was a strong man, but he had never seen anything so horrifying in his entire life. Luckily, Roger hadn't spotted it yet.

"I know about Delilah."

"You do?" She sounded relieved. "My husband loved

her so. My Delly wanted to be a scientist just like him. Had a special interest in birds. Swore that pesticides were going to wipe out the California condor. She would be so pleased to know they're thriving now."

Nick sought to somehow distract and disarm her. "I don't understand why you killed Thad Fisher and Connie Judson," he said, taking one step forward.

"Don't come any closer," said Mrs. Simms firmly. "I'll kill the lot of you." She swung the pistol towards Fox, who Nick wasn't even sure was breathing.

"But why?" asked Roger. A tiny trickle of perspiration slid past his ear.

"It's because of what he did." Her voice cracked. "What he did to *her*! I made them pay. Anthony thought, with his boys dead, that it didn't matter anymore to my girl, so he wanted to stop paying."

"To Ashley or Delilah?" asked Roger, momentarily confused.

"No, not that *Peebles'* girl. She was just a slut . . . a slut, trying to take away my grandchild's birthright. Imagine defiling herself with Anthony Montanari, who was old enough to be her father. Those girls, you know, they wrest every cent out of a man, swearing they will tell his family about their bastard children. Oh, but her child was a perfect little boy. My grandson should have been as faultless as he, but Charlie was spawned in sin worse than hers. I needed to warn Montanari so he would continue paying for his grandson's care."

Roger suddenly convulsed, his eyes finally spotting the horror. His paralyzed mind, seeking to make sense of it all, reminded him of a show he'd once seen on *National Geographic* in which a newborn fetus floated, suspended surrealistically in its own embryonic fluid. It was unbelievable, inconceivable, but there, just above the old woman in a large glass jar bobbed the tiny form of a full-term male infant. Ashley's child had been found.

"I sent him photos of his dead bastard son so he'd understand how the vengeance of God works. My Charlie, he may not have looked like much, but he was a Montanari, though his conception was hideous."

Roger edged closer, sweat sheeting his tense face.

Edith Simms waved her gun at him. "Stay back, Officer. I've nothing else to lose. I'm an old woman with pancreatic cancer and have only a scant six months to live. That's all I was asking for . . . six more months and the promise that my grandson would be taken care of for the rest of his life. But no! Anthony Montanari said he wasn't going to pay up anymore. Said he was having financial difficulties and couldn't continue paying anybody, including that beast of an ex-mayor, who'd found out about Ashley and Anthony's illegitimate son."

"So Thad Fisher *was* blackmailing him?" Nick glanced over at Roger who was fading fast.

"Because he thought *Anthony Montanari* had killed Ashley Peebles! He couldn't have been more wrong. I killed her! After all, I was just receiving what my family was owed after what that monster Anthony Jr. did to my daughter.

"Did to your daughter?" The vision flashed in Nick's brain. Of course . . . the dark head of the rapist had belonged to Anthony Jr., not Anthony Sr.

"My daughter was down by the Monroe River recording her notes on the development of a covey of quail she'd been observing for several weeks. She was only sixteen when he came upon her. Do you know what he did to my little girl, my only child, and the daughter of my heart?"

"I can guess," said Roger sadly. He put a hand out to steady himself, forcing himself to focus upon the mesmerizing voice of the demented old woman.

"He raped her and beat her within an inch of her life. He threatened my sweet angel, promising if she told anyone he would kill her and her family. She staggered off, her dress stained with her own virgin blood. I found her eight hours later, cowering in the corner of my garden shed. She wouldn't tell me who did it and refused to go to the hospital, so great was her shame. I took care of her the best I could and when I found out she was pregnant, I begged her to abort the child. She said that would be evil—a sin compounding a sin.

"So my Delilah dropped out of school and wouldn't leave the house, or her room, for that matter. It was as if her life force had been permanently drained. My husband, fortunately, had died two years previously, and he never had to witness her humiliation. Delilah was all I had, and as her belly swelled, I swore I would get even with the bastard who did it to her. But then, when the baby was born, everything went wrong. The only blessing was that poor Delilah never saw the hideous monstrosity of her son. As she lay dying, I forced her to tell me who the father was."

She shrugged helplessly, the gun nearly limp in her age-spotted hand. Could Nick risk charging her?

Mrs. Simms barked out. "Are you listening?"

"Of course," said Nick soothingly. "It's understandable you would despise her rapist." The gun was so tempting, just a few inches from her dusty gardening shoes. Fox moaned and shifted slightly on the narrow bed. She was still alive!

"By that time, Anthony Montanari Sr. knew what his eldest son was like and informed him he had to enlist or else. He went Vietnam, and there, the avenging angels swooped upon both him and his equally black-hearted brother. I tried to take care of Charlie the best I could and made my younger brother help. That's how you figured it all out, isn't it? Eddie betrayed me!"

"Actually, he didn't. And I believe he really loves your grandson. He only wants the best for him." Roger's voice sounded dry, like a twig waiting to snap any moment.

The woman's brittle face seemed to relax. "I think you're right. Charlie was so special. Sometimes . . . it was as if he could speak . . . and then he would laugh. Oh, how I needed that laughter."

Roger tilted his head slightly to Nick, who was preparing to lunge, not sure he could be of much assistance.

"I didn't have much money after my John died, barely enough to raise my daughter. I was a librarian, you know, and I figured Anthony Montanari could afford to pay for his own grandson's upbringing. And pay he did. I kept him paying and paying, until five years later, he threatened to stop coughing up the needed funds. He started visiting one of the little girls in his wetback camp himself until she got knocked up. Anthony stated he was going to come clean, that Ashley's child was his, and that he was going to take care of her. So I had to warn him."

"By killing her?" declared Nick. He'd managed to inch slightly closer to the rambling old woman.

"You bet, but I made sure that I cut off her finger and kept it as a souvenir in my jar up there."

Some human actions are uncontrollable. Nick willed himself not to turn his head, but couldn't stop his gaze from travelling to where her bony finger pointed, nor stifle the involuntary revulsion as his eyes settled upon the jar. In it, one slender human finger floated daintily.

"But Ashley's finger has been found," he said,

swallowing heavily. Fox moaned again, turning her tightly bound head slightly.

"It's my daughter's, of course. I had to bury the rest of her. There were times when Ashley Peebles', Thad Fisher's and the finger of that whining mistress of his joined hers as well."

"But that doesn't explain why Thad Fisher deserved to die."

"He became too greedy, and when Montanari said he couldn't afford to pay off both of us anymore, I had to take matters into my own hands. After all, *mine* was a good cause—I was taking care of my Charlie. Thad Fisher was using Montanari's money to keep his disgusting mistresses. It was really easy—I called and pretended I was Anthony's secretary. The mayor, flaunting his newest bottle-red mistress, trotted to the Collins house expecting to receive one whopping pay-off so they could leave town and set up house in Mexico. If they hadn't tried to escape, everything would have been easy, but Charlie, well, he got loose, and—oh—it was dreadful. He's so easily upset. The color of that woman's hair and nails really set him off. That, and her screaming. I had so much trouble making her stop."

Sirens sounded in the distance and Mrs. Simms flinched.

"But, Mrs. Simms, is there really anything left to fight for? Charlie's going to be well-taken care of by Social

Services. You won't have to worry about him after your death. There's really nothing left to worry about; not him or this big house." Nick's voice was at his most persuasive.

"But Anthony . . ."

"It's all going to come out now. Trish Fisher will make sure he takes responsibility; I heard her say so tonight. You're tired and need rest. Let someone else worry about Charlie for a change. You've done your duty."

Roger added. "If you put down the gun, Mrs. Simms. We'll take you to where he's staying. It's a lovely place. He'll have no worries or stress there."

Edith Simms smoothed her rose-colored dress and spoke irrelevantly. "You really admired my garden didn't you, Inspector Thayne?"

"I did. It's truly beautiful."

"It's how I visualize heaven to look; all green and fresh, the flowers in constant bloom. We are all reborn there among the zinnias, marigolds, and sweet gum trees. In heaven, those like Charlie are like roses without thorns." Mrs. Simms glanced over at the still form of Lea Fox. "You'll cut a bunch for her from my garden, Inspector Thayne?"

Nick nodded, suddenly divining her intention. He wasn't fast enough to stop the elderly woman from placing the pistol into her mouth and pulling the trigger. Both Roger and she hit the floor simultaneously as Fox remained oblivious to it all.

Chapter 26

Tuesday, September 24th, 2002

Nick kept his word and cut two-dozen pink and red roses from Mrs. Simms' garden for Fox. He also cut some for Susan, who was rightfully furious with him, her black eyes sparking like hot coals. Lea, hunched white and diminutive under the thin sheet of her hospital bed, turned a weary face towards him, squinting because she didn't have on her glasses.

"Nick Thayne," she managed to mutter between dry lips. "Are those *flowers*?"

"They're from Mrs. Simms' garden. She wanted you to have them. You know you're lucky to be alive. That flowerpot she wielded cracked your stubborn little skull. What I can't understand is why you didn't call me. Why did you go out on your own? That was just plain stupid."

"So, now *I'm* stupid? That's rich coming from someone with an intellect like a chauvinistic troglodyte. I least I had it all figured out."

"Well, bully for you. I didn't realize we were in a race.

The least you could do is say thank you, though I'm not sure such words exist within your limited vocabulary. Weren't you aware that Edith Simms was all prepared to add one of your pointed little talons to her finger collection?"

She wiggled her ten digits at him. "I never waste time pondering events that didn't happen."

"Well, at least you're getting better. Your tongue is as sharp as ever!" He placed the flowers on the wheeled meal stand before sinking down onto the uncomfortable hospital chair. "So what *did* happen?"

"I'm not sure I should tell you—being that you're so grumpy."

Nick folded his arms. "Shows how you bring out the best out in me. Okay. I'm all ears. What happened, oh super sleuth?"

"Well, now that you're listening and have acknowledged my superior abilities, I'll tell you. I originally intended only to find out where the tunnel led and then phone you as backup, but unfortunately, Mrs. Simms was in the greenhouse working on her orchids."

"She heard you coming up the steps?"

"I've never been a quiet climber," defended Lea, convinced it was probably the clumping sound of her lame foot that had caused her to be caught off guard. "I barely even recognized I was in the hothouse before I felt the blow."

"So, did your life flash before your eyes?" he mocked

gently.

"Nah. It was more like a guillotine; one swift black slice before La La Land. I'm amazed I even woke up. Didn't expect to be in some damn emergency room."

It was impossible for her to say thank you. Nick wondered how flippant she'd be if she'd opened her eyes to the jars containing Ashley's baby or Delilah's finger.

"So, she killed Thad and Connie? I suspected as much."

"But how?"

"A few things just didn't add up," said Fox. "Remember when she showed me her orchids?"

"On that first day?"

"Yeah. She dragged me to them with such incredible strength I was amazed. That inconsistency never left my mind, nor where she'd gotten all the money for that mansion; it must have been a mighty fine insurance policy on her husband. The final key was discovering her daughter died in childbirth. Where were the photos and paintings of this nameless girl and husband? My F & H pointed me in that direction, but I was so hell-bent on discovering Bouncer's identity that I put off researching her more."

"And look where that got you."

"Almost sharing a headstone with Thad and Connie," she grumbled.

"After all this, I'm thoroughly convinced Philemon

was probably lucky to get away with his life," said Nick snagging a little cup and filling it with water. He bent the straw so she could sip it between her dry lips before continuing. "Of course, Anthony Montanari has now substantiated everything. He's admitted to being blackmailed by Mrs. Simms for over twenty-eight years and Thad Fisher for almost twenty-three. Both blackmailers kept asking him for favors, campaign donations, the scholarship fund, and later, hard cash. It was a nasty story all around, but you know who the real victims were? Mrs. Simms' daughter Delilah and poor Eddie Murdock, who was brow-beaten by his sister into taking care of his great-nephew."

"And what about Chief Rollins' role?" asked Fox.

"I believe Richard was actually afraid that Trish Fisher had something to do with all of it. It's a pathetic issue I'll update you on later when you're feeling better. Let it suffice to say that the current mayor is actively working an early retirement for him since it's clear Rollins did everything in his power to impede justice and stifle our investigation."

"And what's going to happen to poor Bouncer?"

"I'm not exactly sure. While Roger and I are convinced Eddie didn't have anything to do with the murders, he must have suspected his sister got the money from somewhere. We've verified he was actually off the night Thad and Connie were killed, playing pool and drinking at his local hangout. I'd drink, too, if I had his job. That's when Charlie got out and bit poor Connie.'

It was all too revolting to ponder. "And Philemon?"

"A free man—just like Luke Cambridge is going to be real soon."

He gave her another sip of water. Damn, there wasn't much to her under the hospital sheets. "Hey, that reminds me," said Nick trying to perk her up. He waved a check at her. "Roger Chung signed it himself."

"Roger?"

"That's right. He's officially been appointed the new police chief. He's lucky to be alive as well after his stitches broke open. He developed an infection, and Susan nearly killed the both of us after our little escapade. It's addressed to Fox Investigative Agency." The check was for six thousand dollars.

"Well, that ought to help pay a few bills," she said dismissively.

"Yeah, that ought to. But you know what's even better?" He whipped out another check from his suede jacket pocket. "Take a look at this one."

She squeaked, "Twenty thousand dollars!"

"From one Meredith Cambridge. Apparently Luke's mother never believed that Luke and Deke killed Ashley Peebles. Had a private reward sitting in an interest bearing account for nearly 25 years for anyone who could bring the real culprit to justice. Brought the check over last night to the boarding house. She's actually a sweet old girl. That makes a cool thirteen grand each between the two checks. Not bad for less than a week's work."

Lea gulped. That was more than she had made the entire year.

"So, you're staying in town for a while?" asked Lea.

"Why—you a little short on visitors? I think so. Roger and I are going to head down to Modesto tomorrow to be there when Luke is released. Can you imagine sitting in prison for twenty-five years for a murder you didn't commit? Anyway, we are going to work on finding him a halfway house in Sacramento to try to get him back on his feet. I'll be back in a couple of days to see you. Why don't you let me give Bernard a ring? He's been here, hasn't he?"

She frowned. "Of course! I'll see him later this evening."

"Then I'd better skedaddle—wouldn't want to make him jealous."

"As if that's possible!"

"Ooh, she *is* getting better! Later, Fox. We'll divvy up the loot when I get back."

It was too quiet when he left, and she wished Bernard would come.

Nick was as good as his word and showed up two days later with Roger in tow. Behind him stood a grinning Philemon Jenkins, with a Dodger's baseball cap in hand

"The Lord be praised, Ms. Fox."

"I'm glad to see you sprung, Philemon. But I can't be happier than Darcy."

"My Darcy will put double in the plate this Sunday, that's for sure. You don't mind if I help escort you home?"

"Not at all."

So, Philemon wheeled her out of the hospital even though she was quite capable of walking. Lea actually enjoyed being doted on a bit and allowed the three men to fuss over her. Once they had arrived back at her small house fronted by several well-tended rose bushes, she halted abruptly. The triple birch trees swayed gently, shading a perfectly mown lawn and immaculate side planters filled with hibiscus and bottlebrush.

"My yard's been tended."

"It was a pleasure," laughed Philemon.

She smiled gratefully at him before noticing the thin man standing awkwardly upon her doorstep.

"Why, Dr. Koh . . . is that for me?"

Steven shrugged stiffly. He had visited the local florist and instructed the grinning shopkeeper to stuff every species of flowers they sold into the oversized bouquet. It was a marvel indeed.

It seemed only natural to suggest the four men all remain and have a drink. Lea rustled up three of her largest vases as Roger stifled a mischievous grin on his face while pouring fine ten-year old cognac into each one of their snifters.

"I've a proposition for you two," said Roger taking a deep whiff of the spirit and sighing. "As the new police chief of Monroe, it seems to me that I have assembled before me an incredible team of minds, who I'd certainly like to be able to depend on in a crunch."

"Well, that would be news to some of us," snorted Thayne. Lea had changed into a fuzzy olive-green sweater and baggy gray sweats, which were stained at the knees. Her socks were pee yellow. Good grief, the casual Fox was just as fashion-challenged as the business one! Steven, of course, noticed nothing, preferring to examine his drink as if it were chemically infested.

Roger wisely ignored him. "It's occurred to me that Fox Investigative Services and Thayne Private Investigations aren't going to make it on their own servicing the two cities in this county, so I've come up with a plan. The pair of you could form your own investigative agency. You would be able to handle all the business in Monroe and Girard. Shoot, it's only a 50-minute drive between the two towns. Think of all those divorces, cheating wives, bail bond jumpers, and who knows what else. There might be another tantalizing case coming up, just like this one." He pulled a police report out of his coat pocket and spread it out on the oval table. Philemon sipped the strong alcohol gingerly. He wasn't reformed enough to deny himself a celebratory drink.

"That would be unthinkable," summed up Fox, but her

curiosity was pricked. “What’s this?” she asked, leaning forward. Thayne remained mute, acting like a bee had just stung him, the allergic reaction making it difficult for him to breathe. Steven seemed unusually annoyed as well.

“Wow,” she cried. “The packing company in Chancy just 20 minutes down the road from Monroe burned to the ground last night. At first, they thought it was just an electrical fuse, but later discovered a few blackened cans of gasoline near the rear entrance. Sounds like arson. I wonder who stands to profit?”

Nick stayed ominously quiet as Philemon grinned. This was better than Reality TV.

“Let’s face it,” continued Roger. “I’m drastically shorthanded. I’ve got five men, two of whom are rank rookies, an overweight dispatcher hooked on diet pills, a secretary who’s wacko about Jacko, as well as a coroner and forensics expert who makes family meals a weekly ordeal.”

Steven retorted. “I thought you’d appreciate knowing about all the chemicals negligent food companies place in their products. At your age, you should be more concerned about what you eat.”

“The truth is,” continued Roger, “I need some help and could sure use two crack private investigators to help manage my stress level. This is a large county with over two hundred thousand people spread out over farmlands, potato fields, and all the citified nooks and crannies in-between. I’ve already checked with the mayor and she's willing to allocate a sizable portion of her slush fund—and the money saved by having Chief Rollins retire early—to enable you to both work on a contract basis. You could concentrate on those missing kids we can't find, arson cases we don't have the expertise or manpower to solve, and the occasional homicide. I was thinking maybe Thayne and Fox or Fox and Thayne might make a good name for your new investigative team. You each have your own special *gifts* to bring to the table. What do you think?"

Fox was the first to react. She scoffed. "I don't remotely need him, since I've just hired Philemon to help me out."

Thayne turned on her furiously. "But that's impossible—I just hired him! What do you mean you hired Philemon?" He faced the ex-hit man. "Well?" he demanded.

A loud chuckle swelled from deep inside Philemon. "I can't deny it's true—I've promised the both of you I'd work for you'all. Roger said it would be best tactic to get you two together. If you team up, I'll have not made false promises to anyone. I can't lie, you know. Our sweet Savior forbids it."

Nick gnashed his teeth. "What the hell are you up to, Roger?"

"Maybe I'm just tired of lending you money. Come on, Nick. It's the best compromise. That thirteen grand isn't gonna last forever. And she's the only woman I know who won't fall for your charm or fail to tell you when you're just plain full of shit."

Nick's handsome face contorted. "I refuse to work with her! I only teamed up this *once* because she wouldn't give me the information I needed on the Peebles case!"

"I'd sooner drop dead," summarized Lea. "You know, I had this last case all figured out, and then he waltzes in, and to everyone else, it appears like he solved the blasted thing. I knew that Edith Simms killed Thad Fisher and Connie Judson, but who gets all the credit? Him! It was plain as the nose on your face that the old lady was demented."

"And who was all lined up for Mrs. Simms' finger brigade? And to think, you still got half the paycheck!" shouted Nick. "By all rights, I should demand half of the money back!"

The two continued to squabble loudly, Steven's head following the pair as if he were watching Wimbledon. Philemon shifted his glance towards Roger and downed his drink. Man, that cognac was smooth.

"I think it's all going to work out, don't you? I do believe, however, that they just might need a referee appointed by the Lord."

"They might at that, Philemon," returned Roger delightedly.

After five minutes, it was clear there wasn't going to be any sort of truce, so Roger turned to the last ace up his sleeve. He ducked into the arched hallway and returned with Nick's sketch depicting that final, fateful night of Lane and Jeremy Fox. He tossed it nonchalantly upon the dining room table.

Fox went deathly silent as Nick gazed furiously at his friend.

"What the hell, Roger!"

"Where'd you get this?" whispered Lea.

No one answered.

She repeated more loudly. "Where did you *get* this?"

Steven's eyes amazingly filled with tears as Thayne took a fiery gulp of the expensive cognac before answering, "I drew it."

The silence was deafening. She finally said, "You drew this?"

"That's right."

Fox clenched the bottom of the frayed avocado sweater, her mouth twitching uncontrollably.

Philemon examined the drawing. It was damn fine work, though a bit macabre for his taste. He just wished he understood the emotional nuances produced by the terrible scene. Steven refused to look at the picture, instead studying first Lea, then Nick before casting a belligerent glance at his brother-in-law.

No one expected her next question. "You'd consider reopening this case, Roger?"

"It should have never been closed."

Fox turned abruptly to Thayne. "I don't understand your little *gift*, and I'm not sure I want to. But all I know is that I can't sleep at night until I figure out why they were killed. *And* I can't get any consistent answers from *anybody*. Everywhere I turn, it's a dead end. That fat man in the left hand corner being highly entertained by my family's murder . . . You're positive he was present that night?"

"Yes," said Nick shortly.

Her long pause was significant. Finally she said, "Well. I'm not changing the name of my agency."

"Wait a minute. You expect me to work for Fox Investigative Services like some sort of lackey while you remain in charge?"

"That's right. Since my father's death, I've been the only boss of Fox Investigative Services and will remain so."

"Like hell you will."

"What!" She rose to her full 5'2" inches in height. "You expect me to change the agency's name to Thayne's Private Investigations or something and work for you?"

"It's a fine name."

"Well, not for me!"

Steven set down his crystal snifter and frowned menacingly at his brother-in-law before stalking out of the house. The other two immensely satisfied men observed the tiny woman and handsome man argue unceasingly for a couple more minutes before rising to slip unnoticed out the front door. Both of them had devoted wives to return to.

"I'll be seeing you, then," promised Philemon, placing his baseball cap firmly over his graying head. It had turned out to be a fine sunny afternoon.

"I certainly hope so," said Roger, touching a creamy pink rosebud blooming outside of Fox's front door, the petals still damp from its early morning watering. "I *certainly* hope so."

Made in the USA
Middletown, DE
08 January 2023